USA TODAY bestselling author lives in north Texas with her very own hero-worthy husband, three beautiful children, a spunky golden retriever/standard poodle mix and too many books in her to-read pile. In her down time, she plays video games and spends much of her time on or around a basketball court. She loves interacting with readers and is grateful for their support. You can reach her at www.barbhan.com.

Elle James, a *New York Times* bestselling author, started writing when her sister challenged her to write a romance novel. She has managed a full-time job and raised three wonderful children, and she and her husband even tried ranching exotic birds (ostriches, emus and rheas). Ask her, and she'll tell you what it's like to go toe-to-toe with an angry three-hundred-and-fifty-pound bird! Elle loves to hear from fans at ellejames@earthlink.net or www.ellejames.com.

Also by Barb Han

Also by Elle James

Discover more at millsandboon.co.uk

ENDANGERED HEIRESS

BARB HAN

ONE INTREPID SEAL

ELLE JAMES

MILLS & BOON

First Published in Great Britain 2018
by Mills & Boon, an imprint of HarperCollins*Publishers*
1 London Bridge Street, London, SE1 9GF

Endangered Heiress © 2018 Barb Han
One Intrepid Seal © 2018 Mary Jernigan

ISBN: 978-0-263-26573-6

39-0518

MIX
Paper from
responsible sources
FSC™ C007454

This book is produced from independently certified FSC™ paper to ensure responsible forest management.

For more information visit: www.harpercollins.co.uk/green

Printed and bound in Spain
by CPI, Barcelona

ENDANGERED HEIRESS

BARB HAN

To work with an intelligent and amazing editor is a true gift to any writer's career. A huge thank-you to Allison Lyons for being that gift to mine. I'm incredibly grateful for the chance to work with Jill Marsal, an amazingly talented agent.

I have so many writer friends to thank for friendship and encouragement. I'll start with a few: Elizabeth Heiter, Chris Keniston, Kellie Coates-Gilbert and Kathy Ivan. I love plotting books and getting #AllTheWords with you.

To my children, Brandon, Jacob and Tori, who are true lights in my life. I'm excited to see what adventures this year brings for each of you. And I fully intend to hit 1m before you, Jacob. Challenge accepted.
Let the games begin.

And to John, who makes me laugh and keeps me grounded while encouraging me to reach for the stars.
I can't wait to see what this year holds for us.
I love you with all my heart.

Chapter One

Madelyn Kensington glanced at the screen of her phone as it vibrated. Her ringtone belted out. The screen read *Unknown Caller* and the number wasn't familiar. Everyone had gone to lunch on her floor and she suddenly felt vulnerable.

The area code revealed the call came from within Texas. Her muscles corded. She prayed this wasn't her ex trying to trick her into speaking to him by using a different phone. She had no plans to drop the harassment charges against him or ask the judge to lift the restraining order. She was still frustrated with herself for allowing Owen to slip past her jerk-radar. She'd walked away the instant he'd revealed his true colors and, based on his threats, she'd been too late.

A low sigh slipped out. This whole week had been one problem after another, and being without her convertible while the word *skank* had been removed from her hood—courtesy of Owen even though he'd denied it—ranked right up there with the time she'd been stranded for twenty-four hours with no bathroom during a road trip in college.

The ringing stopped and she stared at the device. Tapping her foot, she waited for the voice-mail icon to pop onto the screen. It was taking too long. She absently fingered the small dragonfly dangling from its chain around her neck as she waited. The necklace had belonged to her mother and touching it made her feel connected, comforted when her life felt like it was spiraling out of control. In times like these Madelyn especially missed never having known her mother.

Owen's last words wound through her thoughts. *Think you can walk away from me? You'll never know when I'll strike.* Icy tendrils gripped her spine, shocking her with a cold chill that spread through her body. Either her ex was leaving the longest voice mail in recorded history or this was another frustrating telemarketing call.

Again, her ringtone belted out as the phone vibrated in her hand. The motion startled her. She dropped the device and pushed her chair back as her cell crashed against the tiled floor. *Great*—she probably just broke her phone over nothing. This needed to stop. She was jumping at every shadow ever since Owen's reaction to the breakup.

This probably didn't have anything to do with him anyway. Her father could be trying to reach her. She'd left three messages last week and another this morning to share the good news about her promotion as well as the special ceremony her old high school had planned for her.

Madelyn bent over and clasped her fingers around the phone. She hesitated. What were the chances her father was actually returning the call? It wasn't the first of the month. His calls came like clockwork.

Okay, she'd answer and then get rid of this jerk.

"Hello," she stated on a sharp sigh, deciding on bal-

...ne needed to deal with whatever was on the ...nd of the line.

...pologize for the interruption, Ms. Kensington, ...promise this call will be worth your time." The ...t Southern drawl sounded educated and from ...as. "My name is Ed Staples."

"Okay-y-y." She drew out the *y* as she geared up for her response to the sales pitch that was surely about to come. The name Staples sounded vaguely familiar but she couldn't place him, so she spun around and typed his name into her laptop.

The man seemed to pick up on her frustration. "I'm the family attorney for the Butler estate."

She studied her laptop screen and, yes, received confirmation Ed Staples was telling the truth.

There was a pause and Madelyn felt like he was waiting for some kind of reaction from her.

"Are you familiar with Mike Butler?" Mr. Staples asked.

"Maverick Mike Butler?" she said out loud, not really meaning to. Now she really was confused. Of course she'd heard of Mike Butler, aka Maverick Mike. Her job at the *Houston Daily News* as an investigative reporter assured she would at least be acquainted with the name. His story was no secret—son of a poor crop farmer who beat the odds and made something of himself. He'd done so well that he was one of the wealthiest cattle ranchers in the Lone Star State. His rise to riches was as legendary as his buck-wild reputation. If rumors were true, he won his first ranch at a poker table and lost his first wife to his gambling problem. And that was where his run of bad luck had ended. Everything else the man touched seemed like

it turned to gold. It was no secret that he l̶i̶ ̶ ̶ ̶
own terms, another fact widely known to prett̶y̶
every Texan. Last week, the legend from Cattle Ba̶r̶
had made even bigger news with his death.

"Ma'am," the lawyer said.

The sound of his voice made her jump.

"Sorry—what did you say?" Outside of print, Madelyn had no idea who Mike Butler was. She'd never met him personally and they didn't exactly run in the same circles. "What did you need from me, Mr.—?"

"Staples, but please call me Ed."

Right. He'd already said that. Madelyn was distracted. Thinking about Owen had thrown her off.

"How can I help you, Ed?" she asked, refocusing.

"Can you meet me tomorrow afternoon here at the Butler ranch?" he asked.

"I'm afraid I'm working, but I might be able to arrange something if you tell me what this is about," she responded, still trying to shake the creepy chill from earlier. Owen was right about one thing: he seemed everywhere to her.

"I've been instructed to offer to send a car," he continued, unfazed by her work excuse.

"No, thanks. I have my own. Is there a reason we need to meet face-to-face? I mean, can you tell me what this is about over the phone?" she asked, mildly interested in what he had to say and at the very least thankful for the distraction.

"I apologize. My instructions are clear. If you want to know the nature of Mr. Butler's request you have to be on the property." He was steadfast. She'd give him that.

"Well, then I'm afraid I can't help you," she countered. Her frustration level was already high and she didn't need another person wasting her time. Plus, it wasn't like she could drop everything without a clear reason to give her boss and she didn't cover the crime beat.

"Would it make a difference if I told you that it's in your best interest to come?" he asked.

This guy was persistent. And frustrating with his cryptic message.

"Cattle Barge isn't exactly a few minutes down the road. If you want me to make that drive I need something to go on. My boss will want to know why I need time off to chase down a story outside of Houston," she said. When she really thought about it, the ranch must be swarming with media by now. Any news about Mike Butler's death guaranteed above-the-fold placement in print and major promo for broadcast. "Plus, there must be dozens of reporters at the gate chomping at the bit for something to report. Why tell me? I mean, just walk outside your front door and pick someone if you want to get your story out."

"This is personal," he said. "In fact, you may want to take vacation days."

Days? She decided to entertain him for just a second. "Okay, so let me see if I have this correctly. You want me to take off work at the snap of a finger for a man I've never met and a reason you refuse to tell me? Does that sound about right?"

"I'm afraid it's better than it sounds," he admitted.

"Who wants me there?" Maybe she could come at this from another angle to get an answer.

"Your presence was requested by Mr. Butler."

She waited for the rest of the sentence but Ed Staples would've made a great poker player.

"Pardon my directness, but he's...*gone*. It would be a little difficult for him to ask for me," she stated.

"I'm aware." He didn't give up anything with his tone. And she wouldn't even still be on the phone if he hadn't thrown out the name Mike Butler. But her mild curiosity wouldn't be enough for her boss to green-light an overnight trip. "This matter is urgent."

Hadn't she just read about his oldest daughter being targeted for murder? Was it possible the family wanted an objective reporter to confide in? Then again, that incident had happened after Butler's murder and the lawyer had said this was personal. If it was, wouldn't she at least know Mike Butler? And, again, why her? She exposed neglect in nursing homes and small business fraud.

"I'm afraid I can't help you. I can recommend—"

"Your refusal will come at a hefty cost to you, Ms. Kensington," he said firmly.

"No disrespect, but I have a good handle on what's important to me," Madelyn shot back.

"I didn't mean that as a threat." He sounded frustrated that he couldn't pick the right words to persuade her. A few beats of silence came across the line. And then, "Are you sure you want to walk away without knowing what a man like Mike Butler wanted you to be aware of? Out of everyone he could've picked, he chose you."

Well, when he put it like that she could admit the initial pull was becoming a stronger magnet. Walk away and she might never know what Mike Butler wanted to tell her before he died. Curiosity was growing the more she thought about it and a big exclusive could be huge for her career right now. She could prove to her boss that he'd made a good move in promoting her.

"Fine. I'll talk to my boss," she finally said, knowing full well she could get the time off.

"I'll email the details of your stay." The lawyer sounded pleased and a little bit relieved.

"I'll make my own arrangements." She'd learned a long time ago not to put herself in the hands of a source. And that was just how she'd treat this out-of-the-blue request, like any other news story she was covering.

"Be advised that you'll need to take off several days. I'd suggest a minimum of three," he said.

Wasn't that cryptic? She thanked him and ended the call, figuring she would take it one day at a time. Pretty much her new mantra, she thought.

For the rest of the workday, her thoughts kept circling back to Owen. Not even a hot cup of coffee could thaw the icy chill that crept into her bones when thinking about him. Nor could she shake the feeling of being watched as she walked to her vehicle after work—a feeling that was becoming a little too familiar. Madelyn had always been able to trust her instincts. Until recently. Until Owen. He'd knocked her off balance and she was still trying to regain her footing.

This, too, shall pass. The saying that had gotten her through so many sad or frightened nights as a child provided no comfort.

By six thirty the next morning, Madelyn had eaten breakfast, picked up her convertible from the shop and was on the road. She wanted to get out of Houston before traffic was too bad. The call still had her scratching her head and her imagination running wild. Dozens of scenarios had zinged through her mind when she should've been sleeping. But then, sleep had been as realistic as a unicorn sighting since Owen had made those threats. He'd been stalking her, too, and that had her scanning faces wherever she went, expecting him to pop up at the grocery store, gas station and every other place she visited.

Her thoughts returned to the call from Ed Staples. The lawyer had said this was personal but that wasn't exactly a new tactic to get a reporter's attention. It ensured she'd agree to the meeting without asking too many questions. Her mind ran around the same hamster wheel.

Even though she was a reporter, she didn't work the crime beat. Furthermore, she worked in Houston, not Cattle Barge, although Mike Butler's money seemed to reach all parts of Texas.

Did the lawyer want to leak information to her? Or was this truly personal as he'd suggested? She searched her thoughts and couldn't think of one logical reason she'd plan to stay on for a few days. What could be so important? Why her? Those and other questions that had kept her awake when she should've been sleeping had her yawning as she maneuvered onto the highway. Possibilities churned through her mind.

She tapped her fingers on her steering wheel, keeping time with the music on the radio. There was another good reason to get out of Houston. His name was Owen Lockwood. Dating him had been a mistake. He came from Houston oil money, family money, which she had promised herself she wouldn't hold against him when they first met. He'd been charming and polite on those first couple of dates. And then work had gotten even busier leading up to her promotion. Before she really processed their relationship, he was bringing her six-month anniversary flowers.

When he wanted to celebrate their milestone, all she could think about was how she'd lost six months of her life to nonstop work.

Owen had planned out an elaborate date and said he wanted to talk about their future. *A future?* She'd almost laughed at him until she realized he was serious. Working fourteen-hour days, she barely had time to shower. The last thing she needed was the complication of a real relationship. And, face it, her time with Owen had been winding down anyway. He'd started to become possessive when they were out to dinner and another man smiled at her or looked her way.

When she'd asked why they needed to do more than enjoy each other's company, he'd blown up. His reaction seemed over-the-top. She'd told him as much. That was when everything started heading south.

Madelyn gripped the wheel tighter with her left hand and brought her right to her mother's dragonfly necklace. A migraine threatened and that reminded her even more of those last few weeks with her ex. He'd been the one to point out that she'd been getting them more and more frequently as their relationship had progressed. He'd insisted that she'd been spending too much time at work and insinuated she wanted to be with her coworker Aiden Creed. Owen had demanded that she spend all of her time off with him. And then he'd dropped the bomb that he'd been following her.

They'd fought. She'd told him it was over and he'd come unhinged. A man like Owen was used to getting what he wanted. He didn't take the breakup news well.

She'd filed a report when he broke her bedroom window. Another when he'd spray-painted the word *skank* across the hood of her new convertible. She'd saved an entire year for the down payment on her blue two-door sedan. Nothing had been handed to Madelyn and that was okay by her. She'd learned how to do things for herself at an early age.

It wasn't until she'd filed the police report against Owen last week that she found out about his past. The officer who'd taken the report looked her in the eye and asked if she was wasting his time. It turned out that similar charges had been filed and then dropped before anyone set foot in court.

Madelyn had been indignant and the implication that she'd cave under pressure fueled her determination even more. Owen wasn't getting away with his antics this time. She had every intention of standing up for herself and the other women who couldn't do it for themselves, for future women who would encounter the man.

Anger burned through her as she flexed her fingers around the wheel. Her grip intensified. When she really thought about it, spending a couple of days several hundred miles away sounded like enough time to let Owen cool off and get a grip. His bad deeds had been intensifying lately.

Besides, she really was curious about why she'd be summoned to the home of Maverick Mike. Maybe he'd read one of her pieces and wanted to set the record straight about his personal life. Stranger things had happened.

Madelyn kept her eyes on the stretch of road in front of her, ignoring the tingles of excitement that always came with working on something big—and this had to be huge. Everything involving that man was immense. Traffic had slowed to a crawl and she couldn't see what was up ahead holding everyone up.

On this expanse of highway, she was beginning to see why everyone believed the whole state was nothing but oil derricks and tumbleweeds. The only oil derricks she'd ever seen in the city were on cocktail napkins. And, to be fair, she'd only seen a handful of tumbleweeds on the road so far. The closer she came to her destination the landscape began to change and she noticed there were more cows than she'd ever seen in one place. But then, Madelyn rarely left the city willingly. And she was going to a cattle ranch, she reminded herself. There'd be livestock.

Traffic had finally opened up on the 248-mile stretch southwest on a drive that had crawled out of Houston despite leaving early.

Her job had netted more than a few interesting assignments over the years but this request topped the list, literally coming out of left field. For one, she hadn't been working on a story that involved cattle, ranching or dead maverick billionaires. In fact, she'd had no association with the senior Butler although she might be one of the few women in Texas who hadn't, she thought as she rolled her eyes. What could she say? The man had a reputation.

Speaking of which, Butler's lawyer hadn't given her anything to work with, either. The man who'd identified himself as Ed Staples had kept the call short and sweet, promising her the message he needed to deliver would be worth the trip to Cattle Barge. Not even her editor, Harlan Jasper, could get answers. He'd made a few phone calls to see if he could dig anything up and had gotten zero. He'd thrown his hands in the air, pulled her off her current assignment, a piece on the real story behind the new districtwide alcohol-free campaign being implemented at local high schools, and had told her to make a story out of whatever information came out of the meeting. Even in death Maverick Mike Butler was news. Or maybe she should say *especially* in death. His demise had already created a media circus.

Leave it to a man with a big reputation to go out with fireworks, she thought. And even though her relationship with her own father was strained—well, that was probably a generous way to put it since she hadn't spoken to him in three weeks—she appreciated the fact that she knew what she was getting into with him. He lived in the same bungalow-style house she'd grown up in on the outskirts of Houston. He mowed the lawn at eight thirty every Sunday morning—no matter how many times the neighbors had begged him to push back the time even a half hour later. And he'd never remarried after losing her mother shortly after childbirth to negligent hospital practices, although he had dated the same woman for twenty-six years since. He was as reliable as fall football in Texas. And just to prove it, he still hadn't called her back. Her father phoned on the first day of every month, and any news—no matter how important to her—could wait until their monthly phone call, in his opinion.

Even though she desperately wanted to share her good news, her father didn't operate on the same excitement scale as her. There'd been more than work news. A few days before her promotion, her former high school swimming coach had called to say that she was being inducted into the school's hall of fame. Thanks to generous alumni donations, the school was getting a new wing. They wanted her to bring her family to the celebration. She'd almost choked on her mouthful of coffee. Even though she'd called her father right away, she was still waiting for a response. She seriously doubted he would change his schedule. He didn't like to upset his routine.

Madelyn wasn't sure why she felt compelled to ask him to go with her to the high school event. Maybe it was because he was getting older and she saw less and less time to repair their relationship. And she could never exactly pinpoint how it became broken in the first place. Her father loved her in his own way. She'd never doubted that. Her friend Aiden thought it was because Madelyn resembled her mother a little too much. She glanced into the rearview for a quick second. Did she remind him of what he'd lost?

Exiting the highway, she decided to table the thought. She pulled into the parking lot of a small motel. She was roughly two towns over from Cattle Barge.

Madelyn desperately needed a place to cool off and regroup before the meeting with Ed Staples. It was hot. A drive that should've taken four hours had spread to a hard six and she still hadn't reached her final destination yet. She could already tell that the media circus surrounding the death of Maverick Mike had brought in news outlets from around the country. Traffic had thickened the closer she got to the small town.

Even though it was a very real possibility that Madelyn might be turning around and going right back home tonight, she'd learned a long time ago it was best to grab a room when she had the feeling a big story was about to break, and this one, two towns over, was the only one available.

All these reporters swarming couldn't be wrong.

Where there was smoke, there usually was fire. And she was curious just how big this blaze was going to get.

Chapter Two

The motel room was sparse but had everything Madelyn needed—clean sheets, a decent Wi-Fi connection and a soft bed. She set her overnight bag down, walked into the bathroom and splashed water on her face. There were eight missed calls on her cell with no indication of a return call from her father. She shouldn't be surprised but it was impossible not to be disappointed.

There were, however, repeated messages from her ex-boyfriend's lawyer. What was it all of a sudden with her and lawyers? As for Owen's attorney, no amount of calling or pleas would stop her. She had every intention of following through on the charges she'd filed. The next time she saw Owen Lockwood he'd better be explaining himself to a judge. And apologizing to her and every other woman he'd tried to manipulate and bully. She looked at her hands and realized that she'd been clenching her fists thinking about him.

Madelyn dried her face on the white hand towel before heading back outside and into gnarled traffic.

According to her GPS, she'd be arriving at her destination in thirty-seven minutes. A glance at the line of slow-moving vehicles in front of her said she needed a new system that could adjust arrival times based on traffic jams. In this mess she'd be lucky to get a quarter of a mile in half an hour.

To make matters worse, cars slowed down, stopped and then sped up with no clear reason. It went like this for forty-five minutes as she tapped her finger on the steering wheel. Her patience was wearing thin and especially since an oversize black pickup had been practically glued to her back bumper. She changed lanes. He whipped behind her. She shifted back and glanced in her rearview. There he was again. Was he afraid he was going to miss something? Because she could promise him there wasn't anything going on in front of them. Ten minutes later, they were still doing the same dance and the song was getting tired.

Madelyn pressed her brake, leaving a large gap between her and the car in front. The pickup wheeled around her, pumped his fist as he passed and then cut her off. She steered her blue two-door convertible into the right-hand lane to avoid a collision. Wasn't this turning out to be a red-letter day?

GPS said she still had twelve minutes before she reached her destination, which meant another twenty-five at a minimum. *Fantastic*, she thought sarcastically, looking at the four-lane highway. Before she could celebrate ditching the truck, a sedan came bearing down on her. Rather than tango with another frustrated driver, she put her blinker on to let him know she planned to get out of his way.

As she tried to change lanes, he whipped beside her. She turned to see what his problem was and caught the glint of metal. Shock gripped her. He had a gun.

Pointed directly at her. Panic roared through her. Madelyn hit the brake. The white sedan mimicked her.

What on earth? The driver was going to shoot.

She slammed the wheel right and sped onto the shoulder. Horns blared and she didn't need to look in her rearview to know the sedan was following her. Gravel spewed from underneath her tires as she gunned the engine, her heart jackhammering against her ribs. Adrenaline kicked in and her hands shook. A gun being pointed at her had to be the equivalent of half a dozen shots of espresso.

Eyes focused on the patch of shoulder she navigated, she searched around for her cell with her right hand. She needed to call 9-1-1. The other driver was nuts.

At least this area of road was straight even though scores of angry drivers were going crazy on their horns. A truck popped in front of her, blocking her, and she had to slam on her brakes to avoid a collision. Her tires struggled for purchase on the concrete, spewing rocks.

The white sedan was closing in from behind. With the line of bumper-to-bumper cars to her left at almost a complete stop and the damn pickup in front of her, she had nowhere to go. Except right but that was a field. She spun the wheel, unsure of what to expect once she left concrete. Her vehicle wasn't exactly built for off-roading. Panic seized her lungs as she struggled to calm herself enough to take a couple of deep breaths.

She checked her rearview mirror. The sedan was tracking her. And she was running out of field.

HUDSON DALE WAS on his horse, Bullseye, when he noticed something he hadn't seen in the year since moving to the outskirts of his hometown of Cattle Barge—action.

A pale blue two-door convertible tore across his neighbor's land, kicking up all kinds of dust. Not far behind was a bigger sedan, white. Normally, he'd butt out of other people's business but this looked urgent, like trouble, and was headed his way. Besides, he could admit that his life felt a lot like watching paint dry lately. He was restless.

His experience in law enforcement had his instincts riled up as he watched the scene unfold. The convertible was being chased down and needed an out. As the vehicle passed by, he caught sight of the driver. He couldn't get a good look at her face, not with all that wheat-colored hair whipping around since her windows were open, but he could see that a female was at the wheel. She was getting bounced around pretty well in her small sedan.

Hudson strained to get a good look at the driver of the vehicle pursuing hers. He immediately pulled his shotgun from his saddlebag when he realized the male figure had a gun. Hudson loaded a shell.

"Come on, boy," Hudson said to Bullseye. He'd been named for the brown markings surrounding his left eye, making it look like the center of a target.

The convertible driver had nowhere to go and she seemed to realize it as she spun the wheel and hesitated, facing down the other driver.

Hudson whistled one of his loud, call-the-cows-home signals and motioned for her to head toward his gate. He aimed his shotgun, pumped once and fired a shot at the back tire of the white vehicle bearing down on her. Hudson's chest puffed out a little as he scored a direct hit. He'd been keeping up with target practice, maintaining sharp skills even though he'd never planned to need them again for work.

The convertible driver navigated wide as the other vehicle spun out.

Hudson managed to open the gate while seated on his horse. The pale blue two-door blazed inside the gate and he sealed off the entrance as he hopped off Bullseye, pausing only long enough to tie the horse off. His law-enforcement training had him putting plenty of mass between him and the drivers of both cars in the form of an oak tree.

Red brake lights stared at him from the back of the white sedan. The driver was making a choice.

"Put your hands where I can see them and get out of your vehicle," he shouted with authority, shotgun at the ready and trained on the white sedan.

The numbers on the buyer's tags were impossible to make out at this distance. The vehicle sped off. Hudson muttered a curse as he watched a suspect disappear. He angled toward the blue convertible that was still idling in his driveway.

"Hands where I can see them," he shouted with that same authority to the driver.

She complied.

"Can I move them to open the door so I can come out?" she asked, and there was something about her voice that sent an unwelcome sexual current rippling through him. Damn. It hadn't been that long since he'd had female company. Not really. Sure, it had been too long since he'd had interesting companionship. Everyone he'd dated since returning to Cattle Barge had left him bored and indifferent. What was so special about her?

"Yes," he said as he neared the vehicle.

The door to the driver's side opened and she kept her hands in full view. The woman who stepped out was stunning. Her wheat-colored hair fell around her shoulders in shiny waves. Her body was just as curvy, and, hell…sexy. She had long legs attached to what he could only guess was a sweet round bottom from this angle. Her full breasts rose and fell rapidly, no doubt from adrenaline and fear. She had cornflower blue eyes that were clear and bright. A couple of freckles dotted her nose on otherwise flawless skin. And speaking of skin, her jeans fit like a second layer and were tucked inside red roper boots.

Her hands were in the surrender position and she didn't bother to close her vehicle's door. Good moves. He also noticed that there wasn't a gold band on her ring finger. Didn't always mean someone wasn't married, but was a pretty good indicator. He lied to himself when he said the only reason he'd noticed was habit.

"What the hell was that?" he asked, ignoring his other thoughts—thoughts that had no business creeping in while he investigated a possible crime. Speaking of which, this whole scene had *angry boyfriend* written all over it.

"Thank you for helping me," she said and her voice shook. She also had an almost imperceptible drawl. She was from Texas. "I have no idea what's going on. This guy came out of nowhere aiming a gun at me."

She looked completely rattled. Her eyes—eyes that were almost a perfect match to her convertible—were wild, and she had that desperate look he'd seen one too many times on victims and especially on Misty when…

Hudson refused to go over that again. Not even in his mind.

He could clearly see that this woman's hands shook. And her eyes had that bewildered quality that victims often had when they didn't see a crime coming.

Hudson believed her. "Do you have a weapon?"

"No." She glanced around and his gaze dropped to her jean pockets for confirmation. A serious mistake in his opinion because stray voltage zapped him and a thunderclap of need followed, sizzling through him.

"Where are you headed?" He blew out a sharp breath. Those emotions had no business in this conversation. He'd call the sheriff, turn her over and get back to his day.

"I'm Madelyn Kensington, by the way," she said, offering a handshake.

He took it, and did his level best not to notice the fact that her skin was as silky as it looked. "Hudson Dale."

"What branch of law enforcement do you work in?" she asked, dropping her hands to her sides. He didn't mind the move. There was no way she was carrying a weapon anywhere in those jeans.

Her question caught him off guard. "What makes you think I'm anything more than a rancher?"

She glanced at his legs. "Your posture. The way you hold that shotgun. You walk with your arms out a little, like you're still wearing a holster, and your aim with that shotgun is pretty dead accurate."

He put a hand up to stop her. "I'm no such thing.

What kind of work do you do that makes you notice the way a man carries himself?"

"Me? I'm a reporter from Houston headed to the Butlers," she said, and he was close enough to see her erratic heartbeat pound at the base of her neck.

The last thing Hudson needed was someone who knew how to do research nosing around in his business and especially his past. And there'd been plenty of journalists in the area following the death of Maverick Mike.

"Well, right now, Mrs. Kensington—"

"It's Miss," she corrected.

He gave a curt nod of acknowledgment even though an inappropriate reaction stirred in his chest.

"Is there any chance that white sedan belongs to your boyfriend?" he asked.

"I don't have one, but I do have a persistent ex," she admitted.

Why did relief wash over him when he heard those words? He'd noticed her ring finger a minute ago and tried not to care one way or the other when he didn't see a gold band.

"The guy who just ran you off the road is getting away." Hudson fished his cell out of his back pocket, keeping an eye on the reporter. "So, if you don't mind, I need to make a call to the sheriff's office and see if we can stop him before someone else gets hurt."

"Yes, by all means," she said, taking a step back and leaning a hip against the side of her trunk. She folded her arms and he noticed how the move pushed her breasts against the spring-green cotton shirt she wore. Calmer, her voice was as creamy and smooth as her skin.

Hudson forced his gaze away from the wheat-haired beauty. Getting involved with a woman like her was dangerous. Emotions had no place in an investigation. And he had no intention of repeating past mistakes.

Chapter Three

Madelyn's pulse hammered her ribs. Hudson Dale
might look like a cowboy in those low-slung jeans,
dark navy T-shirt with rolled-up sleeves and white
Stetson, but something—call it reporter instincts and
keen observation skills—told Madelyn that he was hiding something. Would that something put her in more
danger?

The man had that law-enforcement swagger when
he walked but hadn't identified himself as such. He
even sounded law enforcement when he'd instructed
her to get out of the car with that commanding voice of
his—a voice that traveled over her with an inappropriate sensual shiver that ran down her back.

When she'd outright asked, he denied ever working
the job. She'd spent enough time around cops when she
worked the crime beat early on in her career to recognize the voice of authority they used when they spoke
to someone. This guy looked far too young to be retired. The man couldn't be a day older than thirty-two,
which was only two years older than Madelyn.

He was either undercover, or…

He could've been fired. Hiding. Why else would

he move to the outskirts of a small town? Then again, maybe he just wanted peace and quiet.

Madelyn tried not to let her imagination run away with her. Either way, she was grateful that he'd been there to help when she needed it. Noticing the fact that the man was gorgeous couldn't be helped. He was standing right in front of her. They were barely five feet apart, so it was easy to take note that he had the darkest brown eyes she'd ever seen highlighted by sandy-blond hair and a dimpled chin. Her nerves were heightened and that was why her body was having an out-of-place reaction. She also tried to convince herself that the only reason she considered his rippled chest and muscled arms was basic survival instinct. On a primal level she needed to know that this man was strong enough to defend her should the white sedan come back for another round. The fact that he seemed more than capable kept her nerves a couple of notches below panic.

"The sheriff is on his way and you look like you could use a cup of coffee." Hudson motioned toward the ranch-style house. "Since I'm not sure it's a good idea to leave you alone on my property, you'd better come inside with me."

She nodded. The man was unnervingly cool considering he'd just had to shoot out someone's tire to get them to leave his land.

"Your car should be fine where it is," he said, his horse still tied up near the gate in the shade.

"Thank you." She followed the handsome cowboy inside his house. The decor looked comfortable, simple. A couch and matching love seat surrounded a tumbled stone fireplace with a large rustic star over the mantel.

There was a bronze statue of a bull rider on the sofa table and twin lamps that looked good for reading light.

The kitchen was simple—white cabinets, stainless-steel appliances and marbled granite. She leaned against the bullnose edging, trying to absorb everything that had just happened.

"Care to fill me in on what's going on?" Hudson asked, offering her a fresh cup of coffee.

Madelyn took the mug and gripped it with both hands, noticing that she was still shaking. She chalked it up to adrenaline. Owen had nearly run her off the road recently, trying to get her attention. He'd seemed more desperate to speak to her than deadly at the time. But he drove an Escalade, not a white sedan. Of course, logic said he could've rented one.

"I had a bad breakup and he might be following me." She had to consider that possibility, especially since she hadn't gotten a good look at the driver. Of course, with Owen's money he could've hired someone to scare her.

The cowboy's jaw muscle clenched and released. He blinked the thickest lashes. "Is the law aware?"

"A judge in Houston issued a restraining order." She reached for her necklace and found comfort in holding her mother's dragonfly. "I couldn't get a good enough look at the driver to know if that was him. That's not his car."

"Is he dumb enough to drive his own if he pulled a stunt like this?" Hudson asked.

"No." Owen wasn't stupid. "He has a lot of money. Enough to hire someone to be discreet."

"Does he have a record?" Hudson's eyebrow arched.

"Yes," she hated to admit. She sipped the fresh coffee, welcoming the burn on her tongue. "I didn't find out about it until it was too late. I'm sure that he was only trying to scare me before. This is something totally different. I hope it's not him."

The cowboy's steady gaze seemed locked onto an idea.

"What are you thinking?" she asked, realizing that she was gripping her mug so tight that her knuckles were sheet-white.

"That it's him and he's escalating," he said, shooting her a look.

"He's a jerk, I'll give you that, but he's not… I mean, *that guy* seemed like he was trying to kill me. Owen threatened me but he was trying to intimidate me to get back together with him. I wouldn't be able to do that dead."

The cowboy didn't respond and the quiet rang in her ears.

And then it dawned on her that he was probably thinking Owen had decided that if he couldn't have her no one would.

The doorbell rang before she could rationalize that idea. The cowboy set down his mug before picking up his shotgun. He loaded a slug in the shotgun's chamber and readied it on his shoulder. "Whoever it is won't get to you on my watch."

Madelyn was momentarily too shocked to move as another shot of adrenaline coursed through her. Her heartbeat drummed in her ears. Could Owen hate her that much? Could he be that selfish? Yes, he'd crossed a few lines and had gotten away with it until now. But would he go so far as to want her dead? She'd covered stories that still made her shudder to think about them in the same context as her relationship with Owen.

The sheriff walked in and introduced himself as Clarence Sawmill. He was middle-aged, and his eyes had the white outline of sunglasses on otherwise tanned skin. Deep grooves in his forehead, hard brackets around his mouth and his tight grip on a coffee mug outlined the man's stress level. He was on high alert and, from the looks of him, had been since news broke of Maverick Mike's murder.

"Wish we were meeting under better circumstances, Sheriff Sawmill," Madelyn conceded, taking the hand being offered in a vigorous shake.

"I'd like to hear what happened," he said with a polite nod. The sheriff was considerably shorter than the cowboy, who had to be at least six foot three, and he wasn't nearly as in shape. Sawmill squared his shoulders. His forehead creased with concern as Madelyn recalled the events, horrified at the thought Owen could be behind the attack. She wouldn't deny the possibility. And she tried not to notice how intent the cowboy seemed at picking up every last detail of her statement. One look at him said he had to have been on the job. And it might not be her business but she wanted to know more about the quiet cowboy.

Sawmill listened. "Did the driver fire at you?"

"No, he didn't."

"We've had a few similar incidents on the highway lately. Cases of road rage have doubled with the August sun and the town is still in a frenzy over the death of one of our residents." Sawmill's shoulders seemed in a permanent slump and his posture gave away his weariness. No doubt this was the first time he'd dealt with a high-profile murder on what he'd see as "his

watch." The intensity of his expression said he cared
about doing a good job.

Road rage? She prayed it was that simple because
the other was unthinkable.

"Is there a number where I can reach you if I have
more questions?" Sawmill asked.

Madelyn relayed her cell number. "I'm staying at
the Red Rope Inn for a couple of days if you need to
find me."

The sheriff nodded. "I'll make a note on your file."

"Thank you for your time," Madelyn said as she followed him out the door. She scanned the horizon as a
cold prickly feeling came over her, like eyes watching
her. But there was no one around.

Before the sheriff disappeared she'd handed her
empty mug to the cowboy. "Thanks for your help. I'm
not sure what I would've done if you hadn't been there."

He tipped his hat but didn't respond as he followed
her onto the lawn. "Keep watch in case he returns."

"You think he'll come back?" Her heart drummed
her rib cage.

"Probably not. He'll have to fix his tire and regroup," he said. "Doesn't hurt to be extra careful."

Madelyn thanked the cowboy again before sliding
into the driver's seat. Her palms were sweaty and her
heart still galloped but she'd been threatened in her job
before. It would take more than a stressful brush with
road rage—if the sheriff had accurately assessed the
situation—to detour her from finding out what Maverick Mike wanted with her.

Now that she'd almost made it to the ranch, her curiosity was at an all-time high. And she couldn't think
of one reason the man would summon her.

THERE HAD TO be two dozen news trucks lining the street in front of the Hereford Ranch due to Maverick Mike's murder. Again, Madelyn questioned what she was doing here. If there was a story, wouldn't one of these reporters have already sniffed it out?

A beefy security guy stood at the gate attached to a white log fence. He was wearing navy shorts and a matching button-down short-sleeved shirt, and had a gun strapped to his hip.

She rolled her window down and gave her name along with the name of the paper where she worked.

Beefy's dark brow arched.

"I'm expected," she added to clarify.

"Name again, please," he said, checking his tablet.

"Madelyn Kensington." She couldn't get a good look at his eyes through his mirrored sunglasses. The guy obviously worked out but he had nothing on the cowboy from earlier.

Beefy tilted his head to the side. "Main building is straight ahead. Go on through."

"Thank you," she said, pulling away and kicking up a lot of dirt as she navigated into a parking spot near the main building's entrance. She grabbed her purse and stepped out of her car, dusting off her jeans, thinking how much she loved living in the city. The ranch was beautiful, don't get her wrong, but checking her boots for scorpions before she put them on wasn't exactly her idea of fun.

The main building looked like an oversize log cabin. It had more of a Western high-end resort feel with rustic accents. She slipped her purse strap over her shoulder and walked toward the door. Before she could reach for the knob, the door swung open. She had to put a hand up to stop it from smacking her in the face.

"My apologies," the man wearing a taupe business suit with cowboy boots topped off by a cream-colored Stetson said with a smile of appreciation. "We spoke on the phone earlier. I'm Ed."

Madelyn introduced herself as she took his outstretched hand. His shake was firm and quick, his expression concerned.

"Sorry I'm late. I had a difficult time getting here today," she confided.

"Do you mind filling me in on that?" he asked with a raised brow.

"I've already given my report to the sheriff." And then it dawned on her why he'd ask. Ella Butler had just survived an attempted murder. Madelyn shook her head. "No, it's nothing. Sheriff thinks it's a case of road rage." She didn't want to get into the fact that it could've been Owen with a stranger.

"I see. You're no doubt aware of the situation the Butler family is dealing with," he said with a sympathetic look, and she couldn't help but notice that he was scanning her face. But for what? He seemed to be intensely staring at the bridge of her nose and it was making her a little self-conscious. Her nose had always had a slight bump and she'd sworn that she would get a nose job someday as a teenager.

Ed nodded and his lip curled into a faint grin. He was looking at her like she was some piece of artwork to be examined, like he was searching for something.

"Yes. I'm sorry for the loss of their father and for the criminal activity surrounding it," she said honestly. She didn't know the family, but a quick Google search last night had revealed a snapshot of what they'd been going through. No one deserved this kind of attention. She was getting irritated at the way he was staring at her. "Forgive my confusion, but what is so urgent that you needed to see me right away?"

He seemed to catch on when she used her you're-being-rude tone.

"I apologize for my behavior." He shook his head and made a production of walking in the opposite direction toward an office with glass-and-wooden French doors. "I'd prefer to have this conversation in private."

Madelyn glanced around, didn't see another soul. The place was beautiful, though. So far she'd endured a crazy driver, a cowboy who rattled her with his calm demeanor, and now she was with a lawyer who needed to get to the point. She had no idea what was going on with people today, but she'd hit her limit and was starting to get annoyed.

She stalked behind the lawyer into the office. Floor-to-ceiling bookshelves covered the walls. She was almost distracted by the rare book collection when she decided it was more important to know the real reason she was standing in what had to be Maverick Mike Butler's private study. If it wasn't for the day she'd been having, she might actually enjoy all of this. Seriously, this guy was legend and how many times in her life would she actually get to stand in the study of such a notorious, successful and eccentric man?

The problem was that her nerves were still fried from the drive over and her thoughts kept wandering to the handsome cowboy who'd literally ridden up on his horse and saved her. Call it Old West nostalgia, but he did make her pulse race just thinking about him.

That was the thing about living in Texas. Anything could happen.

Ed put on glasses and took a seat in the executive chair. He motioned toward a leather club chair opposite the massive desk. She took a seat, crossed her legs and placed her folded hands in her lap, figuring this day couldn't possibly get any worse.

He mumbled another apology before locating an envelope and making an "ah-ha" sound. He pushed black-rimmed spectacles up the bridge of his nose.

Madelyn realized she'd lifted her hand to her mother's necklace as she fingered the details of the dragonfly.

"Forgive me for saying, but…" He paused and then seemed to think otherwise as he stared at the envelope.

She caught his stare and a feeling rippled through her. She couldn't exactly pinpoint what it was but that look in his eyes sent a shiver racing down her spine, like the kind when people said a cat walked over a grave.

Ignoring the prickly-pin feeling on her arms, she half expected him to get up and walk out of the room when he tossed the envelope in her direction. Many a news lead was "handed" over in similar fashion.

Instead of excusing himself, he leaned back in his chair and continued examining her.

"What's in that envelope is yours to keep. I've been instructed by the late Mr. Butler to advise you to think heavily on it before you break that seal. There'll be no going back once you know what that envelope contains and the information will change your life forever." She listened for something in Ed Staples's tone to indicate that this was some kind of joke. The intensity of his stare said that it wasn't. And now her curiosity really was hitting full peak.

"I doubt that, Mr. Staples." She picked up the white envelope.

"Don't be so sure," he said. "You should take a moment to consider whether or not you're ready."

She ripped open the flap in one swipe and pulled out the 8-1/2 by 11 sheet of paper. It was trifold, so she flatted out the page. "All I'm ready for is a hot bath, a glass of wine and a…"

Madelyn froze. A gasp escaped.

There was no way. This had to be some kind of twisted joke. She glanced up, looking for cameras. Was she on one of those prank shows?

"I can assure you this is legitimate," Ed said, but his voice disappeared in the background noise exploding in her head.

She would know something like this. Someone would've said something to her before now.

"I know who my father is and it isn't Mike Butler." The words were barely audible even to her as she pulled out the legal document that declared her his legal child. Madelyn cleared her throat. "There's been a mistake."

And then Ed Staples said the words she least wanted to hear. "I'm afraid not. It's true."

Madelyn gripped the piece of paper. The edges crinkled in her hand.

"I've never even met this man. This can't be—"

Ed sat there, looking like he had a well of patience to draw on. And then he said, "Who do you think gave your mother that necklace you're wearing?"

Those words exploded in her head. She was on her feet fast and racing toward the door before she could even begin to process. The day her father had given her the trinket popped into her thoughts. He'd looked so grieved when she opened the gift on her fifteenth birthday. Her mother had given him death-bed instructions to make sure Madelyn received it. He'd looked so pained as she opened the box. Until now, Madelyn had always believed that the necklace reminded him of her mother. Could his expression have meant something else? Was it a reminder of the affair she'd had?

Madelyn didn't bother to look back to see if Ed Staples had followed her. All she needed was a quiet room and a way to rewind this crazy day.

With every step toward her pale blue convertible, a little more life escaped from her. A shot of adrenaline was the only thing keeping her legs moving, her flee response having kicked into high gear. Her chest squeezed and it felt like her lungs were seizing.

Hands shaking, she took a few tries to get the letter unstuck from the moisture gathered on her fingers and grip her car key.

She wasn't sure how she managed to get the key in the ignition and start her car. It was all a blur. Was her entire life a lie? A secret this big couldn't be hidden for thirty years...*could it*?

Tears blurred her vision. She blinked them away the best she could and focused on getting the hell out of there. Time seemed to slow as Madelyn tried to process the possibility of Mike Butler being her birth father. Maverick Mike Butler.

One hand on the wheel, she absently fingered the delicate silver dragonfly dangling from its chain as the log-style home shrank in the rearview mirror.

Madelyn parked in front of her motel room. Her

limbs felt like hundred-pound weights and her body sank deeper into the driver's seat. She managed to pick up her phone and dial her father's number.

Of course, he didn't pick up. *Why would he start now*, she thought bitterly.

Madelyn forced herself out of her car and into her motel room. The second she walked in, something felt off. Hadn't she placed her laptop on the second bed, not the one closest to the door? Her overnight bag was unzipped and some of the contents spilled out. On the mirror at the back of the wall were scribbled large letters in what looked like red lipstick: *Walk away or die.*

Taking a couple of steps backward, she stumbled over her overnight bag. She quickly recovered her balance, grabbed her laptop and shoved it inside her small suitcase.

A few seconds later, panting, she was inside her car. She locked the doors and tossed her bag in the back seat. All she could think about was getting out of there and far away from Cattle Barge.

But go where?

Chapter Four

Madelyn thumped the steering wheel, refusing to cry. Then the questions flooded. Who was behind this? How did someone find out she was staying at the Red Rope Inn? How on earth did someone get inside her room? Was she being followed? That was a stupid question. Of course someone had followed her—the white sedan from earlier. The feeling of eyes on her prompted her to scrutinize the parking lot.

All the cars appeared to be empty but appearances could be deceiving. She drove around the building to the motel lobby. She parked, locked her car door and stalked inside, tucking her fears as far below the surface as she could. Like a simmering pot, her emotions threatened to boil over without warning.

Later, she would process this horrific day. Right now, all she could think about was finding out who was behind this threat. A dozen scenarios fought for attention. She'd been so quick to blame Owen for trying to run her off the road earlier. Her thoughts moved in a different direction now. The person behind the mirror scrawl was most likely the driver of the white sedan.

It was obvious that someone wanted her far away from Cattle Barge. Did one of Mike Butler's children know about her? What about Ed Staples? Could she trust him? As far as she knew, he was the only one who knew she was coming to the ranch. Why would he summon her there and then try to hurt her? He had her number, probably her home address. Why wouldn't he just assault her without making himself known? It didn't rule him out, but placed him lower on her possible suspect list.

Nothing else made sense. She'd been nearly run off the road, shot at and threatened.

Madelyn was certain of one thing: someone was watching.

A bell jingled as she swung open the glass door to the lobby and stalked inside.

"Where's Trent?" Madelyn asked the smiling woman as she walked to the counter. A metal nametag pinned to her shirt read *Kelsey*.

"Shift change," Kelsey reported, looking a little taken aback by Madelyn's direct question. "How can I help you?"

Madelyn glanced at her watch. One fifteen was an odd time for a shift change. She debated tactics. Being nice usually got her the information she wanted. What had happened back there in her room had thrown her off balance and she felt violated. There was no better way to describe her emotions. She still couldn't figure out who would have an issue with her. The envelope Ed Staples had handed her was sealed. Based on the way he'd examined her features when she'd first arrived and his knowledge of the origin of her mother's necklace, he had to have known the contents. Personally, she didn't know the man from Adam, so she couldn't get a good read on him. Was he a loyal employee to

Mike Butler? A personal friend? Or was he closer to the family? Did he feel sorry for them and decide to take matters into his own hands?

He'd seemed honest and even a little bit caring, but maybe it was an act. People faked friendly all the time, smiling at strangers when they were really just trying to get their own way. She'd seen people try to manipulate others using charm tons of times in her line of work. Her profession had also taught her that people had two faces, the one they showed the public and the one they kept to themselves. Both were real. And she could never be certain which one she was getting. Until a tipping point happened...

"Who has access to my room?" Maybe Trent was friends with one of the Butler kids and figured he'd be doing them a favor by scaring her off. That was probably the best-case scenario.

"No one." Kelsey blinked.

"Not even the front office?" Madelyn pressed. Cattle Barge was a small town. If news had leaked that she was the daughter of Mike Butler then someone could be trying to protect the family. Heck, it could've been someone in the family, for all she knew. Was her arrival the tipping point? What about the lawyer reaching out to her? Everyone had to be looked at as a suspect now.

"Well, of course, we have acce—"

"And what about housekeeping?" Madelyn's hands were fisted at her sides as frustration and fear built inside her, gathering steam. What if she'd been in the room? Would that person have attacked?

"Well, yes—"

"Maintenance?"

Kelsey nodded.

"So you and countless others *do* have access to my room." Madelyn was almost to the point of hysterical now. She took in a slow breath that sounded like a hiss from a heating coil.

"Did something happen?" Kelsey caught on. Finally, light brightened her eyes as the insinuation dawned on her.

Part of Madelyn—the frightened child inside her—wanted to deny that any of this was possible. She'd like to write off the whole situation as a bowl of crazy, a landmark bad day. She needed a minute to process the day she was having. More than anything, she needed to hear her father's—well, hold on now, was Charles Kensington even her father anymore?—voice. But that wasn't an option. No matter how many times she phoned, he only returned her calls on the first of every month. Today was the ninth.

Madelyn pulled her cell from her purse. She started punching in those three digits reserved for emergencies. This day had *emergency* stamped all over it.

"Ma'am, what are you doing?" Kelsey asked, her voice low.

"Calling the sheriff," Madelyn stated as she turned her back on the front desk attendant.

"There's no need to do that." Kelsey's voice had that quiet calm as she slowly spoke, drawing out her words like she was trying to talk someone out of jumping off the roof.

"How do you know? I haven't told you why I'm here yet." Madelyn turned toward the glass door in time to see a cruiser pull into the parking lot. He was coming in dark, meaning no lights or sirens.

"I'm sorry. You were so upset and yelling at me, so

I hit the panic button my boss had installed under the counter." Now Kelsey sounded nervous.

"Why would I hurt you?" Madelyn heard the irony there. She was being *stalked* and Kelsey had hit the panic button over a few direct words. This time she blew out a slower breath that sounded less like a hiss. "It doesn't matter. Someone broke into my room and I want to file a report anyway. Call and tell them that you hit the button on accident. That we're okay in here."

Silence.

"Kelsey, I'm not in the mood to play games. Would I turn my back to you like this if I was here to hurt you? Make the call." Madelyn swiveled around, hands up. "All I was doing was retrieving my cell so that I could call the sheriff."

Kelsey gave a nervous smile before she picked up the phone.

HUDSON COULDN'T STOP thinking about the stranger, about Madelyn. The sheriff had written the incident off too easily as road rage and hadn't paid enough attention to the fact that she had an angry ex-boyfriend. Even though this wasn't Hudson's business, he put away Bullseye and then climbed into his pickup truck. All he planned to do was drive down to the sheriff's office and put a bug in the man's ear. Sawmill was distracted and anyone could see that he had too much on his plate. Hudson didn't plan to insult the sheriff. He'd find a tactful way to plant the seed about her ex.

Twenty minutes later he was pulling into the parking lot. There was media everywhere and a flock rushed his truck until they got a good look at the driver, realized he wasn't a Butler and dispelled.

He pushed through the mob to the front door, relieved when the lobby was clear. There was a constant hum of chatter from an adjacent room and he suspected that was a "war room" set up for receiving tips and leads on the Mike Butler murder.

"How are you, Hudson?" Doris asked, rolling her eyes at the craziness going on. She was midfifties and the type who made it her personal mission to know what everyone in town—and in his case, just out of town—was up to. She was also an old friend of his mother's before she'd passed away. Lucky for her Hudson's mother had died years before she could be embarrassed by her son. Hudson performed a mental headshake. He wasn't there to think about his own shortcomings and misery.

"Better now that I've had a chance to see you." The line was cheesy as all get-out but Doris didn't seem to mind.

She smiled so hard her cheeks turned six shades past pink.

"And you're a flatterer," she quipped with that smile intact.

Hudson's gaze drifted to the makeshift command post that had been set up in the adjacent conference room. He heard the buzz of intake volunteers taking calls.

"Looks like you're staying busy." He forced his gaze away from the room and back to Doris. He'd read the stories about Maverick Mike and then Ella Butler.

"Us?" Doris glanced around. "Darn right. This town hasn't seen anything like this in all my considerable years. It's a train wreck in here, if you ask me. I don't remember the last time the sheriff left for more than four hours to sleep. His heart won't take it at this pace."

Pens were lined up in neat rows on her desk next to a line of pencils. She had a notepad positioned on her desk in front of her and her computer was off to one side. A woman like Doris was old-school and would prefer to write things down over spending her days glued to a screen. Hudson was sure she subscribed to the old thinking that staring at the TV too long could make a person go blind.

"Are you trying to convince me that you'd let things get out of control?" He perched on the edge of her desk and she immediately shooed him off it.

"There are other, more qualified people in town who could act as a consultant if they saw fit." The insinuation was that he, being from a big city like Houston, would be more equipped to deal with hard-core crimes, like, say murder. Hudson leaned to one side to avoid the proverbial hand grenade being tossed at him. He had no plans to touch that statement. His days in law enforcement were over.

"What brings you all the way into town?" She blinked her eyes up at him like she was ready for him to tell her the sky was falling.

"Can't I check on my favorite person once in a while?" He wasn't ready to tip his hand. Gauging from the chaos in the office, the sheriff didn't have the resources to properly address the reporter's incident. And that worried Hudson for reasons he shouldn't care about. He'd done his part, played the role of Good Samaritan. If he had any sense he'd turn around, walk out that door and let a sleeping dog alone.

Instead, he took a seat across from Doris and leaned forward.

"Thanks for the habanero peppers, by the way. Diced some up and threw them in the pan with a pair of eggs this morning. Best breakfast I've had in months," he said.

"There's something about homegrown that gives 'em that extra kick of flavor." Her eyes lit up. His mom used to joke that her friend grew a garden in small part to feed herself and in large part so that she could stop by and check on her friends on a regular basis. "If you'd come around more often, I'd send you home with all you want. I always grow more than I can use in case someone's in need."

"Now I'm a charity case?" Hudson joked but a pang of guilt nailed him. He'd been content to stick to his ranch. Heck, he'd have his groceries delivered if it meant never leaving his property. The place was the only thing keeping him sane after everything he'd lost and he'd pretty much lost everything.

Once again, he had to ask himself why he was sitting in the sheriff's office.

"Is the boss around?" He glanced toward the hallway.

"Afraid not. Everything all right?" Concern creased her forehead.

"With me? Yeah. I was just checking on a friend," he said.

"Since when do you have a friend in town?" Her brow shot up.

The phone rang. She excused herself to take the call.

Hudson had almost talked himself into slipping out the door while she was preoccupied with the conversation. Until he heard her say the name Madelyn Kensington.

"Where is she?" Doris asked.

Hudson leaned a little closer to Doris's desk.

"The Red Rope Inn, got it," she said low into the receiver. "I'll sure tell the sheriff when he returns. Should be half an hour or so."

Did something happen to Madelyn?

"She's hysterical? What about?" Doris asked into the phone. "Okay. I got it. I'll let him know. Thank you for the call." Before Doris could end her conversation and delay Hudson with questions, he was out the door.

Madelyn was in trouble. He'd heard it in Doris's voice. The Red Rope Inn was eighteen minutes from there, according to his GPS device. He glanced at the route, confident he could make it in ten.

Hudson zipped in and out of cars. The deputy on duty wouldn't appreciate any interference with his investigation, so Hudson needed to think of a good excuse to show up. Mentioning Doris might get her in trouble, and based on his proximity, he had about two minutes to come up with a plausible excuse.

The parking lot was quiet. All the action was going on inside the lobby, Hudson noticed as he searched for Madelyn through the glass. His pulse calmed a notch when he saw her—saw that she was okay—and he didn't want to care as much as he did. He told himself it was the action he missed and not the person who'd occupied his thoughts since she'd driven away.

"I couldn't get ahold of you on your cell." He made a beeline toward Madelyn with the pretense they were a couple. The bell gave away his presence the second the door moved.

Her gaze flew to him and he couldn't immediately discern if his being there was a good thing or not.

"Why are you here?" The shock in her voice gave away the answer...not thrilled.

Chapter Five

Deputy Hank Harley stepped in between Hudson and Madelyn, blocking the path. The deputy's left hand came up, palm aimed at Hudson, and his right remained firmly on the butt of his Glock. He was ready for that split-second decision that might come where he had to pull his weapon and fire. The action was so automatic that most cops kept a hand on their gun even during what many would consider routine traffic stops. Officers knew that traffic stops were right up there with domestic disturbance calls in terms of threat to an officer's safety. Hudson didn't know Harley on a personal level. He'd done his best to keep his presence as quiet as possible since returning to Cattle Barge a year ago, which meant Harley didn't know him or his background. That could be dangerous if Hudson charged in like a bull, so he stopped and made sure his hands were visible to the deputy.

"I'm going to have to ask you to leave, sir." Harley took a step toward Hudson. Most would view the move as threatening. A law-enforcement officer had one primary goal when he left for work—make it home again. Hudson appreciated Harley's motivation. But he was on a mission, too. *Tread lightly.*

"I'm a friend. I just want to make sure she's okay."
Both hands went up to show he wasn't carrying a
weapon. Texas was open-carry and that put some people on edge.

Harley sidestepped, putting Hudson and Madelyn
in his line of sight, and he looked like he was seeking
confirmation from Madelyn.

"I can use a friend right now." She didn't ask the
obvious question: How did he know she was there?

Hudson took her encouragement as a good sign.

"What's going on?" he asked, careful not to infringe
on Harley's investigation. Any random person who
cared about a victim would ask the same question.

"Someone was inside my room and left a message
for me." Her eyes were wild. She didn't need to spell it
out for him. He immediately realized she'd been threatened. He also noted how exhausted she looked. He ignored the inappropriate stir of attraction, chalking it up
to overprotective instincts. Yeah, right. He was being
chivalrous and that was all those feelings were. He
couldn't sell water in the desert with a fake sales pitch
like that. But this wasn't the time to worry about it.

"The white sedan?" Hudson took a purposeful stride
toward her and the deputy didn't protest, which was
the second good sign since he'd arrived.

"That's what I'm trying to ascertain," Harley said as
Madelyn released a panicked-sounding sigh.

"I'm not sure. I mean, I guess. The person from the
sedan makes sense. I didn't see anyone coming and
going from the parking lot." The words rushed out all
at once, almost sounding like they were tripping over
each other.

"Is there surveillance video of the parking lot?"

Hudson moved to her side without protest from Harley. He expected to maybe put a hand on her shoulder to provide some sense of comfort but she shot up and practically pounced toward him. He had to catch her to stop her from crashing into him and she immediately buried her face in his chest.

"I'm sorry." She pulled back after his muscles went rigid.

"It's fine." The feel of her body against his sent a lightning bolt directly to the center of his chest. Not usually the reaction he had with a woman this close but this wasn't the time to break it apart. He pushed the feeling aside as she leaned her head against his chest. His heart pounded and he told himself that it was from the rush of adrenaline that accompanied the possibility of real action and not from physical contact with her.

"There's no video on that side of the lot," the motel worker said.

"I'll check footage of nearby sites," the deputy said.

They both knew that could take days. Hudson thanked Harley anyway.

The deputy told everyone to stay put before he excused himself, presumably to check out her room.

"What did the message say?" There was no way Harley was going to let Hudson trample all over his crime scene, so he'd have to rely on Madelyn. She was trained to look for things out of the ordinary, same as him. But she was flustered and it was her life on the line and that made a difference.

"That I should walk away or die. It was scribbled on the mirror and I have no idea how anyone got inside. I mean, I sure didn't let anyone in my room or leave the door unlocked. You're the only person I know in town." She flashed her eyes at him, sending another jolt of electricity straight to his chest. Being this close to her was like standing on live wires in a thunderstorm.

"I'm guessing the staff denies giving out a key." He glanced toward the clerk.

"Yes. In fact, she's the one who called the law *on me*." Another flash of those cornflower blue eyes. She was scared but there was a lot more going on and he couldn't pinpoint what else it was. Exhaustion...yes. Fear...absolutely. Desperation...and another emotion...

"So far today someone ran you off the road and presumably another person has threatened you?" he asked.

"That about sums it up," she stated, and he didn't like the defeat in her voice.

"Did the deputy give you any indication of whether or not he believed the two incidents were related?" he continued.

"He said that it all seemed suspect and like it could be connected," she answered. There might be defeat in her voice but there was defiance in her eyes.

"*Could* be?" Hudson scoffed.

The bell on the door jingled.

"I'm afraid we should go into the station," the deputy said to Madelyn, and Hudson didn't like the way Harley looked at her.

"Oh, okay." She didn't seem to catch on to the fact this wasn't a good sign.

"My friend here is tired. She's had a long day." Hudson wanted to feel out the deputy. He glanced at his watch. "It's long past dinner time. She's probably starving, so I was thinking that I could bring her by after we grab a bite."

"I can give her a ride. It shouldn't take long for her to answer a few more questions," Harley said.

"Is there a good reason why I can't answer them right here?" She seemed to be catching on to Hudson's hesitation because her brow hiked up.

Harley didn't immediately answer.

"Can I ask a question, Deputy?" Hudson took a step closer to Harley and lowered his voice.

"Yes, sir," Harley said. Back with the "sir" business. What had changed in the last few minutes?

"What did you find in her room?" Hudson made sure his voice was low enough that only Harley could hear.

"Nothing," the deputy said. "Absolutely nada."

MADELYN STRAINED TO hear what Hudson was saying to the deputy and couldn't. It would be difficult to hear anything over the sound of her racing pulse. Yes, because it had been one hell of a day. But also because of the handsome cowboy in the room and it was totally inappropriate to think about that right now. So, she pushed those unproductive thoughts aside.

"What did he say?" she asked as Hudson walked toward her.

His shrug wasn't the most reassuring.

"Are you hungry?" he asked.

"I doubt I could eat anything," she stated.

"He wants you to ride with him to the station." His look of sympathy confused her.

"Why?" But she really wanted to ask why the cowboy was looking at her like she might be a little crazy.

"Because he wants to evaluate your statement and ask the same questions a few different ways to see if he can trip you up." An apologetic look followed but she appreciated his honesty.

"So he either thinks I'm a wack-job or…"

It hit her fast and hard like a bomb dropping out of the sky on a clear summer day.

"He thinks I'm guilty of something? Like what? Why would I scribble a threat on my own mirror?" She glared at the deputy now, putting him in the same category as the front desk clerk. This day was off-the-chain bad. What on earth had she done to deserve such awful luck recently? First, she'd been dealing with a bad breakup. Okay, "bad" was calling it lightly. Then she'd learned that her father might not be her… Never mind… She couldn't even go there right now. In the process of receiving the most earth-shattering news of her life, Madelyn had been run off the road and now her life had been threatened. That should be the worst of it, but, no, this day had somehow managed to get even worse as the deputy suspected *her* of doing something. But what? Yelling at the front desk clerk wasn't exactly a crime.

"There's nothing in your room," Hudson said.

"What do you mean?" She didn't quite absorb those words. "Of course there is. It's written plain as day on the mirror."

Hudson shook his head.

Hold on…

Madelyn knew exactly what that meant.

"What are you doing in *here* when the wack-job who threatened me is out *there*?" she asked the deputy, her anger rising to the surface and bubbling over. "The person who did this is probably right outside staring at us this very second and you're in here...what?...think-ing that I'm nuts?"

Hudson seemed to be on the same page because he was already at the window, scanning the area, and she assumed that he was searching for whoever was behind this. Someone was messing with her, that much was clear.

Ed Staples?

He seemed to know all about her paternity and that was what this was all about. Wasn't it? Being run off the road. The threat. Someone had tried to keep her from coming to town, and now that she was here, that same person wanted her to leave quietly.

"Ma'am, if you don't mind. I'd like to get to the sher-iff's office so we can clear all this up." The deputy's body was angled toward her. "We'll send someone to analyze the scene and they'll find the truth."

He didn't exactly say "crime scene." If Kelsey hadn't hit the panic button, Madelyn doubted he would've shown up at all.

"Am I under arrest?" she asked point-black.

"No, ma'am."

"Then no. I won't go to the station with you." Mad-elyn knew her rights and she didn't have to put up with any of this.

Hudson spun around, and when his attention was directed at her, frissons of heat rippled through her. "You sure about that?"

"I have no intention of running around in circles with a deputy—or anyone else, for that matter—who doesn't believe me," she said. "Call the sheriff. He'll be able to tell you what happened earlier with a white sedan. That couldn't have been in my imagination be-cause the man standing near you witnessed the whole scene. I'm being followed, targeted, and I'm tired of playing games. I already told you what happened here and you can believe me or not. It's your choice. But I'm walking out that door and getting into my own car unless my hands are zip-cuffed."

"Stay in town where I can reach you," the deputy said. She knew enough about the law to realize he had nothing to hold her on. Asking her to go down to the station with him was ridiculous. What would they do there anyway? The place was overrun, and when she really looked at him, the deputy had dark circles cradling his eyes. He was most likely overworked and overwrought, and since he couldn't tell that a crime had been committed, he was grasping at straws.

"Do you know of any hotels where I'll be safe?" She shot an intentional look at Kelsey.

"I have a place in mind." The cowboy stood, feet apart, in an athletic stance. He was almost intimidatingly tall, and a trill of awareness skittered across her skin as she noticed. "My ranch. You can stay with me until this is sorted out."

She wanted to argue against the idea, but, honestly, she was too tired to put up much of a fight. Exhaustion wore her nerves thin, and questions about her family, her heritage, pecked at her skull. But being with Hudson 24/7? Was that really such a good idea?

"You have a problem with the arrangement?" she asked the deputy. Madelyn was still undecided but she couldn't think of a better option.

"I guess not," Harley responded.

If he couldn't come up with an objection, neither could she. So, that had to be a good thing.

Right?

"TELL ME EVERYTHING that happened," Hudson said as he poured a fresh cup of coffee and then handed it to Madelyn. Being back in his kitchen was odd, considering she'd known him less than a day. Rather than analyze it after what had become one of the longest days of her life, she tucked it aside.

The mug warmed her hands and she welcomed the burn on her throat with the first sip.

He already knew the details of the road incident. Then there was the news about Mike Butler, but there was no way she planned to talk about something she had yet to verify or understand. *Although, it could be significant*, a little voice in the back of her mind said.

Madelyn sized up Hudson. Should she really bare her soul to a man who was keeping his identity a secret? She'd had her fill of deceptions for one day. Check that, for one lifetime. Everything she thought she knew could be a lie. This man was a rancher about as much as she was a sous-chef. To be clear, the only thing she knew how to make in the kitchen was toast, and there were no guarantees she wouldn't burn the bread. She could, however, make a mean cup of coffee thanks to pods and machines that basically did all the work.

"I can tell what you're thinking," he said and his voice startled her. "Don't lie to me or hide anything."

"I'm sure I have no idea what you mean," she said lamely. He seemed to know that she was evaluating him, trying to decide if she should ask about his background. Strangers confided in her all the time courtesy of her line of work. But this guy? Everything about his posture said he was a closed book.

So, how could she put her faith in someone who didn't trust her?

Chapter Six

"Do you remember anything about the driver of the sedan that you didn't think of earlier?" Hudson asked Madelyn. She'd been sizing him up while they made small talk and he needed to see if she'd decided to trust him. *Trust* might be a strong word. *Confide* was better.

"No. I couldn't get a good look at his face because of the ski mask," she admitted.

"Which no one wears in Texas, let alone on a day with hundred-degree heat," he stated.

"I didn't notice any white cars in the parking lot, and after this morning I've been watching for that guy to return." She rolled the coffee mug in between her palms before adding, "There were two trucks and a minivan when I arrived."

Hudson had hoped that the coffee would bring some color back to her face. She was still white and her lips purple from a little bit of shock and a healthy dose of fear. "I like that you were watching out for the driver to return. You mentioned a boyfriend before, a bad breakup. Are you still thinking in that direction?"

For a split second her lips thinned, forming a small line.

"Wish I could be sure," she said with a shrug.

What was she holding back? "Why else would a random person want to rattle you or force you to leave town?"

"What makes you think this guy doesn't want me dead?" The whites of her eyes shone brightly against the fluorescent lights in his kitchen.

"My first thought is—" He flashed his eyes at her. "Forgive my bluntness, but he could've shot you on the road."

"True."

"So, this person is worried about hurting innocent people," he said.

"Or he was waiting for a clean shot," she stated.

Okay, he'd give her that, so he nodded. He took another sip of coffee and let the thought simmer. "He might've been trying to scare you."

"Mission accomplished," she said on a harsh sigh.

Why would someone try to scare her? Did the driver assume she hadn't learned her lesson after he'd tried to run her off the road? Did he follow her to the motel, break in and scribble the message once she left? Those actions indicated someone trying to scare her, not kill her. But scare her away from what? Experience had taught him that deep down the victim knew. The trick to breaking open an investigation was helping her realize it.

"Why did you say you were going to Hereford Ranch?" he questioned.

"I didn't."

Hudson took in a sharp breath. "I thought you wanted my help."

"You offered protection and I took it. Not the same thing." She didn't break eye contact. "Can I ask you a question?"

He nodded.

"Why do you care?"

"I don't," he said, selling the lie with a stone-cold glare.

Her shoulders stiffened and she gave as good as she got in the icy-stare department.

Hudson ought to be grateful that she was throwing him a lifeline with the cold-shoulder routine because he was sliding down a slippery slope. He didn't want to give a hoot what happened to her—hell, to anyone. And he considered himself smart enough to pull back when he realized he was fighting a losing battle.

But that look she shot him stung.

And a deep need to break down a few of her walls welled up. For reasons he wouldn't dissect or fight, he stalked toward her. He stopped inches from her. She was shorter than him by almost a foot and had the most delicate lines on her face. His fingers flexed and released as her hand came up to his chest as if to stop him. Instead of pushing him back a step like he assumed she would, she grabbed a fistful of his T-shirt and tugged him toward her. Those gorgeous blue eyes of hers were staring up at him, daring him to take this a step further.

This close, the pull was too much to ignore. So, he dipped his head and kissed her. The taste of coffee was still on her lips.

Hudson braced himself for the rejection he expected to come but didn't. Instead of shoving him away, she drew him closer and parted her lips. He drove his tongue inside her mouth and tasted the sweet mix of her and the bold coffee.

Her hands, which had been fisted in his shirt, released the material before planting on his shoulders. There was so much heat in that one kiss Hudson almost had to take a step back to absorb the blast. He didn't. And so they stood, toe to toe, tongues engaged.

He brought his right hand up to her neck, his thumb resting on the base where her pulse pounded wildly, matching the tempo of his own. With one small forward step the gap between them disappeared. That one move, seemingly so insignificant, was gasoline-poured-onto-a-fire hot. The air crackled around them with the intensity of burning embers.

The kiss, meant to build a bridge of trust, had knocked Hudson completely off balance. Right, extending an olive branch. That was all he was doing and not satisfying a primal urge he'd felt since he first set eyes on her.

Whatever his motive, the earth shifted underneath his feet and his heart shot a warning flare. Keep this up; get into serious trouble.

Pulling back was difficult but necessary. Looking at those pink lips when he did was a mistake but one he made anyway. Hell, why not? He was racking up errors in judgment today. What was one more?

"That shouldn't have happened," he said sternly. She looked at him like she wasn't sure whom he was trying to convince, him or her.

"It won't again," she said with similar conviction.

"Back to the case." He took a step back and searched the countertop for his cup of coffee, thinking that he liked the taste of it on her tongue better. Somewhere along the way, he'd set his mug down but couldn't remember when or where for the life of him. He spied it next to where he stood before the kiss—a kiss that he tried to convince himself meant nothing. Tell that to the beating lump in his chest, hammering wildly against his ribs.

Hudson topped off his mug and took a sip. "Where were we?"

"I was about to tell you something that can't leave this room." Madelyn didn't meet his gaze this time as he examined her.

Difficult truths were more easily admitted sitting down, so he led her to the round table off the kitchen.

She sat there for a minute and he didn't speak. She seemed to be pulling on all her strength to say what was on her mind and he had no plans to intrude. This was the look victims got before they told their stories. Hudson's stomach lining twisted thinking about her in those terms. He didn't like thinking of her in any way other than the strong, capable and intelligent woman she was.

"Ed Staples is Mike Butler's attorney. He summoned me to Cattle Barge with the promise of telling me something I'd want to know." Her voice was even and it seemed to be taking all her energy to keep it that way as she stared out the window. "I thought he was going to give me a scoop, you know, an exclusive. In hindsight, I guess I should've realized that I was being set up."

She stilled and Hudson didn't so much as make a sound. Frighten her away now and she might disappear into the woods like a hunted deer, and never return. For reasons Hudson didn't want to examine, he needed to know why Ed Staples had contacted her.

A sharp sigh pealed from her lips before she continued. "What I'm about to tell you hasn't been confirmed, or, at least, I haven't had any tests run to prove or disprove it."

Hudson nodded encouragement for her to continue. She needed the space to do that on her own terms, so he patiently waited with his eyes cast down.

"And it can't leave this room. I mean, it will get out eventually and will be big news, but I need your word that you'll keep this between us for now," she stated.

"You have it," he responded, making eye contact. She needed to know how seriously he took his promises.

"Basically, if I'm to believe Ed Staples then Maverick Mike Butler is my father." Madelyn crossed her arms tightly. Her shoulders tensed. Muscles around her eyes tightened. Looking at her, it was like a wall was coming up between them. Her face lost expression and he understood that she was distancing herself from what might be the truth, like he'd seen so many victims do while recounting their stories.

The admission sat in the air between them, too thick to wade through at the moment. Money always topped the list of motives. Greed ranked right up there with crime-of-passion killings. Based on her expression while telling him the news, she hadn't seen any of this coming. She was telling him now because she obviously believed someone wasn't happy with this revelation. A good reporter would easily clue into motivation. "Who knows about this?"

"Besides the two of us?" The blank stare overshadowed all the heat and intensity that had been on her face only moments ago. It was like she'd faded out. A washed-out version of her sat in front of him as though someone had scrubbed all the vibrancy and color out of her face. And yet she was still beautiful.

Hudson nodded.

"Ed Staples."

"STAPLES, THE BUTLER family attorney, summoned you to Cattle Barge to tell you Mike Butler is your father?" Hudson asked, and she shared the shock on his face that he quickly tried to cover.

"Yes."

"On your way to receive the news someone runs you off the road." He seemed to be thinking out loud because he was staring at his coffee mug. "And then—what?—you come back to your room to a threatening message."

"That's right," she admitted.

"My question is simple. Why not shoot when the driver had the chance?" Hudson pushed his chair back from the table and leaned forward, his elbows resting on his knees.

"I wondered the same thing." She shrugged.

"Let's go back to the beginning. When I first met you there was a possibility that your ex was behind this. Is there any way, in your mind, he could be involved?" His gaze came up to meet hers and she had to fight with everything inside her not to give away how tenuous her hold on her emotions was. The tether, however small, attaching her to logic and reason was a lifeline she couldn't afford to snap.

"What would he have to gain?" she asked.

"Good question. For now, we'll set him aside as a suspect." He took a sip of coffee before setting his mug on the table. "I need to talk to Ed Staples."

"I doubt it's him. He knew my phone number, and my address was right there on the letter he gave me. Why call me in the first place? I mean, if he wanted to get rid of me I would've never seen it coming. My guess is that someone besides the three of us knows about this…*possibility.*" She didn't bother to hide the frustration in her voice. It wouldn't do any good. The life she'd known for thirty years was over if this was true. Then again, wouldn't it be just like a self-centered billionaire to lie about something just to manipulate the lives of others? But what good would that do now that he was gone? "Before I do anything else, I need confirmation that he's my father."

"Ed Staples didn't provide proof?" His brow shot up.

"I have no plans to take someone else's word on it. I'll need a few days to arrange testing on my terms. I'm not even sure how to go about it yet, so I have to do a little research first," she continued. A little seed of hope that this could all be a bad dream was blossoming somewhere deep inside her.

"What about your mother? Can you ask her?"

"She died when I was born, so, no." The sadness in her voice caught her off guard. Her hand came up absently to toy with the dragonfly necklace. If Mike Butler was her father that meant she knew even less about her mother. Her father had made the subject off-limits, but the knowledge her mother had died because of negligent hospital practices had driven so many of Madelyn's choices. She didn't need Freud to tell her why she'd taken a job as an investigative reporter. She wanted to give answers, peace, to other families. She wanted others to avoid dangerous situations being covered up by hospitals, businesses and crooks. She wanted to protect people from the kind of pain she'd experienced.

"I'm sorry," Hudson said quietly with a gentleness that threatened to crack the wall Madelyn had built to protect herself.

"It's all I've ever known, so..." There had been countless times in her life that she'd wished for her mother. When she was a little girl she used to imagine what it would be like to have a real mom for a few hours, days, years. Madelyn had played the what-she-would-trade game more times than she could count. There were times when she would've traded years from her own life for just a few minutes with the woman. Madelyn had grown up believing her mother had been a saint. She'd built the woman up to angelic status. From a child's eyes, her mother could do no wrong, and she'd carried that belief into adulthood. So, this betrayal hurt like hell and a piece of her still wanted to cling to the fantasy where her mother was perfect.

A thought struck—a dark thought—and the devastation must've shown on her face because Hudson scooted his chair toward her and took one of her hands in his.

"What is it?" he asked.

"I was just wondering if my father knew that I might not be his biological child. Or did my mother have an affair and hide the truth?" A tear escaped because it would explain so much about their relationship. The cowboy thumbed it away. Contact caused her stomach to quiver.

Of course, if her father—could she even still call him that until she knew one way or the other?—had known the truth, it could be the reason he'd kept her at arm's length all these years. Did he resent her for not being his child? For causing her mother to die?

"Is he…?" Hudson didn't seem to want to finish the sentence, so she did it for him.

"Dead? No. He's very much alive." If she could call it that. He maintained the same boring routine since she could remember—up by 5:00 a.m., breakfast, work until after 7:30 p.m., dinner. Bed. Sundays, he worked around the yard and stayed in the garage most of the day.

"But you don't want to ask him?" That brow arched again.

"It's complicated." She blew out a breath.

"So, we focus on who stands to lose if you stick around," he said, and she was thankful that he'd redirected the conversation.

She'd have to deal with her emotions later, and if the revelation was true, she figured she'd be dealing with them on some level for the rest of her life. How did anyone process or reconcile a deception of that scale? Her entire identity had been shattered the minute Ed Staples had handed her that letter.

Madelyn's cell buzzed and the noise made her jump. She scanned the countertops for her purse. Where had she set it down?

"The racket is coming from over here," Hudson said, making a move to get up.

"I got it." The words came out more sharply than she'd intended. "Sorry."

Hudson didn't respond as he gripped his mug and refilled his coffee.

Madelyn located her phone and glanced at the screen. She had six text messages from her ex.

"Everything okay?" Hudson asked.

"Yeah. Fine."

"I've come to learn that word means just the opposite. I take it the messages are from someone you're not anxious to hear from," he said. He leaned against the counter as he studied her face.

She didn't want to be under scrutiny right now. Exhaustion made it difficult to fake a smile, let alone lift up the phone.

"Are you hungry?" he asked.

"Don't go to any trouble," she said. "I doubt I could eat anything anyway."

"I'm not much in the kitchen but I can throw something on the grill. Won't take half an hour and that'll give you time to clean up and rest before supper," he said.

"A shower does sound amazing right now," she offered and under normal circumstances would've enjoyed the quick glance of appreciation. He'd kissed her before but that was most likely to keep her from becoming hysterical. But an attraction? Her body reacted to him every time he was close, and even though they couldn't act on it, she felt satisfied to know that he was having a similar reaction to her.

He was, right?

Or was she just seeing something she wanted to see?

After her relationship with Owen had gone the way it had, she wasn't feeling the most confident in her decision-making ability when it came to the opposite sex. Besides, she'd touched the stove. Been burned. And had no plans to step into the kitchen anytime soon, not even for a man who made her pulse pound wildly by just being in the same room with her.

Besides, she didn't even know the cowboy beyond the surface and a simmering attraction. And her life had just been turned upside down, which was probably why she was fabricating a relationship in her mind with him when she needed to take a step back so she could sort out the craziness.

The worst part?

She was still thinking about how right the world had felt when he pressed his lips to hers and all the background noise disappeared.

"Madelyn?" The cowboy's voice was low, concerned, like if he spoke too loudly he might startle her.

He did and she jumped anyway, quickly reining in her emotions.

"Forensics will most likely find a print in your room and this will be cleared up before you know it," he said. "You're welcome to stay here as long as you need to, but if you stand in that spot much longer I'm going to be tempted to kiss you again."

"Which way did you say the shower was?" she asked.

He pointed to the hallway behind her.

Scooping up her overnight bag, she spun around and marched toward it.

Every ranch-style house she'd been in had the same layout, so she'd only asked to test if she could trust her voice. Because she wanted the cowboy's lips on hers again. But wanting and doing were two different things and she needed to keep a clear head.

It was most likely the stress of the day that had her wanting to feel his big strong hands on her again, roaming her body and getting to know every inch of her.

Or something else that she couldn't afford to consider. Something that had her gripping her bag and trying to decide if she should march into that kitchen or go against every urge inside her and force herself into the bathroom.

Madelyn released the bag, causing it to tumble onto the floor. Then she stalked into the next room.

Chapter Seven

A cold shower went a long way toward cooling Madelyn's skin and helping her refocus. She toweled off and moved into the adjacent bedroom.

She could tell that Hudson wasn't kidding about his grilling skills, based on the smells wafting down the hall while she dressed. Freshly brushed teeth and clean clothes had her feeling like her old self again. *Almost.* A part of her wondered if she'd ever be that person again.

Since going down that road before she had proof was as productive as trying to take notes using a dead branch, she checked her cell. Still no calls from her father and there was an odd comfort in that fact. Well, she guessed he was still her father. What if he wasn't? If Mike Butler was her biological father she had no one left: both of her parents would be dead. She seriously doubted his four children would be thrilled by her presence. Heck, one or all of them could be behind the threat. The guy in the white sedan could've followed her to the motel, written the note when she was on her way to the ranch. The Butlers could've hired someone to chase her away.

Madelyn didn't realize how tightly she'd been gripping her phone until she caught a glimpse of her knuckles, which were bone-white. On a deep intake of air, she pushed off the bed and strode into the kitchen.

"Steaks are ready," Hudson said.

On the table were two plates of steaks, grilled asparagus and mushrooms, along with what looked like hash brown potatoes. So, he was gorgeous *and* could cook. Most women would consider they'd hit the jackpot if a man like him made dinner, and normally she would, too. Now, however, Madelyn's thoughts couldn't stray far from her circumstances.

"Didn't have enough time to bake those." He motioned toward the plate containing the potatoes.

"Are you kidding? Hash browns are my favorite," she said with more enthusiasm than she'd expected. "Sorry, I must be hungrier than I realized."

"You're kidding, right? Because I know you didn't just apologize for appreciating what I cooked," he said with a smile that could seduce a room full of women with one flash. Her included, based on the way her heart fluttered.

She needed to keep that in mind and her emotions in check because an attraction with a man who kept secrets was right up there with asking to be tied up and thrown in the ocean. "Do you normally have two steaks ready to go?"

"Not usually, no." He motioned toward the table, for her to take a seat as he pulled her chair out for her.

And then it dawned on her that he'd been expecting company. Of course he would be. He was gorgeous and with that voice—a deep rumble with just enough cadence to let her know he was full-blooded Texan. His name seemed familiar, she realized now, but she couldn't place the reason and half figured her imagination was at work.

"I'm sorry if I messed up your plans," she quickly added with an apologetic look as her cheeks flamed. He was being kind but he had a life and probably someone special. The thought struck her as odd that this stranger knew so much about her and she knew very little about him. She glanced around the room, looking for any signs of a female presence; a man as good-looking as Hudson must have a girlfriend.

"No problem." He wasn't giving up a whole lot, either.

Madelyn sat at the table, unsure she'd be able to eat half of her plate, so she surprised herself when fifteen minutes later the entire plate was clear.

"You didn't say much during dinner." He motioned toward the plate. "I'm guessing the steak was okay."

"Better than that. It was amazing." Her stomach was happy, the kind of happy that came with a satisfying meal. Being with the strong, capable cowboy settled her nerves enough to relax. The smile he gave warmed her in places she couldn't afford to allow. Those were a few more things she didn't need to notice about the mysterious man.

He cleared his plate.

"At least let me do the dishes," she protested.

"Not tonight. This meal is on me," he said with the smile that carved out dimples in both cheeks.

"I'd like to contribute in some way." Madelyn had learned early on that there was no such thing as a free meal.

"How about making breakfast tomorrow morning? Can you handle that?" he asked.

She shrugged. "I can try. But I'm better at cleaning up afterward."

The deep rumble that started in his chest and rolled out was pretty darn sexy. It took a second to register that he was laughing at her.

"What did I say that was so funny?" she asked, a little indignant.

"It was the look on your face at the suggestion of cooking, like I'd just asked you to lick the bottom of my boot," he said with more of that rumble.

"You may not want to eat anything that comes from a kitchen where I'm in charge," she said.

"So I gathered," he said before his expression changed. "While you were in the shower, I checked in with the sheriff's office."

"Oh, yeah? What did he have to say?" Madelyn took her plate to the sink.

"He apologized on behalf of his deputy. I don't need to remind you how overworked they are over there with everything else going on." Hudson motioned for her to hand it over.

"That's not exactly reassuring," she stated honestly.

"It does make you a lot less safe than I'd like," he agreed. "But you're fine as long as you're here."

She handed over the plate. It was time to fold. Besides, she might not be alive if it weren't for the chivalrous cowboy. "Thank you, by the way. Not just for dinner and giving me a place to stay tonight, but for everything you've done so far."

He shrugged off her comment. His kindness might not be much to him. She figured helping a woman in distress was part of his code. But it meant everything to her. He seemed like a decent guy and she was pretty certain that he was her only friend in town.

Beyond the obvious, she knew very little about him. A shiver raced through her as she searched her memory to see if there'd been a lock on the bedroom door.

"Coffee?" he asked.

"I'd love some but you have to let me get it." She shot him a severe look as he started to wave her off again. "It'll make me feel better about your hospitality if you let me do something for you."

A smile parted his lips and her thoughts immediately zeroed in on the kiss they'd shared earlier. So much heat and…what else?…temptation.

Well, she really didn't need to go there. Her thoughts immediately snapped to Owen, and the emotional burns were still fresh. She refilled their mugs from earlier, trying to push thoughts of her ex out of her mind. Those seemed, she didn't know, out of place while spending time with Hudson.

He thanked her as he took the mug, and sparks lit when their fingers brushed against each other.

"I can't say that I know much about Mike Butler's family." She reclaimed her seat at the table.

"He has four kids that I know of." He shot an apologetic look toward her before adding, "Possibly five but we haven't confirmed that yet."

"I remember reading something about them. There's a set of twins, male. And two females," she said, ignoring the pounding in her chest. She was grateful the cowboy hadn't lumped her in as family. Until she had definitive proof, she had no plans to call herself a Butler. The thought did cross her mind that Mike Butler could've afforded the best medical care on the planet for her mother. Had he known at the time that Madelyn was his? Anger roared through her at the possibility and her hand came up to the necklace for reassurance. She fingered the detail.

"Everything okay?" Hudson asked, shaking her out of her heavy thoughts.

"Yes, sure. We were talking about the Butlers," she said.

"That's right. Ella Butler's the oldest and Cadence is the youngest. Of course, there've been a couple of people claiming to belong to the Butler clan." His one eyebrow arched as he watched her. "Time will tell."

"Well, I'm not one of them," she stated a little too tartly. She started to apologize but he waved her off like it was no big deal. It was. She wasn't normally so rude to someone trying to help her. "It's not okay to come off as a jerk. I've had too much coming at me and I'm still processing."

"It's a lot," he admitted, and she was grateful someone understood. She was clueless as to what to do with the information. Even if she could get ahold of her father to ask what he knew, how would she even approach the subject?

Excuse me, Dad...but are you really my dad? Or, *Did you know Mom was cheating on you?*

Was he from here? "Do you know the Butlers personally?"

"Only from the news, which I don't pay much attention to." He took another sip of coffee before setting the cup on the table.

More questions pecked at her skull and there was no chance of getting answers tonight. At this rate, she'd end the night with a raging headache and that was about all.

"Have you lived here long?" She needed to think about something else to give herself a break.

"Not really."

"Did you grow up here?" Madelyn wanted to know more about Hudson and, let's face it, she wanted to talk about something besides her crazy day for a change.

He drained his cup and stood. "You've already seen your bedroom and you know where the bathroom is. If you need more towels or blankets, you'll find them in the hall closet. I like to run the AC when I sleep. That's all you need to know to get through the night."

With that, he walked away.

Okay. Madelyn rinsed out both cups. She glanced around, looking for something that would tell her more about Hudson Dale. The place seemed normal enough. Even though there weren't many decorations, the few he had were simple and well-placed. She heard the shower turn on in the other room and forced thoughts of him undressing out of her mind. This day had been out of control and the last thing she needed to do was let her imagination run wild. It was her imagination that made her good at her job. She was able to come at a topic from every angle until she fit all the puzzle pieces together. But that same imagination had her wondering if she'd be okay alone in a stranger's house.

Madelyn almost laughed out loud. She knew the statistics. A woman's greatest threat came from those she knew and, in most cases, loved. She found the notion that she'd be safest with a complete stranger ironic. It was true, though.

Even so, she checked her bedroom door for a lock

and was disappointed when she didn't find one. After brushing her teeth, she glanced around the room, looking for anything to secure the door closed. The dresser was a heavy wood piece, significant, and probably too heavy to move on her own. The chair in the corner could work. She repositioned the back underneath the door handle like she'd seen done countless times in movies. Call her crazy but her day had been right up there with one of her worst and, bad as it had been, could get worse if she let her guard down.

A ridiculous part of her said she'd been in way more trouble when she'd locked lips with the handsome cowboy. He threatened to bring a part of her to life that no one before him had.

MADELYN FINALLY UNDERSTOOD what it meant to sleep with one eye open. That wasn't entirely true because she didn't actually sleep. Instead, she drifted in and out, half expecting someone to burst through the door at any second. The night could best be described as fits and starts, and she'd almost thrown in the towel half a dozen times. Relief washed over her when the sun finally peeked through the slats in the mini-blinds and she could get up without disturbing her host.

Her mind kept spinning over the previous day and her possible parentage.

A soft knock at the door came about the time she sat up. She pulled the covers up to her chin as her pulse galloped.

"Coffee's ready," the strong male voice belonging to Hudson said. The sound made her heart stutter.

"I'll be right out." Her gaze flew to her body, making sure every inch of her skin was covered below the chin. And that was silly when she thought about it because he was on the other side of a closed door. Emotion had momentarily overtaken logic. If this was any indication of how well her brain was going to work today, Madelyn was in for a real treat.

She stretched sore muscles, dressed and threw her hair up in a ponytail, trying to bring herself back to center with deep breathing techniques she'd learned in yoga class in college. When that didn't work, she decided she needed caffeine. Like, now. Or sooner.

"Morning," Hudson said, looking fresh as she made a beeline for the coffeepot.

"Same," she grumbled. She was so not a morning person.

"How'd you sleep?" he asked, handing over a fresh mug that smelled out-of-this-world amazing.

"I didn't much," she admitted because there was no point in lying. Her mind had gone round and round last night on the possibility of being a Butler. What if she was? What if she wasn't? How could any of this be true? Granted, her father hadn't been the warm-and-fuzzy type, but he'd always been there for her and she knew without a doubt that he'd loved her. Right? Was he obstinate? Yes. A slave to routine? Absolutely. A bad person? No way. And yet an annoying little voice inside her head kept reminding her that she'd always felt like he was holding back, keeping her at arm's length.

"You didn't like the bed?" That he seemed concerned about her comfort was as sweet as it was surprising.

"It was great. It's me. I kept going over everything that happened yesterday." She bit back a yawn as she took a seat at the table. In a few minutes the caffeine would kick in and her day could begin. In times like these, she wished she had an IV of the brown liquid.

"I'm assuming you're talking about the incident with the white sedan." He took the seat across from her and she ignored the way his nearness made her pulse sprint.

"That and so much more." She made eyes at him before taking another sip.

He didn't seem to know how to react to that and she certainly didn't.

"Did you remember anything else from the events of yesterday?"

"Just what you already know." She shook her head. "I keep going in circles. The white sedan was scary. Being told Mike Butler might be my father completely threw me for a loop. And then there's the 'welcome' message on the mirror. Add to all that the drama I've been experiencing with my ex and it feels like my life has spun out of control."

"That would be a lot for anyone to process." He drummed his fingertips on his coffee mug.

"I just keep asking myself, 'Why? Why me? Why now?' It feels a little like the walls are caving in." She couldn't look directly at him when she spoke. Guilt, or maybe it was embarrassment, assaulted her.

"Bad things happen to good people every day." There was something in his voice she couldn't put her finger on.

How many times in the past few weeks had she tried to convince herself that was true? It didn't stop the black cloud from hanging over her head ever since this whole ordeal with Owen had begun. "I haven't asked for anything from the Butlers, so why would one of them target me?"

"Not yet. But you could, especially if paternity proves true." He made a good point.

"I wouldn't," she countered.

"They don't know that." Right again.

"Granted, they have no idea who I am, but if Ed Staples is to be believed, they shouldn't know about me at all." It was fact and had gotten lost in the stress of yesterday. "The envelope he gave me was sealed and he said he didn't even know what it contained until he took one look at me."

The cowboy sat there, sipping his coffee, contemplating.

Madelyn needed to get up and move. Her nerves were on edge and she needed to keep busy. Overthinking something never made it better. "I promised you breakfast. I hope you have a working toaster."

His eyes widened. "Based on your reaction last night to the thought of cooking, I thought we could go out for breakfast tacos."

"Good call." Madelyn's smile died on her lips. Her mind kept circling back to her problems and who was trying to get rid of her.

"This doesn't look good for the lawyer," Hudson finally said, bringing the conversation back down to reality. "He's the only one who knew when you were coming, that you were coming at all."

"Yes, but I was with him when the note was written on my mirror," she clarified.

"He could've slipped a few bucks to one of the workers at the Red Rope Inn." Hudson drained his cup and rose to his feet. "Let's go find out who was working besides Kelsey and who might've had access to your room. We'll pick up breakfast on the way."

"I'm pretty sure Kelsey isn't going to speak to me again. She'll most likely hit the panic button if she sees me so much as pull into the parking lot." Madelyn followed suit with the cowboy, welcoming the caffeine boost.

"I'd let you wait in the truck but I'd rather keep you where I can see you." He reminded her of just how much danger she was in.

She couldn't argue with his point.

"And then we can talk to the lawyer," he said. "I'll see what kind of feel I get from him."

"What would Ed Staples have to gain from hurting me, though?" She followed Hudson to the garage, where he opened the passenger door of the truck for her.

"Someone's trying to scare you away, keep you silent, and I'm not ready to rule anyone out just yet." He stepped up to the driver's side in one easy motion, whereas she'd clumsily climbed into the passenger seat. He moved fluidly, with athletic grace.

He also brought up another issue.

"The lawyer summoned me, so why would he try to run me off the road?" she asked. "Wouldn't he just ignore his boss's request? After all, Staples is the one who brought this to my attention in the first place."

"Good point. Although, he might've figured news would get out eventually. Or he could be innocent and someone could be monitoring his calls. I'm assuming he used a cell phone?" He navigated down the path toward the gate, and she couldn't help but think that just yesterday morning she'd been on this same road.

"The call had a cell-quality to it," she admitted.

She was used to picking up on things like that in her line of work.

"The Butler estate is worth a fortune. Billions of dollars are on the line. Someone could be monitoring his phone activity." He pulled onto the street and a cold shiver raced down her spine, as she thought about the events that had unfolded the last time she was there.

"I need to get my car." She didn't like the thought of leaving her convertible in the motel parking lot, exposed.

"You can drive it back to the house and park in the garage for safekeeping." He seemed to pick up on the reason for her concern.

"I should find another place to stay. I've already inconvenienced you enough." She pulled out her cell. She could find another hotel using her phone's app.

"At this point, I'd be more comfortable if you stayed with me at the ranch. I'd like to see this through and make sure you're okay. The sheriff's office is too busy to put any manpower on your complaint and it's clear someone doesn't want you here. You could go home and not be safe until this case is resolved." He gripped the steering wheel. "It's your call, but you're welcome to stay at the ranch."

She'd thought that renting a room from a bed-and-breakfast could work but she knew security would be too lax. Then there was a hotel option, which would be expensive. Her budget was tight but she didn't feel right living off the graciousness of a stranger, either. Besides, experience had taught her depending on others was a mistake.

"It's nice of you to offer, but—"

"Think about it, at least," he said. "Hotels aren't the

most secure and your car would be exposed. We have no idea who could be behind this."

She thought about what Owen had scrawled across her hood with spray paint. At the very least she didn't want to deal with him finding her and pulling another stunt like that one. A restraining order wasn't exactly an ironclad guarantee that he wouldn't show up. She'd chew on that a little longer and see how she felt after talking to the workers at the Red Rope Inn.

Her cell buzzed in her hand, startling her. And then she stared at the screen, unsure if she should answer.

"Who is it?" Hudson asked.

"Ed Staples."

"Answer it and let him know that he's on speaker." He'd used his cop tone. He had to have been a cop, right?

"This is Madelyn." She couldn't say for sure what Hudson's background was and there hadn't been any clues at his house, either. "I'm with a friend and you should know that he can hear the call."

"Are you all right?" There seemed to be genuine concern in his voice.

"Why wouldn't I be?" She had no plans to tip her hand about the message on the mirror. If he was involved she might be able to trip him up.

"You tore out of here pretty fast yesterday," he stated.

She couldn't argue with that. "Is that the reason you called? To check on me?"

"I'm concerned at how you're taking the news. I can only guess how confusing this must be." He seemed sincere and honest. But after Owen, she didn't exactly trust her instincts about people anymore and especially men. She tried not to chew on the irony of that thought considering she'd just stayed in a strange man's home.

"All I have is a piece of paper claiming that Mike Butler is my father. That doesn't change a thing, in my opinion," she said as coolly as she could.

"Oh." What was in his voice? Shock. Yes. But what else?

Disbelief.

"What's wrong, Mr. Staples? Are you surprised that I'm not jumping all over a claim to Mike Butler's fortune?" She listened for background noise to figure out his location.

"To be honest? Yes." There was nothing to give away his surroundings. It was quiet and he was most likely calling from that same office inside the Butler camp where they spoke less than twenty-four hours ago.

"Well, then you obviously don't know me very well, do you?" she asked, but it was rhetorical.

He started to say something but she cut him off.

"Guess you had me figured wrong," she said. Was she trying to prove how different she was from a Butler child? Probably. But it didn't stop the little blossom of hope that all this was a bad dream and she'd be getting back to her life—a life without Owen—by tomorrow.

"Not really," he stated, and there was an astonished quality to his voice.

"What's that supposed to mean?" she asked.

Staples hesitated. Then came, "That's exactly what your father would've said."

Chapter Eight

"My father is Charles Kensington until proven otherwise." The slight tremor to Madelyn's voice belied her certainty. She was coming off strong, reassured. Based on Hudson's experience, her house of cards was about to tumble down and she knew it. That was the reason for the tough-guy act.

"Will you be able to stop by today and discuss what this news means?" Ed Staples asked.

"I'll think about it," she said. "I have a few things that I have to take care of first."

"Call me when you're ready and I'll arrange for you to meet the others," he stated.

She hoped he was talking about the Butler kids and not more people like her. How many kids did Maverick Mike have?

"I will."

It took a few seconds of Madelyn staring out the front windshield for her shoulders to relax into the seat after she dropped her phone into her purse.

"How did your father react to the news?" Hudson asked. Years of experience had taught him to recognize when someone was being honest, and Staples had sounded sincere. Hudson wasn't ready to scratch the lawyer's name off his suspect list but he'd moved it to the bottom for the time being.

"I haven't spoken to him yet," she responded.

"Come again?" he asked. That was the first place she should've checked to figure out if Butler was her biological father. A point could be made that the man she believed to be her parent might not have known she wasn't his. But Hudson was jumping the gun.

"He didn't return my call yesterday, okay. It's not like I didn't try." There was so much frustration in her voice that Hudson could tell there was a bigger story. One she didn't seem ready to share. He was smart enough not to poke an angry bear, so he left the subject alone.

They ate in the small breakfast taco shack and then made their way to the Red Rope Inn.

Hudson parked near the lobby's glass doors. "Follow my lead."

"Ask for Trent. He was working when I checked in yesterday," she said.

"What does he look like?" he asked.

"Black hair. Brown eyes. Not too tall, maybe five foot nine. Pretty young, I'd say maybe twenty-three. He had a mole toward the bottom left of his chin. He was reasonably attractive." Her keen observation skills reminded him that he was dealing with a reporter. He needed to keep that thought close when the urge to kiss her tried to overpower common sense again.

A different worker was behind the counter today. He was fairly young, midthirties, and already starting to lose his hair. Hudson made a mental note of his description. Maybe they could get a copy of the schedule.

"Is Trent here?" he asked after taking Madelyn's

hand. Frissons of electricity vibrated up his arm. He did his level best to ignore them, especially since the memories of that kiss from yesterday had been on his mind all night.

"He called in sick," the worker said. "I'm Robert. How can I help you?"

A red flag just shot up in Hudson's mind, and based on the way Madelyn's fingers tensed, the same happened to her.

"Is the manager in?" Hudson asked.

"You're looking at him," Robert said with a curious look. "What can I do for you?"

"There was a woman here yesterday by the name of Kelsey," he continued, wondering why the manager would be behind the counter helping walk-ins. Then again, Red Rope Inn looked like a small operation, so it could be possible.

"Brownish, reddish hair. About yay tall?" Robert held his hand out flat underneath his eyes. He was about five foot ten and was indicating roughly Madelyn's height.

Hudson glanced toward Madelyn, who was nodding.

"Yeah, that's the one," he said. "Does she work today?"

"I'm afraid not and she won't be back." Robert frowned.

"Really?" Madelyn dropped his hand.

"Kelsey turned in her resignation last night," Robert said with a shake of his head. "Said she couldn't handle the job anymore."

"Hard to find dependable help these days," Hudson agreed as more red flags shot up.

"You're telling me," Robert said. "All over some kind of stink made yesterday from one of our guests."

Hudson could guess who that meant. He reached back for Madelyn's hand, found it and ignored the unwelcome charge of electricity pulsing up his arm from contact once again.

"My girlfriend and I wanted to thank her. She and Trent did a great job when we checked in last night," Hudson lied. Didn't sound like Robert knew what was going on. "I guess there's no way you could give us her address so we could stop by on our way out of town."

Robert's head was already shaking. "Sorry. Can't give out personal information of current or former employees. Corporate would have my head on a platter."

"With all the lawsuits going around, I understand," Hudson said in a move of solidarity. "We can't leave a note for her since she's no longer employed here."

"We get paychecks day after tomorrow. She didn't tell me to mail hers when she resigned and she's one of the few who still get theirs on paper, so I'm guessing she'll swing by. I could pass along a thank-you note then," Robert offered.

"Any idea what time that might be?" Hudson asked.

Robert seemed to catch on. He shrugged, like he was trying to look casual, but sweat beaded on his forehead. "Not sure."

"We'll do a note, then." Hudson turned to Madelyn. "Do you want to do the honors?"

She nodded and he could almost see the wheels turning behind her eyes. "Is there a pen and paper I can use?"

Robert produced both and then waited while she scribbled.

They thanked him and left quickly. The door had barely closed behind them when she asked, "Doesn't it seem suspicious that Kelsey quit and Trent called in sick?"

"Absolutely," he agreed.

Her phone buzzed and she looked up at him with a mix of fear and anxiety.

"Might want to see who that is," he said.

She did.

"A number I don't recognize but this is the second time they've called. I figured it was...*him*... I didn't answer last night," she said.

"Is there a message?" His brow shot up.

She nodded. "I forgot to listen to it. My mind's been on a million other things."

He could understand why she'd want to shut down last night. She put her phone to her ear and stilled as she listened to the recording. Hudson glanced at her, ignoring the memory of her lips on his from last night— a memory that had pervaded his thoughts and made sleep impossible. He almost laughed out loud at that one. He hadn't slept a straight eight in more than a year.

"What the...?" She paused. "Oh, you've got to be kidding me."

"What is it?" He pulled out of the parking lot.

"That was Kelsey's lawyer. She's suing me for putting her under duress yesterday," she said, indignant.

"I guess news that you're a Butler is out."

"*Might* be a Butler," she corrected, "and who would do something like this anyway?"

"Now I really wish we had Kelsey's address," he said. "Hold on. I think I might know a person who can help us."

Hudson turned the wheel and headed back to the sheriff's office. A few turns and fifteen minutes later he parked in front of Sawmill's office. The buzz of reporters was everywhere and a few rushed over, swarming his truck. One yelled, "No one important!" and the rest scattered back to their vans with disappointed looks.

"This place is a zoo," she said.

"Keep your head down, eyes forward."

"What are we doing here?" Her eyes were wide.

"Pretending to follow up on your complaint from last night." Hudson took Madelyn's hand, ignoring the spark ignited by contact. It struck him that the reporters dismissing them meant her news hadn't really gotten out. What did that say? Only a few people knew...a few insiders, and that made him think the attacks on Madelyn were coming from inside the Butler camp.

"Doris," Hudson said over the hum of activity in the sheriff's office.

She glanced up and her gaze stopped on Madelyn. A look of shock crossed her worn features. The extra activity seemed to be taking a toll on her but she quickly recovered with a smile.

"How's my favorite person in all of Cattle Barge doing this morning?" she asked Hudson.

"You can't be talking about me since I don't live in town," he said, returning her smile.

"Even so, I rarely ever get the pleasure of your company twice in one week. Who's the pretty lady?" She smiled at Madelyn.

He introduced them.

"Nice to meet you," Madelyn said, breaking their link in order to shake Doris's outstretched hand.

"What brings you into town?" Doris asked with a quirked eyebrow.

"My friend is visiting and had an incident on the highway yesterday afternoon." Could he really only have known Madelyn for a day? Being around her felt natural, like they'd known each other for years instead of hours.

Doris rocked her head. "She's the one?"

"Afraid so." Neither seemed ready to say she was also the one from the complaint at the motel last night.

"The sheriff told me about what happened in our briefing first thing this morning," she said. "Our town is normally a great place to be. I'm sorry your experience doesn't match."

It was good that Sawmill was talking about the incident. Assigning resources was another story and that was where the investigation was falling short. "I know how busy things are around here and a case like hers is likely to be set aside when a murder investigation the scale of Mike Butler's makes news. I thought I might do a little digging on my own. It would be a great help if you could tell me the names of a few employees at Red Rope Inn."

"I can't do that," Doris insisted with a cluck of her tongue.

He'd expected as much.

"There was a girl working last night. Kelsey Shamus," Madelyn continued without missing a beat. "I got a call from her lawyer. She's suing me because she thinks I traumatized her while I was upset about someone gaining access to my room without my permission."

Doris gasped. "What on earth? From what I heard, you were the victim. Why would she...? Never mind...

People surprise me all the time. I should know better than to be shocked by anything these days."

"The person who wrote the threat on my mirror had to have had a key. Kelsey told me no one had access," Madelyn continued.

"What about housekeeping?" Doris clucked her tongue again.

"Exactly. That's what I asked. I'd had a hard day and probably came off a little too strong." Madelyn's conspiratorial tact seemed to be working because Doris was getting visibly upset.

"Who wouldn't?" Shoulders stiff, Doris was indignant now.

"I know, right," Madelyn agreed. "Looking back, I was probably a little too harsh with her but it's not like I cursed her out."

"You had a right to, though," Doris said on a huff.

Madelyn was a damn good journalist. She might not want to admit it, but she'd make one fine lawyer, too.

"A guy named Trent was working when I checked in. Do you know him?" she asked.

"He's the Buford boy," Doris admitted.

And, *bingo*, they had a last name. The fact that Madelyn was a good investigator shouldn't clench his stomach in the way it did. Her curiosity about him would eventually win out and she'd dig around in his background.

"Does he live in town?" Madelyn pressed.

Doris glanced around and then leaned forward. "He rents a house with the Mackey boy over on Pine next door to the CVS, same block."

"Thank you so much, Doris. You've been a huge help," Madelyn said with a satisfied smile.

Hudson took note of the fact that she seemed able to turn her charm on readily in order to get what she wanted. Reporters were bigger chameleons than detectives when they needed to be. He also reminded himself that they didn't have to follow the law and that put them in the same category as criminals in his book.

His back stiffened when Madelyn reached for his hand. He forced a smile, keeping up the charade in front of Doris. The second the two of them left the building he intended to let go.

And that was exactly what he did.

MADELYN HAD JUST scored a major win for the team, so she was caught off guard when Hudson dropped her hand the second they walked into the parking lot.

The drive to Pine Street was quiet and she was left wondering what had changed between them. Something had. But the handsome cowboy wasn't talking and she didn't have the energy to push. He was helping her and she would leave it at that. Plus, they had a lead and that was progress in one area of her turned-inside-out life.

Pine Street had a row of historic-looking houses. She figured they rented for top dollar given the craze for authentic vintage-home charm with modern redesigns and appliances. Hudson walked a step ahead of her and banged on the door with law-enforcement fervor. Whatever had happened back at the sheriff's office had snapped him into cop mode. Although, he had yet to admit his background to her, which begged the question why.

She shelved those thoughts for now. The familiar tingle of excitement that accompanied a break in a big story tickled her stomach. Her pulse sped up, too, along with an adrenaline spike.

If Trent truly was sick, and no one seemed to believe that line, it stood to reason he'd be home.

No one came to the door and there was no sign of movement in the house. It was quarter after ten in the morning, so Trent could be asleep and his room-mate, the Mackey boy Doris had mentioned, might be at work. Didn't normal people mostly have nine-to-five jobs now? Madelyn worked all the time and, as a rancher, so would Hudson. But they were outliers.

Disappointment settled in with the second round of bam-bam-bam. The door rattled.

So close…

And then she heard the creak of pressure on wood floors, a glorious sound. But then nothing.

Hudson pressed his face up to the window and muttered a curse at the same time she did.

"That's him," she said. Trent was trying to run. Her pulse pounded.

"Stay here. I'll cover the back," Hudson said in that authoritative voice reserved mostly for people who wore a badge. She'd been told mothers had that same tone but she'd have to take it on face value given that she'd never known hers.

His heavy footsteps disappeared around the side of the house and all she could hear was him shouting at someone.

Madelyn took off after them, pushing her legs to catch up to the two men running in front of her. Hudson's large frame blocked her view of Trent. Her lungs squeezed as they rounded the corner, reminding her how infrequently she'd used that gym membership she'd bought for herself at Christmas and how little she'd adhered to the New Year's resolution that she'd keep up with the workouts. She pushed through burning thighs as Hudson tackled the guy in front of him.

The two of them were fast, so it took a few beats for her to catch up. By the time she did, Hudson was straddled over the younger man's body.

"It's not him," she said through quick breaths, grasping at the cramp in her right side.

"I told you to stay put," he said, his words angry. He hardly seemed affected by the chase, whereas the young guy underneath him was breathing heavy. There was a small satisfaction in that.

"When you ran, I followed," she said, bending forward and glancing back toward the house.

Hudson made a frustrated sound as he turned his attention to the blond-haired twentysomething guy. "Who are you?"

"Dude, what's your problem?" Blond-hair responded.

"You didn't answer my question." Hudson reared his fist back.

"Hold on a second." Blond-hair winced, readying himself for impact.

"Tell me your name," Hudson shouted.

"Brayden Mackey," he responded, turning his head and squinting.

"Where's Trent?" Hudson's posture tensed even more, his fist a few feet from Brayden's face.

"He's gone, dude. He told me to run out the back door and get as far away as I could while he took off out the front," Brayden said.

They'd been played.

Chapter Nine

A ten-minute conversation with Brayden revealed how little he knew about Trent's activities. Frustration at being so close and the only lead slipping through their fingers nipped at Madelyn as she listened. Apparently, the two had been roommates for the past year. Brayden believed that Trent had switched his days off.

"I don't know what you think he's into but Trent's a good dude," Brayden said.

"I'm sure he is. But in my experience innocent people don't run, Brayden," Hudson said through even breaths. On the other hand, Madelyn was still trying to recover from their late-morning run.

Trent was guilty of something.

Brayden shrugged. "He doesn't *party*, if you know what I mean. That was my biggest requirement for being roommates. I'm not into drugs and wild parties."

"You seem like a straight-up guy. You don't mind if we check out your place, do you?" Hudson asked.

"I've got nothing to hide," Brayden defended.

Hudson hopped to his feet in a smooth motion and offered a hand up to the younger man. Brayden took it and the two of them followed him back to his house. The place looked cleaner than a typical bachelor pad.

Just as Madelyn had suspected, walls had been taken down in order to give the ground floor as much of an open concept as the older construction would allow. Brayden seemed to take great pride in the place. The furniture was simple and modern. There was a surprising amount of food in the kitchen for two bachelors. In the living room, a flat-screen TV flanked one wall and a gaming system of some sort was still on.

"We were playing when you knocked." Brayden motioned toward the screen.

"Popular game," Hudson agreed. A man in battle fatigues held out a gun in the center of the screen. There was a map in the top right corner. Madelyn had heard of the game before but she couldn't remember the title. Something about planting bombs and counterterror attacks.

Two empty cups of coffee sat on the coffee table next to a plate with a few crumbs still on it.

"You don't think it's suspicious that someone knocks on the door and then your friend bolts?" Hudson asked, and he was probably trying to ascertain if Brayden's story could hold water.

"Sure, at first. He said that it's no big deal but he wanted me to run out the back door and distract you. Said he might've forgotten to pay a bill or something and that he'd take care of it later," he said.

"And you believed him?" Hudson asked.

"He's never given me a reason not to trust him until now." Brayden rubbed the scruff on his chin. On close examination, he couldn't be more than twenty-six years old. "Are you like cops or something?"

"You have a nice place," Madelyn said to distract him.

Brayden smiled and she was pretty sure his eyes lit up, too.

Okay, she wasn't flirting but he seemed to take it that way. Hudson stepped in between the two of them, blocking Brayden's line of sight.

"Where's Trent's room?" he asked.

"The bedrooms are upstairs. Follow me." Brayden took the lead. He stopped at the top of the stairs. "I don't feel right letting you in my roommate's private space. I don't even go in there. It's why we get along. We don't mess in each other's personal area."

"Tell him that I gave you no choice. If he's a good guy, like you say he is, there's nothing to hide. We won't find a thing and we'll be out of your hair in ten minutes." Hudson maintained steady eye contact as he spoke, only glancing away when he was finished. He stood tall with his shoulders back, communicating confidence.

"Something you said has been bothering me," Brayden admitted. "Innocent people never run. I've seen that on cop shows and, whatever, just don't mess things up in there. But if you find anything to be concerned about, tell me what it is."

"You have a deal." Hudson offered a handshake.

Brayden took the outstretched hand and then stepped aside to make room for them on the landing.

There were two bedrooms upstairs and a bathroom they must share. Hudson reached for Madelyn's hand and electricity pinged through her with contact. Neither the time nor the place, she thought. He was only making a show of them being together and it meant nothing to him.

Trent's room was messier than downstairs but not

by a whole lot. His wallet was on his dresser along with his keys. Hudson opened it and found the usual: credit cards, license, a few twenties along with a two-dollar bill. A laptop was on his bed and there was a stack of clothes piled next to a hamper. It seemed like every man's room she'd been in, be it friend or more, had that same mound of clothes right next to the hamper. What was up with that?

The covers were mussed on the platform-style bed. There was a fistful of change on the nightstand along with chargers. Hudson had scanned the room as he walked it and now his full attention was on the laptop.

"Do you happen to know his password?" he asked Brayden, who was hovering at the door, looking uncomfortable. Did his pinched expression have anything to do with his suspicion that his roommate might've done something wrong, or was it because he'd just allowed strangers to violate their privacy pact? Brayden seemed like a straight-up guy. She decided it was the latter.

"Can't help you there, dude," he said. "We don't share that kind of information."

Madelyn figured as much.

"What's his birthday?" Madelyn asked, figuring most people's passwords used those numbers.

Brayden shot her an are-you-kidding-me look. "He's smarter than that."

Madelyn had no doubt. It seemed like most twenty-somethings knew ten times as much as she did about technology.

"Most people use a pattern on the keyboard," Hudson said.

"Not likely, but I have no idea and I never ask." Brayden shifted his weight to his right foot.

"Do you have any idea where your buddy might've taken off to?" Hudson asked after three failed attempts to hack Trent's password.

"None at all." He shook his head. "But then, I didn't see any of this coming."

He had a point there. He'd seemed genuinely surprised by the revelations so far.

"What about a girlfriend?" Hudson pushed off the bed and stood. She was reminded again at how intimidating his height could be.

"We don't get into that with each other," Brayden said.

And that seemed odd.

"Surely you'd know if he was serious about someone," Hudson said. "Wouldn't he bring her home with him?"

Brayden shrugged again. "I guess so. He goes out and there've been a few times when he didn't come home lately." His eyes flashed toward Madelyn. "I figured he met someone. But we don't talk about stuff like that. We don't usually work the same shifts, so when we do cross over we're downstairs gaming."

Sounded about right to Madelyn, given their ages.

"Mind if I ask where you work?" Hudson was taking in the scene, leaning a little toward Brayden, and based on the change in Hudson's body language, she figured he wanted the young guy to feel like he was listening.

"I work in the IT department for the Gaming Depot," he supplied. "Everything you saw downstairs we got for free."

"Nice," Hudson said, and she could see that Brayden

was relaxing a little, Hudson was gaining trust inch by inch, and she couldn't help but think that he would've made one heck of a journalist. If he didn't dislike them so much.

"Mind if we head back downstairs?" Brayden asked, stepping aside to let them leave the room and head down the steps. He relaxed a little more once they were in the living room.

"Give Trent a message for us?" With his arms crossed, Hudson's posture was loose and open.

"Sure thing, dude." Brayden swayed slightly, leaning a little closer to Hudson and mirroring his body language. The move was totally on a subconscious level and Madelyn knew that Hudson was gaining ground. She appreciated his skills but the average Joe wouldn't be that good.

"Tell him to give me a call. We just want to ask a few questions. We're not trying to collect on a bill. We just want to clear up what we think might be a misunderstanding. Ask him a few questions." Hudson asked for a pen and paper and scribbled down his cell number. "Have him call when he gets home, okay?"

"I'll pass along the message," Brayden promised.

"Oh, and one more thing. What kind of car does he drive?" Hudson asked, stopping at the door.

"White Jeep. Why?" Brayden asked.

"Just wanted to know in case I pass him in the street. We're not cops. We're not here to arrest your friend or make his life miserable. He doesn't owe us any money. All we want is to ask a few questions." Hudson opened the door and then stopped. "By the way, did he seem sick to you this morning?"

Brayden shot a quizzical look toward Hudson. "Not at all. Why?"

"He's not ill?"

"Seemed fine to me," Brayden said.

"His boss said he called in sick at work today. You guys share rent on this place?" Hudson continued.

"Yeah."

"Make sure he pays up early. Wouldn't want any late fees," Hudson said as he opened the door and walked out.

Damn fine investigative work, if anyone asked Madelyn. Brayden had doubts about his roommate now. From here on out, he'd notice things. She figured that Hudson had plans to circle back in a few days and ask more questions if Trent didn't call, and there was about a fifty-fifty chance Trent wouldn't, based on her experience.

Next time, Brayden wouldn't let Trent run.

MADELYN CALLED HER father's number three times in a row, needing to hear the sound of his voice as she waited to hear back from Ed Staples. He didn't pick up, which wasn't a huge surprise. She pressed the phone to her ear, listening to his recorded message.

"Everything okay?" Hudson asked, breaking into the moment. He surprised her and she quickly wiped the stray tear from her eye before he could see that she was crying.

"Yes. I'm just a little tired. I didn't sleep as much as I would've liked last night." There was no conviction in those words. She couldn't fake being okay. But as she looked out over his expansive property, a sense of calm washed over her. The place was peaceful. She had to give him that. They'd returned to the ranch so that Hudson could take care of his animals and she hadn't heard him walk up behind her until he was right next to her. He folded his hands and rested his elbows on the top railing of the wood fence.

It was hot outside but Madelyn liked the heat. She angled her face toward the sun and closed her eyes. "Ever get the feeling like you're in a nightmare that won't end and you can't wake yourself up?"

"Every day," he said, and there was so much depth to his voice, like a river that had cut its way through granite to carve out its path.

"Where'd you live before?" she asked.

"It's not important," he mumbled, but it was to her. He was as unobtainable as every important man in her life had been. Was that the appeal? The reason her heart fluttered every time he was near?

Madelyn let the sun warm her skin. "My high school coach called to personally invite me to a ceremony honoring my swimming accomplishments."

"Sounds like a big deal," he said.

"It is. The school's planning a whole thing around a couple of us. We're being inducted into the hall of fame," she said. "I called my father to tell him about it and he didn't pick up. He hasn't called back. He calls on the first of the month without fail and nothing in between."

Tears surprised her, burning the corners of her eyes.

"He sounds reliable." Hudson was trying to make her feel better.

"That, he is. Unless you consider that he might have been keeping a huge secret from me my entire life."

So much about her childhood made sense if she wasn't really a Kensington but a Butler.

"I'm truly sorry about your mother." He paused for a beat. "Did your father remarry?"

"Thank you and no. He's been dating the same woman for as long as I can remember. They never married," she stated. "She cooks for him on Thursdays and he takes her out on Sunday nights. Says Saturday is too busy and it's hard to get a table."

Hudson looked out onto the pasture. She expected him to throw a few words on the wall to see if they'd stick, like the few people she'd opened up to over the years always had. They'd say things like, "I'm sure he loved you." Or, "Men are like that sometimes."

Empty words never made a hard situation better.

The cowboy put his arm around her shoulders and she leaned into him.

"Kids should feel loved every day of their lives. They grow up too fast as it is, especially when they lose someone they love so young." His voice wasn't more than a whisper in her hair and yet there was so much comfort in his words.

"Thank you," she said back to him, matching his cadence.

And then she surprised herself in turning to face him, pushing up to her tiptoes and kissing him. His muscles tensed, his back ramrod straight. She trailed her fingers along the strong muscles in his shoulders and gazed up at him.

His eyes darkened with hunger as his tongue slicked across his bottom lip. Madelyn couldn't help herself. She nipped at the trail and he took in a sharp breath.

"This isn't a good idea," he said, and the mystery

surrounding him was most likely half the appeal. She told herself that if they went down that road—the one where they had incredible sex—that would somehow dim the attraction between them. Or maybe she was just searching for comfort, for one night of distraction in this crazy mixed-up world that had become her life. She hadn't truly felt like she belonged in someone's arms in…in… How sad was it that she couldn't remember how long? Maybe never?

And yet being with Hudson on his land brought her dangerously close to just that, a feeling of security.

That hot stove was waiting to burn her, so she took a step back, trying to get a handle on her overwrought emotions. Having her life turned upside down was most likely causing these intense emotions coursing through her, she told herself.

"I know I said going ahead with whatever is happening between us isn't smart but stopping it feels like a decision we'll regret," he said. His voice was low and gravelly, and hinted of great sex.

"Then tell me something about yourself. Something that even Doris wouldn't know. Because I don't want to go there with you, a stranger, without feeling like I know who you are," she said, and her voice came out way more desperate than she wanted to admit. Was this another attempt to heal past relationships? To attain the impossible?

"My mother died when I was barely out of high school. I never knew my father," he said, not breaking eye contact.

It seemed like they had more in common than either of them realized. In so many ways Madelyn didn't feel a connection to hers. What did she know about

Charles Kensington other than surface stuff, like the fact he watched football every Sunday while eating Andy Capp's Hot Fries with a Bud Light chaser.

"I don't even know my father's favorite color. I lived with the man for eighteen years of my life and I have no idea what his favorite flower is. It's like we lived side by side in tandem, but not in sync." She flashed her eyes at him, fighting back the swell of tears threatening. Emotions were taking over and embarrassment heated her cheeks for being so point-blank with a near-stranger. Only Hudson didn't feel like a stranger. "Obviously, I overthink things."

"It's not too much to ask to know little things about the person who is supposed to love you the most," he said, adding, "My favorite color is powder blue, like the early-morning sky in spring and your eyes."

A trill of awareness skittered across her skin.

They both stood there for several seconds and she was certain he was feeling the same thing. She could practically touch the current running between them, lighting her senses and tugging her toward the strong man standing in front of her. She may not know who he really was but her body didn't seem to care.

"Did he talk about your mother growing up?" he asked, his serious eyes intent on her.

"Hardly ever," she said. "He let me keep a picture of her next to my bed, and I talked to it all the time when I was little, like she'd somehow magically appear."

His smile was like stepping into a cool natural spring and out of the heat when the sun started to scorch her skin.

"I'm not trying to make you uncomfortable and force you into talking about whatever you've been through that makes you prefer the company of animals to people. All of this has me wondering if I can really ever trust anyone. Do I really know anything about my past? Or was it all a lie? I'm questioning everything now," she said. It struck her as odd that she might not really know the most basic thing about herself, who her father was.

"What about DNA testing?" he asked.

"I asked Ed Staples about it and he apologized, stating that Mike Butler was cremated. There's no way to get a test now," she said. "I asked about siblings but he doubted anyone would volunteer, although, he agreed to ask. Which leaves me no choice but to go to the judge and ask for a court order."

"And that takes time," he said.

"Money, too," she added. "With the Butler fortune at their disposal, the siblings could tie things up in court for years."

"Leaving you right where you started, with no answers," he stated, turning toward the pasture and clasping his hands again. "We could come at this from a different angle. Why would Mike Butler lie about you being his child?"

"I can't think of one reason. He has nothing to gain and my presence brings shame to his children. I checked online last night and I'm around the same age as his eldest daughter. We both know what that means," she said.

"He was cheating on his wife with your mother."

She turned and gripped the railing. "It also means that both of my parents are dead and I call a stranger 'Dad.'"

Chapter Ten

Dinner came and went, and Madelyn decided it was time to clue her boss in since she might not be returning to work for a while. Harlan picked up on the first ring while she was still debating how much she should share.

"What's the story at the Butler farm?" he immediately asked, a sense of anticipation coming through in his tone. She recognized it immediately because she'd felt it a pair of days ago.

"Ranch," she corrected, and she was mostly stalling for time. He knew the difference and was most likely trying to be funny.

"Is it big or a waste of time?" He skipped right over her comment.

"Turns out, I'm the focus," she said with as even a voice as she could muster.

"A story with Maverick Mike Butler starring you?" he questioned. "I'm not sure that I follow."

"He says I'm his long-lost daughter." The words sounded distant as she spoke them.

"Hold on a damn minute. Are you telling me that you're heir to one of the biggest fortunes in the South—

no, check that, in the United States—and you just found out?" Harlan said with more than a hint of admiration.

"It would seem so," she admitted without much enthusiasm.

"And this upsets you *because*?"

"I haven't checked it out yet. Maybe I don't want to get my hopes up," she lied. The truth was that she wished for the life she believed was true before. Even though she and her dad didn't have a perfect relationship, she'd always known that he'd loved her in his own way. Her life made sense to her and was all she'd ever known. There was simplicity in that. Stability. Now the earth had tilted, shifting underneath her feet and throwing everything off balance.

"So how did your mom know Mike Butler?" he asked.

"Good question." She knew more about her so-called father than she did about her own mother, and this revelation put even more distance between her and the truth. In fact, Madelyn had been so wrapped up in everything, she hadn't gotten in touch with the rage she felt at Mike Butler. What little she did know about her mother was that she'd died while giving Madelyn life. That fact had always burdened Madelyn because she'd felt like her mother's death had been her fault. Her mother had died because, being young and broke, there was no insurance. She couldn't afford to give birth in the good hospital in town. She'd had to go to the county hospital where the machines weren't reliable, nurses were overburdened and she'd bled out.

If Madelyn could believe the story she'd been told, her mother had forced Charles to follow the baby because she didn't trust the nurses. Meanwhile, she'd hemorrhaged and it had been too late by the time Madelyn's father had returned to check on her. Madelyn had always believed that her father had blamed himself... but now? She had to wonder if he blamed her instead.

If she stuck around town and found the truth, could she learn more about the mother she'd always wanted?

"Needless to say, I need time off in order to figure this whole crazy ordeal out," she said.

"Keep reports coming and I'll continue your salary," he stated. He wasn't a bad guy so much as a persistent journalist. This news would be huge if it panned out.

"I'll think about it but what I told you is between us for now." She had to consider whether she wanted her life splashed across all the papers. Which was a good point, actually. Had the news leaked? Someone inside the Butler camp had to know, right? "Give me your word you'll keep this quiet until I say."

His hesitation didn't exactly make her feel warm and fuzzy.

"File a story. It can be about anything you want. Just give me something decent to put into print. And, yes, you know that I would never go behind your back." His tone was softer, the human side of Harlan peeking through the hardened reporter who'd seen pretty much everything in his two decades on the job.

"Okay, Captain." He'd said that he didn't like her calling him that and she knew down deep that he'd been kidding. He loved the attention. Wow, she knew her boss better than her own father. What did that say about her relationship with Charles Kensington?

"Madelyn," he said quietly, as though suddenly realizing the implication. "You want me to do a little digging on the family? They have a lot going on over there in Cattle Barge and I'm not sure I like you being there given the news you just shared."

"I share your concerns. I'll be careful." She decided this wouldn't be a good time to fill him in on what had happened to her since arriving in Cattle Barge, noting the rare fatherly side of Harlan coming through. He was divorced with three children, and by his own admission he'd been too busy chasing stories to watch them grow up. He also said that he had divorce papers documenting how he'd failed his wife, too. Relationships always came with a hefty price tag.

"That jerk leaving you alone, at least?" he asked, and her heart stuttered. And then it quickly dawned on her who he was talking about.

"Owen's been quiet," she admitted. Thankfully.

"Make sure and lock your doors," he warned, his fatherly instincts ever present. He might not have been there for his own kids but he seemed to be making up for it with his reporters. She thought about how little people really knew about each other. She'd worked for Harlan three years and only knew him on paper. Divorced, father of three, boss. Strange when she thought about how many hours she and her high school friends used to spend getting to know every detail of each other's preferences from favorite ice-cream flavor to whether one would pick quitting school over getting to be a rock star.

"I will. Can you dig around into the background of Hudson Dale? He owns a ranch on the outskirts of Cattle Barge and I'm pretty certain he used to work in law enforcement," she said, a feeling of shame washing over her. She should wait until he was ready to talk but had half convinced herself that she deserved to know given that she was staying in his house. She knew the cop-out immediately. "Actually, hold off on that research for a minute."

"You sure about that?" Even though they were in the same state, he sounded a million miles away.

"Yes. Definitely." Was she? She was sleeping in the house of a man she barely knew, but then, based on recent revelations, how well did she know anyone? "Harlan, what's your favorite color?"

"What?" The query was out of the blue and his reaction said she'd caught him off guard.

"Just curious." She found it odd that she knew so little about the man she worked for and yet trusted implicitly. She knew him about as well as Brayden knew his roommate, Trent, and the two lived under the same roof.

"Orange, I guess. Why the sudden interest?" he asked.

"No reason." She paused a beat. "But thanks for telling me."

A soft knock at the door had her ending the call.

"Dinner's ready," Hudson said, and the familiar sound of his voice settled her taut nerves.

"With everything going on today, we forgot to pick up my car," she said after opening the door.

"We can go after we eat," he said as she passed him.

Another fantastic meal courtesy of Hudson Dale and she had no idea how or where he'd picked up his culinary skills. Curiosity was getting the best of her. She wanted—no, *needed*—to know more about him even though she kept her questions at bay on the ride into town.

One look at her car as he pulled beside it and she gasped. The driver's-side window had a hole in it the size of a brick. And that was exactly what had been flung, she realized as she jumped out of the cab of Hudson's truck. Her presence in town might not exactly be welcome, but damaging her property was a whole other issue. Her thoughts shifted to Owen for a split second. Could he have tracked her down?

No. She'd been careful to make sure that only Harlan knew where she'd gone. And she trusted her boss with her life. Literally, countless times, and he'd come through. A little voice reminded her that if she didn't know her own father she couldn't know anyone else, not even her boss. She shushed it and figured half the reason she was sticking around was to find out more about her mother. More lies. They were mounting. Because she needed to know the truth about so many things in her life.

Mike Butler obviously knew about her. Was he even sad when he learned that her mother had died? Relieved? Did he get her pregnant and back out of a relationship, not wanting to take responsibility for Madelyn? Had he sat idly by while she and Charles struggled financially? His legitimate kids growing up with every advantage at their disposal? Money. Education. Respect. If he'd offered to pay for medical expenses, and he'd had plenty of money to cover them, would her mother still be alive?

Anger raged inside her.

"Someone's obviously been here," Hudson said, studying her.

Her hands were fisted at her sides. Frustration nipped at her and she wanted to scream. "It's shocking how little people value others' hard work. I mean, I had to save a long time to come up with the down payment and this is the second time it's been vandalized."

She glanced over in time to see his dark brow shoot up. He deserved to know what he was getting into, so she told him about Owen, the threats and the horrible word he'd scribbled across her car's hood.

"I can certainly see you've had a rough go lately," he said sympathetically. "Is your ex the reason you don't trust people?"

His comment scored a direct hit and she wondered what in his past made him the same way. Of course, every time she tried to get him to discuss anything about himself, he shut her down or changed the subject. It was such an odd feeling, too. Because she barely knew him, he'd scarcely told her two things about him, and yet she felt so at ease with him. "He's one in a long line."

Electricity hummed and sensual shivers raced up her arms every time they touched but that didn't throw her off, either. It felt...natural. Which pretty much proved the mind could trick itself into believing anything it yearned for. Like her belief that her mother had been a decent woman. Seriously, what kind of person cheated on her longtime boyfriend, got pregnant and then came back to let him help bring up the child?

Okay, dying couldn't have been part of the plan, so Madelyn could give her mother a break on that count even if there was a bit of residual anger still there. It hadn't exactly been her mother's choice to leave her, but all these revelations explained so much about why her "father" had never been attached to her emotionally. He'd been in love with her mother, had married her and stayed beside her even with a bastard child.

And then the woman had gone and died on him, leaving him to bring up…*what?*…the constant reminder of her infidelity.

Was Madelyn being too hard on her mother? On the man she knew as her father? *On herself?* a little voice asked.

"Can you handle driving a pickup?" Hudson broke through her heavy thoughts.

"Yeah." She just stared into the night, the wind knocked out of her. It was only a car window, she reminded herself, something that could be replaced. Why did it feel like someone had shattered her soul?

The internal scars racking up wouldn't be so easy to fix.

"Good, because I want you to take my vehicle home and I'll drive yours," he said.

She turned to him. "Can I ask you something?"

"Fire away."

"Why are you helping me? I mean, you don't have to. No one seems to want me around and that can't be good for your social life once I'm gone. Besides, you don't even know me. I'm a total stranger," she said, the words rushing out.

"This will most likely sound strange, it does even to me, but in some ways, I do feel like I know you," he said with a slight shrug.

"What? Like kindred spirits?" she asked, because she felt the same way even though she was too worked up to admit it right now.

"Something like that. You have a familiar lost look," he said.

"I don't need your pity," she shot back, more affected by those words than if she'd been struck.

"It's more of a kinship. I had that same expression when I came back a year ago," he admitted.

"Did buying a ranch chase away your demons?" she pressed, needing to know more. Heck, anything about the man who'd been her link to sanity.

"Not as much as I'd hoped," he said honestly.

"I should pack up, go home and forget all of this happened. Ever since I arrived in Cattle Barge things have only gotten worse."

"Being on my land, taking care of my animals, is a good distraction. Makes me feel like I'm doing something good," he said with such sincerity there was no way he was lying. "But the nightmares still wake me up. No matter where I go, they follow. And yours will, too."

"Then what do you suggest because I feel like I'm running out of options here," she blurted out on a frustrated sigh.

"Stick around. Follow this thing through. Based on what you said earlier about your ex, going home won't give you a break." He paused a few beats. "Besides, there's a way to find out what the Butlers are thinking."

She caught on to where he was headed with this and she wasn't sure she liked it. "I'm the last person they'll want to see."

"You need to talk to them face-to-face. I'll be there and we can put our heads together after and see what we come up with."

She suddenly felt embarrassed. Talk about unwanted—the Butler children certainly wouldn't welcome their father's illegitimate child with open arms and she wasn't sure how much more rejection she could take. "I don't know."

"The best way to conquer an enemy is to look him in the eye." Hudson was right; she knew that. It was also harder than she imagined.

"What makes you so good at investigating crimes?"

Hudson didn't answer. He asked for her keys and told her that his were still in the ignition.

She took the driver's seat and then rolled the window down on the passenger side as he cleared it. "So, we get to talk endlessly about my life but I still don't get to know anything about yours?"

"I'm the one helping you, and knowing the details of yours might just break this case open," he stated, and she could tell that a wall had come up between them.

"Well, then I'm going home in the morning," she said.

"Suit yourself but that'll hurt you a helluva lot more than it will me." Was that true?

Examining his expression, she decided that it was. And that was exactly why she needed to go.

THE DRIVE HOME alone in her car was too quiet, Hudson thought as he contemplated what Madelyn had said. She'd be crazy to leave now and she didn't strike him as such. There was too much at stake here and they still hadn't tracked down Trent or Kelsey.

Hudson missed the sound of Madelyn's voice but it was dangerous to admit it to himself. He couldn't allow himself to care about her more than he already did. He didn't *care*, he corrected. His law-enforcement instincts had kicked in and he missed the job, the excitement.

Being on a horse ranch, on his land, was good for him. Right?

Rather than go round and round about his career choice again, he focused on Madelyn. It would be easy enough to schedule a service to swing by and replace the window. Helping her, feeling useful to someone else, was nice. That was what she provided, a welcome reprieve from the doldrums of routine. His life had become too monotonous and the sexy curve of her hips offered a different kind of distraction. He'd dated since returning to Cattle Barge but he was restless. There was a shortage of interesting women and he told himself that Houston had offered more variety and that was why he'd gotten bored here. He'd been going through the motions. But then, didn't that wrap up his life in general?

His personal motivation had waned and he'd thought about selling the ranch, moving Bullseye to a place closer to the city and settling in Dallas or Austin. A change might do him some good. The only thing stopping him was the thought of not spending 24/7 with his horse. He could admit the land held a pull that the city could never have. Moving to Cattle Barge had been meant to stop the nightmares. It hadn't. He still heard Misty scream as the bullet pierced her barely pregnant belly.

As partners, they'd been keeping their relationship a secret from their supervising officer. To say the pregnancy had been a shock was a lot like showing up to a bullfight only to find an empty ice rink. Hudson hadn't been ready to become a father. The guilt for that would haunt him the rest of his life. Not that it mattered. He'd convinced himself that he loved Misty and had stepped up to ask the big question.

She'd said yes.

The rest was history.

At some point, he thought he'd be ready—excited, even—for the marriage. He'd adjusted to the idea of being a father faster than he'd expected. Love for a child could be so instant and required no work on his part.

He and Misty would've made a good family for the child's sake. They got along and shared the same sense of humor. He'd figured it would be a good foundation. She'd been waiting for her transfer to come through so they could make the big announcement and then get married. He'd been the one to suggest holding off until they'd secured their jobs. Dating coworkers was frowned upon by the department, so the news of a pregnancy and quickie marriage would have hurt both of their careers.

That was what he'd been thinking about and not the fact that Misty had said a million times that she didn't want to be pregnant and unmarried. That her mother had done the same and she'd feared having her mother's hard life and bad choices. Every day as a child, Misty had been told how much of an inconvenience she'd been to her mother. Physical bruises could heal and there'd been a few of those. But words left the biggest marks—marks on the heart.

Hudson had let Misty down, too. And he had the nightmares to prove it.

The bullet that had been intended for him had killed two people with one shot.

And he'd lived with the guilt ever since.

Chapter Eleven

"I know your mind is made up and I respect that but leaving now would be a mistake you'll regret," Hudson said as soon as Madelyn stepped out and closed the door to his truck. They'd made it home in record time and he'd been lost in his thoughts about Misty.

"What do you care about my choices?" she shot back as she spun around to walk toward the front door.

He shouldn't want a reporter to stay with him. Her questions were already mounting and she'd need answers soon. If she dug around in his background, she could kick up a whole storm that he wasn't ready to talk about. His chief had taken pity on him when he'd come clean about the pregnancy and relationship, keeping his name out of the papers. If anyone really wanted to snoop around, a connection could be easily made.

Hudson caught Madelyn's arm to stop her from walking away. She needed to hear what he had to say. Then if she decided to leave, so be it. He would've done his part and his conscience would be clear. He almost laughed out loud at that one. If Madelyn left he was sure he'd get even less sleep than he did now.

"I do care that you seem determined to get yourself hurt or killed." Madelyn and Misty couldn't have been more different. There was more of a comradery between him and Misty than the frissons of heat between him and Madelyn. He and Misty had been co-workers with enough sexual chemistry to make going to bed enjoyable. Had there been sizzle? Spark? Not really. His relationship with Misty had been comfortable. She was funny, hot and had kept an emotional distance. Could there have been more between them? Maybe. He figured that no one could get close enough to her to develop real feelings. And that had shocked him even more when she'd become pregnant, because she was on birth control. At least, that was what she'd said.

Sure, they'd spent time together and they'd made love. But their interludes had had more to do with the fact that they worked the night shift when everyone else slept, and had the same time off.

And then she'd admitted to seeing another guy when she thought things might be getting too intense.

Their relationship had developed out of convenience more so than can't-live-without feelings. He cared about her deeply. Misty had been the last person he'd seriously dated and even that had been more like a friends-with-benefits fling. The fact that his feelings didn't run deeper than friendship didn't stop the pain when she'd been killed; losing her and the baby had left a huge gaping hole in his chest. The only way he knew how to close it was to shut down. And that was exactly what he'd done. Quit his job. Moved to Cattle Barge. Shut himself off to the world.

Madelyn stood there, staring at him with a questioning look on her face. He'd slipped into the past and she seemed to know he'd mentally disappeared.

Her foot tapped impatiently and he had the sudden

urge to haul her against his chest and kiss her until they both forgot what day it was. And everything else, for that matter. If doing so would solve anything, he'd go all in. But it wouldn't erase the real problems they faced.

This seemed a good time to say, "You can't leave until you know what's going on. You owe yourself that much. This will follow you wherever you go. Talk to the Butlers with me tomorrow and if it doesn't help you can pack up afterward and head back to Houston. No harm. No foul. But leave without that conversation and you're always going to wonder."

Her arms folded across her chest and she sighed sharply, her "tell" that he was making headway.

"What do you have to lose? Your car window needs fixing. I know a guy who can get that done in the morning while we visit the ranch," he added. Hudson wasn't sure why it was so important to him to follow this through with her. But it was. A little voice inside his head said that he didn't want her to leave. That losing her brought back feelings he'd buried a long time ago even before Misty had died. But that didn't make sense. He'd convinced himself that he was immune, his emotions had died with Misty and he didn't want to consider other possibilities, like he'd stuffed his true feelings down deep so that he could do the right thing and marry her in the first place.

Dammit. No. He'd cared for Misty. He'd loved his child.

"I'll call Ed Staples and see if I can arrange it as long as you come with me," Madelyn said, and he was grateful for the distraction. Rehashing the past wouldn't change a damn thing. Hudson should know. He'd done that hundreds of times in the past year.

"I'll put on a pot of coffee," he said.

"Save mine for the morning." She looked at him with the saddest eyes as she held up her phone. "I need to make a call and then I'm going to take a shower and go to bed."

She walked away, waiting for him to unlock the door, and that was probably for the best because his damn arms wanted to hold her. He let them both in, locked the door behind them and moved into the kitchen, where he went to work, making coffee and thinking about the questions she should ask the Butlers.

Shower water kicked on in the other room.

He forced his thoughts away from her naked silky skin in his shower. His grip tightened around the mug as he tried to quell the rising tide of hunger welling inside him.

When he heard the water turn off, he stalked toward the bedroom.

"Wish you'd answer my calls. I miss you, Madelyn," the message from Owen began. "I also realize what a jerk I've been. I was hurt and I'm not using that as an excuse but that has to be a little charming, right?"

"It's right up there with being burned at the stake," Madelyn mumbled as she listened to the rest.

"If you'll give me one more chance to prove that I'm not...*that* guy, I promise you won't regret it. We had fun together, didn't we? There's no reason for it to stop because I got out of hand."

"You really know how to pour it on thick," Madelyn said to the phone as she deleted the message.

A knock at the door startled her.

"Hold on a sec," she said quickly, popping to her feet and glancing down to make sure her towel covered everything. "Okay, come in."

The door opened but Hudson didn't enter. "What did the lawyer say?"

Just the sight of him standing at the door, his strong arms resting against the jamb, brought all kinds of sensual shivers skittering across her sensitized skin. She was very aware of how naked she was underneath that towel as heat rushed through her, settling between her thighs.

"He's setting up lunch for tomorrow." Although she shouldn't compare the two, it was impossible not to notice the differences between Owen and Hudson. Owen could be charming but his frame was half that of Hudson. Her host was strong and athletic. He didn't give away much but there was something brooding deep inside him and she wanted to know what it was. Owen talked too easily, too much about things that didn't matter.

She tried to convince herself that her finely honed reporter instincts and professional curiosity had her wanting to know more about the handsome cowboy, but there was so much more to it than that.

"Good. Think about what I said earlier." There was something else on his mind but he didn't seem able or willing to find the right words to say it.

"No matter how long I stay here, I want you to know how much I appreciate everything you've done so far," she said, needing to say the words. "I doubt I'd be alive right now if not for you."

"You would. You're smart and beautiful." He started to turn but stopped. "I'd like you to stay, Madelyn."

Her name sounded sweet rolling off his tongue and her stomach flipped hearing his words.

"Because I do care about what happens to you, Madelyn. More than I should."

"HAVE YOU HEARD anything else from Kelsey's attorney?" Hudson asked the next morning. His jeans were low on his hips and he wasn't wearing a shirt. Madelyn shouldn't notice the ripples of muscles cascading from his chest toward that small patch of hair above his zipper.

"Not yet," she admitted, seeking coffee like a missile homes in on its target. She checked out the window on her way to the kitchen and saw that the glass had been fixed. She thanked Hudson for taking care of it. "I thought we could swing by the motel this morning and check on Trent."

The cowboy issued a rare smile. His cheeks dimpled and she decided she liked his face even more.

Two cups of coffee later, they were on the road.

"We played the part of being two people moving through town the other day with the manager. He'll be suspicious if we walk inside the lobby again and he's there," Hudson said as he pulled into the lot of the Red Rope Inn.

"True." Madelyn glanced around and saw a housekeeping cart. "Let's ask."

She hopped out of the pickup and made a beeline toward the cart, which was positioned in front of an open door. "Excuse me."

An older woman wearing a blue pantsuit stepped

out. She glanced at her cart like she was waiting for Madelyn to ask for more towels.

"I'm sorry to bother you, but can you tell me if Trent's working the front desk today?"

The woman's head shook. "He's sick."

"Thank you." Madelyn walked back to the truck and closed the door behind her. "He's got quite an illness."

"Interesting," Hudson said. "Kelsey's suing you and Trent has caught one helluva virus. Seems like these two know more than they're telling."

"I checked the news last night and no one's reporting the story about me being a Butler," Madelyn said.

"Now all we have to figure out is who knows," he said, pulling onto the highway.

Forty minutes later, he was being waved through the gates at Hereford.

He parked and followed her to the front door.

Madelyn knocked.

"Come in," the woman who'd introduced herself as Ella Butler said from the other side of the door. She hesitated for a long moment before opening it.

"I'm here to see Ed Staples," Madelyn said. Ella looked exactly like her pictures from the society-page stories. Madelyn didn't want to like the woman who was cold-shouldering her, but she did. Even though she'd grown up in the top 1 percent, Ella spent countless hours invested in community projects and volunteer work. She'd been heavily involved in trying to open a new animal shelter, which had put her in the sights of someone determined to stop her because he wanted to buy the land. He'd come close to shooting her to ensure he got it.

Madelyn had combed the internet last night researching each member of the Butler family. She wanted some idea of what she was getting into today. There were four kids—that everyone knew of—two girls and two boys. All had grown into productive, motivated adults, by all accounts, despite having had everything handed to them.

"The family wants to meet you. My sister, Cadence, is recovering from the flu. She thought she could handle all the media attention, so she came home, but it turned out to be too much for her. She caught the first flight out this morning." Something moved behind Ella's gaze that had Madelyn wondering if that were true. A thought struck. Was the media attention getting to the family or was everyone worried now that the Butlers were being singled out and targeted?

Madelyn had read about what happened to Ella. She'd been attacked on a remote piece of the ranch while hiking and had been left for dead. Fortunately, a man on the run had been around to help her recover. A second ambush-style attack had almost killed her but she'd hidden in someone's front landscaping. The details of how she'd survived were unclear except that she'd gone into hiding with the man who'd saved her life and the two had fallen in love. Madelyn introduced Hudson. Ella was courteous but reserved as she greeted him.

Being in Maverick Mike's house was unnerving enough thanks to the tension radiating off Ella. But then, Madelyn hadn't exactly expected the woman to embrace her and call her sister. Heck, Madelyn had been an only child her entire life, so the thought of having siblings didn't exactly bring warm and fuzzy feelings to her, either. Besides, she wasn't there for a reunion. She was there to find the truth.

Slipping into her role as reporter and distancing herself from her own emotions was second nature. She'd done it hundreds of times before, figuring it was so much easier to play a part than to admit to her real feelings of disappointment with family. Damn. That was a little too real for Madelyn.

"Your sister was smart to leave. They won't stop anytime soon." She referred to the vans lining the street.

"Those people out there are like vultures. They'll pick the meat off a carcass and fight each other for the last scrap," Ella said with disdain. "Between them and the people claiming to be a Butler, this town has lost its mind."

Hudson stepped in between her and Ella. "There's no reason to be insulting. Your father summoned her. She had no idea about her heritage before then. And she sure as hell didn't ask to be part of any of you."

He was being defensive and Madelyn shouldn't like that he'd come to her defense as much as she did. Someone sticking up for her was a nice change.

Ella seemed poised to make a comeback.

"It's okay, Hudson," Madelyn interrupted, managing a weak smile as she put a hand on his arm. "I'm sure she wasn't talking about me."

She could handle Ella Butler. From everything she'd heard in the news, Ella was decent and kind. She'd come around to have a civilized conversation at some point.

"Is Mr. Staples here?" Madelyn asked.

Ella seemed to size her up. "I'll get him."

Before she could turn around, footsteps sounded behind her on the tile.

"Thanks for coming," Ed said from the office door. "I apologize for being late. I was held up." His cell was flat on his palm and he shot a look at it. "Crazy thing never stops going off. Please, come in."

Ella unceremoniously turned and walked down the hall without saying another word.

"The boys are waiting in the dining room," Ed said.

She introduced him to Hudson before the three of them made the same trek Ella had moments earlier.

The dining room was beautifully appointed. A long table was the focal point of the room. It looked hand-carved and rustic. Places had been carefully set for six people. But there was not a Butler in sight and she had no idea where Ella had disappeared to.

"I can see that no one wants me here, so this is pointless," Madelyn said, ready to retrace her steps and get far away from the Butler ranch. Being inside made the hairs on her arms prickle. She didn't fit in here and it was obvious. Plus, the whole place set her nerves on edge.

"Give them a chance," Hudson defended, surprising her. "I'm only saying that this has to be as much of a shock to them as it is to you."

"Stay. Please. I'll round everyone up," Ed said. He seemed like the only one trying to build a bridge between them on the Butler side. At least she had Hudson and she'd be lost without him right now.

"Let's sit down and give him a minute to corral the family." Hudson pulled out a chair for her with a wide smile—the smile that was so good at causing her pulse to race and the sensation of birds to flap wildly in her chest.

"Might as well as long as I'm here," she said, returning his smile and hoping she had the same effect on him. One step toward the chair had her rethinking her plan. "On second thought, I might handle them better on my feet."

"Suit yourself." He took a seat next to the one he'd pulled out for her and picked up the glass of lemonade on the place mat.

"That any good?" Her journalism background had her standing behind the chair closest to the exit. It was the trick every journalist knew. Sit closest to the door in order to be the first one out if all hell broke loose. The habit she'd picked up in college had stuck.

"It would taste a hell of a lot better if it was coffee," he stated with a smirk.

Madelyn laughed. She couldn't help herself. Yes, her body was strung tight with so much tension it felt like her muscles might snap. And that was partly why she laughed again.

The click of Ella's heeled sandals cut into the light-hearted moment. Madelyn stiffened as she crossed her arms, steeling herself.

"I apologize for being rude before," Ella started, indicating a seat for Madelyn. The tension in her face hadn't eased in the slightest but her eyes communicated a hint of warmth. "This *situation* is a lot to grasp and seeing you made it all so real. I thought I was better prepared and I realize none of this is your fault."

"For both of us." Madelyn had performed the calculation last night and realized that she and Ella were the same age. Had Madelyn's mother known she was having an affair with a married man? "If it makes you feel any better, I don't want any of your money."

"That wasn't really on my mind." The stress cracks on Ella's forehead said she was being honest. If she was worried about money, it didn't show. "Will we have a chance to meet your mother?"

"She died having me, so that would be impossible," Madelyn stated matter-of-factly. "And, no, I'm not proud of the affair she might've had with your dad."

"I'm sorry for your loss," Ella offered with a look of sympathy. It was too soon to judge her sincerity, but on face value she seemed honest. And then something changed, a split-second reaction.

"Wait a minute. You're not claiming to be a Butler?"

Chapter Twelve

"I don't want to spoil your superior feeling but, no, I'm not," Madelyn stated a little too indignantly. Wearing her emotions on her sleeve was her personal downfall. Professionally, she could hold the line with the best of them. When it came to her personal life she wasn't so skilled at hiding her true feelings.

Ella shot a look at Ed Staples and he returned an I-told-you-so expression.

Two men walked into the room, their boots shuffling on the tiles. They looked almost identical. Tall, probably six feet four inches if she had to guess, and what most would describe as incredibly good-looking, with sandy-blond hair and blue eyes. Madelyn didn't feel a stir of attraction for either one even though she appreciated their good looks. Was it the possibility that they could be related? Did she somehow know they were related?

The first one introduced himself as Dalton and the second as Dade. They were polite, if cautious, as both studied her features. She figured they were looking for any signs of family resemblance. She was, too. And she saw the evidence plainly. All of their hair color was similar and they each had different versions of the same nose. The men had a masculine version, slightly more pronounced. But it was the same nose. A picture on the wall, of Mike Butler surrounded by his children, confirmed they'd gotten the nose from him.

Madelyn absently fingered the dragonfly around her neck with her right hand. Her left searched under the table for Hudson's. She pushed aside the relief she felt when their hands linked, deciding he was the only thing familiar to her in a room full of strangers. Family? It was an odd notion at best.

"I'll just get the sandwiches. I'm sure everyone's hungry and we have quite a bit to discuss after we eat," Ella said, but there was something different about her posture now and Madelyn assumed that it had to do with her revelation.

"I can help," Madelyn offered, standing.

"Oh, okay," Ella said, apparently caught off guard. She was probably used to being in charge and doing things on her own terms, Madelyn guessed.

Madelyn followed her into the expansive kitchen. The place had an old-world-farmhouse vibe, with an oversize single sink, white cabinets and granite countertops. There was a wooden table in the kitchen that looked hand-carved and stretched almost end to end. One side of the massive table looked like it was used for food prep and the rest for eating, with bar stools tucked underneath. Platters loaded with finger sandwiches and fresh fruit were set out on top.

"I think we got off on the wrong foot earlier," Ella said as she picked up a tray. "You want to take that one?"

"Sure." Madelyn had whiplash from the change in her demeanor. "Why are you suddenly being so nice?"

"Ed's an old friend of my father's. He's part of a different generation. One that doesn't talk much. He didn't tell me the whole story about you, and I was concerned about your intentions before I realized you don't seem to want this any more than we do." Ella flashed her eyes. "I didn't mean anything personal by that. You seem really nice. Since my father died, we've had people coming out of the woodwork claiming to be one of us, and you seem offended by the idea."

"And that's what you think I am. Basically, a termite coming to eat your house from the inside out," Madelyn stated a little coolly.

"I didn't know what you were. You look like one of us. That's obvious. But the expression on your face before and what you said…you don't want it to be true any more than we do."

"So you win the big prize. You're right. What next?" Madelyn felt a sting from the zinger.

"You're twisting my words, taking them the wrong way," Ella said, balancing the tray on her shoulder. "I just realized that this is as hard on you as it is on us. That's all. And I can sympathize. Don't confuse that for me welcoming you into the family with open arms."

Madelyn took a minute to think about what Ella was saying rather than react.

"I can see your side of the story and how much your life has been turned upside down. I couldn't see beyond my own nose before when Ed said he had a surprise announcement. The news caught us all off guard. I mean, Dad was no saint, but cheating on our mother? I guess I always blamed my mother for abandoning us, disappearing without any contact. And, yes, he earned his reputation over the years, but I didn't realize he was philandering while he was still married to her," she said. "I'm not ready to forgive her but I'm also realizing how complicated family dynamics can be. Now I'm thinking that maybe she had good reason to leave and not look back." Ella shot a compassionate look.

"I can't argue that families are complex." Madelyn still hadn't figured out what to say to her own father. She picked up the heavy tray, balanced it on her shoulder and walked into the other room behind Ella.

THE LUNCH PLATES were cleared and Madelyn hadn't said two words since going into the kitchen with Ella earlier. Hudson had hoped they'd come to some kind of truce in there but Madelyn returned looking even more stressed. Coffee was served and he took a sip. One look at Madelyn said it was time to wrap this up.

Hudson made a move to stand but Ed Staples waved at him. "Please. Wait. I know it took a great deal of courage for Madelyn to come here today and I also know she has something to ask of the family."

The twins got that "here goes" look on their faces at exactly the same moment.

"I'd like a DNA test for clarification," Madelyn said, wasting no time.

Hudson took another sip of coffee, needing the caffeine boost. Since Madelyn had come to stay with him, things were stirring inside him. Common sense dictated that should make him want her to leave. He didn't.

The twin who'd identified himself as Dalton chuckled and Madelyn shot him a severe look. It looked a helluva lot like the one Ella fired at him and Hudson tried not to read too much into it. He glanced at the picture on the wall of Mike Butler. There was a resemblance.

Dalton held up both hands in the sign of surrender. "Hey. Don't get angry with me. I'm just laughing that you think the old man would make something like this up."

"I didn't know your father, so I have no idea what he would do and why," Madelyn defended.

"Then allow me to apologize. Suffice it to say that my...*our*...old man wouldn't take a claim like this lightly," Dalton clarified. "If he says you're one of us then I'd be shocked if a DNA test proved otherwise."

"That may be true, but I'd still like to know for sure," she said. "I don't want your money or the ranch. I just want to know."

The other twin, who had been quiet up until now, leaned forward and rested his elbows on his knees. "No offense but once it's established that you're a Butler—and my brother is right, by the way, our father wouldn't utter those words if they weren't true—you'll have every right to his money and the ranch. And none of us would stand in the way of his wishes."

Dalton was rocking his head in agreement.

The twins were stand-up men. Ella seemed a little put off that Madelyn rejected her heritage so easily.

"Which one of us do you want to swab?" Ella asked. "Or would you like one from all three to be absolutely certain?"

"One should suffice," Madelyn said. "But how do we proceed? I mean, I want to make sure the results aren't tampered with and I haven't exactly had time to figure all this out."

That comment netted a few angry looks.

"We aren't going to sabotage your test," Dalton said. "But you should learn to trust us. We aren't the self-absorbed jerks the media makes us out to be."

Madelyn tensed. "Not all of us in the media are like the people out there. Some of us expose truths that should be known, that help others."

"Hold on a damn second," Dalton said. "You're one of them?"

"I believe I just said that I wasn't, but, yes, I'm an investigative reporter."

He pushed his chair back and stood. "I'm done here. And, for the record, everything we just said is unofficial. If I see one word of this in print—"

Hudson didn't like where this was going, so he pushed to his feet. If a table wasn't separating them, he and Dalton would be nose to nose, given they were almost equal height. "She's not here for that reason and we all know it, so cool it."

All the warmth in the room disappeared and all three of the Butler children tensed as though ready for a fight. He could give one thing to them: they stuck together.

"She wants something everyone deserves, and that's to know who her father is. Before Ed Staples called and turned her life upside down, she believed it was the man she'd grown up with. Her mother is gone, so she can't ask her," he stated. "So, you guys hold the key."

Ella stood. Her expression was calm but he suspected it was like the surface of water on the stove just before the boiling point was reached. "Ed can arrange everything. You can work with him on the details. We'll comply. In the meantime, I can have a room set up for you here at the ranch. As a Butler, you'll have a right to stay anytime you want."

Why did that offer twist Hudson's gut?

"Do you want to stay here?"

Rancher's Hidden Truth 144

i, want to stay anywhere you want.
When al that that came fraud's and
you and want to stay here?

Chapter Thirteen

"My car's at your place," Madelyn responded to Hudson. She couldn't read his expression. Did he want her to stay with the Butlers? He'd been the one pushing her to come and find answers—answers she wanted but also threatened to shake her foundation to the core.

"It's your call." She searched his face and found nothing to give away his thoughts. His grip was pretty tight on his mug.

"I could stay if it's easier on you," she said, knowing full well it wasn't safe for her to go to a motel in town. But then, a Butler could be targeting her. Sure, they seemed sincere and just as surprised as she had been to learn the news of her possible heritage. On the other hand, she didn't know Ella, Dade or Dalton personally. Any one of them could be putting on a show. Yes, they were convincing and seemed welcoming under the circumstances. Didn't mean they weren't plotting behind her back to get rid of her.

"We still haven't spoken to Kelsey or located Trent. I'd like to hear what they have to say and then there's the vandalism with your car we still haven't reported," Hudson said after a long pause. He was curious about the investigation? "Might be easier to stay put at my place since all your things are already there."

Her heart leaped.

"What's been going on?" Ella asked, a frown of worry apparent on her face. After what she'd been through, it made sense that she'd be concerned.

Madelyn flashed her eyes at Ed. She hadn't told the lawyer. "When did you tell everyone about me?"

"Last night. Why?" Ella cut in.

"Someone tried to stop me from coming here after Ed called," Madelyn said, her attention on Ella now.

Ella drew back and gasped. "Are you all right?" She waved her hands in the air. "Never mind that. I can see you're not physically hurt."

Madelyn relayed the details of the incident on the road and the threat on the mirror.

"Is that why you checked out of Red Rope?" Ed said.

Madelyn's brow shot up and he quickly reassured her.

"I was simply trying to locate you and you weren't answering your cell. I called the front desk, asking to be connected to your room, and they said you weren't staying with them," he clarified.

"Don't look at us," Dade said. "We've been here on lockdown. Ella throws a fit every time one of us so much as tries to leave the ranch."

"We have to take this seriously," Ella said, lines of anxiety etched in her forehead. "I'd like you to stay here where we can be sure you're safe."

"With all due respect, your father was killed on this property," Hudson reminded her.

"Not in the main house. And we've tightened se-curity since then," Ella said. Her demeanor changed the second she'd learned of the threat. "This might not mean much coming from me right now, but I'd like to know that you're safe. No matter what the DNA test reveals—and my money's on the fact that it'll prove what you don't want to hear—I feel like we're responsible."

"How so?" Madelyn asked.

"You said this whole thing started after the call from Ed," Ella said. "If his call triggered this, someone might be listening to our calls." She looked at her brothers. "Is that even possible?"

"Anything goes with technology these days if someone's savvy enough," Dade said. "I'll let Ray Canton know." He looked to Madelyn and said, "He heads up security here at Hereford. He'll be able to tell us if the signal can be unscrambled."

"If someone picked up on Ed's call, they must know what's going on," Ella said.

Hudson reached for her hand, found it. Madelyn wound their fingers together.

"I didn't tell her over the phone," Ed admitted. "Your father had an envelope in a safe in his office. She's the only one who knew the contents once she opened it."

"You already knew," Madelyn countered.

"I had my suspicions. Mike Butler and I go way back. I knew your mother," he said with an apologetic look to Ella and the twins.

But Madelyn had locked onto that last bit…

"How well did you know my mother?" she asked.

"Well enough to know that she isn't from Houston. Your father moved there after she passed away." He seemed to choose his next words carefully. "The minute I saw you, my suspicions were confirmed. You looked exactly how I picture a child of theirs would."

Madelyn wasn't sure if that was a compliment, and she was grateful for the link with Hudson. Their connected hands were the only thing keeping her balanced. "Did you see proof?"

"No. Just what my eyes knew."

"So, it's possible that I'm not his daughter," Madelyn said. At this point, she wasn't sure what she wanted to be true. If she was Butler's illegitimate child then her father's actions were understandable. It would make sense that he'd kept her at a distance her entire life. Otherwise, she had to consider the possibility—the one she'd wholeheartedly feared before this revelation—that her own father didn't love her.

Was that true?

She stood and glanced around the room. It seemed to shrink, the walls closing in. "I need fresh air."

Not one to wait for permission, she darted toward the door and burst outside. The August sun on her face warmed her skin. The blast of heat made it harder to breathe, though. She heard a pair of boots shuffling behind her and was comforted by the fact that Hudson had followed her.

"We don't have to stick around," he said. "We'll get the swab and go."

Madelyn tried to speak but her mouth snapped shut. There was so much she wanted to say, so much that had been bottled up inside ever since she'd heard the news—news that still seemed too crazy to be true. "All my life I've been told my mother was this...*saint*... and I held her up here." She lifted her flat palm as far as she could above her head. "I had this image of her being an angel and looking over me."

"Kids have a way of idolizing a parent who has passed away," he said, and his voice was low. He was standing right behind her. She felt his strong hands on her shoulders and her body responded.

"You can say that again," she said on a sharp sigh. "Anytime I had a bad day—and there were plenty of those, especially in high school when a girl needs her mother—I'd curl up under the covers and envision her holding me. I literally envisioned her with wings, for crying out loud. Now I guess I'm the fool. Not only was my mother no saint but she had an affair with one married man and tricked another guy into marrying her."

"How can you be so sure that your father didn't know?" he asked.

"Because if he knew that explains why he'd been so cold to me all my life. Why he let me cry it out in my room instead of comforting me when I was upset." Her pulse pounded, part anger and part awareness of the strong hands gripping her shoulders. "It explains why he only calls once a month instead of every day. And it explains why he doesn't love me."

Those last few words were daggers to the heart.

Hudson spun her around to face him and she couldn't look into his eyes. She didn't want to see her reflection there—because in his eyes she felt beautiful and loved. More of what she wanted to see instead of reality.

"I haven't met the man, so I'll reserve judgment until I do. But if he turned his back on you or didn't love you it's his loss, not yours." His words were a warm blanket on a frigid night. "You're smart and determined. You have a sense of humor on top of heart-stopping beauty."

Did he just say she was beautiful? Her heart gave a little flip as she struggled against the hot tears burning the backs of her eyes.

"If he really is my father, what does it say about me that he doesn't love me?" The words spoken aloud ripped a hole in her chest.

"Impossible." He ran his thumb along her jawline and sensual shivers rocked her body.

"Maybe not." She dared to look up and his gaze seemed to look right through her.

"We agreed not to do this again, but I'd like permission to kiss you." His brown eyes darkened with need.

Madelyn pushed up on her tiptoes and pressed her lips to his in answer. This wasn't the time for words.

Hudson deepened the kiss, his tongue delving inside, tasting her, and he groaned. He brought his hands up to cup her face and need pulsed through her.

As if realizing they were standing on the Butlers' front lawn in full view of the family, he pulled back. "I won't say it."

"You don't have to. We both know it's true but I want to enjoy this moment anyway," she said.

His quick nod affirmed they were on the same page. They stood there, knowing this couldn't go further, and yet unwilling to let the moment end. He was so close that she could smell the coffee on his breath and remembered the taste of it a few seconds ago. He pressed his forehead to hers and took in a deep breath. "If I could go there with anyone... I would. I hope you know that. There's too much back there and I can't shake it."

"I know." He referred to being able to talk about his past.

"I haven't been in love in a long time. And now I can't," he continued.

"You don't have to explain it to me. I understand more than you realize." There was only so far she could go with a man, any man, and they'd reached that wall. Hudson scared her even more because she could almost envision herself busting down that barrier with him. But shatter it and then what? Hudson wasn't ready to let her in. They both had issues. Not to mention the fact that she had someone trying to run her out of town… possibly *kill* her.

All this emotion could be that they were two lost souls, searching for a temporary reprieve from almost constant pain.

"Being rejected by my father hurt. Losing my mother hurt. All I know is heartache," she said, figuring that she was a magnet, drawing hurt toward her like the scent of honey draws bees. Let the swarm turn on her and it would be all over.

He lifted her chin until their gazes collided. "You deserve so much more than that."

But he'd already admitted that he wasn't the one who could give it to her. And her stubborn heart said it needed him.

She blinked up at him. "We should get back inside."

There was no use trying to convince him that they might be able to give it a shot. She'd tried to make someone love her for her entire life. Granted, it was a whole different kind of love, but that didn't seem important to her at the moment.

"We should tell them we're leaving," he said, letting

go of her and taking a step back. The sharp breath he drew seemed meant to steel his strength.

Part of Madelyn wanted to get lost in him, to forget everything that had happened recently. She couldn't do that any more than she could change her identity with a quick revelation from Maverick Mike Butler. No matter how much her heart protested.

As she started toward the door, it swung open. Ella Butler stood there, flanked by her brothers. They stood more relaxed now and almost seemed sympathetic.

"Ed is arranging the DNA test, unless you want to oversee it," Ella said. "He's planning to expedite the results. I'm sure you don't want to be in limbo any longer than you have to be."

No one mentioned how the result might change things for Madelyn—for all of them, actually. Instead, they all seemed poised to respect her privacy.

"I'm fine with Ed taking the lead," Madelyn said. He had no vested interest in the outcome and seemed to genuinely care about Mike Butler's wishes. There were other pressing questions she wanted to ask him but decided none of them mattered until she received confirmation of what she suspected, feared, to be true.

"He has a kit waiting in the kitchen. We've already been swabbed." She twisted her face into a frown. "If you want us to do it again with you present, we can."

"That won't be necessary." Madelyn needed to establish a little trust. It was tentative at best on both sides, but the family seemed to be making an effort and she should, too. Besides, there was a slight possibility that they would be connected for the rest of their lives and she couldn't ignore it.

She followed Ella and the twins into the kitchen.

"Could I have a minute with Ed?" she asked.

Everyone nodded and left, except Hudson. She'd asked him to stay.

"You said you knew my mother," Madelyn said to Ed.

He stood next to her at the grand wooden table positioned in the middle of the room. His body language was tense, his shoulders rigid and the lines on his face deep.

"Yes, ma'am. I had the pleasure of meeting her a couple of times," he said, and there was so much respect in his voice.

"Can you tell me something about her?" Madelyn wanted—no, needed—to know, and Ed seemed the only one willing to talk about her mother even if his body language said he was reluctant.

"She had your hair and eyes," he said. That, she could gain from a picture.

"What was she like?" Madelyn tried to quell the hope in her voice but was doing a lousy job, by all counts.

Ed gave her a shocked look.

"My father—" she flashed her eyes at him "—her husband never said much about her."

"The loss was probably too difficult," Ed said, but there wasn't a lot of conviction in his tone.

"What was she like? Did she have a sense of humor?" she asked, guiding the discussion back on track.

Ed looked up and to the right, like he was searching deep for memories of her. His gaze shifted, landing on Madelyn. "You have her smile. I know that because she always wore hers. Her laugh could fill a room and she was so darn pretty that it was hard to catch your breath when she walked in."

Madelyn had never considered herself to be that beautiful. Except in Hudson's presence. There, she felt like the most beautiful woman in the room.

"Forgive my saying so, but she didn't take life as seriously as you do," he said.

Maybe her mother hadn't been forced to. Madelyn, on the other hand, had lost her mother at birth and grown up with a father who was loving in his own way and unyielding. She'd learned to work hard at an early age and there'd been no silliness allowed. Coddling, according to her father, would spoil her. He was preparing her for adulthood. And it had begun as early as she could remember.

The contrast between Charles Kensington and her mother, Arabella, struck her. Didn't people say that opposites attracted? If her mother was really that much of a free spirit, then she and Charles, with his rigid view of life, couldn't be more contrary.

"Did she go to church?"

Ed laughed.

Madelyn wondered if that part had been made up so she would ask fewer questions. She'd viewed her mother as a saint and her father, Charles, had taken the easy road by delivering exactly what she'd wanted to hear. Madelyn had been beating herself up pretty hard for her mistakes. Somehow, knowing how imperfect her mother had been lifted some of the heavy weight on Madelyn's shoulders.

"Sorry. I don't mean any disrespect, but your mother wasn't the religious type. She had a zest for life and church would've given her too many rules.

She would've found that way too restrictive." There was so much admiration in his eyes when he spoke about her mother.

"What about this? Why did Mike Butler give it to her?" She toyed with the dragonfly around her neck.

"Ah. I was wondering when you would ask about that," he said with a smile, handing her a cotton swab.

Madelyn took the offering and rolled it around inside her cheek, careful to coat it well. She didn't want the test to come back inconclusive.

Ed nodded toward the necklace as he opened a Ziploc-style baggie. She dropped in the specimen and he immediately sealed it.

"She loved collecting dragonflies," he continued. "She'd go on and on about their magical qualities, something to do with them giving a deeper understanding of life, of self. She felt like they were powerful and graceful at the same time." He blinked. "A bit like you, if you don't mind me saying."

Madelyn tried not to let that thought comfort her. It did. The thought that her mother wouldn't see her as a disappointment let sunshine into dark places inside her heart.

"She'd light up when she talked about them," he continued. "She'd talk about how fast they could move and it was something like thirty or forty miles an hour. But they could also hover like a helicopter and fly backward if they really wanted. But the thing she liked best about them was how simple and elegant they were, like a ballerina, she'd say. She thought they had some kind of mystical wisdom and would always bring light to her."

"Guess it didn't work out so well," she said and

instantly regretted it when the sad look crossed Ed's worn features.

"From what I hear, she'd been forbidden to wear it while she gave birth," he said.

"So, my father knew?" She couldn't hide her shock.

"About the necklace? Yes. I assume he was told the rest." Ed looked her in the eyes and she could see that he was being honest.

"What about Mike Butler? Did he know right away or find out later?" She might as well go for it.

"My guess, and this is only a guess, is that he knew."

A fire lit inside her. A man like Mike Butler could afford a better hospital. Check that, could afford *the best* medical care. Her mother had died because of a negligent county hospital. She could be alive right now if he hadn't abandoned her. He'd turned his back on his daughter, too. If the paternity test turned out positive, he'd left her to be brought up by a man who could never truly love her while his four legitimate children grew up with all this. She and her father had struggled to make ends meet. "So, he didn't love my mother?"

"My friend was a complicated man. I believe that he did love your mother. He'd been talking about leaving MaryAnn, his wife." His gaze shifted to the floor. "Their marriage had been on the rocks and, looking back, it was just as much his fault as hers. He liked to drink and still had wild oats to sow. MaryAnn turned up pregnant and I thought that's why he stayed with her. The only thing my friend ever said when I asked about your mother was that she said she was in love with another man," he said.

"And Mike Butler, a man used to getting everything he wanted, left it at that?" She didn't believe that for a second. "He doesn't sound like the kind of man who was used to letting someone else get his way."

"She married Charles Kensington. What else could he do?" Ed said on a wistful-sounding sigh.

A man she didn't love, would never love.

"But then she died and Mike just left his child for another man to bring up." She couldn't mask the hurt in her voice.

"He visited Charles, asking to see you. The two had words that I was never privileged to hear and Mike left it alone," he stated.

Maverick Mike visited her father? She couldn't imagine how that discussion had gone down. Her hope that her father, Charles, didn't know that she was an illegitimate child was dying a slow death. The question was more like, how could he *not* have known? More questions joined. Why would he keep her? What did he have to gain by bringing up another man's child? Had Maverick Mike bribed her father? Pawned her off on him?

And then she thought about Charles's small business. He'd done okay for a small-time operation. But he hadn't been able to save enough to pay for her college and they'd lived on a shoestring budget. It had taken him years to pay off the hospital bill and he'd insisted on paying every last penny. She'd worked her way through college and had the student loans to prove it.

Thinking about the picture in the dining room with the wealthy smiling family filled her with anger. She had Mike's nose and even she couldn't argue that he was most likely her father. There was absolutely no way she was ready to accept the fact just yet. But that didn't make it less true.

The conversation she needed to have with Charles Kensington couldn't wait.

"Are we done here?" she asked Ed.

He nodded.

She turned to Hudson. "Ready to go?"

"Yes." He put his hand on the small of her back and she couldn't allow the comfort his touch provided.

Ignoring the electricity pinging between them, she led him to his pickup truck parked out front. The grip she had on her cell phone should've cracked the protective case. She climbed into the passenger seat and stared at her contact list. Her finger hovered over the word *Dad*.

She pushed the button as Hudson took the driver's seat.

The phone rang once, twice and then three times. She had no plans to let her father off the hook this time.

His voice-mail recording began and she pushed the button to bypass it.

"I know who my real father is." Madelyn ended the call before her voice could break.

She waited thirty seconds and called again.

"Pull over," Madelyn said to Hudson when her father picked up.

Chapter Fourteen

Hudson made a nosedive for an empty parking lot next to a field. As soon as the truck stopped, Madelyn hopped out and started pacing. She couldn't sit still and take this call. She needed to be moving.

"I know everything, Father. Or should I say Charles?" she asked, not bothering to mask her bitterness. There'd been too many opportunities for him to tell her, to make this right over the years, and he'd chosen to keep her in the dark.

The line was silent.

"What? Don't you have anything to say to me after all these years? Thirty years of flat-out lies?" Her body trembled with pent-up frustration—frustration that was seeking release with no outlet.

A quick glance at Hudson revealed he was leaning against the truck, arms folded, ankles crossed.

"Why don't you come to Friday supper and we can talk about this?" her father said, his calm voice both comforting and infuriating at the same time. Charles Kensington was not an emotional man.

"First of all, someone's after me because I'm a Butler, and the worst part about it all is that I didn't even know I was a Butler. Ridiculous me thought I was a Kensington all this time," she blurted out.

The line was so quiet that she thought her father had ended the call. She wanted to scream, to shout, to get something out of the man to show that he had a beating heart in that ice-cold chest of his.

"You don't sound like you feel well. We should talk when you're better," he said, and she got a lot of pleasure out of a small fracture in his tone.

"How about after I'm dead, like my mother," she shot back, unable to contain the fire in hers.

"It's bad manners to talk derogatory about someone who has passed," he said, regaining that tight lip.

"How so, *Dad*?" She was waving a red flag in the face of a determined bull. In her father's case, the bull was determined not to show any emotion. Par for the course and more proof that he didn't care.

"Should I set an extra place at the table?" he asked.

"Are you kidding me? Don't bother. I won't be coming home ever again. Because you're not my father and I don't want to have anything to do with lies." That should get him riled up.

It didn't.

"Have it your way. Call if you change your mind. Otherwise, there isn't much more to say."

The line died and her heart fisted as the crack of a bullet split the air.

It took a few seconds to register what had happened. A few more to come to grips with the reality someone had fired at them. All of which came too late because the shooter got off another round as Hudson tackled her, covering her with his considerable size as she flew to the hard concrete. Her head almost cracked against the pavement, but Hudson shielded it.

"Stay low," Hudson said, popping up to all fours.

Madelyn rolled over onto her stomach and belly-crawled toward the truck. She barely registered the pain in her hands at clawing across the pavement filled with tiny jagged rocks. This wasn't the time to worry about the ache shooting through her knees.

Hudson muttered the same curse she was thinking as another shot fired. The ping sound of a bullet hitting metal on the truck sent an icy chill racing up her spine. Fear gripped her as Hudson's arm came around her, his hand on her stomach, and lifted her into the passenger seat.

"Keep your head down, eyes below the dashboard," he said sharply. "Get into as small of a ball as you can on the floorboard."

Madelyn did as he climbed over her and into the driver's side. The door closed behind him and the next second he was gunning the motor. She remembered the shotgun tucked behind the seat. She could reach it and fire off a few shots, giving them the distance they needed to outrun the shooter, or she could hide.

"Do you know anyone who owns a rifle?" Hudson asked.

"Yes—more than half the state, according to statistics," she said and then made her move.

"I told you to stay down," Hudson shouted.

"You can't drive and shoot. I'm not helpless. I won't cower on the floorboard when I can make a difference," she stated. "Where's the ammunition?"

"There in the dash," Hudson said.

She bounced around in the seat but managed to gain

purchase on the butt of the shotgun. Next, she located a shell and loaded it. "Who am I shooting at?"

"White sedan. It's the only vehicle behind us."

Hands shaking from a burst of adrenaline, Madelyn opened the little window between the cab and the truck bed, took aim and fired.

The sedan swerved and the driver must've hit the brakes because the hood dipped as the car slowed. She loaded another shell and pumped the action, hoping to blow out a tire this time. From the looks of things, she missed entirely, but the main goal was to slow down the driver so that they could slip away, and that had been accomplished. He backed off and pulled onto the shoulder.

She kept her gaze focused on the sedan until it disappeared completely from view. "He's gone."

"Call the sheriff," Hudson said with more than a hint of admiration in his voice. "Tell him to come to the ranch. Talking to your father will have to wait."

By the time he parked in his garage, she'd given her statement to the sheriff. And it was probably because she'd almost died—again!—that her heart rate was jacked through the roof, or maybe it was the compassion he'd shown earlier and the constant reminders that someone wanted to kill her, but Madelyn climbed over the seat and onto Hudson's lap.

Before he reminded her that this was a bad idea or brought them both back to their senses, she kissed him. The heat in that kiss robbed her breath as she tunneled her fingers into his thick hair.

There was so much heat roaring through her body, seeking an outlet, that her body ached. Ached with need for Hudson. She needed to feel him moving inside her and needed the bliss that would follow getting completely lost with him. She needed to feel her naked skin against his strong, hard body.

He smelled of coffee and outdoors and spice. Just the scent of him turned her on and had her craving *more*. More of him. More of this moment. Just more until they rose to the sky before exploding into a thousand pieces of light and drifting to the earth like confetti during a celebration parade.

His hands searched her body, roaming over her stomach.

And the next thing she realized was the door to the truck flying open and Hudson wrapping his hands around her bottom as he twisted around until his boots were on the pavement. He carried her to the front door, couldn't seem to get the key in the lock fast enough, and then rushed inside. He kicked the door closed and then spun around until her back was against it. She found the lock, making sure they were safe. His body was flush with hers, her legs wrapped around his midsection, and she could feel his thick erection pulsing, denim against denim.

"You're beautiful," he said as he planted kisses along her neck. His hot breath sliding through her, causing a deep well of need to rise from within.

"So are you," she said, and he laughed, his chest rumbling against her body.

She matched his enthusiasm. His lips found hers and she thrust her tongue in his mouth. He groaned as his hands cupped her bottom and he pressed harder against her.

All she could do was surrender to the flames engulfing her. Madelyn gripped both of Hudson's shoulders and he pulled back enough to look her in the eyes.

"We're wearing far too many clothes," she said.

"You're sure this is a good idea?" he asked, the hunger in his gaze almost feral. His voice was low, husky and sexy.

Madelyn answered by urging her feet to the floor and pulling the hem of her blouse over her head.

His tongue slicked across his bottom lip and he groaned as his eyes roamed her body, hungry, seeking. He brought his hand up, using his index finger to outline her lacy bra. Her nipples pebbled and her breasts swelled under his touch.

He cupped her breasts and she reached in back for the release. He slid the straps over her shoulders, groaning again when her breasts were free. He dipped his head and captured her nipple in his mouth. Her body ached for him to touch more. His tongue slicked a hot trail circling around her nipple until he took her in his mouth.

Madelyn tugged at the hem of his T-shirt and he aided her in removing it with one swift motion. Her hands were already on the fastener of his jeans by the time his joined hers. He fumbled with one of the buttons as his hands trembled with the same need coursing through her.

Their rapid breaths mingled and she was ready to taste him. So, she did. Madelyn dropped down to her knees and gripped his length after he stepped out of his denim. She teased his tip with her tongue, drawing a guttural groan from deep in his chest. Working her hand along the shaft as she alternately licked and teased caused his muscles to cord.

"We need to slow down," he said, and she liked being the one in control.

She eased her closed hand around him, sliding up and down in unison with her tongue. And when she brought him to the brink, he helped her up and out of her jeans.

"Hold on," he said, disappearing for a second down the hallway and returning with a condom already secured. His body was perfection as he moved, his muscles flexing and releasing with every intentional stride toward her.

Madelyn had already slid her panties off and tossed them with the pile of clothes on the floor.

Hudson was making a beeline toward her and her heart stuttered at the hungry look on his face. She wrapped her arms around him as soon as he was close and he picked her up. She expected him to ease into her but instead he walked her over to the massive handmade wooden table and cleared it in one swipe. With her back on the table, he trailed kisses down her neck, around her breasts and then farther down still. Down her stomach toward her wet heat. He drove his tongue inside her as he worked her mound with his fingers. Her back arched as pleasure rippled through her from her thighs to her crown as he brought her closer to the tipping point.

When she couldn't take it any longer, she tugged him over her, loving the feel of his muscled body on top of her, pressing her back into the table. She wrapped her legs around his toned stomach as he dipped his tip inside her heat. She was so ready for him, and the second he realized it, he drove himself deep inside. She moaned as the electric current pinging inside her reached fever pitch with each long stride.

Her fingers dug into his shoulders as she tried to

brace herself for the moment when she would soar over the edge. His pace was frantic and she matched each stroke until they both exploded in an inferno of bliss as bombs detonated inside her. She could feel his length pulsing as he reached the same sweet release until all that was left inside them were heavy breaths.

She didn't say that was amazing, but it was. In fact, that was the best sex of her life, and it was so much more than the physical act. The emotional connection she felt brought it to a whole new level, and she hoped—maybe sensed—he had the same experience.

His lips found hers and she got lost in that sensation of being with Hudson. And then he gently wrapped his arms around her bottom as she put her arms around his neck. He lifted her and held her tight as he brought her to his bedroom.

The bed was easily large enough for two people and the room was comfortably furnished. But that was not what she was focused on. All she could think about was how right she felt in his arms and how much she'd needed that release to break the sexual current that had been sizzling between them since she first met him.

She dressed in time for the sheriff to show up and then take their statements.

But when she got back into bed and pulled up the covers, she didn't think about being shot at or the white sedan.

She thought about Hudson as she fell into a deep sleep.

HUDSON PUT ON a pot of coffee. Seven hours was the most sleep he'd gotten since...

He didn't want to go there. Not after having the best

sex of his life and especially not after his heart stirred in ways it hadn't in… He paused. Ever.

A wave of guilt crashed into him. He muttered a curse under his breath. The last thing he wanted to think about was the past when he'd had a short reprieve while he was with Madelyn and, for once, he felt good.

"What's wrong?" Madelyn said from the doorway. The sound of her voice shocked him out of his reverie. He turned toward her and the shot that pierced him was like a bullet to the heart. It also told him that he was in deep trouble. It was too soon to try to figure out what exactly that meant.

"Nothing," he lied, making a straight line toward her and not stopping until she was in his arms and he'd kissed her. All he could think about now was just how shattered he'd been after they'd made love and how much he was ready to do it again.

She pushed up to her tiptoes to deepen the kiss and that was all the encouragement he needed to pick her up and take her back to bed.

They'd made love at a frantic pace last night and this time he wanted to take his time, explore her body and feel her soft creamy skin against his. He broke off the kiss long enough to place a condom on his tip and she rolled it down his shaft for him. All he could think was how much trouble he was in because he couldn't get enough of the wheat-haired beauty as she straddled him and pushed him down on the bed.

This time, she climbed on top of him and set the pace. Long, slow strokes caused the tension to build inside him until he was on the edge again. Her pert breasts bounced as she rode him, and his hands roamed her flat stomach before gripping her sweet bottom.

He could feel the tension building inside her as she increased her speed, grinding her sex on top of him. The sweet feel of her muscles tightening around him and her body cording with tension until she exploded in sweet release.

He flipped her onto her back and she smiled up at him—right then he knew that he was a goner. Once, twice… Hell, three times would never be enough.

She pulled him down on top of her, wrapped her legs around him and he drove himself home. It might be temporary, but it was home.

Chapter Fifteen

Madelyn woke reaching for Hudson and felt cold sheets instead where he'd been. The sun was bright in the sky and she couldn't believe it when she checked the clock and realized that she'd slept until ten thirty, a luxury she couldn't remember when she'd indulged last. She stretched, feeling the happy soreness that always seemed to accompany multiple rounds of back-to-back good sex. *Really* good sex. Okay, mind-blowing sex. And something else?

The feeling was foreign because she'd never been this connected to anyone else or felt this at home. Heck, her own place didn't make her feel this safe and comfortable. Ever since this whole episode with Owen had started, she'd been lucky to get five hours of sleep in a row. And before that, needing to find the truth, to give others answers she'd never known, had driven her to work fourteen-hour days. Her father popped into her thoughts. She needed to circle back and speak to him. She didn't like the way they'd left things. He had been her dad for almost three decades.

Coffee. She needed coffee. She didn't need to overanalyze her life and especially not whatever was happening between her and Hudson. Her heart tried to argue but a strong need for caffeine momentarily silenced all protests. She threw on Hudson's white button-down collared shirt, the one that had been flung over the chair in his room, and fastened a couple of buttons.

A pot was already on, so she poured a cup. The hot liquid burned her throat in the best possible way as she took her first sip. Palming her mug, enjoying the warmth, she moved toward the window to see if she could see him. He was most likely feeding animals, checking the fence for breaks or exercising his horse, Bullseye.

She located him almost immediately in the practice ring, and watched the grace with which the animal and rider moved. Thoughts of the feel of his rugged hands all over her skin brought a tingling sensation to her arms. She moved to the screened-in patio on the back porch, enjoying the bright sunshine and the beauty of the land.

There was something right about being here. Madelyn didn't want to get inside her head about what that meant. She just sat there, admiring the ease with which Hudson guided his horse around the ring. She was on her second cup when her stomach decided food needed to be a priority. It took great effort to force herself up off the comfortable Adirondack chair. She fluffed the pillow and picked up her empty mug, not quite ready to leave the quiet, the stillness of the place. Because she was calm on the inside and she hadn't experienced that since long before Owen. Probably never when she really thought about it and she was reluctant to let this moment end.

She lingered, looking out onto the land.

As she scanned the horizon, she saw someone about Owen's size and build stalking toward Hudson from the tree line. Her heart leaped to her throat. At first, she thought she was seeing things. It couldn't be him. And even if it was, how would Owen know where she was?

A dark feeling came over her as she watched the figure move toward the exercise ring. Did he have something in his hand? A weapon?

She flew to the screen door, flung it open and screamed at Hudson. Her finger was pointed directly at the approaching figure when he looked at her. He froze for a split second before spinning around and retreating.

Hudson wasted no time breaking his horse out of the corral. A shot was fired, and to Bullseye's credit, he didn't panic. Hudson had to stop long enough to open the gate but he was skilled on horseback and broke his mare into a full run toward the trees, aiming Bullseye at the spot she'd indicated. Her heart galloped at the thought he was heading toward the danger. She scanned his white T-shirt for signs of blood.

The figure had disappeared. She searched the trees, looking for any sign of him. He could be anywhere. She regretted yelling out in panic. If she'd kept a cool head, she might've been able to sneak up on him. And then do what? Confront a man who had a gun?

Another shot rang out and Madelyn gasped. Instinct took over and she dropped down to all fours.

If it was Owen, and she couldn't confirm that it was, he'd lost his mind if he followed her to Cattle Barge. Hudson and Bullseye had disappeared into the trees and her heart free-fell at the possibility he wouldn't come out.

It seemed like forever but was probably only ten or fifteen minutes by the time Hudson emerged. He and his horse broke from the tree line at a solid trot. She ran toward them, desperately searching his shirt for blood, but Hudson motioned for her to go back.

"Stay in the house," he shouted. He hopped off his horse and secured Bullseye before dashing onto the porch. "What did you see?"

"A man about my ex's height and build," she started.

"Was it him?"

"I can't be certain. I mean, a lot of men are around five foot ten and a hundred fifty pounds, right?"

Hudson nodded.

"He could come back, couldn't he?" She hated the way her voice trembled.

"Yes. And we'll be ready for him." His jaw ticked.

"How? You can't stay awake all the time and this whole situation is escalating." Her fingers twisted thinking about the danger she'd put him in. "Maybe I should go to the Butler ranch. You could come with me."

He paused like he was considering it. "I can't leave my horses."

"Could Doris stay with them?" Madelyn already knew the answer. He would never risk involving another person, and neither would she, now that she really thought about it. She was having a knee-jerk reaction and needed to calm down so she could think clearly.

Her ringtone sounded in the other room.

"I better answer that." She dashed into the kitchen and located her cell. *Owen.* "You're not supposed to call me anymore."

"I have to see you," he said, and she listened for any

signs of him being out of breath or sounds of nature in the background. If it had been him a little while ago, there'd be something to give him away. Right? Owen was sneaky, a little voice reminded her.

"We both know that's not going to happen." A frustrated sigh slipped out when she could detect nothing. It couldn't have been him. There was no way he'd be this calm and there was no noise other than a TV.

"It doesn't have to be this way, Madelyn. I mean, the restraining order. I was a jerk and said things I didn't mean. I'll never make that mistake again. If you say it's over and you're done I'll respect it. But at least see me one more time," he begged. There was more than a hint of desperation in his tone.

"You're right. We didn't have to get to this place. But this was the path you chose and you need to explain yourself to a judge. If he thinks you should get off for what you did, that's up to him. I'm not withdrawing the court order."

"It's a mistake on your part." Was he threatening her? Again?

"Believe me when I tell you that you need to leave it alone. Walk away," she said.

"I can't. We'll see each other again," he stated.

Didn't that send creepy crawlies down her spine?

"If that was you, Owen, you need to cut it out. Keep your distance or you'll have even more to regret," she warned.

"What are you talking about?" He was either a very good actor or he really didn't know. With Owen, she couldn't be sure.

"I'm telling you to stay away from me," she spelled out for him.

"What do you think I'm doing now?" he shot back. There was a lot of confidence in his tone and that had her leaning toward the trespasser being someone else. But who? One of the Butlers? Someone from the media? A fresh wave of panic washed over her. Another thought struck. Trent?

"Violating a court order," she stated.

"That, I'm not doing. Madelyn, it's me. We had something good together. Don't ruin it now with all this legal mess. Just have dinner with me and we'll talk it out. You'll see that I'm ready and willing to respect your boundaries."

A frustrated sound tore from her throat. "Like you are right now?"

"I'm sorry," he said. "And you're right. I'm trying to get you to agree to see me and here I am being a total jerk. But it's only because I still care about you. That has to be a little charming, right?"

She wasn't about to fall into that trap with him. "I already said that's not possible. Contact me through your attorney from now on."

"You're going to regret this, Madelyn," he said, all the charm in his voice long gone.

"The only regret I have is getting involved with you in the first place, Owen."

The line went dead.

"Who was that?" Hudson asked, startling her.

"Owen."

Hudson's hands fisted at his sides. "Wish you'd let me talk to him."

She had no doubt that Hudson wouldn't take lightly a man who threatened women. "I'm trying to let the law handle him."

"Where was he?" Hudson was most likely thinking along the same lines as her.

"I heard a TV in the background and he wasn't out of breath." She wished there'd been more clues.

"Doesn't rule him out."

"Have you heard word from the sheriff today?" she asked.

"There's no news of the white sedan." Hudson moved to the coffee maker. "You want a cup?"

"I'd like that. Can we take it to go? There's someone I need to talk to this morning."

EVERYTHING WAS HOT this time of year in Texas, from the sidewalks to the rooftops. Lack of rain had left large cracks in the front yard of the house where Madelyn had grown up. She wondered how smart it was to build houses on dry, shifty soil.

She climbed the couple of stairs onto the four-by-four cement porch of her childhood home. She couldn't count the number of times she'd returned since leaving for college. There'd been many. She'd spent so many days of her young life playing on this very porch, in this yard.

Looking around, she found that everything appeared different this time. The place seemed smaller and the flowers out front needed a good watering.

Before she could reach for the handle, the front door flew open.

Charles, her father, stood there. She'd never once seen him get emotional and yet his puffy eyes were glassy and red as though he'd been crying.

"Come in," he said, looking from her to Hudson.

"I can wait here," Hudson offered, but she reached

for his hand, linking their fingers. No way could she do this without him.

Crossing the threshold was like stepping into a time capsule. Her father still had the same brown plaid sofa with twin brown recliners flanking either side, all positioned to take advantage of the TV screen. The back to the TV had disappeared and he'd mounted a flat screen to the wall, adding a console table underneath. Those were the only real improvements. She glanced at the contents, half expecting to see a VHS machine, but she found a Blu-ray player instead.

Her father looked exactly the same as he had as far back as Madelyn could remember. He had a slightly round stomach from too much sitting and a sunburn showing at his V-neck shirt despite owning a clock repair shop and spending much of his time indoors. His light brown hair was graying at the temples. He wasn't wealthy by any stretch of the imagination but they'd had enough to cover the basics. He was the kind of guy who could fix just about anything. But he'd shown no interest in repairing what most needed to be mended in his home—his relationship with his daughter. The irony of that sat heavy in Madelyn's thoughts. He'd spent days off tinkering in the garage, not coming in until supper. He'd park in front of the screen with a TV tray.

Most of the time, Madelyn had read while she ate at the table. Alone.

"I know she was already pregnant when you married her." Madelyn came right out with it, unable to skirt the issues any longer. "The question is, did you?"

"Do you want a cup of coffee?" her father said,

avoiding looking directly at her. Instead he looked at Hudson, who introduced himself.

She didn't really want to waste time but there was something about her father's expression that caused her to think he needed a minute. It was that same look sources got when they were about to tell her something that was difficult for them to say. "Okay."

He disappeared into the kitchen as Madelyn showed Hudson to the round table and chairs near the sliding glass patio door. He scooted his chair next to hers so that the outsides of their thighs touched. There was something so reassuring about his touch.

Charles brought over two full cups, hers and the special one meant for guests. He disappeared into the galley-style kitchen before returning with his #1 Dad mug. She'd saved money she'd earned from chores and received in birthday presents to afford it and remembered being so proud when he opened it that Father's Day when she was eight years old. He'd given her a kiss on the forehead despite his distant expression and then used it every day from then on, as far as she knew.

Her father took a sip of the fresh brew before slowly exhaling, studying the rim of his cup intently. It took everything inside her not to barrage him with the dozens of questions flooding her. But being there in her family home, the one she'd shared with him, brought an onslaught of tender memories. On the table was her baby photo album, the one he'd meticulously put together and given her when she turned eighteen.

There were so many questions swirling. Madelyn pulled on a well of patience she didn't know existed until now. Something in her had changed and she felt a sense of compassion instead of anger for the man who couldn't seem to find the right words to tell her that he wasn't her father.

"I loved her," he finally said before compressing his lips like he had to clamp his mouth shut in order to keep hold of his emotions. "She'd left me because she wanted to go to the city. Said she'd die of boredom if she stayed in Halifax Trail, where we're from."

He paused long enough to take another sip of coffee, white-knuckling the mug.

"I always blamed myself because I refused when she asked me to go with her." He looked up at Madelyn but quickly refocused on the rim. "I was stubborn back then."

A wave of compassion washed over Madelyn. Being here with her father made her remember all those times she'd climbed in his lap while he read the morning paper. He'd bounce her on his knee.

"Told her my life was in Halifax Trail and the city had nothing to offer me," he said. "Looking back, she took that to mean I didn't love her. That wasn't the case at all. But she didn't know how much it broke my heart that she could walk away so easily. I've never been one to show my emotions." His voice hitched.

"Did she lie to you and say the baby was yours when she came back?" Madelyn asked. For some reason the answer mattered very much to her.

"No, she didn't," he quickly countered. "I knew the whole story. She'd gotten herself in trouble with a married man. She needed a place to hide. I knew that her father would disown her if she turned up pregnant and alone, so I asked her to marry me. Told her I didn't have much and my life was here but she could have everything I owned."

Madelyn pushed off the table and got to her feet. He knew. Her stomach tightened. So, he'd loved her mother but not her.

"When I lost her, I felt like the world had ended," he said. "I'd been the one to insist on paying for everything even though—" he didn't look at Madelyn this time "—*he* said he'd cover her medical bills."

Anger rose from Madelyn's chest, licking her veins with white-hot embers. "Is that why you pushed me away? Because I reminded you of *him*?"

"What?" Her father seemed genuinely surprised at her outburst.

"Don't look at me like you don't know what I'm talking about. We both know you were forced to take care of me after Mom died." She paced. The urge to open the door, run outside and keep going until she dropped from exhaustion burned inside her chest.

"You were the best thing that came out of a bad situation," he said with a bewildered look on his face.

"Do you expect me to believe that?" she shot back. "Or is that how you show love to people? Always keeping them at arm's length?"

A few tears streaked his cheeks as he sat there, soberly.

"I had no idea you took it that way," he finally said. "You were so much like your mom when you were little that I figured one of these days you'd walk out, too." His voice broke on the last couple of words. "I've been preparing myself for the day I'd lose you, too, because you were always smart and full of life. Just like her."

The force of those words was a cannon to her chest. She stopped, trying to process the implications of what he'd said. He'd been afraid she'd be the one to leave?

Madelyn whirled around to face her father.

"I've always lived in fear that you would figure out that I wasn't your *real* dad and you'd push me away." He wouldn't look anywhere but at the coffee mug in his hand, staring at it as if he was enthralled, as more tears streaked down his cheeks. "It wasn't a matter of *if* but *when*."

She took in a few deep breaths, praying for the right words. His anguish was evident on his worn face and he looked so old to her then. Fragile. The strong man who'd seemed so impenetrable looked like he might shatter. But the only thing that splintered was Madelyn's anger. She'd never seen her father look so vulnerable and her heart caved.

She started toward him as tears burned her eyes. He met her in the middle of the room. "I'll always love you. Nothing will ever change that. And I need you to start meeting me halfway or our relationship won't work. When I call, I need you to pick up the phone because no matter what a piece of paper says you'll always be my father. And I need you now more than ever."

Her father pulled her into a bear hug. "Forgive an old fool if I promise to do better? I don't want to lose you."

Madelyn embraced her father in the warmest hug she'd ever known.

"I'll admit that I've always feared this day would come, but having everything out in the open is actually a relief." He wiped the tears away. "I couldn't have loved you more than if you'd been my own blood."

"You're my family, Dad."

"Can you forgive me?"

"Absolutely, and I should've talked to you about this sooner." Looking back, she could see how he was the kind of person who had a hard time showing his feelings and she wished they'd cleared the air long ago. She'd confused his fear with a lack of love for her. Now that she realized he'd tried to stay aloof because he was afraid that she'd reject him when she learned of her heritage, she could forgive him. "Even if I had known Mike Butler was my father when he was still alive, you were the one who put on an apron and baked a cake for every birthday I can remember, not him."

"He offered," he defended. "We kept you from him and I never did feel that was right for either one of you. He could've given you things and you deserve to have the world."

"Did you know that I left town because his lawyer contacted me?" she asked.

He shook his head.

"All these years, Maverick Mike kept quiet." It was all she had to say.

"From what I've heard, he wasn't a bad man underneath all the flash and show," her father said, wiping away another stray tear.

"If I'm good, it's because of you. Blood isn't important. Being there every day for a child is." She embraced her father, remembering the look on his face when he'd dropped her off the first day of kindergarten. He must not've realized she was watching him out the window but it was the first time she remembered seeing him get emotional. "Now that everything's in the open there's no more need to be afraid."

"I was stupid." Charles hugged her tighter and for a second she was his little girl again, being comforted by her father's arms. There was only one other time when she'd felt safe and that was in Hudson's arms. But then, he was practically a stranger.

"I love you, Maddie-cake." He hadn't called her that since she was eight years old.

"I love you, too, Dad."

The two reclaimed their seats when the hugs and tears seemed to be over.

"Owen hasn't stopped by, has he?" Madelyn asked.

"Haven't seen him," her dad said with a glance toward Hudson.

She smiled through the awkward moment.

"Steer clear of him for the next couple of weeks. We broke up and he hasn't been taking it well," she said.

"I figured as much." Another quick glance toward Hudson.

"He's a friend." There was no way she was going to try to explain what neither she nor Hudson had attempted to define.

When the coffee cups were drained, it was time to head back to the ranch. They said their goodbyes with promises to be better about staying in touch.

"It was a pleasure meeting you," Hudson said, shaking her father's hand.

Madelyn's moment of happiness was derailed when she saw the back bumper of a white sedan cut a close corner at the end of the street.

"We have to go. *Now.*"

Chapter Sixteen

"Any sign of the white sedan?" Madelyn asked as she checked the side-view mirror.

"Nothing from my view, but just because I can't see it doesn't mean it's not back there somewhere," Hudson warned. "It might not be the one we're looking for anyway."

Madelyn had had the same thought as she double-checked the road. There were a few cars and sport-utility vehicles, none of which were white.

"Your father seems like a good man," Hudson said. "He'll have a hard time forgiving himself."

"Anyone who would take someone else's child and never say one way or the other gets extra points in my book," she pointed out.

"I don't think he saw it like that at all," he said.

"Oh, yeah? How so?"

"Seems to me that you always belonged to him in his heart."

She wondered if Hudson would ever forgive himself for his past. Being with her father brought home a different point. One that she didn't want to apply to her current situation but couldn't stop the comparison. People only changed when they wanted to.

"I'm still touched by your acceptance of him, flaws and all," he stated.

"Perfection is an impossible goal. Love and forgiveness matter so much more." Her cell buzzed and she retrieved it from her handbag. It was a text from Harlan that read, He used to be a cop in Houston. Blood on his hands. Want to know more? Call me ASAP.

"What is it?" Hudson's voice broke through her heavy thoughts. He'd lied to her. He'd been lying to her all along.

"Were you going to tell me that you worked for Houston PD?"

Hudson didn't say a word but she could feel the tension fill the cabin like a thick fog. The rest of the drive was dead silent.

"My past is none of your business," Hudson mumbled, parking the truck in his garage. "And you had no right poking around in my background without my permission."

"Maybe you should've disclosed that before we slept together, Hudson." She hopped out of the truck and slammed the door.

Hudson practically flew around the vehicle. He captured her wrist in his hand and she ignored those infuriating frissons of electricity coursing through her.

"Don't leave. Not like this," he said.

"I can't stick around here anymore and we both know it. Not if you won't tell me anything about you."

"What does it matter? Will it change the way you feel about me?" he asked. He had that same look as her father, the one where he didn't seem to have the right words—only Hudson wasn't trying to find them.

"I'm going to the Butlers'. I can call them once I get

my stuff together. I'm sure the sheriff will speak to Trent and Kelsey and get back to me." She jerked out of his grip and stalked inside to the guest room. Her bag was open and her stuff flung everywhere. Anger roared through her.

He stood in the hallway, his arms crossed as he leaned against the doorjamb.

"What's happening?" he asked.

"You tell me," she fired back.

"I'm not the one packing," he said.

"You want to know what's really going on?" She froze, thought twice about saying the words on the tip of her tongue. It had been an exhausting day already and all she wanted to do was tumble into bed in his arms and sleep. But then what?

"That's what I said."

"I'm falling for you, Hudson Dale, and that's ridiculous even to me because I don't even know who you really are. How stupid is that? I don't know anything about your past or who you are, and you have no plans to tell me, either," she said. "Your life is a mystery and I'm not supposed to ask questions. I'm just supposed to accept everything at face value and it seems to me that if you won't let me in there's nothing I can do about it. And the worst part is that I know you have feelings for me but you'll never let anything develop between us."

"What you said about your father made an impact on me," he began, and she sat on the bed with her back facing him. She didn't want him to see her so close to losing it right then. Tears already streaked her cheeks and her emotions felt wrung out from her earlier encounter with her father. At least that had had a positive outcome.

"There isn't much that can't be forgiven once people start communicating," she said.

She heard him take a step toward her but he must've stopped because all fell quiet again.

"Not everything can," he said before she heard him turn around and walk out of the room.

Whatever he'd done before seemed like it would haunt him forever. She grabbed the handbag she'd tossed onto the floor and made the call to Ed Staples.

There were two problems with staying at Hudson's ranch. One, someone had figured out where she was, and that couldn't be good. And two, sticking around threatened to destroy her when this was all over and it was time to go home.

She'd made a huge error in judgment in dating Owen and she liked to think she learned from her mistakes. Comparing the two seemed absurd to her, even while her emotions were all over the place, but she'd gone into a relationship with Owen blindly, ignoring all the early warning signs of him being a little too possessive.

She'd give him one thing: he'd seemed like an open book, telling her everything about him and his family from day one. Not that it mattered because she and Hudson would never have a chance at a real relationship until he forgave himself.

"Is the offer of a roof over my head still available?" she asked Ed Staples when he picked up on the first ring.

"It is," he said.

"Then I'd like to take the Butler family up on their generosity. I can be there in less than half an hour," she stated.

"I'll alert the guard at the front gate," he said and

sounded happier than she'd expected. Maybe he liked the idea of righting a wrong for his friend.

"Perfect." She gathered the last of her things, shoved them inside her overnight bag and wiped away a few stray tears before stalking into the living room in search of her car keys.

Hudson was in the kitchen, leaning against the granite counter with a mug of coffee in his hand. "Ready?"

She glanced around on the countertop. "As soon as I find my keys I'll be out of your hair."

"You mean these?" He pulled a set from out of his pocket and twirled them around the finger of his free hand.

She made a move toward him but he captured them in his palm, took a big sip of coffee and started toward the garage.

"What are you doing?" she asked.

"Coming with you." He cracked an infuriating smile.

"I didn't invite you."

"Yes, you did. At the Butlers' house and, besides, you made a good point." His intense brown eyes drew her in.

"And what was that?"

"It's not safe here anymore," he said. "We'll stay at the Butlers' until I can secure the ranch."

"What about Bullseye and the other horses?" she asked, her heart betraying her with a little flip at the thought of him coming with her.

"Let me worry about them." He opened the door.

"Are you sure this is a good idea?"

His strong facade broke for an instant and he looked tired. "I don't know what's going on between us. Or maybe I'm not that stupid and I do. I'm not ready to put words to what we have but you in my bed is the first time I've slept in longer than I can remember and I don't want you to go. It's not safe here and I get that, so I'm coming with you."

"I don't need you there. I'll have plenty of security," she said.

"True, but will you have this?" He ate up the real estate between them in two strides, placed his hand on her hip and pulled her toward him until their lips fused together. The earth shifted underneath her feet as a flame engulfed her in two seconds flat, catching her off guard.

She was breathless by the time he pulled back and she could see that he was, too.

"It's the damnedest thing, isn't it?" His face broke into a brilliant show of straight white teeth.

Madelyn couldn't help herself. She smiled, too.

He held out his hand. "Ready?"

The battle between what her heart wanted and her mind warned against raged. She took in a sharp breath. "We're back at ground zero. You haven't told me anything about your past and I still don't know who you are."

"I will," he said with earnest eyes. "All I need to know is if that's good enough for now."

Tentatively, she took the hand he was offering. All logic said she should make him give her something more.

Her heart took over as he pressed a kiss to her lips. This time, the brush was so gentle and yet lit so many fires inside her.

And she was powerless against it. She hoped that didn't come back and burn her.

PULLING INTO THE Butler estate, Madelyn immediately noticed a deputy's SUV parked out front and her heart sank.

"I wonder what that's about." Her first thought was that something else had happened on the ranch and she immediately second-guessed her decision to come. Was anywhere safe anymore?

"Let's find out." Hudson parked and they walked to the front door hand in hand.

It took a couple of minutes for someone to answer. It was Ella Butler and the look on her face dropped Madelyn's heart to her toes.

"Come in." Ella ushered them inside.

Madelyn followed Ella into the same dining room they'd been in yesterday.

Ed Staples immediately stepped forward. "You're going to hear something disturbing, but I assure you no one here knows what's happening."

Madelyn noticed that Hudson had positioned himself between her and the rest of the Butlers. Everyone was standing and Deputy Harley nodded toward her.

"What is it? What's going on?" Madelyn asked.

The deputy angled his body in her direction. "We found traces of lipstick markings on the bathroom mirror where you said someone had written a note. Forensics returned the sample and we were able to identify a brand. It's an expensive lipstick, not something many folks around here would know about or be able to afford. So, the sheriff thought it might be a good idea to come here and ask if anyone knew anything about Rat-tat Red."

He looked to her.

"Never heard of it in my life," she said.

"Neither had any of us, but then we discovered the brand is from Paris and there's only one family in town who would have the kind of money to buy Rat-tat Red lipstick in France, so we stopped by to inquire if there'd been a burglary," he continued.

"And we said that there hasn't been one that we know of." Ella was wringing her hands together.

The deputy agreed with her admission. "And that presents a problem for us because when we looked in Cadence Butler's cosmetic drawer, you can guess what we found."

"Rat-tat Red," Madelyn said.

"That's right. So, if there wasn't a burglary, that means someone with access to her cosmetics wrote that on your mirror." The deputy stood, feet apart, in an athletic stance.

"My sister wasn't even here. She's sick and she's been gone." And then it seemed to dawn on Ella. "When did this happen?"

"Three days ago between the hours of 3:00 and 5:00 p.m.," the deputy responded.

Ella sat down at the table, looking a little lost. "She was here during that window but there's no way she would…"

"Do you know Trent Buford?" Madelyn asked.

Ella's forehead scrunched. "No."

"Your sister might," Madelyn said, looking to Hudson. He nodded. "Seems convenient that Cadence left when she did."

Hudson clasped his hands. "She would have to be working with someone else to pull this off."

"He works at the motel. Doesn't seem like they'd run in the same circles," Madelyn said.

"They could be linked by Kelsey," he said.

Ella grunted. "That name sounds familiar."

"Where is Cadence now?" the deputy asked Ella. "I'll need to speak to her in order to establish a connection."

Madelyn looked at everyone differently now. The few tentative strands of trust had snapped the minute the lipstick was traced to this house.

"I'm not sure," Ella admitted, "but I can call her." She was already looking for her cell.

Dade leaned forward and rested his elbows on his knees. "Looking at this from your perspective, I can see how damaging this seems. We aren't the kind of people who would do something like this. No one is more upset than we are to find this out, and I'm certain my sister isn't involved."

"We'll get to the bottom of this," Dalton agreed.

Madelyn would reserve judgment for the time being. The twins seemed sincere and Ella appeared distraught.

"She's not picking up," Ella said, ending the call. She made a face as she fired off a text. "I just can't imagine that she would be involved in something like this."

"Who else has access to the bedrooms?" the deputy asked.

"May, our housekeeper, but I'd trust her with my life," Ella said, and the twins were nodding.

"We limit people from coming and going ever since our dad was killed and Ella was targeted," Dade said.

Which narrowed down the suspect list to the people in the room and the missing sister.

Madelyn turned to Hudson. "Let's go."

"Don't," Ella pleaded. "At least not until we can clear this up. This is crazy and I don't want you to leave thinking that we're some lunatic family. We're actually pretty decent people, and although we haven't been the most welcoming, we want you to know that we'll adjust. Whether you turn out to be our sister or not, our father wanted you to be part of this family, and we haven't been good at respecting his wishes."

"I'd hate for any of you to put yourself out," Madelyn shot back, leading with her emotions. She reminded herself that staying objective was how a good reporter uncovered the truth. Living that axiom was so much harder when it came to her life.

"What she means is that we're actually a nice bunch who look out for each other," Dade interjected. "Our relationship with our father was complicated."

Ed stepped in front of the French doors. "I was hoping to do this with the entire family in the room, but since that seems impossible with—" he glanced at the deputy "—the current...*situation*, I think this might be as good a time as we'll get. The DNA test results came back."

Chapter Seventeen

"And?" Madelyn didn't want to admit how much she needed the confirmation. She already had proof from Charles. He'd told her that she wasn't his and yet her logical mind needed this evidence. Her hand came up to her dragonfly necklace, fingering the details.

"You're a Butler, Madelyn."

There was something primal about needing to know something so basic, something that most people took for granted, which was where they came from. Knowing who her parents were.

"And as I was going through more of your father's things this afternoon, I found this." He handed over another envelope.

She stared at it like it was a bomb, remembering how much her life had changed when he'd done this before.

"It won't bite. I promise," Ed said softly, urging her to take the offering.

She did and she pulled out the first item, a picture of her about to dive into the water. She remembered that city meet like it was yesterday. "This was senior year. I won that race with a record-setting time. But who took this?"

"I didn't," Ed said. "I believe it was your father."

She dumped a few similar pictures out onto her hand and it was like taking a trip back into the past. Photos of various swim meets, most likely taken with a telephoto lens. There were papers, too. Letters from coaches at various top colleges.

"He's the one who made sure I got into a good college, isn't he?" she asked Ed. "It all makes sense now. And being inducted into the school's hall of fame. The donation didn't come from alumni. It was him."

"Seems like he was very proud of your accomplishments, Miss Kensington." Ed had that same fatherly pride she'd heard in her own father's voice when she'd told him about the ceremony.

A hot tear streaked her cheek.

"Sounds about right," Dade muttered under his breath, and it seemed Charles wasn't the only father who wasn't stellar about sharing emotions.

Madelyn turned her back to everyone and studied the contents of the envelope, not wanting anyone to see just how sensitive she was. There were pictures of her over the years and something she treasured even more, photos of her mother.

Hudson moved behind her and brought his hands to her shoulders, bringing warmth to her tense muscles. It caught her off guard that Mike Butler being proud of her made her emotional.

Had Cadence Butler discovered this? Been jealous? It was convenient timing that she had the flu and was out of town. Had she set all this up to spook Madelyn? To get her out of the way?

Or was someone else trying to protect the family?

So much more made sense about her swimming scholarship that had landed almost out of the blue. Even her coach had seemed surprised and she'd known that he'd been holding something back when he'd delivered the news. Mike, her father—and that still seemed too weird to acknowledge—had obviously set everything up. If his right-hand person, Ed Staples, didn't know about it then he must've done it himself, and that meant more to her than she should allow.

"I think we should go," she said, feeling suddenly awkward in the house, tucking the envelope along with its contents into her purse.

"Please, stay for a little while. At least until we hear back from my sister," Ella said, motioning toward the dining chair.

Madelyn wanted answers. Staying, spending time with the Butlers would give her a chance to get to know them better. And there was another pull to the ranch that she wasn't ready to analyze but it made her feel closer to her mother.

Half an hour later, Ella's phone rang. She glanced at the screen. "It's my sister."

The deputy had already left to continue his investigation elsewhere, promising to follow up on all leads. He'd also asked to be notified when Cadence checked in and said he'd be trying to find her on his own. Everyone was clear that she needed to report to the sheriff's office immediately.

"Where are you?" Ella immediately asked.

"Put the call on speaker," Dade said, no room for argument in his tone. Did he suspect his baby sister of foul play?

"Oh, right, sorry," Ella said. She moved the cell away from her ear and did as he'd asked.

"What's going on, Cadence?" Dade asked with authority. He would've made a great law-enforcement officer.

"Nothing," she said, and there was more than a hint of defensiveness in her tone.

"Don't mess around. This is serious." Impatience edged his tone. "If you did something to Madelyn Kensington you need to speak up because the sheriff's office is involved and there are real consequences."

"What are you talking about? You're going to have to fill me in because I have no idea," Cadence said with a shaky voice that quickly recovered.

"Tell us what you know about Madelyn." He glanced up at her and she didn't know him well enough to figure out what he was thinking.

"I have no idea who that is," Cadence said, but the tremble to her voice said otherwise. Or maybe she really was still sick like they'd said before. She definitely sounded off to Madelyn. But then, maybe she was just reading too much into the situation. It was impossible to stay objective when she was *this* close to the story.

"Sounds like you might," Dade said, and she appreciated his honesty and directness. He certainly wasn't pulling any punches now even though he'd defended his sister fervently before new evidence came to light. "Like I said before, if you know anything about what's going on with Madelyn Kensington—" she noticed he stopped short of calling her their sister, but then she realized that he might be trying to trip Cadence up "—you need to speak up now or face the very real possibility of spending time in jail. Dad isn't here to bail you out this time."

His words were harsh and his stare intent. Even

Ella seemed to feel like he'd gone too far when she shot him a look.

Madelyn looked to Hudson, who stood strong and silent beside her. He stared at the travertine floor intently, expectantly. She thought about his background, his former employment with Houston PD. From what she could see so far, he would've been great at his job. Missing the action was most likely the reason he'd been so eager to help before. Don't get her wrong, ranching life seemed to suit him, but the pace was much slower and there were no adrenaline rushes. Most of the cops she'd known needed them in order to feel alive.

"I already said I don't know her," Cadence said, but there was real fear in her voice now.

"Cadence, who's Trent?"

The line went dead quiet.

"You should come home," Ella said. "Now."

"I'll be on the next flight," she said.

"How long will that take?" Ella asked.

"Hold on." The sounds of fingers on a laptop came through. "I can be home tonight."

"That's too late," Dade said. "We'll send a pilot to pick you up now."

Cadence issued a harsh sigh. "I'm at the lake house in Boulder Mountain. There are fires, so the private airstrip is closed."

Dade didn't seem impressed with the news. "I'll arrange for an earlier flight out of Denver airport. Can you get there within the hour?"

"That should work." She sounded resigned.

"We'll see you this afternoon," he said.

Ella ended the call.

Hudson's hand was on Madelyn's elbow now as he

squeezed. She guessed that he had something to say that he didn't want the others to hear.

"Okay if we take a walk?" Madelyn asked, looking to the concerned eldest Butler.

"Of course," Ella said.

Madelyn walked out with Hudson close on her heels. Whatever he needed to say seemed urgent.

HUDSON FELT LIKE he had a pretty good read on the twins and Ella. All three of them were innocent.

"I don't trust Cadence," he said to Madelyn after making sure they'd walked out of earshot. He glanced behind them, checking to ensure no one had followed. Until they had definitive proof none of the Butlers were involved, they needed to watch their backs. "She's either hiding or covering."

"I got the same impression but I'm curious what makes you think that," Madelyn said, eyeing him carefully.

He hadn't given her much to go on or trust him and she'd shown that she was willing to give him leeway. Thinking about the past, let alone talking about it, had been something he'd been avoiding. Normally, when he thought about it a heavy curtain dropped around his shoulders.

This time was different.

"You already know that I used to be a cop in Houston," he admitted and discovered it wasn't horrible to talk about.

"Most cops I've met would never leave the job." She folded her arms like she was readying herself for the wall that would come up between them. She was a quick learner and he regretted the times he'd done that when he should've forged ahead into uncomfortable territory and talked. "What made you?"

A mix of emotion swirled through Hudson, bubbling to the surface. Talking could make everything a whole lot worse, although his situation—he hadn't really been able to sleep until this beauty had come into his life— didn't seem like it could get much worse.

He could try to reason himself to death or he could go on instinct and tell her what had happened. "My partner was killed."

"And you blame yourself?" she asked.

"The bullet was meant for me," he supplied, waiting for the heavy downpour of emotions that always came when he thought about it, let alone tried to discuss it.

"And he—"

"She," he corrected, and it seemed to immediately dawn on her that the two had been having an affair. "Was pregnant."

"Oh" was all she said at first. She wrapped her arms around his neck, placed her head on his chest and said in barely a whisper, "I'm so sorry, Hudson."

Those words were all she had to say to lighten the war raging inside him because she turned to him when she spoke and that one look she gave shattered another layer of his defenses. There were so few walls left between her and the real him and he felt exposed.

He looped his arms around her waist, aware that another layer was disintegrating. He thought about how helpless he'd been to help Misty and he was in the same boat with Madelyn now, too.

The thought of not being able to protect Madelyn, of the possibility of losing her, too, hit like a physical punch with lightning speed. He glanced around, thinking that someone on this ranch could be threatening her. His own judgment was swayed by his closeness to the case. A good cop never went in alone, like he'd tried to do on the shift with Misty. He was trying to protect her and all he'd really done was end up getting her killed. He'd stopped treating her like a partner and had started looking at her as the woman carrying his child. It had cost him a whole helluva lot. It didn't seem to matter then or now that she hadn't been 100 percent sure the baby was even his. She'd admitted that to him on their dinner break. She'd started seeing someone else when she thought she might be getting too close to Hudson.

Hudson had learned from his mistakes and he wouldn't try to do any of this alone. He and Madelyn needed to involve as many people as possible. They needed to work with law enforcement, the Butlers and anyone else who wanted to be involved in order to ensure her safety.

"You have to go home," he said. "We'll talk to the police in your area and bring them up to date. They're already aware of the restraining order and I'll call my old boss and see if I can plead your case. He'll believe the threat is real, when I explain to him what's going on. You're not safe here. The sheriff is too overloaded. I can't do this on my own and I can't allow anything to happen to you."

This close, he could breathe in the scent of her shampoo, which smelled of citrus and spring.

"I want to see Cadence first. I want to look her in the eyes so I can tell if she's lying." Madelyn didn't budge. She stood there with a fixed, determined look.

"The threat won't stop if it's coming from inside the

Butler camp. They stand to gain millions if you don't exist," he said. "I didn't consider them a serious possibility until today."

"If it's not her, someone also targeted Ella. What if more than one person was involved?" she asked.

"A good investigator follows the evidence and right now that leads to Cadence Butler," he said. "She has motive and had opportunity."

"What about the incident at your place earlier?" she asked. "That couldn't have been her."

"Let me think on this some more." He frowned because she was right. She was also overlooking the possibility that now hit him like a truck. There could be multiple issues at work, converging. The first was her ex. The incident at his ranch and then at her father's house earlier had more of a stalker ring to it. How did Trent fit into the picture? A male figure hiding in the woods, watching. That could be Owen or someone hired by him. This all circled back to the road-rage incident and the white sedan.

Nothing made sense, nothing clicked.

More than anything, Hudson wanted to give Madelyn her life back. Maybe it was selfish but he needed to know that she'd be all right. The feeling in the pit of his gut warned him. And he needed to distance himself from her.

Chapter Eighteen

Hudson stayed within arm's reach for the rest of the afternoon, but he made no physical contact with Madelyn. There was something different about him that she couldn't quite put her finger on. His stance was aggressive and she figured he was going into investigator mode.

Madelyn kept an emotional distance.

At least he'd shared part of his history with her. The constant guilt he seemed to carry made more sense now that she knew, but there was precious little she could do about it.

Dade walked outside and signaled. "Cadence was picked up by the deputy at the airport. She's being taken to the sheriff's office and should be there in fifteen minutes."

"We'll meet you there," Hudson said with a look toward Madelyn. She grabbed her purse and they bolted to his truck.

Twenty minutes later, they were parking at the sheriff's office. Media swarmed the Butler vehicles and Madelyn had the very sobering realization that would be happening to her as soon as news of her paternity got out. There'd be a feeding frenzy when word got out that Maverick Mike's illegitimate child had surfaced. This was her chosen career and she'd always believed in being transparent, in telling the truth. So, why did it feel like the walls were closing in on her?

Because it was her life, dammit, and her professional values just clashed with it. As a journalist, she felt people had the right to know. As a person, she didn't want her life splashed across the news. She shelved those heavy thoughts, kept her head down and walked inside. That would be her life soon enough, but for now she had a little anonymity and she intended to hold on to it until the very last second.

It occurred to her that Hudson's life would be tabloid fodder, as well. His association with her would ensure it. He'd lost a partner, a future wife and a child in the time it took for a bullet to split the air. He'd gone to great lengths to keep his life private. He'd quit his job and relocated to a small town. There was no way he wanted people digging around in his background, and now that she'd be news, it was something she had to consider in order to protect him. He had to come first. She couldn't imagine that he'd be willing to subject himself to media scrutiny for a relationship neither of them was clear about anyway.

None of that mattered now. Madelyn needed to get to the bottom of who was targeting her. And with Cadence already in the sheriff's office, she figured it wouldn't be long before the truth came out. She absently fingered the dragonfly necklace.

Hudson was already making a beeline toward Doris. "Can we watch?"

The older woman grunted. "And get me fired?"

"We both know this office would fall apart without you," he said.

Doris's face flamed. "Are you flirting with me again, Hudson Dale?"

He chuckled that low rumble from his chest that she'd found so sexy. "Guess I am. Is it working?"

Now it was Doris's turn to laugh. "A little bit."

"Then I'm not trying hard enough." He nodded toward the hallway.

Another frustrated sound tore from her throat. "Go ahead. I can always eat cat food if I run out of money once I lose my job."

"You know I'd never let that happen." Hudson motioned toward the hallway but he didn't reach for Madelyn's hand this time.

She followed him to a small room. Next door was an interview room. A two-way mirror allowed her to see clearly and she could listen to the interview through a speaker. Deputy Harley was there, sitting across the table from Cadence. She was petite and her face was very pale. She was hunkered forward, clutching her stomach, and there was a trash can at her feet. Didn't someone say she had the flu?

Based on her looks, it was easy to see that she was a Butler and Madelyn recognized her from the family portrait hanging in the dining room. Madelyn remembered that in the picture, everyone wore jeans and white shirts. They looked to be out on the front lawn. Maverick Mike was in the center and his children flanked his sides. They were younger, maybe early teens, and their father wore a collared shirt along with a white Stetson. From what she could tell, not everyone who smiled in the picture was happy. Obviously, looks could be deceiving. How well she knew that, she mused, thinking back to Owen. This would all be over soon enough and she'd return home to deal with him. The strange feeling in the pit of her stomach surprisingly had little to do with facing Owen and so much more to do with the handsome cowboy she'd grown to care about. Love?

"You said before that you have no idea who might've written the note on the mirror of room twenty-six at the Red Rope Inn," the deputy said, leaning forward like he had to strain to hear Cadence. He was in her face, encroaching on her physical space, a tactic Madelyn had seen used dozens of times in interviews.

"That's right," Cadence responded, but her voice was shaky. The voice, the eyes revealed so much about a person. She was lying.

"Are you sure about that, Ms. Butler, because we're going to subpoena your cell phone records," he continued.

Cadence started working the napkin in her hands and her gaze flew to the floor.

"You'd be surprised the trail people leave behind when they do something wrong. Especially good people who don't normally cross a line like this," he said, dropping his tone to conspiratorial.

"I don't know what you're talking about," she responded, and when Madelyn looked closely, she realized a few tears were streaming down her cheeks. "I'm sorry. I'm tired and not feeling well."

"Where's the white sedan?" the deputy pressed.

Cadence's body language immediately changed. "What?"

"The vehicle you used to run Ms. Kensington off the road," he continued.

"I don't know anything about that." Her head shook

furiously and then a look of panic crossed her features. "Is she okay? Because you already know what my sister's been through."

"How do you know Trent?" he asked.

She froze.

"She didn't do it," Hudson said so low Madelyn almost didn't hear it. She was thinking the same thing and he confirmed her thoughts.

The deputy came at the question from a couple of angles and netted the same response. Cadence had no idea about the sedan. Just as Madelyn started to write the whole interview off as useless, Cadence's shoulders rocked and tears flowed.

"You were here long enough to write the threatening note, weren't you?" the deputy said, focusing in on the area he could make progress on.

"I was," she said. More tears flowed. "I don't know anything about a white sedan or anyone trying to run her off the road but I wrote the message on her mirror."

The deputy leaned back, folded his arms and said, "Tell me exactly how you did it."

Cadence blew her nose into the napkin and bent forward like she was about to retch. She took a sip of the water that had been provided before making eye contact with the deputy.

"I did it to protect my family. All I was trying to do was scare her, though," Cadence quickly added. "I would never hurt anyone or put them in any danger."

"How'd you get into the motel room?" he asked.

"Trent was a year below me in school," she said. "I flirted with him a little bit to get the key and swore him to secrecy."

So, Trent was guilty.

"Then I panicked about the whole episode but it was already too late to go back and fix it. Trent freaked out worse than I did and left work early," she said.

"I have no doubt your cell records will let us know if you're lying."

She pulled her cell from her purse, punched in a few numbers that were most likely meant to unlock the screen and pushed it toward him on the table. "See for yourself. I've told you everything I know. I feel like the biggest jerk for making someone else afraid. It was impulsive and I had no idea that there was a real threat out there. The worst part is that I heard about what my sister went through and I feel awful now for putting someone else through that."

At least they knew how Trent fit into the picture. But what would happen to him now?

"How long have you known Kelsey?" The deputy glanced up from scrolling through her phone. He'd been looking at something intensely and Madelyn figured it was either her call log or text history.

Cadence stared at the wall like she was drawing a blank. "I can't help you there since I don't know a Kelsey."

"You sure about that?" the deputy asked.

Cadence made eyes at the deputy. "I think I'd know if she was familiar."

"Then you don't know that she's suing Ms. Kensington," he stated.

"No, but news she's a Butler must've leaked to someone and I'm guessing maybe that person was Trent," Cadence said.

"Interesting."

"What's going to happen to him?" Cadence asked.

"This is all my fault. Not his. I'd feel terrible if he was brought up on charges."

"We'll let you know when he surfaces," the deputy said.

"Where is he?" she asked.

The deputy shrugged his shoulders.

"Can I call him?" she asked.

"Tell him to come in. He's either a witness or a suspect. If he turns himself in, he's looking at a few hours of community service with a stern warning. If not, he moves to the suspect list. How he handles himself in the next couple of days determines his fate." The deputy folded his hands and put them on the table.

"He'll be in. I'll make sure," Cadence promised.

More questions swirled in Madelyn's mind. She couldn't go back to the Butler ranch, not with Cadence home. If the youngest Butler wasn't connected to the white sedan then someone still had it out for her.

"It's been a long day and I'm tired," Madelyn said, rubbing the spot between her eyes as a headache formed. "I'm ready to go."

Hudson took her by the hand and led her out of the sheriff's office. She ignored the way his strong, warm hand made her heart leap.

He opened the door for her first before walking around and sitting in the driver's seat. He'd excused himself earlier and set everything up with his old boss. Doris had had a friend pick up Madelyn's bag.

The plan was for Hudson to take her home and yet the word seemed so foreign now. Her place had felt comfortable before. She'd always believed that once she knew her mother and improved her relationship with her father she'd finally feel at peace. All the pieces of Madelyn's past had finally been fit together for her, and yet she'd never felt more distance between who she thought she was and who she truly was. That probably didn't even make sense, she thought.

A couple of ibuprofen and a warm shower should make her feel human again. At least she hoped it would.

Being away from Cattle Barge was also supposed to ease the threat. After all, everything had started the minute she'd driven into town. Her apartment should be okay.

But would she ever really feel safe again?

Lack of sleep and the threatening headache had her not thinking straight as she watched the road ahead. Of course she would feel safe. Once her life was back on track and she could put this nightmare behind her.

Hudson was quiet on the ride home. He'd driven her convertible with a plan to return to his ranch in Cattle Barge using a car service. It was long past nightfall by the time they reached her place but it was impossible to miss the activity in the parking lot. There were reporters everywhere. News was out.

Madelyn lived on the second floor because it was safer. She almost laughed out loud. Nothing felt safe anymore.

Hudson circled the block instead of parking. "We could go to a hotel."

"Would that make it harder to protect me?" She'd picked up on the hesitation in his voice.

He parked, took her hand and shielded her from the slew of media rushing toward her. It didn't take long to sweep the place.

"It's okay," he said. He held up the key to her convertible. "You'll be safe while I'm gone. I'll be back as soon as I call on my old boss."

With all these reporters, at least Madelyn would get a break from Owen. There were too many witnesses.

Madelyn glanced around. It was comforting that her couch was in the same spot. There were two chairs positioned around the rug for easy conversation. She'd decorated the place two years ago thinking about all the entertaining she planned to do. When in reality, all she did was work and sleep there. She'd promised herself that she'd get a dog to make the place feel more like home. But all she'd really done was hang a few pictures and arrange the furniture.

Madelyn moved into the bedroom, and couldn't stop herself from double-checking the closet. She peeked under the bed, too. No monsters.

Even so, she waited for Hudson to come inside before she started toward the shower. He mumbled something that she couldn't quite hear and then she turned on the water. Slipping out of her clothes made all the difference in the world. Standing in the shower as warmth sluiced through her caused her to release the breath she'd been holding. It had felt like she'd been holding that breath ever since the call had come from Ed Staples.

The realization of just how much her life was about to change was staggering. And to prove it, she could hear her ringtone in the other room pumping out almost constantly. She thought about Harlan and the promise she'd made to allow him to break the story.

Surely, he would understand. Or maybe he'd fire her. Suddenly, work was the last thing she could concentrate on. A warm shower and her own bed would go a long way toward making life straighten itself out again.

None of which mattered without Hudson.

The bathroom door quickly opened and then closed. The room stilled. The only other sound was the lock.

The mirror wasn't completely fogged up, so she saw him clearly. Owen.

Cornered, Madelyn searched for anything to use as a weapon. She picked up a shampoo bottle and threw it at him but he batted it away. She screamed.

"Your boyfriend is outside with the cops. No one can hear you," Owen said, and there was a strangely calm quality to his voice that sent an icy shiver down her spine.

"We can talk about this, Owen. Settle this out of court." Madelyn kept her eyes on him as she reached for a towel. Thoughts of the self-defense class she'd taken when she was younger ran through her mind.

"You're lying." He took a threatening step toward her. She reacted by jabbing her fist toward his face in panic. And then she felt an iron grip around her forearm as she tried to pull back. He was bigger than her, obviously, and surprisingly strong. His wild eyes said he was long past talking at this point.

"I'm not. I promise," she countered.

"You just had to keep pushing. You wouldn't be happy until my reputation was ruined," he said, and there was so much anger in his voice, his eyes. "This was supposed to be simple. I'd kill you and problem solved. It was perfect. No one would've suspected me after learning that you were a Butler."

"Wait. How'd you know?" The admission stunned her.

"There are spy devices that can be placed on work desks and in homes," he said.

He'd believed her to be having an affair with her coworker. It all made sense now.

His other hand came up to her throat, and in the next moment, the back of her head slammed against the tile of her shower. He was in her face and her body revolted at his touch.

He ran his finger along her jawline and she tried to turn her head away from him but he forced it back. "Look at me, bitch. I want my face to be the last thing you see before you die."

That was all it took for a burst of adrenaline to strike. Madelyn shot her knee up to his groin. Owen's eyes bulged, his grip momentarily weakened but not enough for her to gain the upper hand. He pressed his body against hers, essentially closing off any space for her to be able to do that again, and she wanted to vomit.

Her hands flew everywhere, trying to gain purchase as the room started to spin. She gouged at his eyes and he released a string of curses.

He was too strong and she was losing consciousness. Madelyn couldn't scream. Reasoning would do no good.

But when Owen pressed his lips to hers, she bit and at the same time used all the strength she had for a final push. She bucked off the wall and he took a step backward, caught his legs on the tub and tripped.

Owen splayed out on his back and she jumped over him as she screamed with everything she had inside her. Her neck felt like it had rope burn where his hands had been and she had a hard time catching her breath as she gripped the doorknob, half expecting to be pulled back any second.

The door opened partially before the cold fingers

closed around her right ankle. She tried to shake his hand off but he was too strong.

"Hudson! Help!" she shouted.

"I already said your new boyfriend can't hear you." Owen's other hand caught her other ankle. His hands felt like vise grips.

Madelyn grabbed on to the counter for leverage and tried to kick out of his grasp. Panic had her heart pounding her chest. Panic because she thought she might never see the cowboy again. She grabbed her brush from the counter and threw it at Owen's face. He turned his head in time and she missed. Her hairspray can was next.

With shaking hands, she pulled off the cap and then sprayed it toward his face.

That got him coughing and the distraction gave her a chance at freedom. She dashed down the hall and toward the front door. A chair had been secured under the knob.

By now there was pounding at the door as someone tried to break through from the other side.

"Hudson!"

"Madelyn, can you move whatever's blocking the door?" he asked, and his voice was the only thing calming her racing pulse.

"I'll try." The kitchen chair was secured pretty tightly. Adrenaline and fear had her panicking too much to think clearly. Could she jump out a window? As she glanced left, she saw Owen emerge from the hall. He had something in his hands and she knew for certain if she couldn't get this door open it was all over.

Madelyn pushed at the chair and rattled the door

handle. She'd managed to unlock it but couldn't think clearly.

"Think you can escape me?" A shrill sound tore from Owen's lips. "I'll follow you. You know that white sedan? It's me. The man in the tree line? Me. The cops can't catch me before you get what you deserve."

"Everyone knows it's you. Go through with this and you'll spend the rest of your life in jail," she said.

"You wouldn't drop the charges, Madelyn. My reputation is already over." He dived at her knees, knocking her onto the unforgiving wood floor.

Madelyn screamed as her head made contact. She tried to scramble to her feet but Owen was on top of her, his fists banging against her head, her body. After taking a boot to the midsection, she curled into a ball to protect herself. Another hard kick landed on the back of her head.

Owen was spewing curse words as he beat her.

Madelyn curled into a tight coil, rolled onto her back and sprang toward him. Her feet connected with his knees. His legs buckled and he hit the floor next to her.

There'd been three loud thumps against the door. It exploded open on the fourth.

And then Hudson was there, on top of Owen, wrestling him to the ground. An officer was working beside him, restraining Owen's feet.

Owen got off a good kick and the officer stumbled into Hudson. In the confusion, Owen managed to get free and grab the officer's gun. He came up standing, pointing the gun from the officer to Owen to Madelyn.

"Everybody back up," he shouted, and his expression was feral. "Put your hands where I can see 'em."

All three of them complied as he took a step toward Madelyn. "Wrap a blanket around yourself."

Madelyn pulled the cotton blend from the back of the couch and did as he said.

"Take it easy," Hudson said in a soothing voice, hands up. "We can work this out."

"There's no 'we.' Madelyn's coming with me. She knows what she did wrong." Owen looked at her. "Get over here."

She looked to Hudson, who nodded almost imperceptibly.

"I said, 'Now!'" Owen's gaze narrowed.

"Okay," Madelyn agreed, moving next to him.

He stepped behind her, wrapped an arm around her midsection and placed the officer's gun at her temple.

Madelyn gasped. The look on Hudson's face nearly brought her to her knees.

"It'll be okay," he reassured her, but he looked hollowed out.

All she could think was *How?* She didn't ask. Because it would never be all right again if Owen got her out that door and into his vehicle. Everyone seemed to realize it.

One last glance at the cowboy as she was being ushered out the door and he mouthed three words that renewed her strength and brought a sense of calm over her... *I love you.*

She loved him, too. She'd known it almost from the minute they met. Before that Madelyn had never believed in love at first sight. She believed in attraction. A pull. But never real love. And yet she knew this was special. Real.

If she didn't act fast, her life would be over. She

knew that if Owen got her to a second location there'd be no walking out. He'd have a secure place where he'd torture her to his heart's content before killing her.

The time for action was…

Now!

Madelyn signaled to Hudson with her eyes. And then she dropped to the floor, catching Owen completely off guard. His eyes had been focused behind him at the officer and Hudson.

Before he could react, Hudson dived on top of him and Madelyn clamped her arms around his legs. She heard a snap when Hudson made contact and figured one of Owen's legs had just broken.

He shrieked in pain as he was pinned to the ground outside of her apartment door. Hudson's knee staked his arm and Owen's hand flew open, releasing the gun. Madelyn scrambled to get it before Owen could recover. She gripped it as the officer rushed toward them. She scooted as far away from Hudson and Owen as she could as the two men fought.

Owen was no match for Hudson in a fair fight and the cowboy easily dispatched him. Before Owen could mutter another curse, he'd been flipped over onto his stomach; his face was eating concrete and his hands were being zip-cuffed behind his back.

The officer immediately retrieved his weapon and holstered it. He called it in and helped Madelyn to her feet.

Embarrassed, she secured the blanket around her.

"You can go inside," the officer said, taking pity on her. But she couldn't. She needed to see Owen being taken away in the squad car. It was the only way she'd ever feel safe again.

"Enjoy spending the rest of your life behind bars," Hudson said as he walked Owen to the back seat of his former boss's SUV and personally secured him inside the vehicle.

As soon as they drove off, he turned to Madelyn. There was so much emotion in his eyes as he took her in his arms.

"I thought I'd lost you," he said into her hair, and his voice rolled over her. "Let's get you inside."

Madelyn walked beside him. Her place was a wreck and it felt a lot like her insides. The nightmare was over. It would take a little time to come to terms with that, but Owen was going to jail. He couldn't hurt her or any other woman again.

She threw on yoga pants and a workout shirt and pulled her hair into a ponytail. "Being here is strange."

Hudson had been watching and there was so much appreciation in his eyes. There was another emotion, too, and she couldn't quite pinpoint it.

"I meant what I said before, Madelyn." He walked to her and took her in his arms. His strong heartbeat against her ear brought so much comfort. "I love you."

She looked up at him. Tears threatened. Not tears of sadness but tears of joy. "I love you, too, Hudson."

"I've been waiting for the right words to tell you that I don't want to live without you. I love you and I want you to come home with me to live. Permanently." He didn't wait for a response. Instead, he tilted her face up and kissed her. "But I understand if that's not what you want."

"I'm ready to build a new life with you," she said, and she felt him exhale against her chest. "You should know that I intend to keep working. Maybe not as a journalist but I need to keep writing even if it's a blog. And I intend to make amends with my new family, the Butlers. Can you still love me if I claim my birthright?"

"I don't care what you call yourself as long as we belong to each other," he said without hesitation. "Besides, I know who you really are. You're brave, intelligent, beautiful. And if you'll have me, I'll stick by your side for the rest of my life."

"Forever sounds like a great place to start" was all she said before he picked her up off her feet and held her. "And just to clarify, I'm saying yes."

He kissed her, long and slow. "Let's go home."

And she wanted to tell him that in his arms, she was already there.

* * * * *

ONE INTREPID
SEAL

ELLE JAMES

This book is dedicated to my travel buddies who make every trip fun and exciting. Africa is on our bucket list. We hope to make it there soon. We decided a long time ago not to wait until we retired to travel. I'm glad we made that decision. We've been to a lot of fun and interesting places and have so many more to visit! If I can't get to some places, I read about them and learn. That's the joy of books. Happy reading!

Chapter One

Reese Brantley held on to the frame of the window as the Land Rover bounced wildly over the rugged terrain. "Slow down!" she shouted to the driver.

Mubanga, the Zambian guide, seemed not to hear her. More likely, he completely ignored her as he leaned to the left to look beyond the obstruction of a pair of legs dangling over the windshield from a perch on the roof of the cab. He followed the racing leopard across the ground, heading north into the rocky hills, determinedly keeping up with the beautiful creature.

Ferrence Klein, Reese's client, who'd paid over one hundred thousand dollars for this hunting expedition, clung to his rifle from his position strapped to the top of the vehicle.

"He's not even supposed to be shooting leopards, is he? I thought there was a ban on shooting big cats? What the hell are you thinking?" Had Reese known Klein was coming to Africa to bag a leopard, she'd have told him *no way*. Her understanding was that he was there on a diplomatic mission for his father, the Secretary of Defense.

She wasn't playing bodyguard to an endangered-animal killer. If they weren't traveling so fast and furious, she'd have gotten out of the vehicle and taken her chances with the wildlife, rather than witness the murder of a magnificent creature.

The leopard jagged to the right and shot east into the rocky hills.

Rather than turn and follow, Mubanga kept driving north.

"Hey!" Klein yelled from the front of the vehicle. "The cat turned right!"

Mubanga completely ignored Klein and increased his speed.

The vehicle jolted so badly, Reese fought to keep from being thrown from her seat. The seat belt had long since frayed and broken. If she wanted to keep her teeth in her head, she had to brace herself on anything and everything to keep from launching through the window.

Klein flopped around like a rag doll on the front of the vehicle, screaming for the driver to stop.

"Stop this vehicle!" Reese yelled over the roar of the engine. She reached for the handgun strapped to her thigh. Before she could pull it from its holster, Mubanga backhanded her in the face so hard, she saw stars.

Reese swayed, her fingers losing their grip on the door's armrest. A big jolt slammed her forward, and she banged her forehead against the dash. Pain sliced through her head, blinding her. Gray fog crept in around the edges of her vision. She fought to remain upright, retain consciousness and protect her client, but she felt herself slipping onto the floorboard of the Rover. One more bump, and she passed out.

A FEW MINUTES might have passed—or it could have been an hour, or even a day. Reese didn't know. All she knew was that the vehicle was still and Mubanga no longer sat behind the steering wheel. As her vision and clouded brain cleared, she pulled herself up to the seat, her hand going to the holster on her thigh, pain throbbing through her temple.

Her 9-millimeter Glock was gone.

The door jerked open at her side. Someone grabbed her by her hair and yanked her out of her seat and onto the dirt.

She struggled to get her feet beneath her, but the man behind her swept out a leg, knocking her feet out from under her. Reese crumpled to the ground, her scalp screaming with the pain of being held steady by a handful of her hair.

"What the hell's going on?" she demanded. "Where's Mubanga?"

The men spoke in a language she didn't understand. The goon holding her by the hair kicked her in the side and shoved her away from him.

The relief on her scalp nearly brought tears to her eyes. At last, Reese was able to study her surroundings. Day had turned into dusk. Twenty dark-skinned men stood around her and Klein, each wielding a wicked-looking AK-47 rifle or a submachine gun. None looked like they were part of the Zambia Wildlife Authority. Their clothing was a mix of camouflage and rags. Mubanga was nowhere to be seen.

Ferrence lay unconscious on the ground, several feet away from her.

Some bodyguard she was. Her first international assignment, and her client was most likely dead. Her heart squeezed hard in her chest. Even though Ferrence had been a pain to work with, his father was nice and would be sad to lose his son. The man had paid a lot of money for her services to protect Ferrence, and she'd failed him. Reese hadn't wished ill on Ferrence. He was a job to her, but even more so, he was a human being. No one deserved to die on vacation in Zambia.

Since giving up mixed martial arts fighting, she'd put all her effort into her personal-protection-service start-up. She'd tapped on a few connections she'd gained while in the limelight of her fighting career and landed the job with the Kleins.

Ferrence hadn't wanted a bodyguard, thus, she'd come along at his father's insistence that the younger Klein needed an assistant to make his vacation in Zambia smooth and to his liking. Reese was also to pose as his assistant on his upcoming diplomatic visit to the Democratic Republic of the Congo.

Reese had stressed to both Ferrence and his father that she wasn't for hire for sexual favors. Not that Ferrence had listened to a word she'd said. She'd fought off more than one advance before the private jet had left the ground in New York, nearly crippling her client with a knee to the groin.

Since then, Ferrence had limited his advances to bumping into her whenever he could manage.

Now the spoiled son of a billionaire lay on the ground, still as death.

Reese inched toward him. In her peripheral vision, she kept an eye on the guns waving all around her. When she was only a foot away from Klein, the barrel of a rifle stopped her. She glanced up at her captor, a man with skin as black as the darkest night.

"I just want to see if he's still alive," she said.

"He alive," the man said in stilted English. "For now."

The sound of an engine drew her attention from her captor. That's when she noticed they were on the bank of a river. The motor noise came from a boat barreling toward them as though it would run aground before the driver slowed. Just as it neared the banks where the group of men stood, the driver pulled back on the throttle, and the craft slid to a gentle stop.

Two men reached for Klein, one grabbing his wrists, the other his ankles. They lifted him and slung him over the side of the boat, dropping him to the bottom.

The man beside Reese slipped the strap of his rifle over his shoulder and bent toward her.

Reese could easily take him, now that she was conscious and steadier on her feet. She could make a break for it, and might even make it to the tree line. She reasoned she could make a run for help. But that would mean abandoning the unconscious Klein. She was supposed to be protecting him, and she'd botched the job completely. Abandoning him now was not an option.

When the man reached for her arm, she jerked it away and rose to her feet. "I can walk."

His eyes narrowed, and he stared hard at her for a split second. Then he bent in half, hit her like a linebacker in her midsection and tossed her over his shoulder.

"Bastard!" she yelled. But she didn't fight hard. Her goal was to land in the boat next to Ferrence. When the time was right, and Ferrence was conscious, she'd find a way to escape. In the meantime, she let the man dump her into the boat, her body cushioned by Ferrence's limp form.

As the other men clambered aboard, Reese was able to check her charge for a pulse, which beat strongly. Reese breathed a sigh of relief. At least the man wasn't dead, and they were both tagged with GPS locator chips. She might yet repair the situation, if her captors didn't kill her first.

Three days later

DALTON SAMUEL LANDON, Diesel for short, leaned out of the open door of the MH-47 helicopter. Dusk wrapped around the helicopter, lengthening shadows between the trees and brush below and giving the team the concealment they needed to kick off Operation Silver Spoon.

While being lowered on cables, a Special Operations Craft-Riverine—or SOC-R boat—swayed over the muddy waters of the southern Congo River, before it was released and plopped into the water, rocking violently before it settled.

A bead of sweat dripped down Diesel's neck, into the collar of his shirt. Night swept over the sprawling marshlands of the Congo River in the southern province of the Democratic Republic of the Congo.

SEAL Boat Team 22 had been deployed to Djibouti, on the Horn of Africa, two days ago for this specific mission. They'd gone over the operation, studied the maps and gathered their equipment for what was now "showtime."

"The SOC-R's down!" Diesel shouted, his hand tightening on the rope, which was dangling from the helicopter to the boat below.

Wind from the rotors on each end of the chopper buffeted the craft and water below. One of the gunners hung out the door, searching for combatants, not expecting to find any this far south, but not willing to let his guard down.

"Ready?" Diesel yelled.

A shout rose up from the other members of SEAL Boat Team 22 inside the MH-47. With the helicopter hovering over the SOC-R, Diesel fast-roped from the helicopter and dropped into the boat. Once he had his balance, he took the helm and waited for the others to land.

The SOC-R's four-man crew consisted of one helmsman and three gunners. Two GAU-17/A machine guns mounted in the front of the boat, two side-mounted M240B light machine guns, one .50 caliber machine gun in the rear, two grenade launchers and sufficient ammo to take on a small army gave them enough firepower to withstand a limited war.

Hopefully, by traveling under the cover of night, they wouldn't have to use their supply of ammunition. They'd travel downriver using the GPS guidance system to the last known location of the rebels and their captives.

When all ten team members were on board, those who were designated took up positions behind each of the mounted weapons. The remaining SEALs had their M4A1 rifles with the SOPMOD upgrades in their hands, ready to take on any enemy threat.

Diesel handed the helm over to the helmsman and took up a position near the port bow. The helicopter lifted into the air and disappeared, heading south to await the call for extraction.

The helmsman opened up the throttle and sent the boat skimming through the marshlands of the headwaters of the Congo River.

The hostages had been taken three days ago. Their captors might be getting antsy and ready to kill them and cut their losses. Thus the need for speed, covering as much ground, or river, as possible that night. If all went well and they didn't get lost in the maze of tributaries, they might make it to the extraction location within a few hours.

Diesel and his team had been over and over the maps and satellite images provided by the Military intelligence gurus back in Langley, Virginia. Those were the guys who poured over hundreds of satellite images a day to locate threats or, in this situation, find the location of a kidnapped person being held for ransom. They sat behind their desks, staring at computer screens all day, and sometimes all night, long.

A shiver of revulsion slipped over Diesel. He'd rather shoot himself than man a desk inside an office all day long. Though extraction missions could be tricky and highly dangerous, he'd still rather face the danger than the boredom.

The military didn't always get involved in hostages being held for ransom. "We don't negotiate with terrorists" being the mantra repeated every time the hostage wasn't "worth" saving. But when the captive happened to be the Secretary of Defense's son, strings got pulled and men deployed.

Ferrence Klein, of the Manhattan Kleins, and the son of the Secretary of Defense, Matthew Klein, had been taken hostage by a Congolese rebel faction and was being held for ransom, along with his bodyguard, Reese Brantley.

The official story out of Africa indicated Klein had been on a wild-game hunt and had gotten ahead of his guides, on the other side of the border, in Zambia.

Their vehicle had been set upon by Congolese rebels. Once the SUV had come to a halt, the driver ran away, and the rebels took Klein and Brantley into custody. Some of the witnesses claimed the driver was paid to bring the vehicle to the rebels and was allowed to go free once the deed was done.

A video message was broadcast on the Al Jazeera television network with Ferrence blubbering about paying the ransom or whatever it took to get him out of the jungle and back home to his beloved Manhattan. He didn't mention his bodyguard. The team could only assume Brantley was still alive, so they planned on bringing back two civilians.

Using the GPS, the helmsman navigated the river, speeding along as fast as he could in the growing darkness, skimming past what appeared to be drifting logs in the murky water. Those logs turned out to be crocodiles, floating on the surface. As the SOC-R neared, the crocs dove deep into the dark river, leaving no indication they'd been there other than a gentle rippling wave.

A chill slithered across the back of Diesel's neck. He did *not* want to fall into the water. He'd rather face a dozen Congolese rebels with only a knife than an African crocodile and its mouth full of razor-sharp teeth.

He spent the next couple hours on alert, watching the shoreline for any sign of movement or guards. They passed several villages on the banks with docks jutting out into the water. Unlike back in the States, these little towns were completely dark. Not a single light shining, now that the sun had set. Many didn't have electricity. Those who did conserved the energy, not seeing a need to light the darkness. Dark was meant for sleeping.

Diesel imagined the boat that had taken the two hostages upriver had passed much the same—unchallenged and in the dark, without raising suspicion or providing clues as to its destination.

Time passed slowly. Like a good SEAL, Diesel rested, conserving his strength for the task ahead. If they didn't run into any trouble, they'd arrive well before midnight. That's when the fun would begin.

What seemed like a lifetime later, the helmsman called out, "Twenty minutes to LZ."

Diesel's pulse ratcheted up several notches, and his hand tightened on the M4A1 rifle in his hand. With only twenty minutes until they reached their landing zone, they could potentially run into Congolese rebels soon.

Ten minutes passed, and the helmsman slowed the boat to a crawl, hugging the starboard banks, using the shadows cast by the moonlight as concealment, while he searched for a good spot to tie off. Those who weren't staying with the boat would cover the rest of the distance on foot. That was seven of the ten-man team. They'd push through the trees and bushes of the now jungle terrain to their destination, where the green blips on the GPS location device led them.

A break in the overhanging limbs led to a narrow tributary, just wide enough to wedge the SOC-R into and allow the landing party to disembark.

Before he led the team off the boat, Diesel slipped his night vision goggles into position over his eyes. He scanned the shoreline, searching for any green heat signatures, whether they be man or beast. Life along the Congo River was rife with crocodiles, and if that wasn't dangerous enough, they were getting close to an area known for their bands of gorillas. Now wasn't the time to be wrestling crocs or gorillas. They had a job to do.

Nothing moved, and no green lights glowed in his night vision goggles. Diesel hopped over the side of the boat and landed on the soft, muddy slope of the riverbank. He scrambled up to a drier purchase and provided cover for the others as they disembarked. The SOC-R would remain hidden until the team returned with the hostages. Helicopter backup was a last resort.

Operation Silver Spoon was a covert operation. The Congolese Government wasn't to know the US Navy had sent people uninvited into their country. If members of the team were captured, they were to escape at any cost or disavow their connection to the US Navy and US Government. Though their weapons and equipment were dead giveaways, they each wore solid-black clothing without rank or insignia of any kind, and they didn't carry any identification cards or tags.

Each man knew the risks. He also knew his fellow SEALs wouldn't leave a single man behind—not for long, at least.

As the last man climbed out of the SOC-R, Diesel moved out, following the river, moving several yards in from the shore. He slid from shadow to shadow, carefully scanning the path ahead. He ran quickly and as quietly as possible. Stealth was their friend. If they could get into the camp, subdue the rebels and get out without stirring up a firestorm, they would make it back to Zambia by morning, and Djibouti by lunchtime.

Diesel shook his head. As much as they went through possible scenarios, or practiced different approaches, nothing ever quite turned out like they planned. Sometimes the weather played a role in gumming up the works. Sometimes the tangos they were going up against were a little more sophisticated or armed than they'd anticipated. And sometimes fate dealt them a crappy hand. Bottom line: they had to be ready to roll with the punches.

Diesel spied the first tango fifteen minutes from their LZ. "Tango at ten o'clock, twenty meters." He held up his fist and lowered himself to a squatting position, studying the guard posted near the riverbank.

After a couple minutes of observation, Diesel determined the guard was lying in a prone position without moving. He was either dead or asleep at his post.

Either way, Diesel had to insure he wouldn't raise the alarm.

"I'll take him," Diesel said. "Buck, cover me."

Graham Buckner, or Buck for short, moved up to take Diesel's position. Though he was the team corpsman, or medic, he was an excellent sharpshooter. He knelt on one knee and propped his elbow, staring down the scope fixed to the barrel of his M4A1 rifle. "Got your six. Go."

Diesel shifted his night vision goggles up onto his helmet, slipped his rifle strap over his shoulder, pulled his KA-BAR knife from the scabbard on his ankle and circled wide, coming in behind his prey, who faced the river.

The man woke at the exact moment Diesel pressed the blade to his throat. He didn't have time to shout or even whisper a cry before Diesel dispatched the man.

Slipping his night vision goggles back in place, Diesel studied the area to his north. A small camp had been set up with makeshift tents. Several men leaned against trees, their rifles resting in their laps. By the way the men's heads were drooped to the side, Diesel could tell they were fast asleep. The faint glow of heat indicated two warm bodies in the nearest tent, one in the next closest tent and three more in the farthest tent. One man stood in front of the tent with two people inside. It had to be the tent containing the hostages. The one man stood guard, while all the others slept.

Unfortunately, that one man could easily wake the others, and then all hell would break loose.

"I count eleven tangos, but I can't see the back side of the camp," Diesel whispered into his mic. "Buck, bound to my position. Harm, cover. Pitbull, Big Jake and T-Mac, swing wide and head north to cover the flank."

Each man gave a quiet affirmative and proceeded to spread out.

Once Buck took Diesel's position, Diesel motioned Harm forward. Together, they approached the camp, easing toward the one guard on duty, his rifle held loosely in his hands.

"Cover me," Diesel said.

Harm nodded. He had a silencer on his M4A1. He could drop the man in a heartbeat should trouble erupt. In the meantime, Diesel needed to get to the tent with the two hostages, take out the guard and spirit the hostages away before the rest of the camp got wind of their little operation.

Chapter Two

Reese didn't have much of an opportunity to escape. Their captors had seen fit to leave one of their members in the tent with her and Klein. Not only that, but they'd tied her hands behind her back and bound her ankles. They'd done the same to Ferrence. When he'd surfaced from unconsciousness, he'd been angry and scared. The captors only had to threaten pain and torture to get Ferrence to beg on video for the ransom money they wanted. One of the men had recorded his plea on a cell phone and left to take the video somewhere he could get cell tower reception.

They claimed to be Congolese rebels fighting for the freedom of their country to decide how to be governed, but Reese doubted they were fighting for anyone but themselves. Their leader was a big, bulky black man with a scar on the side of his face. He wore bandoliers filled with bullets, crisscrossing his chest like armor, and carried a submachine gun, waving it at anyone who angered him. His men had called him something that sounded like Bosco Mutombo.

Once their captors had their video of Ferrence's

plea, he and Reese had been left confined to the tent, allowed to go out only to relieve themselves under the watchful eyes of armed men.

Reese had been sized up and threatened with sexual abuse, but left alone when she said they would more likely get their money if both she and Ferrence were not harmed. Otherwise, they'd send in the US Army, Navy, Air Force and Marines to blow them off the face of the earth.

One man translated for the others, and they all laughed, though the laughter had a certain nervous edge to it.

Reese didn't care, as long as they didn't touch her.

A moan sounded from her client's direction.

Inching her way across the bare ground, Reese moved toward Ferrence, careful not to draw the attention of the guard sitting with his back to her. He glanced toward her every two or three minutes, but otherwise, didn't seem concerned that she might find a way to escape. He had an old video gaming device in his hand and seemed more interested in his game score than his captives.

The guard's head came up, and he glanced toward her.

Reese closed her eyes and let her head slump forward like she'd just nodded off.

Through her lashes, she could see the man's eyes narrow. He looked back at his video game. The light blinked out on it, and he shook it, muttering beneath his breath.

Reese almost laughed. She suspected the battery

had died. Since she hadn't heard a generator, and there weren't any other lights on in the camp that she could see through the canvas of the tent, the guard wouldn't be playing his game for the rest of his time there with no way to recharge the battery.

The man stood, ducked his head and stepped out of the tent.

Finally alone in the tent, Reese scooted on her butt toward Ferrence and whispered into his ear. "Wake up."

He moaned, rolled onto his back and frowned when he couldn't move his hands. For a moment, he lay still. Then he asked, "Any news?"

She shook her head, and then realized he wouldn't see the movement in the dark. "None. We can't wait to be rescued. We need to get ourselves out of this mess."

"And hide in a jungle full of snakes, gorillas and who the hell knows what else?" He shook his head. "No way. I'll wait for my father to pay the ransom and be escorted out of here in one of his helicopters."

She snorted. "Wake up and smell the coffee, Ferrence." As soon as she mentioned coffee, her belly rumbled. The only thing they'd been given to eat were a couple of bananas and unbaked sweet potatoes. Fortunately, they'd been supplied bottled water to drink, thus saving their stomachs from parasites. But the last bottle of water had been on the second morning. "It's been three days. If they don't get their ransom money soon, they might decide to kill us and hide the bodies."

"We're still equipped with the GPS tracking devices," Ferrence argued. "They're probably on their way as we speak."

"Are you willing to risk it? Do you really think these men will wait much longer? Just today, they were fighting among themselves. At least sit up and let me see if I can untie the ropes on your wrists."

He did as she asked, scooting around to put his back to hers.

Reese had already tried to untie her bonds or to rub the rope against something coarse, but she was confined to the tent, and nothing inside the tent presented itself as a coarse surface.

She fumbled with the ropes on Ferrence's wrists, finally finding the end and working it back through one of the knots.

She'd broken out in a sweat by the time she'd freed Ferrence's hands. "Now me. Untie my hands."

"When I get my feet done." He leaned away from her and grunted.

Reese grit her teeth. "Think about it, Ferrence. If you untie my wrists first, we can both untie our feet at the same time."

"I've got it," he said, triumphantly, and then turned to work at the knots on her wrists. "Yours are tighter." He blew out a frustrated breath. "I don't think I can get it."

"Try harder," she urged.

Finally, she felt the ropes give, and she shook her hands free. She immediately bent to the task of untying her legs. "If the guard comes back, pretend your wrists and ankles are still tied."

"Like hell. I'm getting out of here."

"Wait until I'm free," she said. "We need to stick together."

"You're fast. You can catch up." He lifted the back of the tent, stared out at the night and whispered, "I don't see anyone out there. I think we can make a run for it."

"Wait—" Her hands still fumbling with the knots around her ankles, Reese couldn't lunge after Ferrence. He was out the back of the tent and gone.

"Son of a b—" The end slipped through the knot and the ropes fell away from her ankles. A grunt sounded outside the front of the tent, and something fell, landing hard against the ground.

Not willing to stick around to find out what it was, Reese ducked beneath the bottom of the tent, rolled out and sprang to her feet. She ran for the nearest trees and bushes.

A shout rang out to her right, and then all hell broke loose.

Shots were fired, men yelled and chaos reigned. Reese didn't slow down, didn't stop, just kept running until she hit a wall. She hit the obstacle so hard, she bounced off and landed on her butt. Refusing to be captured again, she shot to her feet and dodged to the left.

A hand snaked out and grabbed her arm.

She rolled beneath the arm, sank her elbow into what she hoped was the man's belly and hit what felt like solid steel. Pain shot through her arm. She'd likely chipped her elbow.

Whoever had hold of her was wearing an armored plate. Having been caught and tortured before, she refused to be a victim again. She kicked her foot hard, connecting with the man's shin.

He yelled and almost lost his grip on her arm.

Reese took advantage of the loosened hold and yanked herself free.

Before she could run two steps, arms wrapped around her waist from behind, and she was lifted off the ground. She struggled, kicked and wiggled, but nothing she could do would free her of the man holding her.

"Damn it, hold still," a man's voice whispered against her ear, his breath warm and surprisingly minty.

Reese recognized the American accent immediately. "Who are you? Why are you holding me captive?" She fought again. Many Americans hired out as mercenaries. This could be one of them.

"I'm not here to hurt you." He grunted when her heel made contact with his thigh. "Damn it, I'm here to rescue you." He dropped her to the ground so fast, she lost her footing and crumpled into a heap at his feet.

More gunfire sounded behind her. Where the hell was Ferrence? Had the rebels shot him for trying to escape?

This time, when she tried to get up, the man in the armored vest laid a hand on her shoulder and dropped low beside her. "Stay down. You don't know the direction they're shooting." He stayed close to her, and then he said. "Get him out of here."

"What?" she asked.

"We're getting Klein out of here."

"Not without me," she said. "He's my client." Reese

started to get up, but that hand on her shoulder kept her down. "Who are you?"

"My team was sent to get you two out of here."

"Your team?" She glanced around. "Are you Spec Ops?"

"Shh," he said. "Someone's coming."

In the limited light making its way through the canopy of foliage, Reese could make out the silhouette of a man carrying a weapon. She lay low against the ground. The man beside her flattened himself, as well.

Neither moved a muscle as the man carrying what appeared to be an AK-47 passed inches away from where they lay.

More shouts rose up from the rebels in the camp. A motor sounded close by, and flashlights lit up the area.

The man with the AK-47 turned and almost walked over them on his way back to camp. Thankfully, he must have been too blinded by the lights to see what was right next to him.

Once the rebel fighter was out of hearing range, the man beside Reese spoke softly. "Looks like they're getting into their boat."

Reese peered through the darkness. All she could see were flashlights heading away from her and the occasional man caught in the beam. The camp was emptying out, heading for the river.

"They're heading south," the man said softly. "Your direction. Don't wait on me. Get Klein out of here, now. I have Brantley. We'll find our own way back. I'll contact you when we're out of danger. Don't argue. Just go."

Reese was only half-listening to her rescuer's side of a conversation. Some of the men appeared to be climbing aboard a boat. The others turned around, shining lights toward the jungle. She tugged on the sleeve of the man beside her. "We've got a problem." She rose onto her haunches. "Some of them are coming this way with flashlights."

BRANTLEY WAS RIGHT. Diesel glanced around. The men were coming toward them and spreading out, heading south along the river. A shout went up when they found their sentry.

"Follow me. And for the love of God, stay low," he commanded. He led the way deeper into the jungle and turned north, praying he didn't get them lost. He figured, as long as he had a GPS device on his wrist, he'd be all right. If they had to, they'd travel all the way to Kinshasa, the capital of the Democratic Republic of the Congo, and show up on the doorstep of the US Embassy, claiming some lame excuse of being tourists who'd fallen off a riverboat cruise.

In the meantime, they had to get away from the gun-toting rebels who'd just as soon shoot first and ask questions of a corpse later. Especially since they'd found one of their own dead.

A shout sounded behind him. He glanced back at Brantley. Lights flashed toward them. "Run," he urged.

They gave up all attempt at quiet and charged through the jungle. The head start they had on the rebels would help, but they couldn't keep running forever. They needed to find a place to hide.

His lungs already burning, the heat dragging him down, Diesel could imagine the woman behind him had to be dying by now. He reached back, captured Brantley's hand and pulled her along with him. When they arrived at a stand of huge trees with low-hanging limbs, Diesel aimed for them, slowing as he neared.

"Why are we slowing down? They'll catch up to us," Brantley said between ragged breaths.

Diesel cupped his hands. "Climb."

"No. Wait." The woman ripped her shirt and ran away from him.

"Where the hell are you going?" he called out to her in a whisper he hoped couldn't be heard by their pursuers.

In the pale glow from what little starlight penetrated the canopy, Brantley raced to the far edge of the clearing that surrounded the base of the tree and hung the piece of fabric on a bush. As quickly as she'd left, she returned to where Diesel again bent and held out his cupped hands. If they didn't hurry, that little bit of fabric hanging on a bush wouldn't make a difference.

"Go!" he urged.

Still, she hesitated. "I don't know."

"Don't think. Just climb."

Shouts in the jungle behind them had her stepping into the palms of his hands. He boosted her up to the first limb. When she had her balance, he handed her his rifle, and then pulled himself up beside her.

Without waiting for him to instruct her, Brantley climbed from limb to limb, rising high up the trunk to the vegetation that would provide sufficient concealment from the men wielding flashlights and weapons below.

As the men neared the tree, Brantley came to a stop. Diesel followed suit. For the next fifteen minutes, they sat silent in the tree.

Diesel breathed, held his breath and listened.

The sound of footsteps below indicated the men had reached the base of the tree. A light shined up into the branches.

Diesel glanced up.

Brantley hugged the trunk, pressing her body against the hard wood, making herself appear to be as much a part of the tree as its bark.

Diesel had laid his rifle along a thick horizontal branch, and then he laid himself across the branch, as well, bringing his feet up behind him to keep them from dangling over the sides. If he slipped an inch to the left or the right, he might fall off the branch and all the way to the ground. He didn't think about falling. Instead, he focused on his balance and maintaining his silence.

A man below yelled. The flashlights were turned away from the branches of the tree and shined toward the far side of the clearing. Footsteps pounded through the brush, toward the jungle and way from the two people up in the tree.

Soon, the sound of humans faded away, and the creatures of the night sent up their own song.

"They're gone," Reese said. "Should we get down?"

Diesel sat up, his legs straddling the big branch. When he scooted back into the trunk, he found that there was enough room for two people to sit comfortably without falling out of the tree. "We're staying the night here."

"You've got to be kidding," she said.

"I'm not sure which direction the rebels went. If we get down and follow them, they might decide to turn around and head back to camp. If we turn back the way we came, we might run into whoever they left behind."

"Yeah, yeah. I get it. If we go deeper into the jungle, we might be lost for good, and the river is full of its own dangers." She sighed. "I guess being up a tree for the night beats getting shot at or eaten by crocodiles..." Her words trailed off.

Diesel chuckled. "You don't sound very enthusiastic."

"I might be if I wasn't just a little petrified of heights." Her voice shook, and her teeth chattered.

"You're kidding, right?" Diesel shined his flashlight with the red filtered lens up at her.

She remained glued to the tree above him, even though the enemy threat had moved on. As the light touched her face, she opened her eyes and looked down. "Oh, hell." She squeezed them shut. "Shouldn't have done that. No, no, no. Shouldn't have done that."

"What? Shined the light up at you?"

"No," she said, her teeth clattering together so hard that Diesel was afraid she'd chip one.

"No. I shouldn't have looked down." Brantley's arms tightened around the tree. "Now that I'm up here, I might as well stay awhile. I certainly won't be getting down anytime soon."

Good grief, the woman was beyond terrified. "Don't move," Diesel said. "I'm coming up."

"Don't move, he says." Brantley laughed, the sound without amusement. "Trust me when I say, I couldn't let go if I wanted to. So much for all the MMA training. It doesn't help you conquer all of your fears. No, you have to climb up to the top of a giant tree to test the theory. You couldn't just stand on the edge of a cliff. Noooo. You had to climb up a really tall tree in the dark, in a jungle, with an absolute stranger who could be just as much the enemy as the people who kidnapped you."

A smile twitched at the corners of Diesel's mouth at Brantley's long monologue. He knew she was talking to keep from freaking out, but it was funny and kind of cute. She'd kept up with him in their mad dash to evade her captors. And she was a bodyguard and appeared to be capable of protecting herself. To Diesel, that spelled one tough chick.

Until she'd climbed a tree and looked down toward the ground.

Diesel pulled himself up to the next branch and the next, until he finally slung his leg over the limb Brantley was straddling, hugging the trunk with all of her might.

Diesel scooted closer.

Brantley glanced over her shoulder, nervously. "Don't knock me off."

"Wasn't going to." He inched toward her. "You know, there's enough room for two to sit here all night."

"So you say." She didn't let go of the tree trunk.

In the dark, Diesel couldn't see her fingertips, but could imagine them curled into the bark.

When he was close enough to touch her back, she flinched.

"I'm not going to knock you off. I was hoping to reassure you that this limb is big enough for the two of us." He wrapped his body around hers. "You're as tense as a tightly wound rattlesnake with a brand new button on his tail."

Brantley snorted. "Did you just fall off a horse in Texas?"

Diesel chuckled. "How did you know I was from Texas?"

"Lucky guess." She inhaled, her back rubbing against Diesel's chest. Letting the breath out in a long stream, she laughed. "I don't suppose you know of anyone who'd hire a bodyguard who couldn't keep her client safe?"

"Not off the top of my head. But then the odds were stacked against you on this assignment, from what I know."

"Damned guide was in on the kidnapping," she stated. "I should have seen it. Hell, I should have shot him when I realized he was taking us the wrong way." She shook her head. "But I didn't."

"You might have had an international incident on your hands had you killed him."

"Yeah, and he was driving when I considered it, at a breakneck speed, with Klein out front on the hood."

"On the hood?"

"You know, in some kind of seat they rig up for the hunter. He was going after a leopard."

"I thought they were protected."

"Ferrence paid a hefty price for a real safari hunt. I think the guide assured him he could shoot just about anything." The disgust in her voice was evident.

"You don't much care for Mr. Klein?"

"Not really, but that doesn't mean I wish ill on him."

"Then why work for him?"

"I'm not. I work—*worked*—for his father, Matthew Klein. He hired me to protect his son. And a lot of good that did. I wouldn't be surprised if he demands a refund."

"Don't be so hard on yourself."

"Why not? I didn't do my job." She snorted. "I can't even get down out of this tree."

"We'll worry about that in the morning, when we can see what we're doing."

"Hell, I'm putting my trust in a stranger. I don't even know you."

"We can fix that. Hi. I'm Dalton Samuel Landon, but my friends call me Diesel." He reached around her, peeled her hand off the tree and gave it an awkward shake. "And you are?" As soon as she let go, her hand found its way back to the tree.

"You must already know who I am since you were sent to rescue us."

"Reese Brantley," he supplied. "How did a girl like you end up as a bodyguard to Ferrence Klein?"

She stiffened. "What do you mean *a girl like you*?"

He chuckled. "Sorry. I meant how did you get stuck as a bodyguard to the Klein legacy?"

Her body remained rigid for a few seconds longer, and then she relaxed. "His father didn't want him to know he'd hired a bodyguard. He told Ferrence I would be his assistant while he was in Africa. Had he hired a male, Ferrence would have guessed."

Diesel nodded. "And Ferrence didn't want daddy's protection?"

"No. Not when he'd made plans to hunt endangered species." Again, Reese's body tensed. "Had I known he'd come to hunt anything but some plentiful deer, I'd have told his father where his son could go."

"I take it he was more interested in a trophy than food?"

"He was hunting a leopard when the driver veered off course." She half-turned toward him. "By the way, where are we? I have a feeling we aren't in Zambia anymore."

Diesel's arms tightened around her. "We're not. We're in the Democratic Republic of the Congo."

The woman sat stiff. "Okay. Well. We'll just have to get the hell out of here. I don't suppose your team is coming back anytime soon?"

"They will." He couldn't say when. Since they had Klein to get out, the powers that pulled the strings might not want to redeploy the team to extract one SEAL and one civilian. Not in a hostile country. And not when they weren't supposed to be there to begin with. With current tensions between the new presidential administration and international trade relations,

Diesel wasn't sure they'd risk a second insertion into the DRC.

"In the meantime," Reese said, "we'll have to get out of this area, or risk being caught."

A sound alerted Diesel. He touched Reese's arm. "Shh," he said softly. "I hear someone coming."

Chapter Three

Reese froze and listened. The animals and insects were suddenly silent. A slight breeze rustled the leaves around her. Then the snap of a twig alerted her to movement below.

Someone whispered in a language she barely recognized, and didn't understand. Then shots rang out, and the rapid report of a semiautomatic weapon filled the air.

Diesel pressed his body against her, smashing her against the tree trunk. Something hit close to where her fingers dug into the bark, splintering wood fragments over her hand.

As quickly as the burst of bullets began, they ended. Voices below spoke in rapid-fire anger. Then they moved away, heading back toward the camp where Reese and Ferrence had been held hostage for several days. As much as she hated being high up in a tree, she'd rather face the heights than her former captors.

Diesel remained pressed to her back for a couple minutes after the sounds of movement below had dissipated.

The solid strength of his body was unexpectedly reassuring. Reese frowned. She didn't like that she needed reassurance. Having spent the last three years rebuilding her life and confidence, she didn't need a man to reassure her about anything. She was the bodyguard, not Diesel.

Then again, she'd failed in her first real assignment as a bodyguard and had fallen into a situation she'd sworn she'd never allow herself to be in, ever again. She'd been captured. This time, her captors hadn't been as quick to torture and rape her. Had they tried, she'd have died fighting them off. Never again would she allow anyone to violate her, to abuse her like she'd been abused at the hands of the Taliban in Afghanistan.

The mere thought of what they'd done to her had the usual effect on her. She broke out in a cold sweat, her heart raced and she felt as if she might explode if she didn't get away and suck more air into her lungs.

"I can't breathe," she whispered through tight lips.

Immediately, the man behind her eased back. "Were you hit?"

"No," she said and dragged air into her lungs. The desire to move, to get away, took hold of her and refused to let go. At that moment, she had the uncontrollable urge to throw herself out of the tree. But she couldn't. The enemy could return. They might be lying in wait just beyond the clearing around the tree, hoping to capture them as they came out of hiding.

Instead, she bit down hard on her lip, clenched her fists and started counting to one hundred. Her body shook with the effort to control her reaction.

"Are you sure you weren't hit?" Diesel asked, his voice quiet, his mouth close to her ear, his body leaning into hers.

Reese couldn't respond, couldn't utter a word. She remained focused on not losing her cool.

Diesel's hands gripped her arms and pulled her back against his chest. "You're shaking like a paint mixer. It's okay. They're gone," he said, holding her close.

"I'm okay," Reese said, forcing the words out from between her teeth.

Diesel's arms wrapped around her midsection and held on tightly. "Clearly, you aren't."

"You don't have to hold me," she insisted, hating herself for her reaction and the need to feel his arms around her. "I can manage on my own."

"I'm afraid to let go. You might shake yourself right out of this tree."

"I'll manage," she insisted. "Please. Let go."

When he moved his arms away from her, Reese let go of the tree long enough to hug herself to ward off the chills threatening to take over. When she touched her arm where his hand had been, she felt something warm, wet and sticky. Blood? She felt around, but nothing hurt.

Because the blood wasn't hers.

"Hey." She half turned. "Were you hit?"

"I got nicked. But it's just a flesh wound. I'm fine," he said. "I'm more worried about getting us out of here and away from our friends with the AK-47s."

"You should let me look at your wound."

"It's not like you can see in the dark, and I'm not

willing to risk turning on a flashlight for a little scrape."

Reese would bet her best pair of hiking boots the wound was more than a mere scrape. "At least let me apply a pressure bandage to stop the bleeding. Where is it?"

"It's okay," he said, his tone sharp.

"Look, you dripped blood on to my arm. If you're still dripping, you might leave a trail for the goons to follow." She grabbed the hem of her shirt and, carefully and as quietly as possible, ripped off a section. She tried to turn on the tree limb and nearly tipped over the side. Her heart clattered against the walls of her chest.

Diesel held on to her arm to steady her. "Wait until we get down from here."

"For all we know, we'll be up here for a while." She shook her head. "Let me feel for myself. Where is it?" She touched his wrist and moved up his arm.

"Higher," he said.

Reese ran her hand up his thick, solid forearm to the bicep. When her fingers encountered fresh, warm blood, she knew she'd found the source of the leak. "It's more than a scrape. You might need stitches."

"I don't. But if it makes you feel better, you can wrap it up to keep me from bleeding and leaving a trail."

"Damn right I will." Pushing her fear of heights to the side, she maneuvered herself around to face him, her knees touching his, making it hard for her to reach his arm. She bent close, but still couldn't get to the spot she needed to reach. "Could you lean closer?" she asked.

"Oh, for Pete's sake." He grabbed her hips, lifted her off the tree limb and deposited her onto his lap, her legs straddling his hips.

Heat rushed into Reese's cheeks and farther south to her core. She'd never sat in a man's lap quite like this before. The angle of their contact was more than intimate, and completely befuddled her thinking. Thankfully, it also took her mind off the fact they were over twenty-five feet in the air, perched on a tree limb.

With his arms holding her firmly around her waist, she went to work wrapping the fabric around his injured arm. The fact he could move it as well as he did was proof it wasn't as bad as she'd thought. But any injury in the jungle and subsequent blood loss could be life-threatening, especially if it became infected. She did the best she could in the dark. The sooner they got her rescuer to a health-care facility, the better.

"That's as good as I can manage, without seeing the actual wound," Reese said. "You can let go, now."

"And if I don't want to?" he said, his voice rich and thick like smooth heated chocolate, spreading into every pore of her skin.

Reese's breath lodged in her lungs, and a thrill rippled through her, culminating at the point where her bottom rested on his thighs. Good Lord. She could *not* be having lusty thoughts about a complete stranger, while facing one of her most irrational fears in the canopy of a jungle tree.

Diesel's arms tightened around her for a moment

and then loosened. "I'll balance you, while you turn around." He grabbed her around her waist and eased her backward.

Reese rested a hand on his broad shoulder, until she was forced to release it and turn to clutch at the tree's trunk.

A second later, Diesel moved from behind her and dropped to the limb below. Once again, he wrapped his strong hands around her waist. "When I lift you, wrap your arms around my neck and slide your body down mine. Your feet will land on another limb."

"C-can't we wait until morning?"

"The more I consider it, the more I'm afraid that if we wait until morning, the men in the camp will see us. We need to get as far from them as possible tonight."

Reese knew what Diesel said was valid, but climbing down from a tree was so much more frightening than going up. The warmth of his hands gripping her waist gave her the courage to let go of the tree trunk and transfer her hold to his neck. She wrapped her arms around him so tightly, she was sure she practically strangled him.

He settled her feet onto the limb in front of him and urged her to ease up on the stranglehold around his neck. Once he had her sitting on the lower branch, he leaned close. "See? Not so bad."

"Easy for you to say," she grumbled. But it wasn't so bad. She still couldn't see the ground, and maybe that was a blessing.

"I'm going all the way to the ground," he whispered into her ear, his warm breath stirring the loose hairs against her cheek. "Don't move a muscle, until I return with the all clear."

She nodded, wanting to tell him to be careful, but knowing it was a wasted sentiment. The man was obviously trained in tactics and evasion. He knew how to steal through the night like a shadow.

He slipped away before she could change her mind or cling to him and beg him to stay. While Diesel was gone, she counted her breaths, praying he didn't walk into a trap and get himself killed.

He was gone for what felt like an eternity. When she'd about given up hope of his return and started to consider her own descent from the tree, she heard the soft rustle of fabric and a gentle grunt. Diesel pulled himself up to the limb below her, his head on level with her thigh. All she could see was his black silhouette against the dark backdrop of the jungle and the pale whites of his eyes.

"Miss me?" he asked.

She snorted. "Hardly," she lied. "What took you so long?"

"I went back to the camp. The men there had settled in for the night. The ones that took off on the boat hadn't returned."

"God, I hope they didn't catch up to the rest of your team." She prayed Ferrence made it back to civilization without further incident. Then, at the very least, she wouldn't be responsible for his death.

"Don't worry. There are enough of them to take on anything those rebels have in store. It's you and me I'm worried about."

"Any ideas?"

"We head north, following the river. Hopefully, we will run across someone who can help get us to safety. But first, we have to get you out of this tree."

"I can do it by myself," she said with a lot more confidence than she felt.

"Okay then. It's tricky in the dark. If you need to hold on to me, I'll be here."

Taking a deep breath, Reese leaned on to her belly and dropped both legs over the side of the limb she'd been sitting on.

A hand on her bottom steadied her and helped guide her to the branch below. Once she had her feet firmly on the thick limb, she dropped to a sitting position. Using this method, she slowly eased herself to the lowest limb.

Diesel dropped to the earth and touched her thigh. "Swing your other leg over and drop. I'll catch you."

"I'm a full-grown woman, not a small child. If I throw myself out of this tree, I could hurt both of us. Besides, you're injured."

"Do you always argue this much? If we don't hurry, those goons will be on top of us. Now do as I said," he commanded.

Reese closed her eyes, swung her leg over the limb and slid out of the tree.

True to his word, Diesel caught her. Granted, he staggered backward several steps until he got his feet under him. Still, he held her in his arms.

"You can put me down," she said. "I can stand on my own feet." She touched his arm where she'd tied the cloth around his wound. It was soaked with blood. "Damn it, Diesel, you're still bleeding."

He let her feet drop down, and she slid down his muscular front, feeling every line, ripple and indentation as she went. By the time her feet touched the ground, her body was on fire. What was it about this man that awakened in her something she thought died back in Afghanistan?

Reese quickly stepped away, her breathing ragged, her thoughts flustered. She was glad for the darkness, as she figured it would hide how red her cheeks must be. "We need to get you to a doctor. You might need stitches and antibiotics."

"I'll live. I won't need any of that if we don't get out of here ASAP." He grabbed her hand and took off, running north of the camp.

Reese ran with him, doing her best not to trip over branches and fall flat on her face. They didn't have time for broken legs. The few shafts of starlight making it through the canopy were all she had to light her way. She prayed they didn't run into any crocodiles or gorillas in the darkness.

DIESEL KEPT UP a grueling pace, determined to get as far away from the camp of Congolese rebels as he could before daring to slow down.

To Reese's credit, she did a good job keeping up with him. Based on the brief moments he'd held her in his arms, he could tell she didn't have a spare ounce of flesh on her. Her body was honed, her muscles tight and well-defined.

Eventually, they slowed and moved at a fast walk, following the river, keeping it within twenty or thirty yards—close enough to maintain their bearings, but hopefully not too close they would run into a crocodile lazing on the bank. The river twisted in undulating curls, making it hard to follow exactly. Despite the meandering nature of the waterway, Diesel felt confident they were still within fairly easy reach of the water.

If only they could come across some sort of civilization—someone who had a telephone would be great. The river had villages along the way, but Diesel had no idea of how far it was between each. They couldn't remain on the run for long. And as soon as they stopped, the mosquitos would eat them alive and spread who knew what kind of diseases. Fortunately, he'd packed a lightweight mosquito net in one of his cargo pockets. As soon as he felt they'd gotten far enough away from the rebels, he'd find another tree big enough for both of them to sleep in.

They'd been fortunate thus far that they hadn't run into any other wildlife. That luck couldn't last forever. Big cats, gorillas, hippos and crocodiles were just a few of the dangers that lurked along the banks of the Congo. The two-legged creatures could be every bit as treacherous.

After they'd been on the move for two hours, Diesel could feel his energy waning. The wound on his arm hadn't stopped bleeding and had begun to throb. They needed to stop and rest soon.

He came across a clearing in the jungle, where the

trees on the edges were large enough to provide shelter for them.

When he stopped beside one of the trees, he turned to Reese.

"Please tell me you're just stopping to catch your breath," she said, bending over to rest her hands on her knees, her breathing labored. "You know how I am about heights. It's not something I'll ever outgrow."

"It's the safest place to sleep. If you want to stay on the ground, you're welcome to it. You might be sharing it with snakes, big cats, warthogs and gorillas. The mosquitoes alone might kill you. I'm going up. And I have a mosquito net."

Reese straightened and slapped at her cheek. "Mosquito net? What armed aggressor carries a mosquito net into an operation?"

"One who's going into the jungle. I brought the very basics for survival, in case I was separated from my team."

"How fortuitous. I don't suppose you have a cell phone in one of your pockets?"

Diesel could see the pale outline of her face in the murky darkness, but not the expression in her eyes. "We were equipped with two-way radio headsets, but we're too far away from my team to communicate, and the chances of finding a cell phone transmission tower in the jungle are slim to none. The cell phone I have probably won't work until we make it all the way to Kinshasa."

Reese tipped up her head. "I really hate climbing trees," she muttered and grabbed a hold of a low-hanging branch. "And what will keep a big cat from climbing the tree with us?"

"I think we can fend off a big cat in a tree easier than we can on the ground. I do have a weapon."

"With that weapon, couldn't we fight off everything on the ground, then?" Reese pulled herself up onto the first branch.

"We need to get some rest. You might not like heights, but I'm not fond of snakes. I'd rather take my chances in a tree than on the ground."

"Fine. I'm climbing. But don't expect me to like it," she grumbled.

He chuckled and climbed up behind her. "I didn't expect you to." He handed her a tube. "Drink."

"Where did you get water?"

"I have a water container on my back. Standard issue. Beats the hell out of canteens."

She sipped and then sat back. "I didn't realize how thirsty I was. As humid as it is, you'd think we wouldn't need to drink."

"All the more reason to keep hydrated." He tucked the tube away and tipped his head up. "Wait here."

She raised her hand. "I'm not going anywhere."

Diesel climbed higher, found a fork in a sturdy branch, broke off some boughs full of leaves and twigs and laid them in the fork. He figured if the gorillas could make nests, he could too. Soon he had a relatively secure place for them to sleep through the remainder of the night. He hooked the mosquito netting from a branch above and camouflaged it with leaves.

When he was satisfied, he turned to climb back down, only to find Reese scooting out on the limb.

"I got tired of waiting," she said.

The meager light that found its way through the canopy gave just enough illumination for her to see what he'd been working on. "Looks like a cocoon."

"It is, in a way. Crawl on in."

"You sure it'll hold me?" she asked, still hesitating.

"I've been all over it. It's pretty sturdy."

Reese eased beneath the netting and stopped. "Can we be seen from below?"

"Won't know until daylight. Go ahead. Get some rest. I'll take first watch."

"No way. You're the injured party. I should have been up here doing all this while you rested."

"I'm fine. It's just a—"

"Flesh wound," she finished. "You men. You could have a sucking chest wound and you'd still call it a flesh wound. At least let me do a better job on the bandage, now that we're far enough away from our pursuers."

"If it'll get you inside, okay." He slipped into the nest beside her and turned his arm toward her.

"Got a flashlight? I'd like to see what I'm working with."

He handed her a small flashlight with a red lens. "Better than nothing and not as visible from a distance."

She nodded, wedged the flashlight into the netting and pointed it at Diesel's arm. Then she tried to untie the knotted bloody fabric.

Every time her knuckles grazed the wound, Diesel flinched.

"It's getting red and puffy around the wound. You need medical attention."

"Why? I have you." He winked.

She frowned.

"Why the frown?" He touched her cheek.

Was she frowning? Reese schooled her face, ripped off another strip of fabric from her shirt, made a pad with part of it and pressed it to his wound, maybe a little harder than she should have.

He flinched. "Mad about something?"

"This whole situation. I'm supposed to be on a diplomatic mission with Ferrence Klein, protecting him from threats, not alone in the jungle with a stranger, far from my client."

"Sometimes plans change. Missions change. You have to learn to roll with the punches."

She glanced at the nest of branches. "I'm rolling." She nodded toward the makeshift bed. "You sleep. I'm taking first watch."

"I don't need much sleep. You can go first."

Her lips curled on the corners. "Do you always argue this much? You've lost blood. You need to rest." She switched off the flashlight and remained in an upright position, refusing to lie down beside him.

Diesel could tell by the stubborn tilt of her chin that he couldn't change her mind. Used to catching Z's wherever and whenever he had the opportunity, he'd make use of this time to refill his internal store of energy. "Have it your way. But wake me in a couple hours. You need to sleep, too. We might have a long trek ahead of us tomorrow." When he woke, he'd figure a way out of the jungle and back to his normal routine.

He lay staring up into the darkness, wide awake, wondering about this woman he'd rescued from the rebels. She wasn't like most women he knew. "How did you end up hiring on to protect Klein?"

"I had some connections," she replied.

"What's your background? What makes you qualified to protect Klein?"

She hesitated only for a moment before firing back, "What makes you qualified to recover him?" She was feisty and gave as good as she got.

Diesel chuckled. "I'm in the navy. My team was tasked with the mission to rescue you and Klein."

Silence stretched between them.

"Four years active duty in the army and two years on the MMA circuit."

"MMA?" he asked.

"Mixed Martial Arts."

"Why the army?" he asked.

"Why the navy?"

"Family legacy. My father was a marine, my grandfather was in the navy. I guess you could say it was in my blood. I like a challenge," Diesel said. "Your turn. What's your story?"

"Why do you care?" she said.

Diesel sighed. "Look, I'm just trying to get to know the woman I'm sleeping with in the jungle."

Again, she was quiet for a few moments before speaking. "My parents died in car wreck a few days after I graduated high school. I had nothing keeping me there, no home to go to. A recruiter said, *Join the army, see the world.* So, I did."

"But you didn't stay in the army."

"No." The one word was spoken in a tight, sharp tone.

"Deploy?"

"Yes. And when I got off active duty, I became an MMA fighter."

Diesel stopped suddenly, his brows rising. "Seriously?" He touched her arm. An MMA fighter was the last thing he expected to come from her mouth. "I mean, you're in great shape and all, but I didn't picture you as someone who'd fight for sport. Why the MMA?" he asked.

"I had some anger management issues I needed to resolve." She shifted. "Are you finished with the interrogation?"

"I am."

"Good, because you're supposed to be sleeping."

Diesel suspected there was a lot more to Reese's story than she was sharing, but he wouldn't push her more. If she wanted him to know more, she'd tell him. He had enough to go on, for now.

He'd hoped talking would make him less aware of her tight body. When she'd been in his lap, he'd been so turned on, he'd thought for sure she'd notice. Her body was honed, her attitude determined, but she was vulnerable enough to make him want to protect her. And if that meant holding her in his arms through the night, so be it. He swallowed a groan on that last thought. Maybe it was a good thing they split the watch and slept in shifts. Nowhere in his life did he have room to fall for the long-legged, curvaceous bodyguard, even if she was pretty hot in the red glow of the flashlight. And she had gumption. No. He needed to complete this mission and move on.

He lay on his back, unable to ignore the warmth of her thigh pressed against his. Swallowing a groan, he focused on sleep. He'd never had trouble falling asleep before he'd met Reese. Why start now?

Chapter Four

Reese sat beside Diesel in the nest of boughs and stared through the gaps in the camouflage he'd applied to the netting. Every time the man moved, he brushed up against her, making her heart race and her body light up. What was wrong with her? Even if she wanted, she couldn't begin to sleep with her thoughts running wild over her rescuer.

When Diesel had flashed his smile and winked at Reese, butterflies had erupted and swarmed in her belly, and heat had spread from her center outward. Not only was the man as hard as a bodybuilder, he was charming and sexy, too. A triple threat to her libido. She shook her head. She was in a tree, in a jungle with a man she'd met only a few hours ago. How could she be having lascivious thoughts about him when they were both covered in sweat and dirt?

She could hear the steady breathing of the man beside her. Darkness kept her from studying him. Time passed slowly with nothing but her thoughts to keep her company. Every sound made her tense up until her back ached. In the wee hours of the morning, her head dipped, and sleep threatened to overtake her.

She didn't want to wake Diesel. He was the one who was wounded. His body needed time to recover.

Guilt made a knot in her gut. She'd already botched her first assignment. Ferrence's father would fire her as soon as she got back to civilization. She wouldn't have a job, and word-of-mouth about her failure would see to it she never had another bodyguard client. The least she could do was watch over the navy SEAL.

But she was so darned sleepy.

The man lying beside her moved. A second later, a hand touched her shoulder, and Diesel pressed the drinking tube against her fingers. "Drink and then sleep."

She didn't argue. Too tired to do anything but what he commanded, she sipped from the tube, the liquid soothing her dry throat. Then she lay on the bows and closed her eyes.

Reese must have fallen asleep right away. When she opened her eyes, she could make out all the shapes and shadows within the nest Diesel had created.

One thing she couldn't see was the man himself.

Reese bolted upright and listened for the reassuring sound of him moving around outside the mosquito netting.

She heard sounds, but they weren't the sounds she expected. Something was moving down below—a lot of somethings. And there were several grunts and other sounds she couldn't quite place. She leaned forward and pressed her face to the netting. In the clearing below, dark shapes moved about. Some big, some smaller, but none of them human.

Her heart leaped into her throat, and she fought back a gasp.

A troop of gorillas had moved into the clearing and appeared to be setting up camp. Even from her perch high above them, Reese could tell they were big. Mothers sat preening their babies. Adolescent gorillas romped in the clearing, wrestling and tumbling.

Reese looked for the alpha male but didn't see him. He had to be there. All troops had an alpha male, and the alpha could be extremely fierce.

Where was Diesel?

"Shh," came a soft whisper close to her ear.

The sound was so quiet, she almost didn't hear it. Reese turned toward Diesel on the other side of the mosquito net.

He pointed down and mouthed the words *alpha male*.

Reese gulped. She worried that, if the alpha male caught their scent, he could climb the tree and rip them apart. Holy hell. And she thought being caught by Congolese rebels was bad. At least they hadn't been capable of ripping her apart with their bare hands. There would be no reasoning with a male gorilla.

Reese remained still, afraid to move and disturb the branches of the nest Diesel had built. Thankfully, they were at least twenty-five feet from the floor of the jungle. More importantly, they were twenty-five feet from the male gorilla. At the very least, they had a head start at climbing higher.

Her heart raced and her hands grew clammy. How good would she be climbing if her hands were slick with nervous sweat?

Silence and minimal movement were the orders of the day. Reese settled back and observed the social structure of the troop. Never had she ever imagined she'd have a front-row seat at a family gathering of giant apes.

They ate, groomed and dozed in the morning heat, in no hurry to move on to a different area. The strong scent of their bodies drifted upward to where Reese sat, but she didn't let that bother her. The social dynamics of the group of gorillas was fascinating.

For a couple of hours, the gorillas sat. Reese grew uncomfortable and needed to relieve herself, but she didn't dare move. She wondered how much longer the troop would be in the area.

Suddenly, the bigger gorillas sent out a disturbed cry. Mothers gathered their offspring and herded them to the other side of the clearing, disappearing into the jungle. The male gorilla left his position beneath their tree and powered out into the center of the clearing.

Men erupted from the shadows, yelling and firing AK-47s, aiming for the larger gorillas.

Reese gasped. "What are they doing?"

Diesel's lips pressed together. "Poachers. Gorilla hands and feet sell for a lot of money on the black market." He lifted his rifle into his hands and straightened from his position next to the nest. "Stay down."

Her heart grinding to a stop, Reese stared from Diesel to the men below. "What are you going to do?"

"I'm going to stop the carnage."

"But they outnumber you. You'll be killed."

"They don't know I'm here." He slipped off the limb and lowered himself to the one below, moving away from where Reese hunkered low against the branch, wishing she had a weapon.

The smallest gorillas screamed and ran ahead of their mothers. The alpha male ran toward the two men bearing weapons closest to him, roaring loud enough to make the leaves shake in the trees.

Before the men could yank their rifles up, the gorilla swept out a mighty hand and knocked the two men across the clearing.

Once the other men realized what was happening, they turned their rifles toward the huge silverback and fired.

With every bullet that hit the big ape, Reese flinched. The gorilla had done nothing to deserve this attack. Even though he could just as easily have killed her and Diesel, he hadn't, and all he was doing was protecting his troop.

Reese pressed a hand to her chest as the big gorilla charged the men shooting at him. In her heart, Reese hoped the big ape killed the men trying to kill him. It would serve them right for what they were doing to the endangered species. She wished she still had a gun.

A yell suspiciously similar to the ones from the old Tarzan movies sounded below, and shots rang out from beneath the tree in which Reese hid. Diesel, covered in leaves and camouflage, charged out of the shadows, firing his M4A1 rifle. He ran toward the group of poachers like a creature straight from hell.

"Are you insane?" Reese shoved aside the netting and climbed out on the limb. "You'll get your foolself killed."

The group of men hadn't expected the gorillas to fire back at them. Apparently, they were so stunned by Diesel's appearance, they shot rounds into the air on reflex, then turned and ran into the jungle.

The huge gorilla spun around and roared in Diesel's direction, but the man had already ducked into the brush, completely blending into the foliage.

Blood oozed from the gorilla's wounds, but he was able to run after his troop, into the woods.

Minutes later, the clearing was empty and nothing moved.

Reese counted to fifty, praying Diesel hadn't been hit by a stray bullet. Why wasn't he coming back to the tree?

Then she noticed a movement at the far end of the clearing, where the two men had been knocked out by the male gorilla.

They rose, grabbed their weapons and spoke to each other in hushed tones. Then they walked around the clearing, their rifles held out in front of them, ready to shoot anything that moved.

Reese stared at the two. They were both darkskinned—possibly Congolese. And one of them had on a shirt she remembered from her time in captivity with the rebels. She wondered if these thugs could be the same people who'd captured her and Ferrence?

She remained still, refusing to move a muscle. Since she could see them clearly, they could potentially see her, if they looked up.

The two men frowned, shrugged and started in the direction the others had gone, when suddenly a twig fell from the tree below where Reese hovered.

The men spun around and aimed their weapons up at the branches.

Reese knew the exact second the man in the shirt she recognized spotted her. His eyes widened, and he said something to the man beside him. Then he tipped his rifle upward, aiming directly at her.

The man beside him did the same.

With no way to protect herself, she stood transfixed.

A shot rang out and then another.

Reese braced herself for pain, but none came. She pressed her hand to her racing heart and stared at the ground.

Then the two men below crumpled to the ground below her, their weapons falling from their hands. They lay still.

Finally, Diesel emerged from the brush, but followed the shadows up to the point he had to step out into the open to check the two men.

"They're dead, but their buddies might circle back to check on what the gunfire was all about." He glanced up at her in the tree. "Need help getting down?"

She shook her head. Sure, she was still petrified of heights, but what had just happened was more intense than getting out of a tree. She worked her way down, slipping from limb to limb, until she reached the last one. Then she dropped to the ground and ran to where Diesel stood over the bodies of the two men.

"Are they dead?"

"Very." He drew in a deep breath. "We need to keep moving."

"Do you think the male gorilla will survive?"

He shook his head. "I don't know. He took quite a few hits. But he's a big guy. Hopefully he'll make it."

Reese hoped so, too. She stared at Diesel's arm. "That was a reckless stunt. You could have been killed."

He grinned. "Would you have missed me?"

"Yes, damn it. You're supposed to be rescuing me, not ditching me in the jungle. And you're bleeding again." She started to rip the hem of her shirt again, but his hand stopped her.

"You won't have anything left of your shirt at that rate." He shed the vest with the metal plate and his outer shirt, then he pulled the black T-shirt from the waistband of his pants. "You can use this." He yanked the T-shirt over his head and handed it to her. Then he reached into a scabbard on his calf and handed her a knife.

Her heart thudding against her ribs, Reese focused on slicing off the bottom four inches of the shirt, refusing to focus on Diesel's naked, tanned chest. If she thought his muscles were sexy in the shirt... Reese dragged in a shaky breath and let it out slowly. The man had no idea what he was doing to her libido. His being hot, sweaty and covered in jungle grime didn't put a dent in his appeal. If anything, it made him appear even more rugged and badass.

Her hand slipped, and she almost cut the tip of her finger.

"Hey." Diesel grabbed her hand and the knife. "Careful. One person injured is more than enough."

"It's okay. It didn't break the skin."

"I'll be the judge of that." He studied the finger and then lifted it to his lips.

Reese's breath caught in her lungs, and her eyes widened.

Diesel kissed her fingertip and winked. "You're right. You'll live."

Only if she remembered how to breathe. Reese pulled her finger out of his grip and glanced down at the T-shirt. What was it she was doing? Oh, yes. She was playing combat medic to Diesel's wound.

His hands closed around hers. "Want me to do it?"

"No," she said. "No. You can't dress your own arm." She shook her head free of her lusty thoughts and directed her attention to Diesel's arm. The skin around the wound was an angry red, and the sore oozed. "We have to get you to a doctor ASAP. This gunshot wound is infected."

"I'm all for finding a doctor, only I'm not sure where to start." When she finished binding his arm, he shrugged into his shirt and stuffed the tail into his trousers.

Reese folded the remainder of his T-shirt and tucked it into her blouse for use later, if needed.

A finger touched her beneath her chin and tipped

her head up. Her gaze skimmed across his lips, noticing how full and firm they were. Dragging her glance from his mouth, she stared into Diesel's eyes.

Bad move. She hoped he couldn't tell what she was thinking by where her gaze had lingered. At that moment, she wanted nothing more than to kiss the man.

"Thank you for taking care of me," he whispered. His head lowered, his lips hovering over hers. "I can't help it. I have this insane urge to kiss you." And he did. His mouth claimed hers in a deep, mind-melding kiss that rocked Reese to her very core. She'd placed her hands on his chest, but they found their way to the back of his neck, pulling him closer.

The jungle, the bugs, killer animals and dangerous men faded into the background as she pressed her body to his.

His tongue darted out, skimming the seam of her lips, urging her to open. When she did, he slipped his tongue inside, caressing her tongue with his in a long, sensuous swirl.

When at last Diesel lifted his head, Reese's head was spinning. Her thoughts fogged, and she dragged in a steadying breath. She wiped the back of her hand over her swollen, pulsing lips. "Why did you do that?"

He chuckled. "I've wanted to since I found you in the rebel camp." Diesel brushed her cheek with the tips of his fingers. "I'd kiss you again, but we need to move before those jokers return." Diesel, dressed in his shirt and vest, took her hand and led her out of the clearing, heading north again.

Reese hurried alongside him, pulse racing, heart

tight in her chest and lips tingling from his kiss. What had started as an escape from enemy territory had almost changed into an exotic adventure with a man whose mere presence made her body burn with desire.

How could this be? They were in a life-or-death situation where anything could kill them, from raging hippos to angry rebels. Not to mention, they could die of starvation or dehydration, infection or disease before they found some form of civilization where they could seek medical attention. And here she was thinking about what else was beneath the clothes this man wore.

Hell, she didn't even know him!

Pushing hard to keep up with him, Reese didn't have much breath available to ask questions, but she tried. "So, what exactly is this team of yours? Army, navy, marines?"

"If I tell you—"

"You'll have to kill me." She sucked in a deep breath and double-timed to keep up with his longer stride. "Cut to the chase. I'm in this with you, and I can keep a secret."

"We're navy SEALs."

That would explain why he was so well trained and in remarkable physical condition. Whew. Not only was he hot, he was one of America's elite forces. Wow. Talk about every woman's dream—to be swept off her feet by a navy SEAL. And she'd been swept off her feet more than once. Well, she couldn't let that happen again. Navy SEALs were bad boyfriend material, and even worse at marriage. Not that she was thinking about marrying the man. Hell, she hadn't even had a date since she'd been released by the Taliban. She hadn't really been interested in men, and wasn't sure she ever would be again. A relationship with Diesel was completely out of the question. Reese marched forward, determined to keep her head out of the clouds and her feet firmly on the ground.

DIESEL COULD TELL his revelation about being a navy SEAL wasn't welcomed by his jungle escape partner. Most women found it exciting to be with a SEAL. Why was Reese different? He realized he didn't know much about the woman he'd rescued from the Congolese rebels. "What made you become a bodyguard?" He glanced down at her. "Don't tell me it was a dream of yours as a little girl."

She shook her head and stared at the path in front of her. "No. I kind of fell into it."

"You're in good physical shape. You had to have worked up to that."

Reese shrugged and kept moving. "The physical regimen kept me sane. I had some things to work out of my system." Her voice was tight, her body stiff.

Diesel wasn't going to let her end her life history on a statement like that. "For instance?"

She walked faster, as if she were being chased by demons. And maybe she was. Diesel had a few demons of his own. A SEAL didn't live through so many battles without something bad plaguing his nightmares.

He reached out and snagged her arm, bringing her to a stop.

"We need to keep going," she said, pulling away from him.

Diesel didn't release her. "What are you running from, Reese?"

"None of your business. And who said I was running?" She jerked her arm free of his hold and glared up at him, defiantly.

He cupped her face, his heart tightening. She'd been hurt. "Whatever it was, I'm sorry it happened."

She slapped his hand away. "Why should you be sorry? You didn't do it. The filthy Taliban did it. And I swore I'd never let anyone capture me again, but it happened." She sucked in deep breaths, blowing them out through her mouth. The color was high in her cheeks, and her eyes shone with moisture. "I swore," she whispered.

Diesel cursed and pulled her into his arms. "Babe, whatever they did is done. You're a wonderful person and a strong woman."

"Not strong enough," she said into his shirt, her fingers curling into his chest. "And not strong enough to keep those men from taking me this time. What do I have to do? Where a suit of armor, rigged to electrify anyone who lays a hand on me?"

Diesel chuckled. "I for one am glad you're not wearing an electrified suit of armor." He held her at arm's length and stared down into her eyes. "You don't have to tell me what happened unless you want. I'll just know that you were hurt, and I'll do everything in my power to keep you safe from harm."

She shook her head, a single tear rolling down her

cheek. "But you don't get it. I should be capable of defending myself. Otherwise, what was all of this good for? Mixed martial arts are only good if you're conscious."

"Is that what happened? You were knocked unconscious?" He hugged her again, running his hands down her back. "You can't always plan on being conscious, can you? But I'll bet that if you had been conscious, they'd have wished you were out cold. You'd have given them a run for their money."

Reese drew in several deep breaths and pushed away from Diesel. "Sorry. I haven't had a meltdown in a long time."

"You call that a meltdown?" Diesel laughed. "Far from it. Most women I know scream, kick and sob buckets of tears in a meltdown."

She sniffed and tilted her chin up. "I'm not most women."

"I'm beginning to understand that about you. And I like it." He held out his hand. "Ready to find civilization?"

"More than ready." She hesitated before placing her hand in his.

Together, they set off, moving upriver. The heat was debilitating, and they soon ran out of drinking water. With all the water flowing beside them in the Congo, they didn't dare drink it.

Though she put up a good front, Reese was slowing down. Lack of food and fluid was taking its toll on her and on Diesel, as well.

He worried that if they didn't find help soon…well, he didn't want to think about the alternative.

Several times, they strayed too close to the riverbanks and had to hurry out of the way of giant crocodiles and wading hippos. The sun hit its zenith and plunged toward the opposite horizon, and still they hadn't found a village or other people.

Just about the time Diesel was considering where they would sleep that night, he spied someone in a dugout canoe, paddling by on the river. Hope surged through him, and he stopped, bringing Reese close beside him. He ducked, staring through the branches to the river beyond. "See that?"

She nodded.

"He's not in a motorized boat. He can't be too far from a village."

She sighed. "That would great, as long as the villagers are friendly, and the village is on this side of the river."

"We'll have to ease up on it before we announce ourselves." Diesel set off, moving with more care and an awareness that they could walk right out of the jungle and into a village before they realized it. The jungle often crept in on villages if they didn't fight it back on a regular basis. Nature had a way of reclaiming what was hers.

Twenty minutes later, people's voices and the hum of a generator were like sounds from heaven. Diesel pressed a finger to his lips. They were in luck. The sound was on their side of the river.

Reese nodded and followed him, doing what he did,

moving from shadow to shadow, until they stood at the edge of an encampment scraped out of the jungle. A dock had been erected, jutting out into the river. Several small skiffs with outboard motors were tied to the jetty, and canoes lay beached on the banks nearby. People moved about the small village, some carrying what appeared to be bags of grain. Others had handmade baskets filled with a variety of fruits and vegetables.

Diesel's mouth watered, but he didn't dare step out of the jungle until he knew for certain they were not in danger.

Reese tugged on his shirt and pointed to the far side of the village, where a large white tent had been erected with the words MEDICINS SANS FRONTIERES written across the sides. She grinned at him and mouthed the word "Bingo."

An older woman with white hair, wearing blue jeans, a T-shirt and a yellow-and-white jacket stepped out of the tent and stretched her back, staring out at the river.

Diesel backed away from the village, far enough that their voices wouldn't carry. "We need to get to that tent. Hopefully, whoever that woman is speaks English and can tell us how to get a ride out of here."

Reese nodded.

"Follow me." Diesel led the way, making a wide circle around the camp, coming up from behind the medical tent. He couldn't see straight into the tent. The back was closed off, with only the front opening for an entrance.

Fortunately, the white-haired woman stepped

around the tent with a bucket of water and walked toward the jungle. Just as she swung her arms back to empty the bucket, Diesel spoke. "Hey, do you speak English?"

The woman yelped, dropped the bucket and stepped backward. "Who said that?"

Reese stood, exposing her position to the woman. "We did. Hi, I'm Reese and this is Diesel."

Diesel rose to stand beside her. "Ma'am, are you American?"

She nodded, pressing a hand to her breast. "You scared the bejeezus out of me." The woman frowned. "I'm Martha Kowalski. And yes, I'm American. Why are you hiding in the jungle?"

"My friend was held captive by Congolese rebels. I helped her escape, and they might be looking for us." Diesel glanced behind the woman.

The woman looked over her shoulder and back to Diesel and Reese. "You're right to worry. We've had to be very careful. If it weren't for the fact they need us here so badly, I'm sure we would be in more danger than we are. How can I help you?"

Reese spoke before Diesel. "He's been shot and needs medical attention." She pointed to the bloody scrap of T-shirt on his arm.

The woman moved closer, frowning. "We have the medications and bandages you'll need. But to get you into the tent to take care of it will alert the village to your presence." She bit her bottom lip and narrowed her eyes. "Wait here. I have an idea."

Diesel and Reese ducked low into the foliage and waited for the woman's return.

Several minutes passed. Diesel began to think she wasn't coming back or had run into trouble. But then she appeared around the side of the tent, carrying an armful of packages. A man followed her, just as old and white-haired as the woman, carrying more sealed packages.

They walked into the jungle and kept going until they were well outside the perimeter of the camp. Diesel and Reese followed.

"Reese, Diesel, this is my husband, Dr. Jerry Kowalski."

The man nodded and set his packages on the ground. "These suits will get you into the tents, past the other patients and their families, no questions asked."

They tore into the sealed packages to discover personal protective suits. "We had these shipped in recently because there have been several reported cases of the Ebola virus. We use these suits to protect medical staff from patients infected with highly contagious diseases or viruses."

Diesel grinned. "And they will cover us from head to toe." He reached for one of the packages and winced. He hadn't said anything to Reese, but his arm had become increasingly sore and achy over the past few hours. He suspected infection had set in. He handed one of the suits to Reese. "Suit up." The sooner he got the arm treated, the sooner they could be on their way back to civilization and safety.

Then he and Reese would part ways. Somehow,

that end goal didn't make him happy. He'd dated other women, but none he'd considered going out with more than once or twice. Reese would have been another story. He could see spending time with her and enjoying it. But what else could he do? His job would be done, and she had hers to resume.

Chapter Five

Reese pulled the yellow-and-white jumpsuit of synthetic fabric up over her legs, hips and torso, then pushed her arms through the sleeves.

Diesel seemed to struggle into his, barely using his injured arm.

Reese suspected the wound was infected and could turn septic if they didn't get it cleaned out and fill him with antibiotics quickly.

Martha held up a hand. "Wait." She helped him remove the shirt and the bandage, exposing the wound. She clucked her tongue and shook her head. "We need to tend to it immediately." She helped him into the suit and slipped the head gear over his face.

Martha and Dr. Kowalski suited up, as well.

Once they were all fully covered, the four of them walked out into the open, led by Martha and Jerry. They walked around to the front of the tent and entered.

Cots lined the walls inside, and a section in the very back was blocked off by walls of waterproof tent material with a zippered door as an entrance. Martha unzipped the door and held it to the side as Dr. Kowalski,

Diesel and Reese entered. Martha entered behind them and zipped the door shut again. No one could see in or out of the small area.

As quickly as they could, Martha and Dr. Kowalski shed their protective suits and went to work. Martha switched on a battery-powered light hanging from the ceiling and set up a tray of medical equipment, gauze and a bottle of clear saline solution. Dr. Kowalski washed his hands, slipped into a surgical shirt and mask and stepped up to Diesel. "Have a seat." He indicated the end of the cot with a tilt of his head.

Diesel didn't argue. His wound was hurting, the pain radiating throughout his arm.

As a former soldier, Reese knew as well as anyone what happened to wounds that were left untreated. She hoped they weren't too late to fight the infection.

The doctor irrigated the site and cleaned it thoroughly. Martha handed him what he needed, without having to be asked. They worked well as a team. When they had the site completely cleaned of dirt, dried blood and pus, Dr. Kowalski sewed the skin shut, applied a bandage and held it in place with adhesive tape.

"Now lie down," Martha said.

Diesel obeyed.

Martha set him up with an IV of clear liquid and added something to the tube.

He frowned. "You're not giving me a sedative, are you?" he whispered, careful not to let his voice carry beyond the thin walls of the tent.

She shook her head. "No. Just an antibiotic to ward

off infection. You need to have your wits around you if those rebels show up in the village."

He smiled at the woman and her husband and mouthed the words "Thank you."

The smile melted everything at Reese's core. She had to turn away to keep him from seeing how it affected her by the heat rising in her face.

Martha patted his shoulder. "The fluids will help keep you from dehydration." She glanced at Reese. "I'll bring you water and food. In the meantime, you look like you could use some rest." She switched off the overhead light, plunging the room into darkness.

Reese hadn't realized how late it had gotten.

Martha and the doctor dressed in their protective suits and left the isolation room, zipping the door behind them. A faint light shined through the thin tent wall.

Reese scooted a cot close to Diesel and lay on her side, staring across at him, wanting to be near him. "Feel better?"

"I will when the infection dies down." He pressed his lips together. "We can't stay here long."

"I know. But let the antibiotics get into your bloodstream and the additional fluids. Then we can decide what to do next."

Diesel held out his free hand, capturing hers. "Are you sure you're all right?"

She snorted. "I'm fine. A few blisters and a little heat rash, but nothing a bath and a pedicure won't fix." She winked.

"I can't imagine an MMA fighter getting a pedicure."

She laughed softly, though her heart was flip-flopping at the way his fingers rubbed hers. "You'd be surprised what's required. Not only did we have to have our hair and makeup perfect, but we had to have neatly manicured nails. We had to look good while we pounded each other's faces into the mats."

He touched a finger to the tip of her nose. "Is that why your nose is crooked? Not that it isn't cute, but I wondered."

She stiffened. "No." Her nose had been broken by the Taliban.

"Was it always crooked?"

"No." Reese released his hand, rolled onto her back and stared at the ceiling. The last thing she wanted to think about was her experience in Afghanistan. She prayed her current situation didn't end up similarly. Hopefully, having a navy SEAL around would help keep her safe.

"Sorry. I take it I'm stepping into no-man's land again."

She shrugged and lay for a while without speaking, breathing in and out to calm her racing heart.

DIESEL CLOSED HIS eyes and drew in a deep breath.

Reese had some baggage she carried around. Trying to talk to her about it was like walking through a minefield. He suspected she'd open up eventually, if he was patient.

His fists clenched. The men who'd captured her in

Afghanistan must have done horrible things to her. He wished he could find them and strangle them with his bare hands. Any men who mistreated women were barbarians who didn't deserve to live.

Then out of the darkness, Reese's voice sounded in a barely discernible whisper. "I was a driver in a convoy transporting supplies to one of the forward operating bases, when we were surrounded by Taliban fighters.

"The first vehicle hit an IED, killing the driver, the passenger and the gunner. The explosion disabled the truck, blocking the road. I tried to turn around, but we were rushed by men carrying rifles and machine guns.

"My passenger didn't even make it out of the truck to lay down return fire before he was shot and killed. I was hit in the arm. I couldn't hold my weapon in my left hand, much less shoot straight." Her whispers grew strangled.

Diesel didn't stop her or try to offer words of encouragement. He let her talk, the darkness providing her a little anonymity. His chest tightened with each of her words. He wanted to reach out and take her into his arms and hold her until all the bad memories disappeared.

Reese was silent for a few moments. "They grabbed me and hauled me off to one of their villages deep in the hills." She snorted. "That's when the fun began."

Diesel heard the pain in her voice.

"Let's just say, they don't treat women well…" Her voice seemed to fade. Diesel almost didn't hear her when she said, "And I'll never be able to have children."

Diesel had suspected the Taliban fighters had raped

and tortured her. But hearing her quiet admission about children hit him like a punch to the gut. He swallowed the bile rising in his throat, his heart aching for the young woman so badly abused by her enemy. If he could, he would have taken away all of her pain and killed every one of the bastards who'd done the damage.

She gave a harsh laugh. "I was one of the lucky ones. A Delta-Force team had targeted that village to eradicate the Taliban hiding there. They found me and took me back to the nearest medical facility. From there, I was flown back to the States, where I had an almost 'full' recovery, but I was processed out on a medical discharge for PTSD."

Diesel lay for a while, unsure of what to say. Nothing seemed appropriate, and he couldn't get up and wrap his arms around her with a blasted IV in his arm.

"I was out of the army, out of a job and angry. I vowed never to be vulnerable like that again. So, I worked out, took self-defense and martial arts lessons. One day, a woman approached me about joining the MMA circuit. She thought I had what it took to succeed in the arena. I had so much hate and anger simmering below the surface, I needed an outlet."

"That's a tough job," Diesel commented.

"You're telling me. I gave it two years. When I was tired of broken fingers, cracked ribs and having my bell rung more times than I could count, I retired and started my own bodyguard business. That's where Ferrence's father came in. He was my first, and possibly my last, client."

"You'll have more. You can't blame yourself for what happened while you were unconscious."

"Yeah, I could have insisted we avoid the situation all together."

"Hindsight is always twenty-twenty. You have to move on. Learn from your past, but leave it in the past."

She grunted. "Easy to say, not to do."

"I know." And he did. He'd lost several of his buddies in operations that had gone south. For months afterward, he second-guessed his every move during newer assignments. When it began to impact every new operation, he sought help. Not with anyone in the military. One of his friends had a wife who was a psychologist who specialized in treatment for soldiers with PTSD. She'd helped him to come to grips with his past, to allow him to move forward into this future. Without her help, he'd still be hesitating when he should be acting, and possibly costing more lives due to indecision.

To Diesel, Reese sounded like she hadn't found her way to the future. She was still beating herself up over the past, afraid to think there was a future for her.

War had a way of breaking perfectly healthy individuals.

Before Diesel could think of anything to say that would make everything better for Reese, Martha unzipped the door and entered, carrying a tray of food. Light shined in from the other tent compartment. Martha still wore the protective gear and remained in it until she closed the zippered door.

She reached for the overhead light, turned it on and set the tray on the end of Reese's bed.

Reese sat up.

When Diesel also tried to sit up, Martha shook her head. "Lay still. I'll bring it to you."

"You don't have to wait on us. We're hungry and able-bodied," Diesel reassured her, careful not to talk too loudly.

"You need to let the antibiotics do their job," Martha warned him.

"Right now, food is as important as the antibiotics." Reese licked her lips, staring at the crackers and peanut butter Martha proffered.

Other items were packaged like the US Army's Meals Ready to Eat or MREs. Even those sounded good at that point.

Diesel's mouth watered.

"Go ahead, then." Martha smiled. "Eat and then rest. The doctor and I will keep watch."

Reese grabbed for a cracker, slathered peanut butter over the surface and handed it to Diesel.

He waited until she had one for herself and then bit into it like it was a delicacy.

"I'd offer you some of the local cuisine, but I'm not certain your bellies could handle it right now. Eat what's there, and I'll get more."

"Mrs. Martha," Diesel said.

"Yes?"

"Is there a way to get to a larger town? One with a telephone or a cell phone tower?"

Martha nodded. "The boat comes once a week, carrying supplies and mail. You're in luck. It's due to arrive tomorrow."

Diesel glanced over at Reese. "Do you think we can barter for passage on the boat?"

"Certainly. It's how we got here and how the locals get to and from the market upriver. Do you have any Congolese currency?"

Diesel smiled. "As a matter of fact, I do." He reached into a pocket of his cargo pants and pulled out a plastic bag filled with different currency notes.

Reese chuckled. "Another item from your survival kit?"

He grinned. "Absolutely. You never know when you have to bribe your way out of a situation."

Martha smiled. "You are a resourceful man."

"I try," Diesel said. "Will this be enough?"

Martha thumbed through the bills, separated a few and held them up. "Don't offer more than this. If they know you have more, they'll charge you more." The older woman checked Diesel's IV, fussed over his bandages and then slipped her hood back on and left the compartment.

Diesel and Reese didn't talk for the next few minutes. Instead, they ate, concentrating on filling their empty stomachs.

Martha had gone to the trouble of heating some of the packages. Diesel found one of macaroni and cheese and ate every last bite.

Reese dug into one marked beef stew.

When they'd eaten their fill, Diesel lay back on the cot and stared up at the light dangling from the ceiling. "I didn't realize just how hungry I was."

"Me either." Reese lay down beside him, closed her eyes and yawned.

"You should sleep. You heard our host. Martha and the doctor will warn us if the rebels find their way to this village."

"At this point, I'm not sure I could keep my eyes open." Reese yawned again and tucked her hand beneath her cheek.

Diesel stared over at her, admiring the way her lashes formed dark crescents beneath her eyes. She'd kept up with his grueling pace and hadn't complained. She'd been through hell and back on more than one occasion and hadn't cracked. Reese was one tough cookie. *On the outside.* But she was soft and vulnerable on the inside.

"Diesel?" she whispered.

"Yeah, sweetheart?" he answered.

"What I told you," she yawned, "I don't want anyone feeling sorry for me. I'm okay. And I never told anyone else."

"Gotcha." Diesel's gut clenched. "Your secret is safe with me."

"Thanks," she said on a sigh. Soon the sound of her steady breathing let him know she'd fallen asleep.

He watched her until his own eyelids drooped. He needed sleep as much as she did to continue their journey.

Diesel reached across to the other cot and took Reese's hand in his. For now, all he wanted to do was hold on to this amazing woman. Tomorrow, they'd be on their way toward civilization and freedom.

REESE WOKE WITH a start. She lay for a moment, trying to determine what had disturbed her sleep.

Shouts outside the tent made her jerk to a sitting position. Light through the tent panel from the other compartment gave the room a deep gray, just-past-dusk feeling. She could see well enough, but not all the nuances.

Diesel was off the cot and standing in two seconds flat, ripping the IV from his arm. He touched her shoulder. "Sounds like we might have company. There's a raid on the village."

Gunshots were fired outside. Men yelled. Women and children screamed in the night.

Diesel dragged the rifle out from beneath the cot, as the zipper on their compartment was yanked up. He aimed at the intruder only to lower his rifle when a woman's white head poked inside.

Martha's eyes were rounded, her face flushed. "Suit up. They're headed this way. Dr. Kowalski won't be able to hold them off for long." She already wore the protective suit without the hood. She nodded toward the pile she'd placed in the corner. "If they come in, look like you're half-dead. I'll make an excuse for a patient to be in a suit. Just don't talk."

"Yes, ma'am," Reese said. She grabbed a suit and jammed her feet into the legs, pulling the jumpsuit up her torso as quickly as possible. Once she had hers on, she helped Diesel into his. She'd just settled the hood over his head, when loud voices sounded from the entrance to the tent.

Reese slipped her hood over her head and lay on the cot.

Diesel lay on the other, his rifle tucked beneath his leg, completely covered by the baggy synthetic fabric.

"You can't go in there. Those patients are infected with the deadly Ebola virus," Dr. Kowalski said.

"We will go where we please," a deeply accented voice said.

"Let him go, Dr. Kowalski. It's his life. If he wants to die of Ebola, let him," Martha said. She unzipped the compartment and held back the flap door. "Go. See for yourself."

Reese lowered her eyelids almost all of the way. She could just see through the slits.

A big black man with a camouflage outfit and a vest filled with loaded magazines leaned through the doorway with two others similarly attired. He stopped short of entering. Instead, he brandished his rifle at Reese and Diesel. "Why are they wearing these clothes?"

Dr. Kowalski stepped up beside Martha. "The two in there are hyper-contagious, we had to put them in suits to protect the other patients from getting the virus. They come from a village where all the other people have perished."

"Perished? What is this?" the rebel demanded.

"Died," Martha cried. "They all died." Then she turned and sobbed against Dr. Kowalski's chest. "Every last man, woman and child are gone from their village."

"Then why are they here? Why didn't you leave them to die with their people?" the rebel demanded.

"We couldn't leave them," Dr. Kowalski said. "They

were still breathing. Our jobs are to help those in need, no matter how sick."

"You should shoot them so they don't infect everyone else along the river." The rebel raised his rifle.

Reese tensed. She had no weapon to defend herself. If Diesel pulled out his rifle, they'd have all the other rebels on top of them in seconds.

A shout from outside made the man with the gun swing around. "Get them out of here. They shouldn't be around to infect the others."

"We'll do our best," the doctor promised.

"And if you see a white man and woman pass through this area, you are to send word to us immediately. Do you understand?"

Martha sobbed, and Dr. Kowalski nodded, holding her close to him. "We understand."

Then the man with the gun was gone, taking his sidekicks with him.

Diesel rose to his feet, ripped off the hood and held his rifle at the ready.

Reese realized that if the rebel leader and his goons returned, they might not get a second chance. Again, she wished she had a weapon of her own.

As if he'd read her mind, Diesel reached into a pocket and pulled out a small pistol. "Hang on to this. It won't stop an eight-hundred-pound gorilla, but it could ruin a man's day if he tries to hurt you."

She clutched the pistol, ejected the magazine in the handle and slammed it back into the grip. It was light and almost felt like a toy. But like Diesel said, it could ruin a man's day at close range.

Martha sobbed until the shouting outside faded into the distance. When they were finally alone, but for the patients in the outer compartment, the doctor and his assistant entered the compartment.

Martha righted the IV stand and collected the empty bag from the floor. "You'll have to go as soon as the morning boat arrives. It usually gets here early. We're the last stop before it heads back to the closest big town. If the rebels are gone when it arrives, you should have no problem boarding. If they hang around, you might have to miss this boat and wait for the next, a week from now."

Diesel's gaze met Reese's. If she read it right, they were in agreement. They would be on that boat come hell or high water. Reese was ready to be done with the jungle, mosquitos, crocodiles and anything else that could eat her in the night. She needed to get back to Ferrence. Despite their detour, they still had a political agenda to fulfill. The time they'd set aside for his safari was nearing an end. If she had any chance at all at redeeming herself, she had to get back to civilization and back to her client, Ferrence Klein.

Martha and the doctor stripped out of their protective gear and left Diesel and Reese alone in the quarantine compartment. On the other side of the panel, the medical workers checked their patients, calming them after the rebel fighters' visit.

Soon the noise in the village ended, lights were extinguished and the little town slept.

Not Reese and Diesel. They sat on the edges of their cots, listening, waiting for the morning light of dawn and the sound of a boat engine.

THE BOAT ENGINE arrived as the gray light of predawn filtered through the white walls of the tent.

Martha and Dr. Kowalski unzipped the compartment and entered, zipping the door back up behind them.

"A different boat arrived at the dock. We think it might be American," Dr. Kowalski said.

"You might want to check it out from the safety of the jungle," Martha suggested. "Perhaps they are friends?"

Reese stood and stretched, tired to the bone, but curious. "Do you think it might be your team?"

"Maybe." Diesel tucked his rifle down the leg of his protective suit, settled the hood over his head and nodded to Reese. "Let's go see."

Reese slid the hood over her head and nodded. Together, they left the tent and rounded to the back, walking deeper into the shadowy jungle. When they were far enough away from the encampment, they stripped out of the protective gear and hurried around the perimeter to the shore of the river, keeping an eye out for crocodiles and snakes.

When they reached a position where they could see the dock, Diesel chuckled. "It's them." He started for the dock.

Reese shot out a hand. "Are you sure it's safe?"

"Sweetheart, there's enough firepower on that boat to level this village. The Congolese rebels wouldn't stand a chance against them."

Reese and Diesel walked out of the jungle and through the makeshift shelters of plywood and shipping containers that housed the villagers who lived around the dock.

A rugged-looking metal boat with machine guns mounted on all sides rested up against the dock. Several men dressed similarly to Diesel stood on the dock, rifles in hand, ready to take on anyone.

The village was just waking up.

As Diesel stepped out into the open, a couple of the men spun toward him, aiming their weapons at his chest.

Reese started to jump in front of Diesel, but the men with the guns lowered their weapons and grinned.

One stepped forward. "Diesel, you old son of a bitch, figures you'd find a way to vacation with a pretty girl." The man engulfed him in a bear hug, pounding him on the back.

"Hey, Buck." Diesel flinched and backed away, flexing his injured arm. "Watch the arm."

The man Diesel called Buck frowned. "Were you hit?"

"It's nothing, just a—"

"Flesh wound?" Buck's frown deepened. "I'll take a look at it when we get underway."

"No worries. It'll hold until we get to where we're going. The doc here patched me up and fed me antibiotics. I'm good to go."

Buck looked beyond Diesel to where Reese stood. "You must be Reese Brantley."

Reese nodded, suddenly feeling like she'd been rolling in a pigpen. She needed a shower and a change of clothing.

"We heard all about you from Klein." Another, taller

man stepped up next to Buck. "I'm Jake." He held out his hand to Reese.

Wincing inwardly, she took the big man's hand and shook it. "I'm sure it was all bad."

"Not at all. He was worried about you."

"Don't lie to the lady. He was worried about who he would take with him on his political tour of Kinshasa." Another man stepped up on the other side of Buck. "Percy Taylor, but my friends call me Pitbull. And we call Jake, Big Jake, on account of his excessive height."

Reese shook the man's hand, a smile playing at her lips.

Pitbull turned to Diesel. "Thought we'd lost you, man."

Diesel shrugged. "Couldn't get back to the boat, so we took a stroll through the jungle."

Buck snorted. "Some stroll. I'm surprised you weren't eaten by a lion or crocodile."

"We were actually more worried about the poachers, our Congolese rebel kidnappers and the gorillas."

Buck's brows rose. "Gorillas?"

"Just a small troop of around twenty." Diesel gave a nonchalant shrug that almost made Reese laugh.

"No kidding?" Pitbull asked, his eyes alight. "Aren't they dangerous?"

"A little." Diesel tipped his head toward the boat. "We should be going before the rebels return. They were here earlier. And we were supposed to be in stealth mode. Why did you come now?"

"We were going for that no-man-left-behind adage," Buck said.

"Right," Pitbull added. "The team just didn't feel like it was firing on all cylinders without our Diesel."

Diesel hooked Reese's arm with his hand and guided her to the boat. He helped her aboard and stepped in after her, ushered her to a seat on a hard metal bench and then he stepped up behind one of the mounted machine guns.

"No way, man." Buck shook his head. "You're injured. You can sit this one out for now."

"I told you, it's just a flesh wound."

"Yeah, and a flesh wound in Africa can go south in a heartbeat." Buck's lips twisted. "Humor me, will ya?"

The man at the helm waited until every man on the team was aboard the boat before he turned the craft around and headed north.

"Why aren't we going back to our helicopter pickup point?" Diesel asked.

"The chopper went on to an airstrip in Zambia where a private plane will carry Klein to Kinshasa for the African Union convention. We're supposed to head down the river to the next big town. Apparently, there is a bush pilot who can take Miss Brantley the rest of the way to Kinshasa. Once we leave her there, we'll head back down the river to our previously scheduled pickup point."

"And the stealth mode?" Diesel asked.

"We hope to be off the Congo in the next twenty-four hours." Yet another one of the SEALs turned away from his position manning a machine gun. "We'll leave the cover-up for the politicians and diplomats."

Diesel settled onto the bench next to Reese, his rifle

resting across his legs, one hand holding it, ready to put it to use, if the need arose.

"Navy SEALs, huh?" Reese asked, staring around at the men on the boat. "I guess that accounts for the boat."

"Not all navy SEALs are trained for riverine missions," Diesel said. "We're from a Special Boat Team. We train on these kinds of boats for missions requiring extractions via water."

Reese studied the members of the team. Each of them appeared to be fit and intent on their mission, as the boat raced along the Congo River. The helmsman maintained a steady speed, even as he rounded the curves in the winding river, skidding sideways across the surface of the water. When they came upon hippopotamuses in a wide area of the river, he skirted the beasts, giving then a wide birth. They passed canoes, dugouts and small boats with outboard motors. At one point, they passed what appeared to be the weekly supply boat, heading toward the village where Martha and Dr. Kowalski performed miracles as part of the Doctors Without Borders effort.

Three hours later, they neared a small town on the edge of the river. The jungle had been trimmed back to allow for fields of agriculture and a small airstrip.

As the fully armed boat approached the dock, people scattered, running toward town.

"Harm, Buck, Pitbull, be ready to accompany me to escort Miss Brantley to the airstrip," Big Jake said. "A plane will be waiting to take her to Kinshasa."

Diesel stood. "I'm going with her."

"Stand down, Diesel," Big Jake said. "You're in no condition to provide for her protection."

"I'm going," Diesel insisted.

To be honest, Reese wanted him to come. They'd been together for the past couple days. Going on without him would feel strange. But then, she wasn't in Africa because she needed protection. She was there to protect Ferrence Klein.

Reese laid a hand on Diesel's arm. "It's okay. These men can escort me to the airfield. I'll be all right."

Diesel touched her cheek. "You're my responsibility. I'm going." He glared at Big Jake and stepped off the boat onto the dock. Then he held out his hand to Reese.

She rested hers in his and let him assist her off the boat. Harm, Pitbull and Buck, armed with rifles, gathered around the two, and they moved as a unit across the dock and through the small town, to the field on the edge where a small plane awaited. Three armed men stood guard around the aircraft. A person wearing jeans, a white polo shirt and a baseball cap pushed away from the side of the plane.

As Reese and the team closed the distance between them, she realized the person in the jeans was a woman with long sandy hair pulled back in a ponytail behind her.

The woman held out her hand. "Hi, I'm Marly Simpson, your pilot."

Reese almost laughed at the expression on Diesel's face.

He was practically scowling at the woman. "You're the pilot?"

She nodded, her lips twisting into a wry grimace. "I am. Got a problem with it?"

Pitbull chuckled. "Only if you don't know how to fly the plane."

She shot a glare at him. "I have over twenty-five hundred hours flying in this plane and others. You're welcome to review my logbooks." Her gaze darted around the landing strip. "I suggest we get this plane in the sky. The longer it sits on the ground, the more chance of it being shot at, hijacked or stolen."

Reese tensed, her belly knotting. "You've had that happen?"

Marly sighed. "More times than you can imagine." She planted her fists on her hips and stared at the group. "Because I have a load of cargo, I can only take three passengers and no luggage. Who's coming?"

Reese stepped forward. "As far as I know, I'm the only passenger." It was time to say goodbye to her rescuer. Diesel was an integral part of the military. Surely he had better things to do than escort her around the Democratic Republic of the Congo. She turned to thank him. "Diesel, thank you for getting me out of the jungle alive." She held out her hand to shake his, her heart clenching in her chest. "Without you and your men, who knows what would have happened to Ferrence. Thank you."

He took her hand and refused to let go.

Chapter Six

With Reese pretty much telling him to shove off, Diesel's pulse rocketed. Before he could think through his decision, he said, "You're welcome. But I'm coming, too."

"What the hell?" Buck sputtered. "That's not part of the plan."

"I'm not letting them go without someone to ride shotgun," Diesel said. "You heard Marly, the plane and the people in it are subject to being hijacked. I'm not turning Reese loose without an escort all the way to Kinshasa."

Buck stared at the men guarding the plane. "What about them?"

Marly followed his gaze. "They're only contracted for guarding this airstrip. They're not coming with me."

As far as Diesel was concerned, Marly's words sealed the deal. "I'll find my way back to Djibouti. I'm not ditching Miss Brantley now. We've come too far together for me to walk away."

"I can take care of myself," Reese insisted.

"You're not in the States," Buck argued. "This is the

DRC. The current government is run by a tyrant refusing to allow democratic elections. He could imprison you without cause and no chance for a trial."

Reese lifted her chin. "I'm here on a diplomatic mission and to protect Ferrence Klein, not to have you or anyone else protect me."

"Tough," Diesel said. "I'm coming with you. End of argument."

Marly frowned at them. "Please tell me you aren't going to argue the entire trip?"

"We aren't." Reese crossed her arms over her chest. "Because he's not coming with me."

"Do you always argue this much?" Diesel shook his head and gripped her arm. "Sweetheart, we've come too far together. I can't just let go. I need to know you're safe. You'd do the same if the situation was reversed."

Reese stared into his eyes, her mouth pressed into a thin line. After a moment, her stance relaxed and the corners of her lips twisted into a wry smile. "Given all that's happened, I would appreciate someone having my back." She glanced at the members of his team. "But what about your team?"

"They have to get the boat back to the pickup point. They'll need all men on deck in case they run into trouble." Diesel looked to Big Jake for concurrence.

"Right." Big Jake shook his head. "We just got you back with the team, but I get it. We'll get the SOC-R back to the rendezvous location and ship it back to Djibouti. I'll work with the commander to cover your sorry ass. But once you get to Kinshasa, you need to hightail back to Djibouti. My bet is there's another mission awaiting our attention."

Diesel drew in a deep breath and let go. He was pushing the envelope on his duty to the current mission and his loyalty to his unit. But he just couldn't let Reese leave without an armed escort. "Now that everything's settled…" He clapped his hands together. "Let's go."

The pilot climbed into the plane and took her position behind the yoke.

"I'll sit in back since you're the only one carrying a high-powered weapon," Reese volunteered.

Diesel handed Reese up into the seat behind the pilot and then laid his rifle in the front seat, before stepping up into the plane. He winced when he reached for the safety harness and pulled it across his shoulder.

Reese leaned forward. "Are you sure you're up to this? You haven't given your arm a chance to heal."

"I'm fine," he said through gritted teeth, as pain rippled through him.

"About the gun…" Marly's eyes narrowed. "You'll have to hide it when we stop for fuel along the way. I've had a special compartment built into the floor between the seats. It should fit there."

Diesel closed the door, waved at his teammates and fumbled trying to get the flight headset over his ears without contorting his sore arm.

Hands reached out from behind him and settled the headset over his ears. "How's that?" Reese asked.

He laid his hand over his shoulder to grasp hers. "Thanks." Once he was strapped in, he dismantled the rifle into two large pieces and stuffed them into his backpack. He then placed the backpack into the storage compartment between the seats.

Marly checked her instruments, started the engine and the single propeller spun. "Hang on," she said into her mic, the sound carrying through to Diesel's ears.

He'd been up in so many different helicopters and large airplanes, but never a fixed-wing, small-bush plane. His gut knotted as the little craft bumped over the dirt landing strip, picking up speed with each passing second. At the end of the strip was the dense jungle. If they didn't lift off the ground soon, they'd plow right into the trees.

Diesel's fingers curled into fists. He couldn't close his eyes, even though his death appeared imminent.

Just when Diesel thought they couldn't possibly live through the takeoff, the little plane lifted off the ground, climbed into the air and barely missed the tops of the trees.

A chuckle filled his ears, and Marly shot an amused glance toward him. "Gives you a rush, doesn't it?"

"More like a heart attack," Reese said from the back seat, her voice shaking in Diesel's ear.

Marly laughed. "The runways in the jungle can be pretty short. Even I have to hold my breath and pray." She settled back with one hand on the yoke. "Might as well get comfortable. Next stop is Kananga to refuel."

Though he tried to stay awake during the flight, the hum of the motor lulled Diesel into sleep. Not until the engine slowed did he wake to find the plane descending into an airport with a flight tower and a couple of landing strips.

A small town was off to the side of the airport. On the road leading into the town, a plume of smoke rose from what appeared to be the hull of a vehicle.

Diesel leaned toward the window, his eyes narrowing. A truck loaded with men drove toward the airport. They appeared to be wearing green camouflage uniforms, and they carried weapons. From the distance, Diesel couldn't tell exactly what type of weapons, but he didn't have a good feeling about it.

"We might have some trouble here, but I don't have many choices on places I can land," Marly said. "We need fuel to continue on to Kinshasa. If you can, stay in the plane. If you have to make a trip inside to use the facilities, make it quick. The sooner we're back in the air, the better. The DRC military has had clashes with the Congolese rebels. The battles can get bloody and neither side has much of a sense of humor these days."

"I hate to say it, but I need to use the facilities," Reese said from the seat behind them.

Marly nodded. "I do, too. We'll have to make it quick." She contacted the tower, received landing instructions and set the plane down on the runway, taxiing to the point at which she could purchase fuel.

Diesel was first to climb out, then Marly and finally Reese. While Marly negotiated for fuel, Diesel escorted Reese into the dingy terminal in search of a toilet.

Several people wearing brightly colored clothing waited inside with bags and boxes. When Reese and Diesel walked through the door, the people stopped talking and stared at them. Three men in Congolese military uniforms, carrying rifles, turned with narrowed gazes and watched as Reese walked across the floor toward what appeared to be a ladies' room.

Diesel needed to relieve himself, but he wouldn't until he knew Reese was okay. The bag of fluids Martha had given him had worked their way through his body. He waited outside the ladies' room for Reese to emerge, keeping an eye on the men with the weapons.

"Your turn," a voice said beside him. Reese smiled and tipped her head toward the room marked with a figure of a man.

"Are you sure you'll be okay?" he asked without shooting a glance in the direction of the men holding the rifles.

"I'll be fine. But you'd better hurry before that truckload of potential trouble arrives."

"On it." He entered the bathroom, relieved himself, washed up and was back out in less than two minutes.

The three armed men had left their position by the door and strode toward Reese.

She gave them a brief, but uninviting glance and turned toward Diesel with a huge smile. "There you are." Hooking her arm through his, she walked with him to the door leading out onto the tarmac, where the plane stood. "Isn't it a lovely day for flying?" she asked.

"You bet," he responded. And the sooner they were back in the air, the better. Out of the corner of his eye, he could see the truckload of Congolese soldiers nearing the airport.

Marly was overseeing a man who was pumping fuel into the plane, when Reese and Diesel walked up to her.

"Watch him while I head inside. The fuel tank is almost full."

"The truckload of soldiers will be here within the next few minutes," Diesel warned.

"Then I'll make it fast." She jogged toward the terminal and disappeared inside.

The man pumping fuel into the little plane eyed them, but didn't say a word.

Diesel wished they could be in the plane and ready by the time Marly returned, but he wasn't sure he trusted the man fueling the plane. He kept an eye on the fueling process with glances toward the building the truck of soldiers had neared.

Moments later, Marly trotted out of the building, slowing her pace, probably so that she didn't appear anxious. She moved as fast as she could without raising too much suspicion. She shot a glance at the man who'd provided fuel and spoke to him in a language Diesel didn't understand. After a quick inspection of the exterior of the plane, she climbed inside.

Reese entered and took her seat. Diesel closed the door and took his seat beside the pilot.

He'd barely sat when Marly started the engine and contacted the tower. Moments later, Marly set the plane in motion, and the aircraft rolled down the runway.

They were just picking up speed, when suddenly several men carrying rifles burst through the doors of the terminal and ran out onto the tarmac.

"Come on, Betsy, pick up speed," Marly muttered, her words barely audible in the headset.

Diesel twisted in his seat, staring back over his

shoulder at the men running for the runway. They aimed their weapons and fired.

"They're shooting at us!" Reese yelled.

Marly didn't slow the plane. She pushed the throttle as far forward as it would go, picking up speed. Then she pulled back on the yoke. The craft left the ground and climbed into the air.

Soon the Kananga airport was a speck in the distance.

Marly glanced at the array of instruments in front of her and sighed. "Doesn't look like they hit anything." She sat back and smiled. "Well, I bet you've never been on a vacation as exciting as this one, huh?"

Diesel shook his head. "I hope never to repeat it."

Marly pushed her sandy-blond hair back off her forehead. "You and me both." She grinned and shot a glance over her shoulder. "Next stop is Kinshasa."

Diesel remained awake and alert for the remainder of the journey to the capital city of the DRC. They didn't encounter any more difficulties or anything that would slow them.

Reese fell asleep in the back. She needed the sleep after her capture and subsequent escape into the harshness of the jungle.

Though Diesel's arm ached, it didn't feel as painful as it had before Martha and the doctor had worked on it. Hopefully he was well on his way to recovery. He couldn't afford to be down the use of one arm. Not when Reese still needed him to get her to the hotel where she would meet up with Klein.

Diesel leaned forward as they approached the Kinshasa International Airport.

The large, sprawling city of Kinshasa stood in stark contrast to the lush, green jungle surrounding the south and central areas of the Congo River.

The plane touched down on the runway and rolled to a stop in the general aviation area, away from the larger aircraft and the modern terminal.

"Thank you for delivering us safely." Diesel held out his hand.

Marly took it. "The pleasure was all mine. My usual route keeps me in Zambia, where it's not nearly as exciting."

"I could deal with a little less excitement," Reese said. "But right now, I'd settle for a shower and clean clothing."

"I hear you. I'm on my way back to Zambia. You two be safe." Marly shook Reese's hand and sat back, giving them the time and space they needed to get out.

Diesel grabbed his backpack from the compartment in the floor, exited the aircraft and held the door for Reese, helping her out onto the tarmac.

"Reese, darling, you don't know how happy I am to see you."

A man hurried forward, wearing a business suit, his neatly combed hair barely being ruffled by the wind.

Diesel stepped between the man and Reese. "Stop right there."

The man frowned, pulled himself up to his full height, which came to a few inches shorter than Diesel, and puffed out his chest. "I'm Ferrence Klein. Miss Brantley works for me. Kindly step aside."

"I don't care who you are. Until I'm sure you're not carrying a weapon, you're not getting anywhere close to Miss Brantley."

"Seriously?" Klein's upper lip pulled back into a sneer. "You're standing in the way of work that must be done."

Diesel crossed his arms over his chest. "You're not getting past me until you empty your pockets and submit to a pat down."

The frown on Klein's face deepened. "Fine. Whatever it takes to see my employee." He opened his jacket, displaying the crisp white shirt beneath and no shoulder holster with a gun.

"Turn around," Diesel commanded.

"For the love of Mike." Klein turned.

"Spread your legs," Diesel said.

Klein did as asked. "Where did you find this goon, Reese?"

"In the jungle," Reese answered, a smile tugging the corners of her lips. "He's pretty determined. I suggest you do as he says."

Diesel patted the man's legs and hips, searching for weapons. When Klein came up clean, Diesel stepped back. "Miss Brantley has had a difficult few days. Don't delay her from the shower she so sorely deserves."

Klein glared at Diesel and stepped around him to face Reese. "What took you so long getting back? The Freedom and Human Rights Conference is tomorrow, and the ball is tomorrow night. I almost had to hire another assistant to attend with me."

Reese's eyes narrowed. "And who would that be?"

"How should I know? I couldn't go to the event without someone on my arm."

Diesel bit down hard on his tongue and clenched his fists, fighting the urge to smash Klein's face. What a jerk. The woman had been through hell and back in captivity and on the run through a hostile jungle. She was lucky to be alive. From what Reese had said, Klein didn't know she was more than an assistant.

"I need to get cleaned up. I don't suppose you had our luggage sent up from Zambia?"

"Thankfully, I had the good sense to have it flown to Kinshasa. All of my suits made it here undamaged."

Diesel's gaze met Reese's. She had to put up with the man as part of her job; otherwise, Diesel would have taken her hand and walked her away from the selfish bastard and seen to it she had what she needed.

"Did my luggage arrive with yours?" she asked, her tone even.

"Yes, yes, of course. Come on, the car is waiting." Klein sniffed. "Although, perhaps you should take a taxi. My dear, you smell awful."

Diesel hooked her arm. "She'll take a cab." And he'd be her escort all the way to the hotel.

Reese shook her arm free of Diesel's. "We'll take a taxi and follow you to the hotel. I can be cleaned up within an hour."

"Good, good." Klein walked ahead of them toward a gate leading off the flight line. "The sooner you're ready, the better. We have a social this evening with some of the members of the European and African Unions. I'll need you there with me to make notes about anything we need to follow up on." Klein kept talking all the way to the limousine he'd hired. Two guards stood on either side of the long white vehicle, each carrying a rifle and dressed in the military uniform of the Congolese Government.

"Did the Congolese president provide these men for you?" Reese asked.

Klein barely glanced at the men. "Yes, thankfully. There have been protests and run-ins with the rebels near the city. He's assigned guards to each of the diplomats attending the delegation."

"How close to the city have the outbursts been?" Reese asked.

"I don't know. Perhaps on the edge of the eastern suburbs. There was a scuffle in the downtown area last night, a few blocks from our hotel, but the military put a stop to it pretty quickly."

"What kind of scuffle?" Diesel asked. He didn't like what he was hearing. Kinshasa didn't sound much safer than the villages along the southeastern Congo River.

"Several thugs threw Molotov cocktails into a building."

The chauffeur opened the back door to the limousine.

Klein slid in. "I'll see you in two hours. Meet me at the bar in the hotel."

"Same hotel as on our original reservation?" Reese asked.

"Yes." Klein settled back in his seat. "Don't be late."

"Don't you want to wait and let us follow you to the hotel?" Reese asked.

"I have phone calls to make. If I wait for you to find a taxi, I might not have time to make those calls." The chauffeur closed the door, slid into the driver's seat and drove the limousine away.

Diesel shook his head, his gaze following the man in the fancy car. The two Congolese soldiers climbed into a camouflage SUV and followed. "That man is a piece of work."

"You're telling me." Reese sighed. "I can't protect him if he doesn't stay with me. I don't think he realizes that being in a city doesn't necessarily mean he's safe."

"I'd rather fight an army of ISIS than deal with political mumbo jumbo on a daily basis." He gripped her arm and started walking. "We can catch a cab in front of the airport terminal."

Now that they were in a civilized area, Reese was more aware of her dirty clothes, matted hair and filthy skin. She couldn't do anything about it until she got to the hotel. They walked to the terminal, found a cab and gave the driver the address of the hotel.

Diesel settled back against the seat, though his gaze scanned the roads and streets they passed, looking for any signs of trouble, his hand resting on his backpack.

Reese's lips quirked upward on the corners. She admired the man's dedication and complete awareness of his surroundings. He was smart, physically fit and determined to see her to her destination.

Kinshasa, home to over eleven million people, was

perched on the southern side of the wide Congo River. High-rise buildings stretched toward the sky in the downtown area, and the slums spread south and east.

Traffic was slow as the taxi driver wove through the streets, dodging pedestrians, motorcycles and bicycles.

When the cab pulled up in front of the hotel, Reese's heartbeat kicked up several notches, and her chest tightened. Now that she had reached her destination, what would Diesel do? Would he hop back into the cab and return to the airport to catch the next flight out to Djibouti?

Though she'd only known him a couple days, Reese wasn't ready to part ways. They'd been through so much together. He'd helped her survive. *That counted for something.*

She stood in front of the hotel and realized she didn't have any money to pay the taxi driver. "I'll have to go find my luggage before I can pay him."

Diesel touched her dirty cheek and stared down into her eyes as though she weren't covered in jungle filth. "I've got this."

"But you shouldn't have to pay for my cab ride."

His lips curled upward, and his eyes twinkled. "I was in the cab with you."

"But you were escorting me."

He chuckled and tapped a finger to the tip of her nose. "Do you always argue this much? Oh, and you have a smudge on your cheek." With a wink, he turned to the cab driver and handed him a credit card. Once the transaction was completed, the cab driver left.

"You aren't headed straight for Djibouti?" she asked.

Diesel touched a hand to the small of her back and shook his head. "Nope. Not yet. I want to make sure you're safe."

"Hey, frogman," she whispered. "I've got news for you. *I'm* the bodyguard."

"To Klein. For now, I'm *your* bodyguard. Now hush and let's get you checked in and see if they have a spare room for me."

"You're staying?"

"I figure I have a couple days of leave I can use. And I'm not going anywhere until I get cleaned up." He wrinkled his nose. "I stink."

Reese didn't think so. The man smelled of the jungle and outdoors. Perhaps she smelled too much like him to know whether or not it smelled bad, but she didn't care. They were alive.

At the front desk, the clerk raised brows at their appearance, but went to work clicking the keyboard to find Reese's reservation. "Madame, you're lucky to arrive when you did," he said in a heavy French accent. "The hotel is completely booked, and if you had not come soon, we would have given your suite to someone on the standby list. Fortunately, your luggage was delivered this morning. Now, how many keys would you like?"

"The hotel is completely booked?" Reese asked.

"*Oui,*" the clerk responded. "Many delegates from the European and African Unions, and others from all over the world, are here to attend the Freedom and Human Rights Convention. We've been booked for months." He ran a plastic key card. "One key or two?"

"Two, please," Reese responded.

Chapter Seven

Diesel's groin tightened. For a moment, he'd been considering where else he'd have to look for a hotel. In the next second, Reese had solved his problem and raised his body temperature.

The clerk nodded and ran another card through the machine. He handed both cards to Reese. "Enjoy your stay, madame, monsieur."

As they walked away, Diesel leaned close to Reese. "I can get a room somewhere else."

"Don't be silly. If they are full here, they'll be full all around here. Besides, I have a suite. You can clean up while you decide what you want to do next."

"Yes, ma'am." Diesel swallowed a chuckle, feeling lighter and happier than he had in days. Only steps away from a shower and walking beside the woman who'd been at his side for the past few days, things were really looking up.

With no luggage to carry to the room, and Diesel carrying his own backpack, they didn't need a bellman to show them the way.

The elevator took them to their floor, and moments

later Reese pushed the door open to a beautiful, clean suite. She walked across the smooth white tile floor to the floor-to-ceiling windows at the far side of the sitting room, so that she could look out upon the Congo River. The sun was on its way toward the horizon, painting the sky in lovely shades of mauve, orange and purple.

"This high up, you can't really see the internal struggle of the people of the DRC," she said.

"No, but it's there. We experienced it," Diesel said, his attention captured by Reese, framed in one of the floor-to-ceiling windows, the sunset giving her a glow of faint pink and orange. Despite her disheveled appearance, the muted light managed to enhance her beauty and strength.

Reese nodded and glanced over her shoulder at him. "If you don't mind, I'll go first in the shower."

"That works. I'm going to duck out and find some clean clothes." He had nothing but the outfit he'd worn to storm the kidnappers' camp.

Her eyes widened. "I'd completely forgotten you came without anything other than what you're wearing."

He shrugged. "No worries. I'll be back in less than an hour. Don't let anyone into this room until I return."

Her lips twisted. "Even my boss?"

Diesel snorted. "Especially your boss." He bent and brushed his lips across hers.

She stared up at him. "How can you do that?"

He lifted his head slightly, his gaze on the lips he wanted to take again. "Do what?"

"Kiss me when I'm so filthy?" she said, her voice airy, as if she couldn't quite catch her breath.

"In case you hadn't noticed, I'm just as dirty." He swept his thumb across her cheek. "I think you're beautiful."

She laughed shakily. "Seriously? What other drugs did Martha give you?" Reese shook her head. "Never mind. Go. Get some clothes and get back." Reese grabbed her suitcase and rolled it into the bedroom. "If you don't hurry, I'll use up all of the hot water."

"Going," he called out, on his way toward the exit. He paused with his hand on the doorknob and glanced back at Reese as she closed the door to the bedroom.

Everything had changed since they'd left the jungle. The city, the hotel, the modern conveniences were as different from the harshness of the jungle as night was from day. But his gut told him that it was no less dangerous. Yeah, they didn't have to worry about crocodiles so high up in the hotel, or gorillas climbing up to rip them apart. But the trouble in the Democratic Republic of the Congo was real.

Maybe he was being overly protective or paranoid, but Diesel couldn't leave Reese alone for long until that feeling went away. But if he was going to stay with her, he had to be dressed for the part. His combat clothes had to go.

REESE STARED AT the bedroom door, her heart suddenly racing. Her first inclination was to run after him and tell him to stay. Logic prevailed. The man was only going out to buy some clothes. He'd be back. What could happen to him in the city that was any worse than what had happened in the jungle? The man was a survivor.

Willing her pulse to slow back to normal, she dug through her case for toiletries, panties, a dress and shoes and carried them into the bathroom. After she peeled her torn, dirty clothes from her body, she shoved them into the wastebasket and turned to stare at herself in the mirror. Holy hell!

Dirty was putting it mildly. Her face was streaked with dirt and sweat, her hair looked like a rat's nest and she had bruises and cuts on just about every surface. She turned the shower on and stepped in, watching the clear water turn murky as the dirt mixed with the water and swirled down the drain.

Squeezing out a sizable glob of shampoo into her hand, she attacked her hair. Then with a fresh bar of soap, she went to work on scrubbing all of the jungle grime from her body. When she was done, she did it all again. Finally, the water running off her body was clear and clean.

Feeling like a completely different person, she turned off the water and stepped out onto the bath mat to dry off. Brushing the tangles out of her hair was harder than scrubbing the dirt off her body. She lost several clumps of hair to the bristles before she smoothed out every last knot. This time, when she glanced into the mirror, she almost recognized the woman staring back at her. Only, she was somewhat different. The time she had spent in the jungle with

Diesel left her feeling strangely hopeful and optimistic about the future.

Whereas her captivity at the hands of the Taliban had left her very broken and angry, the time with Diesel had made her feel empowered and capable. Yes, he'd saved her life, but he'd appreciated the fact she could keep up with him. All the training she'd done to make her body strong and to be able to defend herself had paid off.

Being captured by the Congolese warlord had been nothing but bad luck. Had she not been thrown against the dash and knocked out, she could have forced the Zambian driver to stop before they drove across the border into the DRC.

She had managed to free Klein and escape captivity herself, before the SEALs showed up. They had helped to make good her escape, but she had no doubt she could have survived on her own.

But she was glad she'd had Diesel to help get her out of the jungle. A shiver rippled down her spine in the air-conditioned room. On second thought, it had taken both of them to get through the jungle. Alone, she might have been the target of a hungry lion. And she never would have considered climbing a tree. No, Diesel had been the main reason she was standing in the hotel, fresh clean and alive.

Reese slipped into her bra, panties and the cocktail-length black dress she'd brought along for the social event that evening. When she stepped out of the bathroom, she glanced at the clock on the nightstand. She had exactly fifteen minutes before she was to meet Ferrence at the bar. Over an hour had passed since Diesel had left to find clothes.

She frowned at the door, willing it to open to the man she worried about. A nervous chuckle rose up her throat. Why she worried about Diesel, she didn't know. The man could clearly take care of himself.

Back in the bathroom, she brushed her teeth and then plugged in the blow-dryer and dried her clean hair. The long strands fanned out across her shoulders, the rich auburn tresses curling slightly at the ends. She wondered what Diesel would think of her hair now that it wasn't covered in dirt and dust. *Would he think it was pretty?*

Reese bent to place the blow-dryer beneath the cabinet and straightened to see another person in the mirror's reflection.

Diesel stood behind her, clean, freshly shaven and wearing a dark business suit, the white shirt beneath it making his tan seem even darker.

Reese's heart fluttered. The man was so handsome it almost hurt her eyes to look at him. "How?"

"The gym in the basement of the hotel had a shower. I knew if I showed up at a store to try on clothes, they'd run me off. So, I showered before I left." He held up his arm, displaying a price tag hanging from his sleeve. "They missed one."

Being so close to the man made her body temperature rise and heat rush into her cheeks. "I've got a pair of fingernail scissors in my bag," she said, her voice fading as her breath lodged in her lungs. He really was too handsome. He was causing her thoughts to scramble. "I'll just get it," she said, and started to brush past him.

His arm snaked out, blocking her path out of the bathroom. "Wait. You have something on your chin."

Her eyes widened, and she raised her hand to her chin. "Where? Here?"

He took her hand and kissed the fingertips. "No. Here." Then he pulled her into his arms and kissed her chin, then migrated up to her lips.

Her hands rested against his chest, her fingers curling into the fabric of his new suit.

When he traced the seam of her lips with his tongue, she opened her mouth and let him in.

He claimed her in that kiss, crushing her body to his, sweeping her tongue in a long, sensuous caress.

Reese forgot everything outside the circle of his arms. Forgot she had a job to do. Forgot the past and all the horrors it held for her. In Diesel's arms, she was who she was meant to be and more. She slid her leg up the back of his calf, pressing her hips closer to his. How she wanted to shed her clothes and take him to her bed to make sweet love to him. Surely that was the reason they'd made it through the jungle and back to this hotel.

A knock on the door jolted her out of the fog of lust threatening to consume her.

She lifted her head and stared into Diesel's deep brown eyes. He had a speck of gold in one of them, making him even more attractive and a little mysterious.

Another knock sounded on the door. "Reese? Are you in there?" Ferrence's muffled voice sounded through the paneling, jerking Reese back to reality. "I have to go."

"I'm going with you," Diesel said, his tone firm.

She frowned. "I'm not sure I can get you in," she said. But she'd try. As long as he was still there, she wanted to be as close to him as possible. "Perhaps Mr. Klein can pull strings."

"Let's find out." Diesel brushed a kiss across her forehead. "You're beautiful."

She smiled, warmth spreading through her chest and everywhere else in her body. "You're not half-bad yourself."

He touched a strand of her hair. "I didn't know you were a redhead."

She laughed. "It was hard to tell with it being so dirty." Reese nodded toward the door. "We'd better go before Ferrence has housekeeping come unlock the door to check for dead bodies."

He glanced down at her feet and smiled. "I'll get the door, while you find some shoes."

Her cheeks heating and her core on fire, Reese hurried to the bedroom and slipped into the strappy silver stilettoes she'd chosen to go with the black dress. She prayed Ferrence could get Diesel into the social event, and maybe afterward, they'd come back to the suite and pick up where they'd left off on that kiss.

DIESEL BRACED HIMSELF against annoyance and opened the door to Ferrence Klein.

"Oh," the shorter man said and frowned. "I must have the wrong room."

"No, Mr. Klein, you have the correct room." Reese walked up, carrying a light silvery clutch in her hand. "We're ready to go, if you are."

"We?" He stared from Reese to Diesel and back. "I only have invitations for the two of us."

"Is there someone you can talk to about getting Mr. Landon in? I believe it would be worth a try. He's proven quite helpful in seeing to my safety. I'm sure he will be equally helpful in looking out for the both of us."

Klein's frown deepened. "I don't know. If the dignitaries think I don't have confidence in their ability to see to my well-being, they might not want to negotiate with us."

"He could come as my fiancé," Reese said. "They don't have to know he's here to provide protection."

Diesel loved the irony of the situation. Klein didn't know Reese was there to provide for his protection, and here she was volunteering Diesel to be their backup, as long as their hosts didn't catch wind.

The diplomat's face hardened. "I had hoped to have you acting as my date."

Reese crossed her arms over her chest. "Considering your wife is at home with your children, perhaps it would be better if my fiancé tags along, don't you think?"

Diesel almost raised his hand to give Reese a high-five, but he restrained himself and let her manage her boss. Knowing her, she wouldn't appreciate him butting in or punching the man in the face, as he sorely wished he could.

"Well, I suppose you're right. But I need you to be with me at all times in case I miss something. You are my assistant, after all."

Reese nodded. "Yes, I am. And I'll be with you throughout the evening."

"Well, then, let's get this over with. We'll make an appearance, talk with the president and call it a night. The convention starts tomorrow. It'll be a long day of meetings."

Reese followed Klein out of the suite and to the elevator.

Diesel was glad he'd gone to the trouble of getting the suit. Had he not, he'd be waiting in the suite, cooling his heels while Reese was off with the lecherous Ferrence Klein.

He clenched his fists and reminded himself that Reese was perfectly capable of handling her boss. It was the rest of the delegates he should be concerned about. Some of the countries represented at the convention had little to no respect for women, their rights or their safety.

The elevator took them to the second floor, where half of the ballroom had been sectioned off to provide a more intimate space for the smaller social gathering of a few chosen dignitaries.

Diesel didn't recognize any of them. Most wore expensive, tailored suits or long, elaborate robes, depending on their faith or the country they represented. Although there were some women in the room, the preponderance of people there were men. And they appeared to be businessmen, many of them white.

"I thought this was supposed to be a summit of the African Union," he said.

"This social is for the businessmen who have interest in the DRC. They want to make sure their interests are being represented in these meetings," Klein said. "There's the president. I want to speak with him before the room gets too full." Klein hurried across the room with Reese at his side.

Diesel followed at a slower pace, taking in all the guests and the military men dressed in neatly pressed uniforms, but still carrying their rifles. He didn't like that he'd had to hide his own rifle in the suite, still stashed in his backpack.

If one of the military guards started shooting, it would be a massacre in a matter of seconds. A chill rippled across the back of Diesel's neck. The ball would be held in the same place the next night. He wondered if they would have the same military presence stationed throughout the room. He also wondered if the exterior of the building was being guarded as well.

Diesel hurried to catch up to Klein and Reese. Perhaps he'd been involved in too many skirmishes. He thought too much about different scenarios. With as many dignitaries in town, the president of the Democratic Republic of the Congo would have heightened security, especially since there were rebel factions stirring up trouble in the country, based on what Klein had told them.

Diesel had read about the president of the DRC and how he was known to be heavy-handed with his use of military force. Though the president was an elected position, the current one wasn't keen on giving up the job. He'd delayed the elections, claiming the country was not stable enough to hold them when they were supposed to be held. The truth was he didn't want to be voted out of office.

And he was the host of this event. He had a lot of riding on his ability to maintain the peace and keep the dignitaries safe while they were in Kinshasa.

As Klein and Reese reached the president, a scuffle broke out behind Diesel. He turned to see the guards holding a man at the door. The man appeared dressed in a ceremonial uniform and headdress. He struggled against the guards holding him back from entering the room.

He shouted something across the room toward the location where Reese and Klein were standing.

Diesel couldn't understand his words, as they were spoken in one of the languages indigenous to the Congo.

The president's chin lifted, and he answered in French, the official language of the DRC.

Diesel had taken French in high school, but he could only pick up on a few words. One of them being *brother* and the other being *go*.

He knew the president of the DRC had a brother who'd planned to run in the next election. It appeared the brother hadn't been invited to the social and was attempting to crash the party.

The president excused himself from the people gathered around him and walked across the floor and out the door with his brother.

Diesel joined Reese and Klein.

"Well, that wasn't helpful," Ferrence complained. "I wanted to speak with the president since I couldn't get a meeting alone with him while I'm here."

"Why are you so intent on meeting with the president?" Diesel asked.

"The mines in the Congo are rich with minerals everyone in the world wants," Ferrence said, his voice hushed in the crowded room. "We need to make sure we have a stake in the mining industry. The Russians and Chinese have been funding development of the mining operations. We can't let them take everything. We need the copper, gold and other minerals for our own country's needs."

Diesel watched the door, waiting for the president's return. "And what does that have to do with the US?"

"We suspect President Jean-Paul Sabando sold half the interest in one of the major copper mines to an undisclosed party," Reese continued. "Ferrence is here to find out if he sold it and to whom."

"And if he did, then what?" Diesel asked.

"We attempt to find out who has it and try to purchase it from them."

"Since when does the US negotiate purchases of mine interests with foreign countries?"

"Since we need those minerals in the production of our weapons," Klein said. "And the US won't be the ones to purchase the interest. It would be one of our primes who provide the materials we need for weapons production."

"The president's brother, Lawrence Sabando, is running on the platform of returning the profits to the people of the DRC," Klein said. "Rumor has it he's got the backing of Bosco Mutombo, one of the major warlords responsible for attacks on the mine."

"Bosco Mutombo?" Reese frowned. "I could swear he was in charge of the men who abducted us."

Klein's brows drew together. "In which case, we're lucky to be here."

Reese's lips thinned. "Luck had nothing to do with it. Diesel and his men got us out of there."

Klein nodded. "Yes, yes, of course."

"And Lawrence decided it was a good idea to crash his brother's party?" Diesel shook his head. "Sounds like a recipe for trouble."

Klein craned his neck to see over the crowd, watching the entrance for the president's return. "Like I said, there was an incident involving Molotov cocktails last night at a building not far from here."

"What building?" Reese asked.

"The headquarters of Metro Mining Company, one of the state-owned mining companies of the DRC," Klein said. "They are responsible for the mining of the copper mine the president sold half interest in."

Diesel shook his head. "Are you sure it's a good idea to be in the DRC right now?"

"I'm here on my father's behalf to establish a conversation with the president." Klein lifted his chin. "My father would be here, but he's tied up with the troubles in Libya. The US president wanted him in Washington if anything broke out."

"So you're here, in a hostile environment and have

already been kidnapped once by Congolese rebels and held for ransom." Diesel didn't like it. "Why?"

"From what my father told me, they were demanding a lot of money. Money the US government could have handed over to free me. I suspect they wanted the money to fund their supplies to keep up the fight." Klein stood straighter. "As far as President Sabando is concerned, I was never kidnapped or held for ransom. My father didn't want to give the rebels any more credit than we can help."

"Okay," Diesel said, "But what's to keep the rebels from making another attempt on your life, or one of the other delegates here for the convention?"

"I'm glad you asked." Klein gave him a hint of a smile. "Since you insisted on coming to this social, it's given me an idea. I'll work with my father to see if we can get more help here to protect the people at the convention. Of course, whoever helps would have to be undercover. We couldn't let Sabando catch wind we don't trust his security forces. I bet my father could get the team that rescued me to provide the support we need for tomorrow."

"Only if we get on the phone now. It takes time to get them from where they are to Kinshasa, and they'll need appropriate attire for the mission. Combat gear would be a dead giveaway." Diesel's brows pulled together as he worked through the logistics in his head.

"I'll see what I can do to make it happen." Klein pulled out a shiny new cell phone and walked off to a deserted corner of the ballroom to place his call.

Reese and Diesel followed, but stood far enough away to give the man privacy for his call.

"Do you think your team could be here and in place by tomorrow?" Reese asked.

"You'd be surprised how fast they can deploy. And since they're already on this continent, they could be here by morning."

Klein rejoined them, his lips forming a thin line. "It's done. Your team should be receiving orders within the hour."

Chapter Eight

Reese was beginning to think they'd bit off more than they could chew in the DRC. With warring factions pushing the limits and warlords looking for ways to fund their war machines, Ferrence Klein, the son of the US Secretary of Defense, was a prime target.

Her experience as both a soldier and an MMA fighter would be precious little protection if they were cornered again by Congolese rebels.

President Sabando didn't return to the social event. After waiting for him for the next hour following his departure, Klein called it a night.

Fortunately, he and Reese had rooms on the same floor. His room directly across the hallway from Reese's made it possible for her to hear if he was being attacked. On the other hand, he was right across the hall from her. Which meant little privacy. The three of them rode the elevator up to their floor. When they reached Klein's door, Diesel asked for his key.

Klein frowned. "Why?"

"Let me make sure your room hasn't been compromised. Anyone of the maintenance staff could let himself in. And they could have been bribed to let someone else in."

Klein handed over his key and waited in the hallway with Reese as Diesel searched his room for intruders or booby traps.

When he emerged, he handed the key to Klein. "I'll be across the hall if you should need me. Lock the dead bolt and don't answer the door unless it's one of us."

"I arrived before you two," Klein said. "You'd think if anyone was going to do something, they already would have."

"Except Diesel's team got you out of the jungle with the express purpose of keeping your rescue on the down low," Reese reminded him. "If the same folks who ordered the kidnapping were going to sabotage your room, they wouldn't have known you'd show up when you did. They might still have been under the impression you were secured in the jungle somewhere."

"No one was expecting you to arrive," Diesel said. "Now that you've shown your face at a gathering, they'll know you escaped. You're back to being a target."

"Great." Klein shook his head. "I guess I'll be sleeping with one eye open tonight."

"Again, we're across the hallway."

"Why not stay in my suite?" Klein suggested.

Reese held her breath. It made sense to have Diesel stay with the Secretary of Defense's son. But she didn't want him to. She wanted him in her room, doing what he'd done earlier, and more.

Diesel shook his head. "We set the precedent. I'm

here as Miss Brantley's fiancé. If you suspect someone is trying to break in, and you think I won't hear it, you can call. I'll be there."

Klein nodded. "Okay, then. I'll see you two in the morning." His eyes narrowed. "Don't do anything I wouldn't do."

Reese refused to rise to his taunt and smiled as the man closed the door. "Which means the sky's the limit," she muttered and turned with her key to open the door to her suite.

As soon as she crossed the threshold, butterflies erupted in her belly, and her body tingled all over. She was alone with Diesel, and they weren't being shot at or threatened by a troop of gorillas. The possibilities exploded in her head, and her core heated.

She didn't turn around, afraid Diesel would see the desire in her eyes. *What if he wasn't feeling it as deeply as she was?*

She heard the door close behind her and felt a hand catch hold of hers, spinning her around.

"Come here," he said, his voice low, throaty and sexy as hell, melting every bone in her body. *How did he do that?*

Reese hadn't been with a man in so long... She tried not to think about the last time. She'd been raped by Taliban fighters. As far as she was concerned, it didn't count. She pushed the memories to the back of her mind and concentrated on the real electricity firing off all of her nerve synapses, sending fire to her center.

And took back ownership of her body.

Since her abuse at the hands of the Taliban, she'd

thought she wasn't capable of feeling the intensity of lust and desire. "I was wrong. So very wrong," she whispered.

His head dipping low, Diesel stopped before his lips reached hers. "Wrong?" He leaned back and stared into her eyes, his brows knitting. "Did I read you wrong? Are you not feeling what I'm feeling?"

She laughed and wrapped her hands around the back of his head and pulled him down for a quick kiss, before saying, "No. I was wrong. I thought I would never feel what I'm feeling now."

"And what are you feeling?" he asked, tucking a strand of her hair behind her ear.

She drew in a deep breath and let it out. She told herself that he wouldn't be holding her like he was if he didn't feel the same. "Every cell in my body is on fire."

"I hope in a good way." He brushed his lips across her forehead.

"Only the best." She smiled up at him, but the smile faded. "You need to know something, though."

"Shoot. After our trek through the jungle, and facing the wrath of a giant gorilla, I think I can handle just about anything."

Reese dipped her head and stared at the tips of her toes in the stilettoes. "I haven't had sex with anyone since I was a Taliban captive."

Diesel drew in a deep breath and let it out slowly. Then he gathered her in his arms and held her, stroking the back of her head, his lips pressed to her temple. "Sweetheart, if I could, I'd kill every one of those bastards."

"You and me both." She laid her cheek against his chest and listened to the beat of his heart. "When I was liberated, the army ran me through all the tests for STDs. I'm clean, but because of how rough they treated me, I'm damaged. Remember, I told you before, I'll never have children."

"Oh, Reese, darlin', you're not damaged. You're perfect. Don't let anyone tell you differently." He tilted her chin up and stared into her eyes. "You're strong, brave and you have a big heart." He smiled down at her. "In my eyes, that's perfect."

"I always felt dirty after that." Her eyes filled with tears, but she managed to grin. "Until I showered earlier, I hadn't realized how much cleaner I've felt since I met you. Inside and out. And you're making me feel things I never thought I would feel ever again."

"Like you're on fire?"

She nodded. "Like a flame is burning inside, making my blood warm and my heart beat faster. Please tell me I'm not silly. Am I the only person who has ever felt like this?"

"No, you're not." He threaded his fingers through her hair and brushed his lips across hers. "I'm feeling it, too. It's like electricity is humming through my body, and it's all because of you. I can't seem to get close enough to you."

Reese knew exactly what he meant. Their bodies touched from their lips to their thighs but it wasn't enough. She wanted to be closer.

But first...the kiss.

He claimed her mouth, thrusting his tongue between

her teeth to sweep alongside hers, caressing it in long, slow swirls.

Reese gave as good as she got, wrapping her hands behind his head, threading her fingers through his short hair. The longer the kiss went on, the weaker her knees became. She wrapped a leg around his, rubbing her aching center against his thick, muscular thigh. She wanted him inside her, filling the emptiness that had been with her since she'd left the military.

When Diesel broke the seal of their kiss, he pressed his forehead to hers.

Reese dragged in breaths, filling her lungs. Her heart raced and her knees wobbled. This man had such a profound effect on her, she couldn't control her reaction. Before she could think or talk herself out of it, she pushed his jacket off his shoulders. By the time the garment hit the floor, her hands had moved to the buttons on his shirt, sliding them through the holes, her fingers shaking, eager, desperate to reach the skin beneath.

When one button got stuck, she tore at it.

"Hey." He chuckled and laid a hand over hers. "I need this shirt for tomorrow."

"Sorry. It's just…you have on too many clothes." She glanced up at his face, her brows drawing together. "Are you just going to stand there and make me do all the work?" She brushed his hand aside and attacked the button again. "I can't get you naked fast enough," she muttered beneath her breath.

"Sweetheart, we have all night." He pushed her hand aside and deftly flicked the button through the hole. He repeated the action with the next three buttons, his motion pulling the shirttail out of the waistband of his trousers.

Reese was already working on the button on his trousers. She then proceeded to slide the zipper down.

His shaft jutted out of the opening into her palm, and she looked up, giving him what had to be a goofy smile. "Commando?"

"Always," he said.

"I should have guessed." She wrapped her hand around his length and tried to remember to breathe. This was what she wanted, him naked, inside her, thrusting, filling, becoming a part of her. She hooked her thumbs in the waistband of his trousers and shoved them down his legs. God, she hoped she didn't freeze at the wrong moment. Deep inside, she knew she was ready, but that PTSD stuff had a bad habit of debilitating her when she least expected. A sexual situation would be the most likely to trigger her into a downward spiral.

Diesel toed off his shoes, bent to remove his socks and stood in front of her completely naked. He was the most beautiful man she'd ever seen.

He arched his brows. "You're overdressed for the occasion."

Trying not to salivate, Reese turned her back to him, her entire body shaking.

His fingers curled around her shoulders, and he pulled her back against his front, his staff pressing against her bottom. "Tell me if I move too fast. Just say *no*, and I'll stop."

"Are you kidding me?" She laughed shakily. "I just

stripped the clothes off your body. Does that say *no* to you?" Dear sweet heaven she wanted him, and he was taking far too long to get her naked.

His hands slid downward, gripped the zip on the back of her dress and lowered it to the base of her spine. She tilted her head back, letting her hair brush across her back, liking the way it felt.

Then he skimmed her shoulder blades with his fingertips and slipped them beneath the straps, inching them over her shoulders. The little black dress slid down to pool at her hips.

Diesel leaned over and kissed the curve of her neck, pushing her hair aside to nibble on her earlobe.

Reese shivered and leaned her head to the side, giving him full access to her neck. He accepted the invitation and laid a trail of kisses along the length and back to the curve of her shoulder. Meanwhile his fingers lowered to the clasp of her bra, and he unhooked it.

Tied in knots and eager to get the show on the road, Reese shrugged out of the bra and let it slide down her arms to the floor. Then she raised her hands to the dress gathered around her waist.

Diesel beat her to it and pushed the dress over the swell of her bottom, slowly, letting his hands ride down her hips until the dress slipped to the floor in a puddle of black fabric.

He hooked his thumbs into the elastic of her panties and dragged them down her legs, going down on one knee to reach her ankles.

When she stepped out of them, she started to reach for the clasp on her shoes.

"Don't," he said and pressed a kiss to one of her lower cheeks, and then the other. Rising, as if in slow motion, he kissed the small of her back and dragged his hands up her thighs to rest on her hips.

His shaft pressed against her bottom, hard, thick and hot.

"I can't wait any longer," she whispered, her core so hot, she feared she'd spontaneously combust before they actually made it to the bed.

"Me either." Then he scooped her up into his arms and carried her into the bedroom.

This was it, this would be her first time since…

And her only thought was if it felt this good now, it could only be better when he finally came inside her.

DIESEL LAID HER on the edge of the bed, parted her knees and hooked his arms beneath her thighs. He wanted to thrust into her, hard, fast and all the way to the hilt. But this woman had suffered at the hands of their enemy. A horrible, tragic abuse of her body. She needed to know it didn't have to be that way. He wanted her to know and feel how good making love was when the person doing it cared.

Drawing in a deep breath, he released her thighs and bent over her to kiss her lips, long, slow and gentle. He'd bring her to the brink, to that pinnacle of desire before he slaked his own.

Reese wrapped her arms around his neck, arched her back and pressed her breasts to his chest.

She was going to make it hard for him to hold back.

He unwound her arms from around his neck and

pressed her back against the mattress. "Let me show you how good it can be."

"Just don't take forever. I'm really a quick learner, and I want you. What more do we need?" she said, her voice quivering.

"If you have to ask, you don't know." Then he kissed a path across her cheek and down the side of her neck. He didn't stop until he brushed his lips over the swell of her breast, taking the nipple into his mouth. He tongued the tip until it formed a hard, little bead that he then rolled between his teeth.

Reese moaned. She cupped the back of his head and guided him to the other breast, where he then performed the same treatment. When he had her squirming beneath him, he moved down her torso, flicking his tongue across her skin, dipping into her belly button and then moving lower to the tuft of hair at the juncture of her thighs.

Her body stiffened.

"Are you afraid I won't stop?" he asked and blew a stream of air across the curls.

"No, I'm afraid you *will* stop. Please, don't." She widened her thighs, giving him better access to his goal. He dropped to his knees and looped her legs over his shoulders. Then he parted her folds with his thumbs and touched the strip of nerve-packed flesh at her center with the tip of his tongue.

She gasped and arched her back off the bed. "Oh, please."

He chuckled. "Please, what?"

"Do it again."

"As you wish," he said, breathing warm air over her heated flesh. He flicked her again, this time staying long enough to swirl his tongue the length of the nubbin, drawing from her a long, low moan.

He swirled and pressed a finger to her entrance, pleased by how damp and ready she was. Still licking and flicking, he slid a finger inside her channel.

Reese bucked off the mattress and laid a hand over his.

He froze, afraid he'd scared her.

When she curled her fingers around his hand and urged him deeper, he wanted to yell *hallelujah*. He sent another finger into her and then another, stretching her and pumping in and out to prepare her for when he came to her.

Her juices drenched his fingers, making him so hard, he couldn't hold out much longer. He flicked and swirled until she raised her feet, still wearing the shoes, and dug them into the mattress. Sweet heaven, she was sexy, pushing her hips up as her body pulsed and trembled with her release.

Diesel didn't stop what he was doing until her bottom lowered to the bed. Then he pushed to his feet, reached into the nightstand for the accordion of condom packages he'd stashed there earlier when Reese had been in the bathroom. He tore one off, opened it and rolled it down over his throbbing shaft.

Then he hooked her knees in his arms and pulled her bottom to the edge of the bed, nudging her soft, wet entrance with his hardness. "Are you okay with this? I can stop now."

"Oh, please, whatever you do, don't stop now." She wrapped her legs around his waist and pulled him into her.

He entered her slowly, giving her body a chance to adjust to his length and girth. When he'd sunk all the way to the hilt, he stopped, breathing in and out, afraid he'd scare her if he went too fast.

"Faster," she said on a gasp. "Faster and harder. I want to feel every bit of you."

He obeyed, sliding out and then back in, increasing the pressure and the force with every thrust.

Reese flung back her head and arched off the bed, tightening her thighs to bring him deeper.

He pumped in and out of her until his body tensed and heat radiated from his center, sending electric tingles out to the very tips of his fingers and toes. Diesel thrust into her one last time and held her tightly against him, his shaft throbbing inside. His heart was pounding so hard in his chest, he thought it might break his ribs.

When he finally came back to earth, he gathered Reese in his arms and scooted her up onto the bed, laying her head on a pillow. Then he dropped down beside her, spooned her body from behind and cupped a breast. He kissed the curve of her shoulder. "Are you okay?"

"I don't think I'll ever be okay again," she said, her voice sexy and gravelly. She wiggled her body against his. "I'll forever be fabulous. *Okay* is for underachievers." She laid a leg over his and wrapped his arms around her. "Thank you."

Diesel chuckled.

"What?" She turned her head in an attempt to look at his face.

"Nothing. You just make me happy." He pulled her closer, kissed her temple and reflected on how incredibly lucky he'd been to find her in the jungle.

His life couldn't be better than at that moment. Tomorrow they'd have to sort through what had just happened, but tonight was everything he could have dreamed of.

"Diesel?" Reese said, her voice barely above a whisper.

"Yeah, babe?" He brushed her hair aside and kissed her shoulder.

"Do you really think Sabando's brother will try something stupid while the delegates are attending the conference?"

"I don't know. But there are a lot of important people here from all over the world. If his brother is desperate enough, he might."

Reese lay quietly for several minutes.

Diesel thought she'd gone to sleep.

"Diesel?"

"Yeah, babe?"

"Do you think your team will get here in time?"

He chuckled. "You bet. It might be overkill to bring them here, but I'd rather have overkill and nothing happen than do nothing and innocent people die."

Silence settled in around them. Sleep was just a blink away.

"Diesel?"

"Mmm?"

Reese yawned and stretched her lithe, sexy body against his. When she settled back into him, she sighed. "What's going to happen tomorrow?"

"At the conference? I have no clue."

"No," she whispered. "Between us?"

"I don't know, but we'll figure out something."

She hugged his arm around her and pressed it to her breasts.

Diesel's body jerked awake, his groin tightening at her touch. He willed his desire to recede.

Reese needed her sleep, and so did he. Tomorrow might be more of an event than even the attendees anticipated. At least his team would be there to provide backup.

Chapter Nine

A firm knock on the door in the outer room of the suite broke through the dead of sleep Reese had fallen into. For a moment, she lay comfortable, surrounded by the luxury of clean sheets and an incredibly soft mattress. She didn't want to wake up, but the incessant knocking forced her to open her eyes.

Diesel was already out of the bed, running for the other room, stark naked. Through the open bedroom door, Reese could see him snatch up his suit trousers from the floor where he'd left them and jam his legs into them. Half running, half hopping, he made it to the door on the third round of knocking. A quick peek through the peephole, and he flung the door wide.

"Damn, you guys got here fast," he said quietly and opened the door wide, grinning.

Five hulking men, dressed in dark pants and T-shirts stretched tightly over broad chests and massive biceps, tumbled into the room.

Reese yelped, rolled out of the bed and dropped to floor on the other side, where she'd laid her suitcase. She dug through, searching for her workout clothes and sports bra. While lying on the floor, she dressed quickly, her heart pounding, and her cheeks on fire.

When she was convinced all pertinent parts were covered, she straightened, pretending that getting up off the floor of a hotel room was a natural occurrence. She could have been exercising for all they knew.

And pigs might learn to fly.

Diesel's men would all know she'd been in bed with their teammate as soon as they caught sight of the discarded clothing on the sitting-room floor.

The man she'd made love with stood in the middle of the group of men, each back-slapping and filling each other in on the other's stories.

Reese stepped into the room and cleared her throat.

Diesel turned, grinned and held out his hand for her.

She took his and allowed him to draw her into the circle of his friends.

"Guys, you remember Reese Brantley. Reese, this is just part of my team. Apparently, they only got clearance to send them, no more. Which is probably for the better. Too many SEALs in a public place would raise red flags all over the world."

Reese remembered most of their faces from the boat ride the day before. "Hi. I'm sorry, I don't remember your names."

Diesel pointed to a man about the same height as him with black hair and brown eyes. "This is Harmone Payne."

He held out his hand. "Harm."

"I don't understand." Reese took his hand, a frown

drawing her brows together. "I have no intention of harming you."

Harm laughed. "The team calls me *Harm*."

Heat climbed into her cheeks. "Oh. Sorry. Harm, it is."

"You remember me, Graham Buckner." A brown-haired man with bright blue eyes held out his hand. "You can call me Buck."

"Percy Taylor." Another hand was shoved toward her by a man with short dark hair and hazel eyes. He was stockier than the others and built like a freight train. "But you might remember me as Pitbull."

"On account he looks like one," Diesel said.

"And smells like one," Buck added.

Pitbull swung a fist at Buck, hitting him hard in the shoulder.

Reese flinched, imagining the pain of that meaty fist on her own shoulder. But Buck didn't seem to notice.

"I'm Trace McGuire." A man with dark auburn hair and blue eyes held out his hand.

Buck leaned close. "That's T-Mac to most."

The biggest man in the room stepped forward. Reese remembered him. "Jake Schuler." He had dark blond hair and gray eyes. He tipped his head toward his buddies. "You'll remember me as the one called Big Jake."

Reese smiled at the men. Even at five-foot-eight, she felt dwarfed by their size and extra-large, alpha-male personalities. "Have you been up all night?" she asked.

"We have," Big Jake said. "We could use some shut-eye, but the front desk said the hotel was full.

We thought we'd let you know we were here before we looked for other accommodations."

Diesel shook his head. "You aren't likely to find anything nearby. Not with the convention in town."

Buck glanced around the suite. "There's enough room here. We could catch a few Z's."

The corners of Reese's mouth quirked upward. "On the floor?"

"Lady, we've slept on worse," Buck admitted. "The floor would be heaven."

Harm nodded. "We only need a couple hours to recharge our batteries."

"Do you mind?" T-Mac asked.

Reese laughed and frowned. "Not at all. Are you sure you'll be all right on the floor?"

"Perfectly," Big Jake yawned. "I could sleep on a bag of rocks about now."

"Hopefully it won't be that bad." Reese hurried for the bedroom. "I'll get some pillows and whatever blankets I can find. But you might want to keep it down. The hotel staff will kick us all out if they find out I've got six men in my room."

Diesel grabbed their clothes from where they'd landed on the floor and tossed them on the bed. Then he helped her gather the spare blankets and pillows from the closet, and a couple from the bed, and carried them out to the five men stripping out of their shirts and boots.

Reese's eyes widened at all of the muscles on display. She was in every woman's paradise.

Diesel nudged her with his elbow. "Hey, don't get any ideas. I'd like to think you're all mine."

She smothered a giggle. "You can't blame me. It's like looking at works of art." Reese dropped the pillows and blankets on the sofa. "I believe that sofa folds out into a bed."

"I call it," T-Mac said.

"Sorry, dude. I'm pulling rank on this one." Big Jake nudged the auburn-haired SEAL out of the way. "You can have the cushions."

"Deal. Actually, that sounds better anyway." T-Mac gathered the cushions from the sofa and carried them to a corner of the sitting room.

Pitbull snagged a pillow and stretched out in front of the floor-to-ceiling window. He didn't ask for a blanket or a spare sheet. He lay down and closed his eyes. Within seconds, his chest began to rise and fall in deep, restful breaths.

Harm draped his body over a large chair and was snoring within seconds.

Buck grabbed a pillow. "Do we need someone to stand watch?"

"Not tonight," Diesel said. "We'll come up with a plan in the morning. I'm not sure I can get all of you into the convention center. But having you close by will be a relief."

Buck nodded to Diesel and Reese. "Okay, then. I'm catching a few Z's. See you two when the sun comes up." The big man found an empty space near the door.

Big Jake unfolded the bed from inside the sleeper sofa and dropped onto the thin mattress. He gave Diesel a salute, crossed his arms over his chest and closed his eyes.

Diesel clasped Reese's hand in his and led her back to the bedroom and closed the door.

"How do they do that?" Reese asked, amazed at how quickly they settled in for sleep.

"Do what?"

She shook her head. "Go to sleep so fast?"

"Part of it is that they're tired. That, and they're used to grabbing a nap whenever and wherever they can. You never know when you'll get to sleep again."

Reese nodded. "Like when we were in the jungle."

"Exactly." He pulled her into his arms and kissed her soundly. "As much as I'd like to make love to you again, we should get some sleep, as well."

"Yeah, you two need to sleep," Buck called out from the other side of the door. "We don't need reminders of how lonely we are out here."

"Speak for yourself, dirtbag. You can always snuggle up to me," T-Mac said.

"In your dreams," Buck shot back.

Reese's face heated, but she chuckled. "Sleep it is." She could have gone for another round of lovemaking with her handsome SEAL but not with an audience of five of his buddies on the other side of what appeared to be a paper-thin bedroom door.

Diesel stroked his thumb along the side of her cheek. "Do you want me to sleep out there with the guys?"

She frowned. "Hell, no."

"Does it bother you that they know we're sleeping together?"

Reese stood on her toes and pressed a kiss to his lips. "I'm a grown woman. What I do and who I sleep with is my business, and I don't give a damn what anyone else thinks."

"You tell him, Reese," Buck said.

Diesel growled. "Go to sleep, Buck."

"I would, if you two would stop yammering," Buck grumbled.

Reese took Diesel's hand and led him to the bed. She lay down, fully dressed in her workout clothes.

Diesel stripped out of his trousers and slipped beneath the sheets, pulling her body against his.

She touched a finger to his chest. "I want to get closer, but—"

"Shh. There are far too many men in this suite. Go to sleep knowing that at least you're safe."

She pressed her ear to his skin, listening to the strong, steady beat of his heart, her own swelling inside. This was a man worth keeping. Someone she could easily fall for. Too bad they were in such difficult jobs. They'd never find time to be together. She'd have to settle for what little time they had together for the next couple days. Her memories would have to carry her for a long time. Finding someone like Diesel would be impossible. He'd set the bar for her. No one else would ever do. Eventually, exhaustion claimed her, and Reese slipped into a troubled sleep.

DIESEL LAY FOR a long time, wishing the guys hadn't come as soon as they had, but glad they were there.

He wanted to make love to Reese again, but the

others would hear and give him and her hell. Until they made it through the conference and got Reese and Klein on their way back to the States, he would just have to abstain. But it was hard. Really hard.

When he finally went to sleep, it felt like only moments before an alarm blared on the nightstand nearby.

Reese reached out and turned it off, and then rolled over into his arms and kissed him. "They can't hear if I kiss you," she whispered, and did it again.

Diesel gathered her close and took her mouth, thrusting his tongue past her teeth to spar with hers. He could get used to waking up every day to this strong, beautiful woman.

But he was a SEAL. He would always be on call and deploy at the drop of a hat. He'd seen too many SEALs divorce within the first few years of marriage. Their wives couldn't stand the uncertainty, never knowing when they would be home, or if they would arrive in a body bag.

Reese deserved better. After what she'd been through at the hands of the Taliban terrorists, she deserved someone who could be there to protect her every day, not just a part-time lover who would enter and leave her life at the whim of the navy.

He kissed her hard, wishing they could stay in bed for the entire day, but knowing they had a job to do. He smacked her bottom. "You can have the bathroom first. I want to work with the guys to come up with a plan."

"I want to be in on the planning, too," she insisted.

"Then you better hurry. Your boss's meetings begin

in less than an hour, and my guys will want to grab something to eat before the fun begins."

"Going," she said, grabbed his ears and pulled him to her again for another kiss. Then she scrambled from the bed and raced to the bathroom.

Diesel pulled on his suit trousers and walked out of the bedroom.

T-Mac crouched by the window, unpacking items from a duffel bag, laying them out on the floor.

Harm was checking out the coffee maker. "One lousy cup. Why bother?" He glanced up as Diesel entered the room. "We have to make a run for coffee."

"We will, after we discuss the mission." Big Jake pulled a polo shirt over his head and tucked it into his khaki pants. "What are the chances of us getting into the conference?"

"I'd say slim to none," Diesel replied. "From what I've seen so far, only the attendees will be allowed into the auditorium. I assume they'll have tight security around the conference center."

"We had orders to come provide any help we can," Big Jake said.

"But we aren't supposed to be here, so we weren't allowed to carry weapons," Harm added.

"What good can we be without firepower?" Pitbull asked.

"You can let us know if you see, hear or smell trouble," Diesel said.

"That means we'll be the eyes, ears and noses." Buck lightly backhanded Diesel in the belly as he passed him and bent to the equipment T-Mac was laying out on the floor. "I'll take one of those."

"I figured you might have lost yours in your run through the jungle." T-Mac handed Diesel one of the tiny radio headsets that fit in the ear and that would pick up the sound of his voice, providing two-way communication.

"Great. Did you bring an extra for Reese?" Diesel asked. "I probably won't be allowed into the conference center with her and Klein, but I'd like to keep in contact."

"I'm a step ahead of you." T-Mac held up a small earbud that would fit easily into her ear. "She could cover it with her hair."

Diesel took the earbud. "I believe we have a couple hours before the actual conference begins. I'd like to recon the area around the convention hall, find all the entrances and where they lead. If something goes down, we need to get Reese, Klein and as many of the attendees out of harm's way as quickly as possible."

"We can do that first and then find coffee," Big Jake said.

"You're hurting me, B.J.," Harm said.

T-Mac handed him a headset. "You'll live."

"Not unless I get a cup of coffee soon." Harm pressed the earpiece into his ear and slipped his arms into a button-down, short-sleeved cotton shirt. "Let's get this recon done soon. I have a date with a cuppa jo."

"I could do with a cup of coffee, too." Reese stepped out of the bedroom, wearing a sleek, gray jacket and slim-fitting, stretchy skirt that wouldn't hamper her movements.

All six men turned in her direction.

Diesel frowned at the hungry looks in their eyes. Hell, he couldn't blame them. She was beautiful.

She left her hair hanging down around her ears and shoulders, and she wore matching gray high-heeled shoes.

"Wow, you look like you could take on the United Nations in that getup," Buck said.

T-Mac whistled. "Dang, Diesel, I'd have gone for a run in the jungle if I'd known Reese was going with me, too."

Diesel's fists clenched. "Knock it off. She's here to do a job." He smiled. "Though, you do look like you could take on the entire conference and kick ass."

Reese blushed and smiled. "Thanks. All of you." She glanced at her watch. "I need to touch base with Ferrence. We'll probably go to breakfast in the hotel restaurant. I'd invite all of you to join us, but then everyone would know you're with us."

Buck sighed. "Have a couple of eggs over easy for me, will ya?"

"And a cup of black coffee for me," Harm said, giving up on the coffee maker the hotel provided each room.

Diesel handed Reese the earbud headset. "Try this on."

"What is it?"

"A two-way radio. You'll be able to contact us, and we can contact you."

She nodded and settled the communication device in her ear.

"Go ahead and try it," T-Mac said, pressing a similar earbud into his ear.

"Testing," Reese said. "Testing."

"I can hear you. Let's see if you can hear me." T-Mac stepped outside the hotel room and walked down the hallway.

Diesel closed the door.

Reese stared at Diesel, tipping her head to the side. "I can hear you," she said, smiling.

T-Mac opened the door. "You're good to go."

Reese tapped her ear. "Thanks." She glanced at Diesel's bare chest. "Are you coming with us?"

He nodded. "As far as I can."

"I doubt I can get you into the conference, but you can join us for breakfast, since we've already established you as my fiancé."

"Fiancé?" Pitbull grinned. "Something you aren't telling us, dude?"

"Would you care to explain, while I finish dressing?" Diesel passed by Reese on his way to the bedroom.

Behind him, he heard Reese clear her throat. "Staying here was all part of his cover. Otherwise, he would have had to get a room somewhere farther away."

"Uh-huh," Buck said, a knowing grin spreading across his face. "Perfectly reasonable."

Diesel jammed his arms into the shirt, pulled on his socks and shoes and tucked in his shirt, in a hurry to get back to the sitting room before his teammates could further embarrass Reese. He buttoned his shirt and returned to the other room, handing his tie to Reese. "Could you?"

She wrapped the tie around his neck and made quick work of the knot at his throat. When she was done, she stood back. "Ready?"

He nodded and held out his arm. "I'll contact you guys later. Let me know what you find."

"Will do." Big Jake gave him a mock salute.

On his way out of the room, Diesel hung the Do Not Disturb sign on the outer doorknob.

Reese stepped across the hall and rapped on Klein's door.

Her client opened it, carrying a plain black briefcase and wearing a tailored charcoal-gray suit. "I was just about to come get you. I scored a breakfast with President Sabando's chief of staff. I hope to come out of breakfast having scheduled a meeting with the president himself." He handed the briefcase to Reese. "I'll need you to take notes."

"Do we need a translator?" she asked.

"No, he speaks English, having been educated at Harvard."

Diesel followed Reese and Klein to the hotel restaurant, where they met with Sabando's chief of staff, a tall, thin, dark man. He spoke English with an American accent.

A waiter led them to a table in the corner.

Diesel gave half of his attention to the conversation, while scanning the occupants of the restaurant.

So far, no one stood out as a threat. But then he

didn't expect to find one yet. If anyone wanted to make the news, they'd wait until all the foreign dignitaries had arrived for the conference. Based on the number of Congolese soldiers at the social the night before, the conference center would be well guarded.

Still, Diesel felt better knowing part of his team would be there should anyone make a move on the delegates, Reese or Klein. He only wished they could have come armed. But then, how would they explain navy SEALs at a conference to which they weren't invited? The African Union might consider it a sign of aggression if they came in with their guns a-blazing. No, it was better they were unarmed and supposedly there on vacation. They didn't need to cause an international incident. And he knew his brothers—they'd have knives strapped to their ankles. They wouldn't be completely unarmed.

By the end of breakfast, Klein had his meeting scheduled for the day after the conference. He rose from the table, appearing quite pleased.

Sabando's chief of staff excused himself, claiming he needed to be available for the president when he arrived at the conference center.

Klein paid the bill. The three of them left and walked down the long hallway to the huge conference center attached to the hotel. Every twenty feet, they passed armed soldiers.

Other dignitaries and their entourages walked the long hall, as well. The conference would begin in less than thirty minutes. Dignitaries and their assistants hurried into the auditorium to take their assigned seats.

Reese and Klein checked in with the registration desk and were given badges to clip to their collars.

Diesel bent to kiss her and whispered. "I'll be waiting out here. But I'll be with you all the time."

She nodded and stood on her toes to kiss him again. Then she entered the auditorium behind Klein.

Diesel stood back far enough not to attract attention from the guards standing on either side of the entrance, weapons held at the ready.

Other members of dignitaries' entourages remained outside the auditorium, claiming seats on benches against the walls or pacing the corridors, talking quietly into their cell phones.

"Comm check," T-Mac said through Diesel's radio.

"Diesel here," he responded.

"Reese here," a whispered feminine voice said.

Diesel's heart swelled at the sound. "Damn, you sound sexy," he answered.

"Thank you. My momma always said I had a lady-killer voice," T-Mac responded.

"Jerk," Diesel said, a smile tugging at his lips.

He heard a feminine chuckle in his headset, warming him all over. Knowing they were in communication made him feel better about being separated from her, but he'd rather be seated next to her, in case someone got trigger-happy.

Other members of the team checked in, one by one.

"Pitbull here, sweetlips."

"Big Jake here," Big Jake reported. "Our check of the exterior of the conference center yielded three entrances—all heavily guarded by Congolese soldiers."

"Buck, here. Harm and I walked the connecting hallway earlier and counted three more entrances from inside. One of the doors leading off the far end of the hallway leads to a staircase down into the parking garage. As does an elevator. Parking garage has four levels below the convention center."

"They have guards at each of the levels checking people getting on and off the elevators or staircases."

The team had done well on their recon mission. Now all they could do was stand around and wait for something to happen that raised concern. They were men of action. Waiting would be a challenge. But, if Diesel had his way, they'd wait all day for nothing.

He'd rather have the day pass uneventfully than see problems arise with the conference attendees. Especially one named Reese Brantley.

Diesel paced the hallway, passing each of the three interior entrances. All three were guarded by two soldiers each. Minutes passed into one hour, and then two. Diesel didn't like being on the outside, away from Reese. What if someone had gotten past the guards? What if the fight started from within? None of the delegates were armed. They'd be cut down like fish in a bowl.

The longer he waited, the more worried he became, until he found himself standing in front of the door in which Reese and Klein had entered. The guards narrowed their eyes and tightened their grips on their weapons.

Chapter Ten

Reese sat beside Ferrence, silently watching the proceedings, listening in one ear to the interpreter through the headset she'd been given, while also straining to hear news on anything going on outside the conference center.

She'd studied the Congolese military men when she'd stepped through the doors of the auditorium. Two guards on the door didn't seem to be a lot. But then, she'd heard the team's report on those on the outside. Still, for the number of delegates at the meeting, she would have thought Sabando would have had more of a show of force in the streets.

"Harm here. I'm going farther out from the conference center to see if anything's happening in the streets. I'll circle around two or three blocks out."

"We'll cover the corners of the exterior," another one of the men reported.

On edge from the potential of hostilities, Reese was slightly comforted by the knowledge the SEALs were watching their backs. Though they were unarmed, they would provide a significant warning system should trouble arise outside the building.

"As the president of the Democratic Republic of the Congo, what are you doing about the human rights violations happening at the Metro mines?" The English interpreter translated the words of the female representative from Rwanda, who spoke directly to the DRC president in French.

Reese focused her attention on the president's response. He answered in French, the translation coming through moments later from the English interpreter.

President Sabando leaned into his microphone and answered with authority.

The interpreter translated, "I have my people looking into this."

"While your people are looking into it, men, women and children are dying. Young children under the age of ten are dying in those mines and have been for years. Why are you not doing anything to prevent this?" the woman asked.

Sabando lifted his chin, narrowing his eyes just a little before answering, "Policy moves slowly in this country. I am working on it. These people make their living working the mines. If we take away their living, they will starve."

The representative from Zambia spoke in English, "Food aid is available. Small children do not have to work in harsh conditions to eat."

"The rebels intercept the rations to these people. They are part of the problem," President Sabando replied.

The woman from Rwanda met Sabando's glare with a steady, unbending one of her own and spoke in rapid-fire French. The translator struggled to keep up, but the message was clear. "Rumor has it your military is intercepting the rations, not the rebels."

President Sabando pounded his fist on the table in front of him and fired back. The interpreter translated with the appropriate intonation. "Bosco Mutombo is responsible for stopping the food to the people. He steals from the people of the Democratic Republic of the Congo!"

"He claims he steals from your forces, taking the food away from them to give back to the people." The president's brother, Lawrence Sabando, entered the auditorium in full military regalia of the Congolese Army, speaking in English.

"He lies!" President Sabando stood so fast his chair fell over behind him. He pointed his finger at his brother and shouted in English. "And you would spread these lies because Mutombo works for you!"

"Tell the people of the African Union why you won't allow elections." The president's brother shook his fist. "Tell them!"

President Sabando stood tall, his chest puffed out, his chin held high. "Because the nation is unsettled. An election now would cause riots in the streets."

"There are already riots in the streets," his brother reasoned. "You can't control the change happening in our country. The people will prevail."

Riveted by the power struggle going on between the two brothers, Reese almost missed the change in stance of the guards surrounding the room. "We might have trouble inside the auditorium," she whispered, hoping the mic on her headset was sensitive enough to pick up her voice.

"Holy crap. Harm here. We have trouble coming in from the streets. A massive movement of people, who appear to be led by rebel forces, are on the march toward the conference center. Rebels are armed. Civilians have whatever they could get their hands on, from hunting rifles to axes and pitchforks. Must be a couple thousand."

Reese's heart leaped, and she stared around the room full of dignitaries, for a moment, at a loss for what to do.

"ETA?" Diesel's reassuring voice sounded in her ear.

"Two or three minutes before they arrive," he said, sounding as if he were running. "I'm closing ranks with the team."

"What should we do?" Reese asked.

"Get Klein to the south door," Diesel said. "The one to the far right of the door you entered."

"What about the rest of the delegates?" she asked.

Ferrence leaned close to her. "What's going on?"

Reese brought him up to date in a whisper. "We need to get out of here and seek shelter."

"If we stand up in the middle of the Sabandos' arguments, we'll draw too much attention."

"Did you hear that?" Reese asked into her mic.

"I don't care," Diesel said. "Get up and leave before

things get hot on the inside, as well as the outside, of the auditorium."

"Going," Reese replied. Then she gripped Ferrence's hand tightly and shot him a stern stare. "Either you come with me now, or risk being trapped in this building when all hell breaks loose." She let go of him and gathered her notebook and pen, smiled at the people next to her and stood, hunkering low to keep from being too obvious.

She didn't get far before the shouting became more intense.

"You *will* hold elections on time, or the people will have their say," the president's brother yelled, fist waving in the air.

The president remained firm. "These people do not know what is good for them. They are uneducated. The country is not stable. Elections will cause chaos, I tell you."

"By not holding the elections as is mandated in our constitution, you will bring chaos down on all of us." Lawrence nodded toward one of the guards by the door.

The man raised his weapon and started firing over the heads of the crowd of delegates.

As soon as Reese saw the man raise his weapon, she grabbed Ferrence's arm and pushed him to the floor, covering his body with hers. "Get down," she yelled as loudly as she could. "Shots fired," she said, as if Diesel might not have heard the gunfire.

President Sabando dropped to the floor. "Are you insane?" he yelled to his brother.

"No, I'm determined to return the power to the people. This is a democratic republic, not a dictatorship. It is time for the tyrant to step down and be held accountable for his crimes!"

"This cannot be happening," Ferrence said, from his position beneath Reese. "I have an important meeting with the president tomorrow."

"Really?" Reese said, sliding to the side to poke her head up and assess the situation. "That's all you can think about when your life is in danger?" People were screaming and dropping to the floor.

"My father sent me here for one purpose. If I'm not successful, for whatever reason, I'm a failure in his eyes."

"Cry me a river, Ferrence. I'm getting out of here alive, even if I have to take out a few of these gun-toting terrorists myself." She eyed the door Diesel had said to head for and mentally estimated forty feet between her and the door. "Look, Ferrence, we're getting out of here, either you come with me and stand a better chance of living, or stay here and die."

"Either way, I doubt I'll get that meeting with Sabando. I wonder, if his brother takes over, can I meet with him instead?"

"For the love of Mike!" Reese cursed.

Ferrence struggled to his feet, bent over and followed Reese as she crossed the room toward the south door.

More shots were fired, echoing off the walls. Delegates cried out and rushed for the doors, pushing Reese and Ferrence in front of them.

Two men with guns blocked their path, pointing their weapons toward them.

Reese pretended to trip, falling into one of the men, shoving his weapon toward the ceiling. She performed her best side kick, aiming for the other man's hands. His weapon jettisoned out of his hands and clattered to the floor. Meanwhile, Reese fought for control of the guy pointing his weapon toward the ceiling. He elbowed her in the side of the head, knocking her earbud out. Knowing she was running out of time and the other men with weapons would start firing at her across the room, she shoved her thumbs in the man's eyes and lifted her knee with a swift upward jerk, kneeing him in the groin. The man went down, his grip loosening on the rifle. Reese wrested it from his grip and flung it away.

His partner lunged for Reese, but one of the delegates blocked him by swinging his briefcase up, hitting him in the nose. Blood spurted, and the gunman's eyes watered. He went down, clutching his face in his hands.

With nothing standing between them and the door, Reese grabbed one of the rifles from the ground and rushed forward. She shoved through the door and ran out. While the rebels focused on the delegates and the president still back in the auditorium, Reese ran for the door on the opposite side of the wall. From what the SEAL team said, it would lead to the parking garage below. Reese held the door for Ferrence. "Go down as far as you can and hide. I'm right behind you."

Before she could follow him, delegates shoved her out of the way, ran through the door and hurried down the stairs. Then the president of the Democratic Republic of the Congo appeared in front of her. "Who are you?" he demanded in English.

"Does it matter? If you want to be safe, follow me," Reese commanded.

The president nodded and hurried down the steps after her. Reese glanced over her shoulder. The last one through the door above was the president's brother, Lawrence Sabando.

She knew it would mean more trouble, but she had to get these people and Ferrence to safety. She'd deal with the troublemakers later. Then the door to the auditorium slammed shut, and no more delegates emerged. Several men dressed in shabby rebel camouflage uniforms rushed toward them.

Reese ran down the stairs, following the slower moving delegates. At the rate they were moving, the terrorists would catch up and shoot her first. And since the president was with her, she might as well have a bright red target painted on her back.

All she'd been paid to do was keep track of Ferrence Klein, be his assistant and protect him. Had she known she'd be at the center of a national coup attempt, she might have told the Kleins where they could go with their money. But second-guessing herself wouldn't get her out of the current situation. She had to use her brain and her fighting skills to see herself through and get Ferrence safely back to the States.

She didn't have time to think about Diesel and his teammates, unarmed and at the mercy of the terrorists. But she couldn't help wondering if they got out all right, or if they were in the midst of the fighting.

A loud crashing sound echoed down the stairwell. Voices shouted above, and someone fired shots that pinged off the concrete steps.

"Go! Go! Go!" Reese shouted to the people in front of her.

The people up front had reached the bottom of the staircase and spilled out into the lowest level of the parking garage. It wouldn't take long for the gunmen to get to them. They had to find a place to hide.

"Ferrence!" she yelled, anxious to get to him. Her job was to protect him, and she couldn't do it with all the others in the way.

"Over here!" Ferrence shouted. He held open a door marked with red lettering in French and English—Authorized Personnel Only.

With nowhere else to go but being out in the open in a free-for-all coup, Reese had no choice. "Get inside! Go!" She waved at the delegates and the president as if they were children who were slow to come off the playground. No one seemed to understand the urgency but Reese and Ferrence.

The squeal of car tires screamed off the concrete walls of the parking garage, heading lower in the building. They only had seconds to get everyone through the door and find some way of locking it behind them.

WHEN DIESEL HEARD Harm's assessment of the outside situation, he'd immediately told Reese to get out. He walked up to the doors and was barred from entering by the two guards dressed in DRC uniforms. He saw no other way to get past them but to start a fight. As he balled his fists, ready to throw the first punch, gunshots rang out inside the auditorium.

The guards turned toward the doors, weapons at the ready.

"What's going on in there?" Big Jake asked.

"Shots fired inside the auditorium. I'm going in." Diesel shoved the guards from behind, pushing them into the melee of the auditorium.

More shots were fired from similarly dressed guards on the inside. The president of the DRC was running low to the ground, shouting orders like a football quarterback, while the delegates either lay flat on the ground or ran screaming for the doors.

Through the chaos, Diesel had a hard time locating Reese. Then, he spotted her on the far end of the large auditorium, taking out the two guards blocking her exit. She'd done as he'd told her and made for the south exit. *Good girl!*

Diesel would have cheered out loud at her skill and bravery, but bullets flew, and he had to get down or get shot. As soon as he was certain Reese and Klein made it out, Diesel backed toward the doorway he'd entered.

"The north end of the building has been breached," Big Jake said into Diesel's radio headset. "I repeat, the building has been breached."

"We need weapons," Buck lamented. "Without them, we're useless."

"Do your best to get the delegates to safety," Diesel said. "There are only a few gunmen in the auditorium."

"There are a lot more people with guns rushing the north entrance," Harm said.

"Get into the auditorium and block the entrances," Diesel said, heading for the north door where he took out the gunman, and used his rifle to jam the doors shut.

"That might mean taking out some of the DRC military guys," Buck said.

"Do what it takes, otherwise this event will turn into a serious international incident," Big Jake said.

"Roger," Buck replied. Harm, T-Mac and Pitbull chimed in.

A moment later the outside doors burst open, and the team stormed in. They only took a few moments to disarm the guards inside, and then they locked the doors from the inside.

Within seconds, voices shouted from outside, and people banged on the metal doors.

"We have to get the delegates out of here, before they try blowing the doors open," Diesel said. "I'm going for the south exit. Pitbull, T-Mac, come with me. The rest of you, herd the dignitaries to the south exit."

"Where's Reese?" Buck asked.

"She made it out, and I'm guessing she headed down the stairs to the parking garage. I haven't heard from her. She might have lost her comm."

"There were rioters pouring into the garage on the north side," Harm said. "They were swarming the streets like ants. Without weapons, we'll be lucky to make it out of this alive."

"Don't be a Debby Downer, Harm," Big Jake said. "We'll make it, and these delegates will, too."

"Not this one," Buck hovered over a man lying on his back, staring up at the ceiling. "No blood. Looks like he suffered a massive heart attack."

"Do what you can for those who've been injured," Diesel said, "but get those who can move up and out of here as soon as we clear a path."

"Where's President Sabando?" Big Jake asked.

Diesel's heart sank. "He must have made it out with Reese and Klein." Which meant he'd draw the fight to him and Reese. The rebels might not be discriminating when shooting at the president. Reese could become collateral damage.

Diesel crossed to the south exit, took a deep breath, unlocked the door and peered out. Several terrorists dressed in ragged camouflage uniforms were crowding into the stairwell leading into the garage.

One of them spotted Diesel and swung his rifle around too late.

Diesel rushed across the hallway, pushed the rifle up toward the ceiling and punched the man in the throat. He fell, clutching at his shattered windpipe, gasping for air. The man behind him spun and fired off several rounds without first aiming. The bullets hit the wall. Diesel hit the shooter, knocking him backward and down the stairs, taking out two more men already on their way down. That sent them tumbling to a heap at the landing, their weapons flying to the side.

Before they could scramble to their feet, Diesel,

T-Mac and Pitbull had their rifles and were pointing them in their faces.

Diesel left the others and continued down the steps. T-Mac and Pitbull would spend a few precious moments tying their wrists and feet with the zip ties T-Mac always kept handy.

Diesel hurried downward, listening as he went. He could hear the squeal of tires and the sounds of footsteps pounding on the concrete floors at the upper levels, but he couldn't hear the sounds of voices from the fleeing delegates or Reese.

He worried he'd come the wrong way, except the rebel fighters had been on their way down, as well. They had to be after someone. From the sound of footsteps on the stairs below, there might be some of the rebels getting too close for comfort to the woman he'd made love to the night before. He couldn't let anything happen to her. Now that he'd found the feisty, former MMA fighter, he didn't want to let her go. She was everything he could ever want in a woman—independent, strong and determined. Only a confident woman like her, familiar with the military life, stood a chance of making a relationship with a SEAL last. Perhaps he could find a way to make something between them work—if only he were given the chance.

Chapter Eleven

Reese rammed the pointy heel of her shoe into the door-jamb and closed the door hard, hoping to slow her pursuers. When she turned to survey the room she found herself in, she frowned. Pipes hung from the ceiling, and machines filled the room. These were the heating, air, water supply and other mechanical devices necessary to operate a huge hotel and convention center.

In the middle of the room, Lawrence Sabando faced off with his brother, Jean-Paul, the president of the DRC.

"If the rebellion is successful," the president said, as he poked a finger at his brother's chest, "you will be responsible for this country's disastrous fall into chaos."

"Better than being ruled by a tyrant," Lawrence responded. "Your time is finished as president."

"The country isn't stable," Jean-Paul argued. "Having an election will cause great unrest."

"We are brothers, but we must do what we must." Lawrence held out his hand, as if to shake his brother's.

The president's eyes narrowed, but he took his brother's hand.

Lawrence gripped his brother's hand and shook it.

"A man must do what a man must do." Before Jean-Paul could pull his hand free, his brother twisted his free arm up behind his back and pulled a pistol from beneath his jacket.

Reese was too far away from the two men to interfere with what was happening.

Jean-Paul cried out, "What is this?"

"I'm taking the country back for the people."

"You do not know what you are doing." The president stood on his toes to relieve the pressure on his arm. "My army will slaughter your rebels."

"Not if you tell them to back down," his brother replied.

"I will not."

"Then you will die, and our people will elect a new leader."

Reese couldn't believe what was happening. As if they didn't have enough problems outside the door to the room they hid in. Inside could get just as messy. Reese had to do something before the situation spiraled out of her control. "Uh, sirs."

Ferrence stepped forward, closer to the two men than Reese. "Maybe we can talk this out peacefully."

Lawrence swung his gun toward Ferrence. "All you want is to get your hands on our minerals. You don't care about our country."

"I care about getting out of this alive," Ferrence said. "As I'm sure your brother does."

Reese glanced around the room at the frightened dignitaries. "Look, there are a lot of people in here," she said. "Could you take your argument where others won't be hurt?"

Lawrence snorted. "Foolish woman. Other countries have hovered like vultures, preying on our natural resources, raping the lands of what is ours. The people of the Democratic Republic of the Congo deserve to be free of oppression from my brother, from the countries that would force our people into slavery, and make our children work in the mines from the day they learn to walk to the day they die. This ends now."

A shot rang out.

Reese dropped to the ground. Only, the sound came from behind them. Pounding sounded on the door, and then the door burst open, her shoe having done little to keep the rebels out.

Three men rushed in, pointing rifles at the dignitaries huddled in a corner.

Lawrence said something in Lingala and then waved his gun toward the hostages. "You will follow these men out of this room and into the van waiting in the parking garage."

Reese glanced around the room, looking for anything she could use as a weapon.

Lawrence's eyes narrowed. "If you do not do exactly as I say, my men are instructed to kill one delegate at a time to gain your compliance." His gaze settled on Ferrence and then Reese. "Who will be first?"

Reese held up her hands. "I'll do whatever you say. Just don't shoot these people."

"I'm not arguing," Ferrence said. "You want me

to go into a van? I'll go." He started for the door and stopped when a man blocked his path.

Reese gasped when she realized it was Diesel, standing on the other side of the threshold. "Don't try anything," she called out. "They have their weapons trained on the delegates."

Diesel ducked back out of the doorframe.

Seconds later, a shot was fired, whizzed past Reese's ear and splintered the doorframe, inches from where Diesel had been standing a moment before, but was now gone.

Reese gasped and held her breath, praying the bullet hadn't ricocheted off the door and hit Diesel.

"Stay close together," Lawrence said.

His men shoved their rifles into the backs of some of the dignitaries, herding them out of the room and into the garage.

A dark van skidded around a corner and came to a stop, steps away from the door.

When Reese stepped out of the room, she shot a glance around, searching for Diesel. He was nowhere to be seen.

"Don't try anything, or we will shoot the delegates," Lawrence called out in English, and then in French.

More rebel fighters filled the garage, surrounding them. Outside on the street, sounds of gunfire made it feel like an all-out war was going on.

"You will not get away with this," the president said. "My men will kill you and your rebels."

Lawrence shook his head. "Not if I have you as a hostage." He pressed the handgun to his brother's head. "Get in the van," he called out to the delegates.

One by one, they climbed into the van, until it was packed with people. Then four armed men climbed in with them.

When Reese and Ferrence started to get in, Lawrence stopped them.

"No. You two will come with me and my brother." Lawrence nodded toward a group of men. "Follow me."

A mob of armed men gathered around Lawrence, his brother, Reese and Ferrence. Together, they reentered the conference building. In their strange little huddle, they walked down the long hallway, passing other members of their rebellion, until they reached the elevator bay.

Lawrence touched the button with the barrel of his pistol.

When the door opened, Lawrence shoved his brother in first, holding tightly to his arm, with his gun pressed to his head. He turned and nodded toward Reese and Ferrence. "Get in, or I kill my brother, and then I'll kill one of you."

Ferrence and Reese entered simultaneously, and five of the rebels crowded in behind them, all carrying wicked-looking guns. The doors closed.

"Take us to the top, brother," Lawrence said. "I know you only reserve the best with the people's money."

"I don't have my key," Jean-Paul said.

"Then I suppose you will die." Lawrence pressed the gun harder to his brother's head and started to squeeze the trigger.

"Okay, okay, it's in my pocket. Don't shoot!" the president cried. With his free hand, he pulled his key card out of his pocket, waved it in front of the control panel and hit the button for the top floor.

As the elevator rose through the building, Reese wondered when and where this would end and whether Diesel had been hit. If this was the end for her, she wished she could see him one last time.

Reese wouldn't let this be the end for her or her client. She'd been to hell and back and survived. She'd be damned if it was all for naught. She had to think she was in this position, at this time, for a reason. And that reason was to get her client out of hot water and get herself back home.

When they emerged from the elevator, Lawrence urged them to climb the stairs to the rooftop, where a helicopter touched down in front of them.

Lawrence waved Reese and Ferrence toward the helicopter. Once they were inside, he shoved his brother into a seat. Two other guards climbed in and pointed their rifle barrels at Reese and Ferrence.

As the helicopter lifted off the roof, Reese sat back in her helicopter seat, buckled her safety harness and went through every scenario that would get her and Ferrence out of this mess. She would not go down without a fight. First, they needed to be on the ground again, where they had a chance of escaping. Then she'd have to convince Ferrence to go along with her plan. Whatever that plan might be. She couldn't wait for the SEAL team to find her. They might not make it in time.

"T-Mac, TELL ME you still have GPS tracking on Klein and Reese." Diesel, T-Mac and Pitbull managed to get the hell out of the parking garage before the rebel forces converged on them.

"I've got Klein. Last night, while you were picking your noses, I snuck into Klein's room and planted a tracker in his watch," T-Mac confirmed.

"You have the GPS tracking device?"

"In my duffel bag back, in the hotel room." T-Mac stopped and stared at the hotel surrounded by the mob of rebels and civilians. "How the hell are we going to get inside?"

"Service entrance." They worked their way around the crowd of rebels converging on the hotel to the back, where trucks were backed up to loading docks, their drivers having deserted the area. The team entered through an open overhead door and slipped down a service hallway.

Ahead, they saw a crowd of people heading their way.

"In here." Diesel ducked into a huge laundry room. T-Mac and Pitbull darted through the door and turned to see who was coming.

"I'll be damned," Pitbull said and opened the door right as the first person in line passed the door. He reached out and grabbed a man, dragging him into the laundry room. The man came in fighting.

Pitbull ducked a punch. "Buck, it's me," he said.

Buck stopped with his arm half-cocked, ready to throw another punch. "Pitbull?" He glanced around. "Damn, where did you guys come from?"

"Long story," Diesel peeked out into the hallway, where more delegates stood, worried frowns on their faces. At least these hadn't been bundled into a van and carted off to who knew where. "Where's Big Jake and Harm?"

"That you, Diesel?" At the back of the group, Big Jake looked over the tops of the delegates' heads.

"Bring them in here," Diesel said.

Big Jake and Harm herded the dignitaries into the laundry room.

"I think they'll be all right in here until the riot dissipates," Diesel said. "We have to find Klein and Reese."

"I thought you had them covered," Buck said.

"Until Lawrence hijacked them. He loaded a van full of delegates going to who knows where."

T-Mac held up a hand. "I slapped a magnetic GPS tracker on that van as it was driving out of the parking garage."

Diesel grinned. "Damn, you're good. But that doesn't account for Reese and Klein. We need to get the tracking device."

"We passed the utility elevator on our way through. Come on." Buck checked the hallway and waved to the others.

The team ran for the elevator, while Big Jake stayed back to warn the dignitaries to stay put until the rioting was over. By the time the elevator had arrived and the five men had stepped in, Big Jake came around the corner and hopped on board. The elevator rose to their floor at what felt like the pace of ice freezing. By the time the doors opened, Diesel had ground the enamel off his back teeth.

Reese could be anywhere in the DRC. The longer it took to find her, the farther away she could be.

Inside the suite, Diesel raced T-Mac to the duffel bag and waited for his teammate to dig out the tracking device and turn it on.

He frowned down at the screen. "It appears as though Klein is right on top of us."

"What do you mean?"

"The tracker is two-dimensional. They could be at the bottom of the building, the top or on any one of the floors." His frown deepened.

"What?" Diesel demanded.

"They're moving."

"As in, driving out onto the street?" Buck asked.

"No. As if cutting across the city, going fast." T-Mac turned toward the window. "There!" He pointed to the sky.

A helicopter flew past the window and away toward the east.

"Damn!" Diesel pulled his cell phone from his suit jacket.

"If you're hoping to get more help, they won't send any more assistance from Djibouti," Big Jake said.

"I'm not calling Djibouti." He scrolled through his contacts and found the one he was looking for. "I'm calling Marly."

"Bush flights, Marly speaking," a voice answered on the second ring.

"Marly, it's Diesel. Please tell me you're still at the airport."

"I am. I just finished filing my flight plan back to Zambia."

"File another to somewhere east."

"I have to be a little more specific."

"Pick a city. I don't care. Reese and Klein have been taken by Sabando's brother in a helicopter headed east. I need you to follow them."

"They could be going anywhere. By the time you get to the airport, they will be long gone."

"We have a tracker on Klein."

"Well, why didn't you say so?" Marly said. "Get your ass to the airport ASAP. I'll have the plane ready to go."

"Will it hold six men plus you?"

"Easily. Why?" she asked. "Did you make some friends in Kinshasa?"

Diesel glanced around at his teammates, glad they were in this together. "You could say that."

"Bring them. I'll be waiting." Marly ended the call.

While T-Mac gathered their equipment into his duffel bag, Diesel shed his suit, slipped on jeans, a T-shirt and the boots he'd purchased when he'd been out the day before. In less than two minutes, he was heading for the door, backpack in hand, carrying his dismantled M4A1 rifle. "Let's go. We have a damsel in distress to rescue."

"Oh, so now we're in the knights-in-shining-armor business?" Pitbull asked. "Do we get to bring out our weapons for this one?"

"You bet." Diesel ran for the utility elevator and

punched the down button. Fortunately, the elevator doors opened immediately, and the men piled in.

On the ride down, Diesel clenched and unclenched his fists, his insides knotted so tightly, he could barely breathe. Why had Lawrence separated Reese and Klein from the dignitaries? And why did he feel the need to take them with him to wherever he planned on disposing of his brother?

"How are we getting from the hotel to the airport?" T-Mac asked.

"We'll get clear of the riot and see if we can grab a taxi," Big Jake answered.

Diesel was thankful his team was there with him. They helped to keep him together when he felt like coming apart at the seams. Normally level-headed when going into a dangerous situation, he was completely out of his element now. All because of a woman who'd slipped beneath his defenses and stolen a part of him.

Holy hell.

Diesel shook his head. Could it be? Had she stolen his heart in the few short days they'd known each other? Falling in love could not have happened so fast. Before Reese, he wasn't sure he even believed love existed. Lust? Well, yeah. But love?

He felt as if someone had sucker punched him in the gut. Was that what love felt like? Why would anyone want to feel like that?

Reese had been taken away in a helicopter to God knew where. If they didn't find her quickly, it might be too late.

The doors opened, and Diesel rushed out. He led the way to the loading docks and down backstreets not already crowded with rioters or rebels. He could hear the reassuring sound of footsteps pounding behind him, and he felt glad his team had his back.

Four blocks from the hotel and conference center, they were able to hail two taxis. The drivers promised to hurry toward the airport.

Hurry was relative. In the congested streets, nothing moved fast.

By the time the taxis dropped them at the airport, Diesel was so wound up, he leaped out of the cab and ran for the flight line where Marly's plane sat waiting for them. Marly stood outside of the aircraft, talking to several DRC soldiers wielding rifles.

Diesel slowed to a more casual walk and waved at Marly. "What's going on?"

"These men want to take my plane, but I explained to them we're about to take off on an emergency flight to save a life."

"You are the doctor?" one of the soldiers asked.

Diesel met Marly's gaze, and then the soldier's. "Yes, sir."

"And these men?" The soldier glanced over Diesel's shoulder.

"All in the medical field." Big Jake stepped up beside Diesel. "An entire village has come down with the Ebola virus. We're on our way in to help." The man towered everyone standing on the tarmac. "Would you care to accompany us?"

The leader of the DRC soldiers tipped his head up

and squinted at Big Jake for a long moment. Then he shook his head. "No, we will find another airplane. Carry on."

Marly waved to the plane. "You can store your bags in the wing compartment. The sooner we board, the sooner I can get clearance from the tower."

T-Mac loaded his duffel bag into the wing, and the men climbed aboard the aircraft. Diesel sat in the co-pilot's seat beside Marly, settled the headset over his ears and held the GPS tracking device like a lifeline to Reese.

Marly started the engine, contacted the air traffic controller and waited for clearance to take off.

Moments later, they were airborne.

"Which way?" she asked.

"East."

She rolled her eyes. "I don't suppose you can be more specific?"

"Not really. Right now, it appears they are flying due east and they have a sizable head start on us."

Marly nodded. "That works for now. I filed flight plans to Kananga, which is due east. Let me know if their direction changes."

They passed over farmland, jungle and rivers. Every so often, Diesel would inform Marly of slight changes to their route.

She adjusted and pushed on.

By nightfall, their fuel was getting low, and the helicopter ahead of them was slowing. They were about thirty minutes behind the craft carrying Reese and Ferrence.

"I need to land at an airport, where I can refuel," Marly said. "There's one in Kamenbe."

Diesel checked the tracker. "They stopped."

Marly glanced at the device. "Even if I could land there, I wouldn't have enough fuel to take off again and get to the nearest airport with facilities to refuel. I'll have to overshoot their landing area and go on to Kamenbe."

Diesel nodded, his fingers clenched so tightly around the tracker, his knuckles turned white. Marly was right. They couldn't land where the helicopter did, even if they had enough fuel. "T-Mac, you don't happen to have a parachute hidden away in that duffel bag of yours, do you?"

"Wouldn't matter if I did—it's stored in the wing."

"Damn. I hate being so close, but so far," he said. "Can we at least fly over the landing site so that we can see what we're shooting for?"

Marly nodded. "You bet. But if you don't mind, I'd rather not get in range of small arms fire." She reached into a compartment and extracted a pair of binoculars. "Here."

Diesel pressed the binoculars to his eyes. As they neared the location where the green blip was on the tracking device, Diesel glanced out the window.

The terrain had changed from jungle to huge scars on the land, where open-pit mining craters had been dug.

He could see the helicopter below. A couple of SUVs were pulling away from the aircraft.

The helicopter rose slowly from the ground, rising into the air.

"That's our cue to get the heck out of here. That chopper has guns on it." Marly increased the plane's speed, sending it on its way to Kamenbe.

All the while, Diesel studied the land, the roads leading into and out of villages along the way. He noted several trucks full of men in military uniforms, carrying rifles and what appeared to be rocket-propelled grenades. The trucks stirred up dust along the roads, heading toward the mine. Diesel wondered if they were part of Jean-Paul's army or the rebels fighting with Lawrence? Either way, they could stir up more trouble for Reese and Klein.

Since the helicopter was taking off, and the green blip wasn't moving with it, Diesel thought it could be safe to bet Ferrence and Reese were still on the ground. Their best plan would be to get to Kamenbe, rent, borrow or steal a vehicle and get back out to the mine, and soon, before they could move the captives again.

Chapter Twelve

Reese wished she had on a sturdy pair of trousers and her hiking boots. Dressed in a skirt suit, barefooted because she'd ditched her heels in order to run and jam a door, she wasn't in any condition to make good an escape.

What she didn't understand was why Lawrence had brought them all the way across the country to what appeared to be an open-pit mine. If he were going to kill them, wouldn't he have done it already?

She didn't want to get her hopes up, but Lawrence might not be as bad as she originally thought. Perhaps he only wanted to teach his brother and the greedy Americans a lesson. Reese hoped that was the extent of his plan and that he would then turn them loose.

In the meantime, she wasn't counting on it. She had to have a plan B.

The helicopter was met by two Land Rovers. Lawrence, his brother and two soldiers climbed into the first with the driver. Rebel soldiers nudged Reese and Ferrence with the barrels of their weapons, herding them toward the other SUV. Now would be a good time to fight her way free, but she didn't have shoes, and the rebel fighters didn't appear to have a sense of humor. They'd probably shoot rather than ask permission. Reese and Ferrence climbed into the back seat with one of the fighters. Another fighter sat in the front, turned around in his seat with a pistol and pointed it at Ferrence's chest.

"I hope we don't hit any major bumps along the way," Ferrence whispered.

"Quiet!" The soldier beside Ferrence hit him in the jaw with his elbow.

Ferrence pressed a hand to his jaw and closed his mouth. They drove several miles, deeper and deeper into the maze of open-pit mines. The sun had long since descended from its zenith, now casting long shadows, as it raced for the horizon.

The vehicle in front of them finally halted in front of what might once have been a white tent. The white canvas was stained a muddy red from the dust kicked up by vehicles and mining activities.

Rebel fighters crowded around the tent, shouting something in Lingala. Lawrence ushered his brother, whose hands had been bound behind his back.

A cheer went up from the fighters, and shots were fired into the air.

Reese cringed. All it took was one careless fighter to swing a weapon their direction, pull the trigger and boom. Reese held her breath as she was escorted into the tent. Once inside, a rebel fighter bound her wrists in front of her with a strap and bound Ferrence's behind his back and forced him to kneel so that they could bind his ankles. *Apparently, a woman in a skirt suit wasn't as scary as a man.* Reese counted her blessings. She was one step closer to escape. She could easily untie Ferrence's restraints, and he could return the favor, as soon as their captors left them alone for any length of time.

"I don't understand why you have brought me here. If you're going to kill me, why not get it over with?" The president had been bound much like Ferrence, his wrists behind his back. He sat on the ground, with his knees drawn up and his ankles tied together.

"I want you to see what you have done to this country by your actions or, rather, inaction. You have sold this country to the devils." Lawrence glared at Ferrence and Reese. "The Americans will know, too, what price our people have paid. When the sun rises again, you will see."

Lawrence left the tent and gave brief orders to his men in Lingala.

From the shadows on the outside of the tent, Reese could tell there were two rebel fighters left as guards, one on either end. The two guards inside the tent sat on boxes, facing them, their rifles resting on their laps.

As the sun sank below the horizon, the interior of the tent went from gray to black. The inside guards stood, stretched, said something in their language and headed for the tent's flap door.

Outside, they spoke to the guards on the front and then left.

As soon as the inside guards left the tent, Reese tore at the bindings on her wrists with her teeth, working the knots in an attempt to loosen them. She stopped when one of the two guards standing outside ducked his head into the tent and shined a flashlight at the captives.

Reese raised her hands to block the glare.

The guard stared at her suit and snorted. He then left the tent and said something to the other guard, and they laughed.

Reese hoped her skirt suit gave them some form of entertainment that would keep them occupied long enough for her to tear the knots loose. There were several SUVs outside the tent. If she could get to one of those, she and Ferrence might have a way out—if she didn't get lost in the maze of roads through the mining operations.

Reese struggled with the strap, but no matter how hard she tried to pull with her teeth, the strap wasn't coming loose. She'd looked around the tent, while there was still light left from the sun, but hadn't found anything that appeared to be sharp enough to cut through the leather. If she could get to the wooden crates the guards had used as seats, she might be able to rub the straps against the coarse edges of the wooden slats.

Someone outside the tent lit a fire, giving just enough light for Reese to find her way. Not sure if the campfire would silhouette her movements against the tent, she crossed the dirt floor on her knees, a little at a time, until she was next to a crate. Thankfully, the boards it was made of were rough-hewn and provided a serrated edge to rub her bonds against.

"What are you doing?" Ferrence whispered.

"Trying to get us out of here," she answered.

"And how far will we get?" Ferrence asked. "You're barefooted, and we're surrounded by men with guns."

"They will shoot you if you step one foot outside of this tent," Jean-Paul said, his lip pulled back in a sneer. "You should wait for my army to come to our rescue. They will be here soon."

The president had confidence his troops would find him and carry him back to Kinshasa and safety.

Reese, not so much. The riots in the streets of the capital city were evidence the country was already in turmoil. The president had not helped matters by delaying the elections. He'd angered his people and possibly some of the members of the country's armed forces. They might let this be a lesson to anyone who tried again to circumvent the constitutional elections.

"We can wait for morning and whatever Lawrence wants us to see, and then be shot, or get out in the dark of night and maybe live to tell our grandchildren about our adventure." Reese pushed harder against the crate. The leather strap seemed to be thicker and stronger than she'd originally thought. At the rate she was going, it would be morning before she broke through.

Ferrence scooted across to where she sat and turned his back to her. "See if you can untie mine."

She stopped long enough to work at the strap they'd used to tie Ferrence's wrists together. His was some kind of synthetic material, but equally strong. The knot was so tight, no amount of coaxing with her fingers so close together would work it loose.

"You'll have to rub yours on the crate, too." Reese went back to scraping her strap against the wood.

Ferrence turned his back to the second wooden crate and started rubbing his bindings against the wood. He faced Reese as they worked. "Do you think your fiancé will be able to find us?"

Her heart fluttered at Ferrence's reference to her fiancé. Diesel wasn't her fiancé, but the sound of the word on her client's lips almost made it seem real and exciting. *Foolish*, she realized. "I don't know. We've come a long way. They'd have had to find someone to fly them here."

"I saw how you handled the guards in the conference center. And you got us out of the last situation like a pro." Ferrence stared at her in the limited lighting, his eyes narrowed. "You're not just an assistant, are you?"

"You father hired me to be your assistant on this trip. That's what I am," Reese hedged. Why did it matter now that she'd been hired as a bodyguard? Once again, she felt she'd failed her client. She hoped she would be as fortunate this time as she was the last time, and that they were able to get out of hot water and back to safety. If they ever got back to the States, she'd really have to rethink her career choice and come up with a better plan.

Time passed, and she still hadn't managed to tear through her restraints. Hunger gnawed at her belly, and exhaustion wore her down. Still, she rubbed until her wrists were raw and her eyelids closed of their own accord. Her last thought was of Diesel. She prayed he'd gotten out of the city alive and that his team made it out, as well. She also prayed she'd see him again. She'd tell him how much their short time together had meant to her, even if it hadn't meant as much to him.

MARLY LANDED THE little plane at the Kamenbe Airport, just after dusk.

Big Jake was able to rent a large enough black SUV to get all of them inside. Diesel took the wheel, too wound up, and in need of something to keep his mind off what could be happening to Reese, to sit in the back seat, gnawing at his fingernails.

The roads back to the mines started out paved, but quickly became gravel, and then dirt. Dust sifted through every opening of the SUV, even though they traveled with the windows up.

Big Jake rode shotgun and T-Mac sat in the middle, holding the GPS tracker in his lap, while studying the one provided at the rental car agency. They'd paid for the insurance, unsure as to what shape the vehicle would be in when they returned it— *if* they returned it.

"We should have called back to Djibouti for air transport," T-Mac said.

"We never were supposed to be in the DRC," Big Jake said. "Transporting the SOC-R onto the Congo River was a huge risk. Bringing helicopters to the big cities would draw even more attention, and it could end up on the nightly news."

Diesel didn't say anything. He was with T-Mac, wishing they had a faster, more direct way to get to Reese. Instead, they were stuck on dirt roads, traveling through the night, hoping they were going the right way. As the roads narrowed, they had to do some back-tracking, which wasted even more time.

In the early hours of the morning, T-Mac nodded off, his head dipping so sharply, it woke him immediately. He yawned, stretched and glanced down at the tracking device. "We should be getting pretty close."

"Close, as in a mile or two, or close, as in within the same continent?" Diesel asked, getting crankier by the minute. Time was passing all too quickly, and they still hadn't made it to the mining operation. Everything appeared so different in the dark. He might drive off the edge of an open-pit mine for all he knew.

"As in, within five miles. We might consider hiding the SUV and going the rest of the way on foot soon. We don't want the rebel fighters to open fire on the strange vehicle entering their space in the dead of night."

"Let's get another mile closer, and then we'll ditch the vehicle," Diesel said.

"Turn out the headlights, then, so they don't see us coming," Big Jake suggested.

Diesel slowed almost to a stop before extinguishing the headlights. He took a few minutes to allow his eyesight to adjust to the darkness.

"Guys, wake up back there." T-Mac twisted in his seat. "Get the night vision goggles out of the duffel bag. We might need them sooner than you think."

Diesel glanced in the rearview mirror at his teammates.

Pitbull, Buck and Harm sat up instantly.

Harm reached behind the seat and pulled the duffel bag over into his lap with a grunt. "Damn, T-Mac what *don't* you have in this bag of tricks?" He passed forward a pair of night vision goggles.

T-Mac handed them to Big Jake.

Jake slipped the night vision goggles over his eyes and scanned the road ahead.

Now that his sight had adjusted to nothing but the limited light from the stars overhead, he picked up speed, eating up the next two miles.

"They're close," T-Mac said.

Diesel found a good spot on the side of the road where he could hide the SUV. They'd go in on foot from here. Finally, he'd be able to help Reese.

Once they covered the SUV in brush and branches, the team took off through the trees and bushes, paralleling the road, still following the GPS tracker. When they were within half a mile of the bright green dot on the tracking device, they slowed and took even more care to locate any outlying sentries.

Harm, Pitbull and Big Jake manned the night vision goggles and spread out, searching for anyone lying in wait of people entering the perimeter of the mining camp.

"Got a heat signature near the road, fifty meters ahead," Pitbull reported.

"Another on the opposite side of the road. Appears to be lying down. Could be asleep," Big Jake said. "Going in."

"Same here," Pitbull acknowledged.

"On three," Big Jake whispered into the radio. "One…two…three."

Without night vision goggles to see the green heat

signature of bodies moving ahead, Diesel had to rely on his own eyesight. All he could see was a couple of gray shadows moving in the woods, and only because he knew what he was looking for.

"Target subdued," Big Jake reported.

"Make that two," Pitbull seconded. "All clear up to the camp. Bound forward. We have your six."

With Big Jake and Pitbull covering, Diesel, Harm, Buck and T-Mac bounded forward, almost to the very edge of the camp.

The camp was a mass of tents and shacks made of discarded plywood, pieces of corrugated tin and other trash.

At the far end was a large white tent, tinged blue by the moonlight.

"Based on the tracker, Klein is in or very near that tent," T-Mac said.

"And, if they kept them together, Reese should be with him," Diesel said, thinking optimistically. Though they really had no reason to keep her alive. She wasn't the bargaining chip. She didn't have a father with a vast fortune to negotiate her release. Still, Diesel wouldn't give up hope. Reese had to be with Klein. And he'd bet his last dollar she had an escape plan.

"Our biggest problem now is getting past all the people between us and the white tent," Big Jake said.

Diesel stared at the dark camp. "What do you mean?"

Big Jake moved up beside Diesel and handed him the night vision goggles.

Diesel stared through the lenses. "Damn."

In amongst the tents, plywood shacks and garbage were people—whether lying beneath a shelter, out in the open, or sleeping in any space available. The ground was littered with the green heat signatures of bodies of living, breathing humans.

"There must be hundreds," Pitbull reported.

"Maybe even thousands," Diesel agreed. "But we have to get in."

"Then we'd better make our move before the sun comes up," Big Jake advised.

Already, the eastern sky had lightened to a dark gray. The sun would rise within the next hour, and they'd be exposed to the mass of people surrounding the white tent.

Diesel squared his shoulders, handed Big Jake the night vision goggles and took a step forward. "Let's do this."

The team moved forward. While three provided cover, the other three bound, eating the distance thirty yards at a time, swinging wide to the rear of the encampment.

When they were within one bound of the white tent, they paused to regroup and plan their next move.

The light of dawn continued to push the black and gray of night toward the western sky, filling the horizon with rose gold and orange hues. They only had moments before the entire camp was awake and they would have missed their opportunity to rescue Reese and Klein.

"Uh, folks, we might have bigger problems than we thought," Big Jake said into Diesel's headset.

Diesel tensed as the meaning of Big Jake's warning became clear.

Chapter Thirteen

"Reese," a voice came to her in her sleep.

She blinked open her eyes and wondered if she'd really opened her eyes or was still asleep. The darkness was so profound, she couldn't even make out shapes.

"Reese," that same voice said. Only now she knew her eyes were open and the voice had to be that of Ferrence Klein, lying on the ground beside her.

"Ferrence?" she whispered.

"I got my hands loose," he said.

Any lingering fatigue vanished, and Reese bolted upright to a sitting position. "Do mine," she urged, feeling her way in the darkness toward him.

His hands touched her fingers and settled on the knot securing her wrists. For what felt like forever, he worked at the strap. Finally, he managed to slip one end through the knot, and the band fell away.

Her heart skipped beats as she worked the bindings at Ferrence's ankles. When they were both completely free, she rose to a squatting position.

Without light to see, she'd potentially walk over Jean-Paul and awaken him. This thought led to an important question: Should she free him, as well? Or should she focus on getting herself and Ferrence out of the camp and back to safety?

The president had been so certain his troops would find and free him. Had he changed his mind?

"President Sabando?" Reese felt her way to a lump on the tent floor.

"You're wasting time," Ferrence said sharply. "He wasn't willing to risk a run for it last night. Why should he do it now?"

"He's as much a prisoner as us. I can't just leave him here," Reese said. "Sir."

The man emitted a soft curse in French, and then mumbled in English, "What is it?"

"Do you want us to untie you?" she asked.

"You foolish girl," he said, his voice husky from sleep. "If you attempt to escape, you won't get out of this camp alive."

"Nevertheless, we have to try," she said. "This is your last chance."

He sighed. "Yes, I would wish you to untie me, so that I might face my brother in dignity."

Feeling the seconds ticking away at an alarming speed, Reese worked at the knot on Jean-Paul's wrists, while listening for sounds of the camp awakening. Already, the darkness was graying into predawn and she could make out shadowy shapes in the tent's interior. Dawn would bring the camp alive, and any chance of escape would be gone.

Just when she thought she couldn't get the knot untied, the end of the rope pushed through, and the binding fell away. When she started to rise to her feet, Reese was stopped by a hand on her arm.

"They will kill you if you try to escape," Jean-Paul said. "Let me negotiate your release. I would not like for a visitor to my country to leave in a funeral procession."

"We can't bank on your brother's good nature. Not after what happened in Kinshasa," Klein whispered. "You can't guarantee our safety."

Jean-Paul sighed and pushed to his feet, massaging his wrists where the rope had rubbed them raw. "I understand your hesitation." He held his hands out. "I wish you well in your pursuit of freedom."

Reese moved to the door of the tent and pushed aside the flap just enough to peer through the opening into the soupy gray of predawn.

Already, people were moving, if not awakening. A guard lay across the entrance to the tent, blocking her path. She would have to go over him or make another exit out the back. Closing the flap, she tiptoed to the opposite end of the tent. The darker gray lump lying over the other end indicated another guard sleeping at the back. Then she spotted a rip in the canvas at the base of the right side of the shelter.

Reese knelt on the ground, took both sides of the rip and pulled gently, easing the opening higher, trying to minimize the sound of ripping canvas. When she had the tear three feet high, she waved for Ferrence. "It's now or never."

He nodded.

Reese popped her head out. The predawn light was

enough for her to determine there were no guards on this side. She slipped through the opening and made her way to the back, where the guard lay sleeping soundly, his weapon lying in his lap, his chin dropped to his chest. Beyond him was a jumble of brush and trees. If they could make it to that bunch of bushes, they might have a chance at escape. Reese glanced back.

Ferrence had his head through the gap.

She waved for him to join her.

When he had, she whispered. "You go. I'll hang back and make sure the guard doesn't wake and decide to start shooting."

Ferrence nodded, drew in a deep breath and tiptoed past the guard, toward the brush in the distance.

Before he was halfway there, a loud clanging sound ripped through what was left of the night.

The guard beside Reese jerked awake, his hands tightening around his rifle.

Reese could tell the exact moment he saw Ferrence by the way the sleeping man rolled to his feet and shouted something in Lingala.

Reese performed a side kick to the man's middle. She hit him so hard, he flung his weapon as he pitched to one side and landed hard, jolting his head against the ground. Reese pounced on the man, grabbed his arm and wrenched it up between his shoulders.

When she looked up, Ferrence had stopped halfway to the tree line.

"What are you waiting for? Go!" she shouted.

Instead, he lifted his hands in surrender.

Reese wanted to shake the man, but she had her

hands full of the guard, squirming beneath her. Why didn't he run? He could get away. She'd find a way to get free and catch up to him.

Then she spotted a familiar figure coming up from behind Klein, running toward him with a rifle in his hands.

"Diesel?" she whispered, her heart flooding with hope and relief. He'd found her. Five other men appeared around him.

But they weren't the only ones. Dozens of people emerged from the woods. Emaciated men, women and children hurried toward the camp from every direction, including the tree line. Small children clambered around the legs of the SEALs, hands held out, begging in a language Reese could not understand.

Diesel and his men couldn't take a step without bumping into a child or a woman with his or her hand held out in piteous need.

Another clanking sound filled the air, and the men, women and children abandoned the SEAL team and continued toward the center of camp.

They swarmed the camp like ants, their arms and legs so skinny, Reese couldn't fathom how they held them upright.

Before Diesel and his men could reach her, men carrying rifles emerged from around the tent and pointed their weapons at Ferrence and Reese. They shouted in Lingala.

Another voice shouted in English, "Put down your weapons, or we will kill the Americans."

Diesel ground to a halt, hesitated a moment, probably gauging whether he had half a chance to shoot the guards and get to Reese. More guards surrounded Reese in that moment of his hesitation, all pointing weapons in her direction.

Forced to release her prisoner, Reese pushed away from him and stood, her chin held high, her mouth set in a firm line, her heart racing. She prayed her captors wouldn't open fire.

"I should have guessed you would try to escape," Lawrence's voice sounded behind her. "I've heard from my sources you are a determined woman, who is not easily imprisoned, and that you have a team of men at your disposal."

"Don't hurt Mr. Klein," Reese said. "It was my idea to escape, not his."

"I have no intention of hurting either one of you, or these men who so foolishly thought they would rescue you." He tilted his head toward the camp. "In fact, to show you I am serious, they can keep their weapons, as long as they promise not to shoot me or my men." Lawrence raised his brows, giving Diesel a pointed stare.

"We won't shoot, if you won't shoot," Diesel promised.

Lawrence nodded. "So be it." He lifted a hand and said something in Lingala. His guards lowered their weapons, though they didn't appear happy about it.

Diesel and his men relaxed their holds on their rifles and came forward.

"Mr. Klein, I brought you and my brother here to see for yourselves what greed and corruption is doing to the people of our great nation." He swept his hand to the side. "Come." Lawrence waved to the SEALs. "You, too, will benefit from what you will see."

Reese waited for Diesel to join her, and then walked with Lawrence to where a guard held his brother at gunpoint.

Lawrence touched the man's weapon and gave him a low, brief command. The man stepped back, pointing his rifle at the ground.

"You might think my methods were extreme, but what you will witness is a different kind of extreme." Lawrence swept his arm wide. "Behold the men, women and children of our country." Lawrence lifted his head and gazed at the swarm of people lining up in front of a giant cauldron.

A man, using a long wooden paddle, stirred a mash of some kind of grain in the cauldron, barely heating it before ladling out portions into the bare, dirty hands of those waiting. Men, women and small children took what they were given and licked their fingers clean of possibly the only nourishment they would receive that day.

"What is this?" Jean-Paul asked. "You have brought me to see people eating?"

"I've brought you to see the people employed in our country's mines—people who are more or less enslaved from the misfortune of their births, until the day they die." Lawrence's brows furrowed. "Look at them. Men our age reduced to skin and bone. Women who can't feed their children. Children who must work for the food they receive. They dig with their hands, carry bags of dirt and minerals heavier than their own weight, and die in the heat and humidity, their bellies empty." Lawrence drew in a deep breath and let it out. "This is your legacy, my brother."

Reese's heart squeezed in her chest when a toddler with the distended belly of the malnourished, missed his portion because he couldn't hold his little hands together.

The mush plopped to the ground. The little boy scooped up what he could, dirt and all, before he was pushed out of the way.

Reese wanted to gather the child in her arms and feed him as he should be fed.

"I do not approve of these conditions," Jean-Paul said.

Lawrence snorted. "But you allow them to be. When was the last time you visited a mine?"

"I visited one last year." Jean-Paul's frown mirrored his brother's. "These were not the conditions I witnessed."

"The people you employed to run the mine showed you what you wanted to see, not the truth," Lawrence said. "Now that you've seen reality, what do you plan to do about it? Surely you realize now why the people want a democratic election. They are tired of their needs being ignored. Tired of their children dying in mines when they should be going to school. Our country will not move into the twenty-first century at the rate we are killing our people."

Jean-Paul pounded his fist into his palm. "There will be change."

Lawrence crossed his arms over his chest. "Starting with allowing the election?"

Jean-Paul scrubbed a hand down his face and nodded. "Starting with the election. But understand, brother, there are factions who would rather take this country by force and keep it stirred up and fighting from within."

"These people cannot go on as they are," Reese whispered.

"You think I want them to?" Jean-Paul demanded.

Diesel cupped Reese's arm. "The working conditions are deplorable."

"It's all they have. Without this work and what little food they receive, they have nothing," Lawrence said. "The problem cannot be resolved by banishing them from the mines."

"I will do what I can until the election," Jean-Paul swore. "In the meantime, we must get more food to these people. I will work on a program to get the children out of the mines and into schools."

Lawrence turned to Ferrence. "I know you are here to negotiate interest in our country's natural resources to include the products of this mine. If you are truly interested in securing access to our treasures, you must be willing to invest in the infrastructure that will provide jobs for our people, not the kind that employs our children."

Reese held her breath, wondering what her client would say about what he'd seen. *Would he continue to be the privileged rich-man's son, concerned only about his own well-being, or would he be the man and dip-lomat he needed to be?*

Ferrence nodded. "Although I can't condone your method of bringing us here, I understand your desire to shed light on the situation. I will convey your message to my father and will work to insure we will help, not exacerbate the problem."

"That is all I ask," Lawrence said.

"My brother," Jean-Paul stepped forward. "What is in this for you? Do you wish to take my place as president of the Democratic Republic of the Congo?"

Lawrence shook his head. "If that were to happen, I would do my best for all of my people. But that is not why I brought you here. I brought you here because I could not allow this to continue. I have nightmares about the children I've seen die in the mud and dirt, just trying to work enough to be fed." He shook his head again.

Reese pressed a hand to her growling belly, her own hunger almost an embarrassment in light of the mine workers' plight. They needed food, clothing and shelter—the very basics of human needs.

The thump-thump of rotor blades whipping the air drew Reese's attention to an incoming helicopter.

"Your transportation back to Kinshasa has arrived." Lawrence stepped back to glance at the aircraft as it hovered over a bare spot on the ground. As it descended toward the ground, a loud bang ripped through the air.

The fuselage of the chopper exploded, sending the craft reeling to the side.

People screamed and ran to get out of the way of

the blades as they hit the ground, broke off and were shot through the air.

Automatic weapon fire sounded from the direction of the road. Several trucks filled with men carrying rifles and rocket-propelled grenade launchers raced toward the camp.

"Get down!" Diesel yelled.

Bullets sprayed the dirt near Reese's feet. For a moment, she froze, not sure what was going on, or where she should run.

Diesel curled his arm around Reese and herded her toward a rise in the ground. He shoved her behind the berm and touched his hand to his ear. "Report." He listened for a moment and then responded. "Get the Sabandos and Klein to cover. I'll lay down suppressing fire until you're ready."

Diesel stretched out on the ground and aimed his rifle toward the men leaping from the backs of the trucks. He popped off several rounds. With each shot, he took out a rebel fighter. The men rushed toward them, more bodies than Diesel could fend off with just one rifle.

Soon, his shots were joined by others. The SEALs moved into defensive positions, forming a line, along with Lawrence's guards.

Reese kept her head low, feeling defenseless, unable to contribute to their survival.

One of the men who'd piled out of the back of the second truck took cover behind the truck. He carried what appeared to be a rocket-propelled grenade launcher. The man lifted the weapon to his shoulder.

"Holy hell." Reese touched Diesel's shoulder and pointed. "That man's going to fire an RPG."

Diesel redirected his aim to the rebel fighter as he shifted the weapon to his shoulder.

Reese held her breath, praying the rocket wouldn't launch before Diesel had a chance to take out the operator.

Diesel squeezed the trigger, hitting the man in the chest. He fell forward. His hand must have been on the trigger, because the RPG launched, hit the ground in front of him and exploded into a fiery blaze that shook the ground. The explosion pierced the truck's fuel tank, sending fuel spewing over the nearby fighters.

The battle had barely begun when it ended, but Reese couldn't remember a more intense fifteen minutes in her entire life.

The few remaining rebel fighters turned and ran for the woods.

Lawrence's guards gave chase.

When the dust and smoke settled, the SEALs rose from their positions.

Reese glanced around, taking a headcount before she let go of the breath she hadn't released since she'd started counting. All six SEALs were alive and unharmed. Klein hesitantly pushed to his feet, along with Jean-Paul and Lawrence Sabando.

"You see," Jean-Paul said, more calmly than one would have expected after the gunfire, "there are factions who would take what they can." He walked to the two abandoned trucks and stared down at the dead men scattered around. He nudged one of the men with the toe of his shoe. "At least one of their leaders is now accounted for."

Reese rose from her position and stood beside Diesel. He took her hand and led her to where Jean-Paul and Lawrence stood beside the dead man.

She recognized the man with the scar across his right cheek. "That's the man who kidnapped me and Mr. Klein," she said.

"Bosco Mutombo," Lawrence confirmed.

The DRC president shot a glance toward Ferrence. "What is this?"

Reese and Ferrence met gazes.

Ferrence nodded and looked directly into the president's eyes. "We didn't tell you about the incident because you had enough on your mind with the conference. And we came out of it all right."

The president looked around at the SEALs. "I take it your friends assisted your escape?"

Ferrence nodded.

"Do I want to know what qualifies them to assist in your liberation and our battle today?" President Sabando asked, his brows furrowing.

Reese and Ferrence shook their heads.

The president studied Diesel and his team for a moment, his eyes narrowing. Finally, he snorted. "Americans."

"Well, from my perspective, we would not have survived without them." Lawrence strode to Big Jake and held out his hand. "How can we send our thanks?"

Big Jake shook the man's hand and let go. "We'd prefer you didn't."

Lawrence nodded. "Brother, does this convince you that Mutombo's men were not working with me?"

Jean-Paul drew in a deep breath. "It does."

"And, having seen the wretched conditions of the mining operations, do you see the need for change?"

The DRC president frowned in the direction of the able-bodied miners who were headed into the mines to work. "I don't like it when I don't know what's going on in my country. But it appears I have missed a lot. As far as I'm concerned, your rescuers were never here and my military succeeded in removing one of our country's greatest enemies."

"With Bosco out of the picture, we will no longer waste resources on hunting him." Lawrence stared down at the dead man, and then looked out at the mining camp, where some people tended to the wounded before getting back to work. "We should be able to concentrate on helping our people."

The president followed his brother's gaze. "And we will." Then he faced Reese and Ferrence. "For now, perhaps our guests would like to return to Kinshasa?"

Lawrence glanced at the crashed helicopter. "Unfortunately, that helicopter was our transportation."

"I can have the presidential helicopter here in a few hours," the president said. "All I need is a telephone."

"President, sir," Diesel stepped forward. "My men have transportation waiting for us at the Kamenbe Airport. However, I would like to accompany Mr. Klein and Miss Brantley back to Kinshasa with you, if that's possible."

Jean-Paul nodded. "With my brother's approval, I

will send my men to accompany your men and see to it you don't run into any other rebel fighters."

Big Jake held out his hand. "Mr. President, we'll see you back in Kinshasa."

President Sabando shook the man's hand. "We will be there before nightfall."

The three hours it took for President Sabando's helicopter to arrive gave those who remained ample time to tour the mining camp and take stock of the deplorable conditions.

By the time they loaded into the helicopter, the president had put in an order to deliver food and provisions to the site. He made arrangements to make unscheduled visits to other mining sites in the near future and sent word to his cabinet members to move forward with preparations for the election to take place on schedule.

Reese was able to settle back in her seat beside Diesel. With her hand held tightly in his, she slept all the way back to the capital city, putting off thought of what would happen next. She didn't want to think of leaving Diesel and never seeing him again.

Chapter Fourteen

Diesel loved the way Reese leaned her head on his shoulder and felt safe enough to fall asleep against him. He wished he could have slept as she did. Instead, his entire body was tense with thoughts of having to leave Reese soon.

At most, he'd be in Kinshasa long enough to see Reese and Klein on to the first airplane out of the country, which could be as soon as the next day. That gave him only one more night with Reese. One night to cram a lifetime of memories.

He couldn't believe he'd known her for just a few days. But those few days might as well have been a lifetime. Deep in his heart, he knew she was the woman for him. But did they have a chance in hell of making a relationship work? Hell, did she even feel as strongly as he did about her? Yes, he could bring her body to life, but body and heart were two different things.

Lawrence Sabando assured the president he'd released the dignitaries he'd herded into the van back in Kinshasa, shortly after they'd been taken away. None of them were harmed. His actions and those of his supporting fighters had been designed to frighten more than harm the people of the conference. He'd only wanted to make a statement that would be heard around the world and draw attention to the plight of the people of the DRC.

Lawrence couldn't promise his brother he'd go free after what he'd done, but he would work to insure his brother's safety.

Diesel had listened to the brothers speaking in English. The president had news that the rebellion in the city had been brought to order. By the time they landed on the grounds of the Palais de la Nation, where the president of the DRC lived, the city was calm, and people were back to their normal work and routines.

"You are welcome to stay here for the night," President Sabando offered. "But my driver is on standby and can take you wherever you would like to go."

For once, Ferrence looked to Reese first.

"I'd like to go back to the hotel. My luggage is there," Reese said.

Ferrence's brows dipped. "I too would like to go back to the hotel, as long as it's safe."

The president nodded. "My people assure me the uprising has been dealt with and the city center is back to normal. I will order the car around."

"Thank you."

The president's brows rose. "Mr. Klein, do you still wish to have the meeting with me?"

Ferrence's lips pressed into a thin line. He glanced from Jean-Paul to his brother, Lawrence. "Mr. President, I would love to, but I believe you have your hands full with the needs of your country. I won't deter you from taking care of your people first."

Diesel could have been gobsmacked. After all of Klein's determination to get a meeting with the president of the DRC, it shocked Diesel that the man declined—and politely, too.

Both the president and his brother nodded.

"Thank you for understanding," Lawrence said.

"I will put in a good word for you with my successor," the president offered.

"Thank you." Ferrence drew in a deep breath. "Please, don't let us keep you."

One of the president's assistants hurried out onto the lawn. Moments later, Reese, Diesel and Klein were ushered to the drive, where a long white limousine awaited them.

Shortly after, they were deposited at the entrance to the hotel.

"Allow me." Diesel scooped Reese up into his arms and carried her into the hotel. They stopped at the desk for key cards to their rooms. The hotel staff was apologetic about the events of the day before and offered to send a bottle of wine to their rooms, which they gladly accepted.

"If it's all the same to you, I'll call down for room service rather than go to dinner," Ferrence said, as they rode the elevator up to their floor.

"Good, because I don't think I can go another step," Reese said, her arm looped around Diesel's neck. She gave him a pointed glance. "However, I can stand on my own two feet."

"I know," he said with a smile. "But there might be broken glass or something sharp in the carpets."

"We're standing on tile," she pointed out with a smile.

"Humor me, will ya? I'm trying to be a gentleman. I don't get much practice."

Klein shook his head. "I'll arrange for our flights to leave tomorrow, and then I think I'll call my wife."

Reese's smile faded. "If we aren't meeting with the president, we really have no reason to stay." Her voice trailed off. Though she had answered Klein, her gaze met Diesel's.

Diesel's heart sank to the pit of his belly. Tomorrow was finally coming, the day he'd have to say goodbye to Reese. His arms tightened around her. If he could make the night last forever, he would.

The elevator arrived at their floor. Klein waved Diesel through first. The walk down the hallway to their rooms was accomplished in silence. At their doors, Diesel final set Reese on her feet.

Diesel held out his hand for Klein's key card.

For once, the man didn't argue. He handed over the card and waited in the hallway, while Diesel made a quick perusal of his suite.

Nothing seemed out of place or disturbed. In fact, the hotel staff had cleaned and made the bed. Everything was as it should be. When Diesel came out, he handed over the card. "You're still a target. If you need to leave your room for any reason, let me know. I'll go with you."

Klein nodded. "Thank you. You and your team have

been invaluable to this event. I'll be sure to put in a good word for you."

Diesel's lips twisted. "We were never here."

Klein's mouth turned up on the corners, and he nodded. "Right. Then, I'll see you two in the morning, for the ride to the airport."

Klein entered his room, closed the door and locked it.

Alone at last, Diesel turned to Reese. "This is it."

Reese nodded. "Our last night together." She ran the card over the reader and opened the door. "I don't know what I would have done without you." She stepped across the threshold.

Diesel followed and closed the door behind him. Then he took her hand, spun her around and clamped her body to his. "Let's make this night count."

She laughed, the sound ending on what could only be a sob. "Damn right, we will."

"But it won't be our last," he said, as he lowered his mouth to hers."

"No? But, I'm leaving tomorrow," she whispered against his lips. "I won't see you again."

"But that's only tomorrow." He touched her lips with his in a feather-soft brush. "We'll be back in the States soon."

"And?" Reese reached for the hem of Diesel's shirt and dragged it up his body and over his head, and then tossed it to the floor.

"And, though I'm stationed out of Mississippi, I have a car. I can hop on a plane." He ran his fingers through her hair and cupped the back of her head. "I'm coming to see you." Then he kissed her and slid his hands down her neck and into the lapel of her suit jacket. With little effort, and a little help from her, he had that jacket on the floor in seconds.

Reese laid her hand along the side of his face and sighed. "Long-distance relationships never work." She reached for the button on his trousers and worked it free, and then dragged the zipper down ever so slowly.

With his body on fire, and his need for her rising with every move she made, Diesel fought back the urge to pound his chest like an eight-hundred-pound gorilla. She was special, and he needed to show her just how special she was. "Then I'll ask for a transfer to Virginia. It's closer to DC." He frowned. "Come to think of it, I don't even know where you live."

She shrugged. "I can live practically anywhere they have a need for bodyguards. Do they need them in Mississippi?"

"Only to fight off the alligators." He tugged the blouse from the waistband of her skirt and pulled it up over her head.

Reese raised her arms. "Alligators?"

"Yes. We train on the river and in the swamps. There are snakes and alligators."

Reese shivered. "Are they as bad as the crocodiles here in the Congo?"

Diesel shook his head, released the button on the back of her skirt and dragged her skirt down over her hips. "And there are no gorillas in Mississippi."

Reese's skirt fell to the floor.

Diesel slid his hands from her waist over her hips to

cup the backs of her thighs. Then he lifted her, wrapping her legs around his waist. "Unfortunately, there's probably not much use for bodyguards, unless your client is having a Bubba feud with his neighbor. But Mississippi is probably a lot safer than here." He kissed her long and hard before he broke it off and sighed. "Please tell me your next assignment isn't to Africa."

Reese chuckled and held on as he carried her through the bedroom and into the bathroom. "I don't even know if I'll have another assignment. Not after all that's happened here in the DRC."

"You'll be overwhelmed with work." Diesel set her on her feet beside the shower and tucked a strand of her hair behind her ear. "But do me a favor and save a little time for me."

"Really?" she asked, her eyes wide, shining with a layer of moisture. "Because I'm willing to give this long-distance thing a go, if you are." She brushed her thumb across his lips. "You see, I kind of like having a knight in shining armor swoop in to rescue me."

"Heck, I know you. You're perfectly capable of taking care of yourself, but please promise me you won't take on any more assignments in the jungle."

She shook her head. "I can't make any promises I can't keep. What if my next assignment takes me to the wilds of Costa Rica or Honduras?"

Diesel's fingers tightened on her arms. "I'll be crazy with worry."

"What if you are sent back to Afghanistan or Syria? I'll be nuts with worry."

"So, you care?"

She frowned. "Damn right, I do." She clasped his cheeks in both hands. "You don't get dragged through the jungle by a sexy man and not come out without forming some sort of attachment."

"Attachment, is it?" He liked the sound of that. "However we make it happen, promise me you'll see me again when we get back."

"That I can promise. If you can't come to me, perhaps we could meet halfway." She tipped her head. "What's that, someplace in Georgia?"

Diesel gathered her close, crushing her body to his. "We have the entire night to ourselves. No rebels, no teammates, no bosses. Just you and me, babe. Make love with me."

"Now you're talking." She wrapped her arms around his neck and pulled his head down so that she could meet his kiss with the fierceness that Diesel had learned he loved about this amazingly strong woman.

If they only had the night, he would make it the best night of their lives. But he wasn't ready to say goodbye. And he wouldn't. He'd find a way to see her again, stateside.

In the meantime, he had a job to do. He had a woman to please, and he wasn't going to waste a single minute he had with her.

He scooped her up into his arms and carried her into the shower, where they would begin their long night of forever.

* * * * *

LET'S TALK
Romance

For exclusive extracts, competitions
and special offers, find us online:

f facebook.com/millsandboon

◉ @millsandboonuk

🐦 @millsandboon

Or get in touch on 0844 844 1351*

For all the latest titles coming soon, visit
millsandboon.co.uk/nextmonth